One Deadly Rhyme

The Number Mysteries

Other books by dusty bunker:

Numerology and the Divine Triangle (with Faith Javane)
Numerology and Your Future
Numerology, Astrology and Dreams
Birthday Numerology (with Victoria Knowles)
Quintiles and Tredeciles: The Geometry of the Goddess
Dream Cycles
One Deadly Rhyme: The Number Mysteries
The Two-Timing Corpse: The Number Mysteries

One Deadly Rhyme

The Number Mysteries

dusty bunker

Writer's Showcase
San Jose New York Lincoln Shanghai

One Deadly Rhyme
The Number Mysteries

All Rights Reserved © 2000 by dusty bunker

No part of this book may be reproduced or transmitted in any form or by any means, graphic, electronic, or mechanical, including photocopying, recording, taping, or by any information storage retrieval system, without the permission in writing from the publisher.

Writer's Showcase
an imprint of iUniverse, Inc.

For information address:
iUniverse, Inc.
5220 S. 16th St., Suite 200
Lincoln, NE 68512
www.iuniverse.com

Any resemblance to persons living or dead is purely coincidental.

ISBN: 0-595-10063-5

Printed in the United States of America

For April, Melanie, Matthew and Sarah

Epigraph

One a penny, two a penny, hot cross buns;
If you have no daughters, give them to your sons.

> Nursery Rhyme: *Hot Cross Buns*

Acknowledgements

An endless stream of thanks to my son, Matthew, whose technological genius saved my computer from a shattering death through the sun porch windows and out into the back yard.

Thanks also to my Doppelgänger and cousin-in-law, Joan Hansen, who sat through a reading of the entire manuscript many times, over the course of months. She picked up a number of errors, and laughed in all the right places. I'm still surprised at how much alike we are.

I couldn't forget to thank daughter Melanie who, above the screams of her two-year-old son, patiently took my phone calls as that great Bugaboo, Indecision, plagued me. She made countless worthy title and cover suggestions.

Thanks also to my LifeSaver, editor Nancy Marple.

A hug for my sweetheart, Skip, who sat through a reading when he would rather have been mountain climbing or canoeing.

And finally, thank you, Charlie.

Prologue

HE worked under a ragged lampshade the color of dead leaves. To his left, a recent issue of *Time* magazine lay in shreds. Like his past, he thought, scissors poised in midair.

His eyes slid toward the shiny numbers and letters spread to his right in neat rows and over the bottle of Elmer's glue and package of generic white paper.

Focusing once again, he cut around the letter G, held it at arm's length, and squinted.

Damn it! The crossbar was uneven.

He tossed it aside and pulled over the slashed magazine, recalling his childhood fury at going outside the lines of his coloring book. Not that anyone cared.

His foot tapped as he jabbed at the bottom corner of the right page with his forefinger.

His finger slipped.

He licked his finger and jabbed again.

Page, after page, after page!

Then he found it! An ad with a thick black border dotted with white fish icons. Inside lay a message from Deuteronomy 8:11-20. "Be careful that you do not forget…"

Right on. They won't forget this.

"…that you will surely be destroyed."

Ain't that the truth.

The 'g' in forget was perfect. He placed it with the others, then reached for his cigarette and took a tug.

He gazed out the grimy window over the wheat-colored grass and the dying crocuses his dead mother had planted at the corner of the toolshed. Wraith-like arms of mist curled around the weathered boards. Ghostly reminders. He visualized spring clawing up through the cold New Hampshire ground.

Sizzling in the frying pan behind him in the smoky room, a steak sucked at his taste buds. He laid the smoldering cigarette in a mayonnaise cap that served as an ashtray, and with his forearm, wiped the tiny rivulet of drool from the corner of his mouth. Then he began murmuring the words to "Pretty Woman" in synch with the foggy voice of Roy Orbison that issued from the radio. He liked Roy. Even Elvis had fashioned his style after the man in black.

Setting the magazine aside, he pulled a piece of paper from a package and smoothed it a few times, feeling the hard wooden surface beneath. Through clear rubber gloves, he could see new hair sprouting on the back of his hands. Time for another plucking session.

Gracie watched his every move. Let her watch. She didn't bother him. He scratched the center of his chest.

This note would be a work of art, word perfect. He snickered at the pun. Yes, If you're going to do a job, do it right. He mumbled the message his mom had pounded into him for more years than he wanted to remember. Not that he'd ever listened.

An excruciatingly pleasant tingle rippled from his scalp, over his shoulders, and down to his groin. He waited for the hardness to subside.

Then he got up, stepped over to the avocado stove, and waved a hand over the black skillet to dispel the smoke. Carefully turning the thick steak with a long pointed fork, he laid in three slices of Bermuda onion. With a padded oven mitt on his hand, he shimmmied the heavy pan and watched the fat dance and sparkle like fireflies in the gloom.

Satisfied, he reached for the ruler and number one yellow pencil and marked off both sides of the paper in one-and-one-quarter inch increments. Seven light horizontal lines completed phase two. He held the sheet before him.

Yes! You will approve.

From the back of the book jacket propped against the wall, she smiled back at him.

Placing the sheet of paper back on the portable desk, he rolled his stiff shoulders, then slowly cracked each knuckle.

Smoke from the cigarette spiraled serpent-like in the diffused light. He picked up the white cylinder, twisted it between his fingers, stared at the ash gray tip. Mom never smoked. Mom detested the filthy things. But mom never knew about this vice.

A long drag brought on another coughing jag that nearly rendered him unconscious, but he would never submit to those black fugues again. He had learned control.

He replaced the cigarette in the jar cap sitting on top of a stack of magazines.

Gracie's eyes were on him again. She wanted him. With an impatient sigh, he went to her.

"What is it? Are you hungry?"

She didn't move. She liked toying with him.

He sneered. If she didn't respond, she wouldn't eat. That's all there was to it. It was her own fault.

Now for the message that would set this New Hampshire town on its ear.

Back at the table, he used a pair of tweezers to turn the first number over onto a clean sheet of paper, spread a few drops of Elmer's glue with a Q-tip, and watched the second hand on the greasy wall clock lurch over black sexagesimal wedges.

Fifteen seconds.

He tapped his foot as he recited a nursery rhyme his mother had taught him.

One a penny, two a penny, hot cross buns.
If you have no daughters, give them to your sons.

Laughter bubbled up in his chest.

Time's up. The glue will set better now.

Thus began the satisfying job of lining numbers and letters evenly on penciled lines.

Funny how strokes of ink on paper can send chills down your spine. His eyes narrowed. *Well, mom, what do you think of your son now?*

When he was done, he scooped up all traces of his work, placed them inside the portable desk, and moved to his bedroom, where he slid the desk under his bed. This was his room. No one was allowed in. He locked the door.

He returned to the kitchen where his steak awaited. Rare. The only way to eat a fine cut of meat.

When he was through eating, he'd lock Gracie in his room and clean up the kitchen real good so nobody could tell he'd even been there. The kitchen was a woman's place, after all.

He sliced a piece of meat into a perfect triangle, speared it with the fork, and held it before his eyes. He examined its grain. Saliva collected at the corners of his mouth as he anticipated the tangy feral taste.

He held the fork before his eyes for a long time. Discipline, restraint, and anticipation carried their own rewards.

Slowly he put the meat in his mouth as interior cells rose up to embrace the raw flesh like a black widow welcoming her mate. He chewed it slowly, sensually.

He cut another triangle.

Wait.

Eat.

Another. And another.

He seemed unaware of the blood dribbling down his chin. As he got into a rhythm, his thoughts shifted to the note hidden in the portable desk under his bed. His groin moved.

He grinned. This was what he was born for.

Chapter 1

"Sam. We got a problem. A big one."

"What's wrong, Charlie?" Samantha Blackwell sank back into the sofa cushions on her sun porch. Nick had just left for work, and she was munching an apple and gazing out into their wooded back yard, trying to quell an uneasy feeling that had arisen moments before the phone rang.

"It'll be all over the papers tomorrow," Charlie said, "and for certain on Channel 9 tonight. And you're right in the middle of it."

Lifting drowsy lids, she responded, "What did I do? Forget Selket's leukemia shot? Is that a police problem?" She pulled an ash blonde hair from the arm of her nightshirt and watched it float to the floor. She didn't want to hear any bad news.

"Forget the cat, Sam. I'm serious. It's Doug Hammand. Lenny and I found him dead in the frozen fish section of McCutty's Market. With a note pinned to what was left of his suit jacket."

The apple fell from her hand as she bolted upright. "No! What happened?"

The cat periscoped up, her head swiveling.

A note pinned to Hammand's chest. That had to mean murder. Doug, a model of plaid and chino, wasn't the kind of man to run to the grocery store in his one suit with a note attached to his lapel.

Crazily, Sam thought back to the time when her two daughters had climbed the steps of the school bus with those identifying manila tags attached to their buttons as if, in case they got lost, they could be dropped into the nearest mailbox. She pulled herself back to the present as a 5.8 registered across her shoulders.

Charlie was still talking. "McCutty went back to the store last night around 11:00 because he thought he forgot to turn on the alarm. You know he had that alarm installed a few years ago when he noticed problems with shoplifting. Well, he took a walk around the store like he always does, just to double-check things, and that's when he found Hammand, fish-eyed with the frozen flounder. Had some kind of flower stuck in his buttonhole. McCutty almost had a heart attack. Called 911, then fainted dead away behind the cash register. That's where we found him."

"My God! Doug Hammand." She unconsciously patted her chest as if that would still her quaking heart. Selket, sensing danger had abated, settled down once more.

"Yeah," Charlie said. "I got the call around 11:30. Found Doug with his legs sticking out of the freezer case, colder than a witch's teat, wearing a cowberry necklace. He was strangled." His voice wavered a bit. "And cut up some. By the time we finished with the crime scene, it was 2:00 A.M. Didn't think you'd appreciate a call at that time in the morning."

Sam wondered why Charlie would call *her* from the crime scene, but all she could say was "Cowberries?" Her childhood friend was now the chief of police in their town, but he didn't consult with her on cases.

"Well, they're fake, but they're definitely cowberries. Probably got them from one of the lampposts in town."

The windows of her mind fogged. *Why are we talking about cowberries?* "What about the note, Charlie? What did the note say?"

"Here's the kicker, Sam. The note mentions you."

Sudden clarity! An 8.1 rumbled. Sam clutched at her nightshirt as the blood drained to her feet. "Me? Why me?"

"The note is in some kind of code. Numbers and letters, glued on a piece of white paper, cut out of a magazine most likely. At the bottom, it says: 'Catch me if you can, Sam Blackwell.'"

"Oh, my God!" She swallowed hard and scanned the doorways, her mind searching for a place to hide.

"Sounds like some kind of psycho that reads your numerology column or books. Not that people have to be nuts to read your stuff," he added quickly.

Her knuckles were white around the phone. "You think it mentions me because of the code?"

"Don't know. There's no rhyme or reason with some of these guys. Maybe this guy's got a crush on you from that sexy picture on the back of your book jacket. Maybe he wants to match wits with you. Maybe he likes blondes or wants his picture in the paper. Maybe he's one of your clients. Who knows? I've been through a thousand reasons why since midnight."

Sexy, all right, Sam thought, relieved to switch gears, if only momentarily. Good thing the picture was taken before she gained the thirty extra pounds. She looked down at the mound of red plaid belly resting on her lap then berated herself for thinking about her looks when poor Douglas would never have to worry about such things again. Her mind ping-ponged between fear and disgust.

"Gonna be there for a while?" Charlie asked. "I want to show you this note."

Just four hours earlier, Samantha sat at her desk, chewing on her thumb, thinking about drinking Piña Coladas on a velvet beach in Aruba, sailing a dhow to Zanzibar, even going grocery shopping. God! She *was* desperate. She wanted to be anywhere but here. Her mind was as blank as the computer screen before her.

Arching her fingers over the keyboard, she typed:

Georgetown, NH
Column 5-4, April
I've Got Your Number
by Sam Blackwell

Well, that's a start.

She leaned back, clasped her hands behind her head and rocked in her black swivel chair wondering if it had been Flaubert, the famous French writer, who would roll around on the floor for days looking for just one right word. She needed a whole bunch of them right now.

Her eyes drifted toward the bank of sun porch windows that wrapped around to face both south and east into her back yard. Outside, white pines bumped and ground against each other as if in some primal mating ritual. Behind them, against the rousing dawn, bare maple and oak arms swayed, choreographing the ancient dance. True to its New England roots, March had stomped in blustery and cold and was still at it.

Then Sam remembered yesterday morning.

Her self-taught fingers flew over the split keyboard, ninety words a minute.

> A bell in the church's clock tower struck five times. Seconds later, a solitary bird burst into song. I lay in bed relishing the moments, listening to nature's aria, so full of joy and anticipation. My mind searched for the memory of an ancient Egyptian prayer that went something like, 'I go forth each morning, my heart awash with laughter.' Yes, it is a magical time of day. The birds know that.
>
> It's now 5:38 AM and I'm at my computer on the sun porch. The house is quiet; the family sleeps, healthy and happy. My new feline friend, Selket, dozes on the bookcase by the windows. I think this is heaven.

Never mind that her two daughters were snug in a new apartment in Portsmouth ten miles away. A little poetic license never hurt anyone.

My mind, polarized, immediately leaps to images of hell and the number that has terrified the faithful for centuries, 666. What is it about this number that causes such fear?

She hesitated.

She could continue pounding away at the keyboard, but ever since childhood she'd had a death grip on progressive order. Whether it was a blessing or an obsession depended entirely on the assessment and the assessor.

A book, she had announced to her parents after she had read her first sentence from her mother's copy of the *Dick and Jane* primer, was meant to be read from the very first page, in order, to the last page—including the publishing date, title page, dedication, contents, introduction, and so on. This philosophy was reinforced by the creation of the world in seven days. After all, she told her mother, what would have happened if Day Three preceded Day One? The world would have been plunged into chaos. Elizabeth Blackwell couldn't argue with that logic. Basically, Samantha Blackwell's need sprung from the fear of missing something.

Sighing, hating to interrupt the roll she was on, she nevertheless got up to find the exact quote. Selket's lime eyes, half-slit ovals, observed her movements.

From the low-slung maple bookcases under the windows that skirted the perimeter of the outer wall, Sam pulled the old Bible she got from Sunday School in Norwood, Massachusetts. The red edges were faded and water stained. She ran a hand over the cover's pebbly black surface. HOLY BIBLE, WITH HELPS.

Sam carefully turned the thin pages of the Bible and found the pale gold lock of hair that she had cut with her mother's manicure scissors and tied with red embroidery floss when she was seven. So long ago.

Enough.

This was as bad as preparing to wallpaper, spreading out all the newspapers and finding yourself on your hands and knees reading last year's news.

Where is that verse in Revelations?

Finding it, she used her finger as a marker, returned to her desk, opened the Bible, and weighted it down with a blue Scotch tape dispenser.

She ran a hand through her uncombed hair before typing the verse verbatim.

> We find 666 in Chapter 13 of the last book in the Bible, Revelation, verses 16-18: 'And he causeth all, both small and great, rich and poor, free and bond, to receive a mark in their right hand, or in their foreheads: And that no man might buy or sell, save he that had the mark, or the name of the beast, or the number of his name. Here is wisdom. Let him that hath understanding count the number of the beast; for it is the number of a man; and his number is Six hundred, threescore and six.

Sam yawned and leaned back. Brahms played softly in the background. She looked up. A dust web on the paddle fan above her head wavered slowly. A bit thicker and monkeys could swing from it.
I should wipe that down, she thought. She looked back at the monitor. *I should also be out exercising, but…my ankle.*

It twinged in support. As she wiggled ragg socks on the wooden footrest Nick had made for her, she thought about the time she missed the last stair at exercise class and sustained a sprain that the orthopedic surgeon said was the worst one he had seen that year. She'd hobbled around on crutches for eight weeks without complaint. Her ankle was now a reliable barometer for the weather, and a convenient excuse for avoiding the impassioned pleas of her husband to exercise because he loved her and wanted her to be healthy.

Her fingers fell back onto the keyboard as Selket stirred in her Timberland boot box. The cat's whiskers twitched in a kitty dream.

> Some historians feel the Bible speaks in code. The art of interpreting numbers and letters, or gematria, is known from ancient Babylonian inscriptions. Numbers have meaning beyond their use for measurement. Given that premise, let's look at the number six.
> On the sixth day, woman and man were created; Key 6 in the Tarot is the Lovers; six is the first perfect number in mathematics.
> Doesn't sound so beastly yet.
> Then there is the reference to wisdom: the three vowels in the word Solomon reduce to 666. (O is the 15th letter in the alphabet, 15=1+5=6). And that's a story for another column.
> While collecting information on 666 over the years, I discovered that the atomic number of carbon is 6 and that the carbon 12 atom is composed of 6 electrons, 6 protons, and 6 neutrons, or 666.
> Hang in there.
> Carbon exists in two forms: soft carbon, like pencil lead, and a hard crystalline variety, a pure form of carbon, transparent and flawless, which is the diamond.
> Still with me?

Sam leaned back. *I like it.*

Wondering if the reader would, she pulled at the neck of her red and black plaid nightshirt, then vigorously massaged her scalp, taking pains to avoid the green sponge rubber roller in her bangs.

This information was important. She'd stick some personal stuff in the column before finishing.

Gently sliding the old Bible back into the bookcase, she headed for the kitchen, stopping to straighten her favorite print, *Repose on the Flight into Egypt,* by Luc Olivier Merson. Mary, cradling her baby, looked so peaceful nestled between the paws of the Great Sphinx.

Sam could still remember both times those warm bundles were placed in her arms. Tiny creatures with luminous eyes. The memory still took her breath away.

She sighed as the large ficus by the doorway caught her attention. A knuckle in the soil tested moderately damp. Sam wondered how all her plants actually flourished. Sometimes she swore she could hear their parched screams for water. How many times had her daughters chided her about the veritable jungle in which she worked while she insisted plants cleaned and oxygenated the air and made her feel better? NASA had done a study.

With her foot, she straightened the braided rug in the breezeway and glanced at the thermometer outside the diamond-paned windows. Forty-four degrees in the shade. Had to be colder with the wind chill.

In the kitchen, she winged a finger on the refrigerator door and yelled, "Damn it." The gingerbread-man magnet clattered onto the tiled floor; a photograph floated after it.

As blood trickled, Sam grasped the middle finger that she had diced yesterday along with the carrots. The throbbing reminded her once more that quick movements often lead to trouble. She ran to the bathroom and grabbed the last Band-Aid out of the Johnson & Johnson box.

She marveled that she was such a wimp when it came to small things. Yet she had stoically endured two pregnancies, with the accompanying bouts of morning, afternoon, and evening sickness, and hours of labor, so she felt entitled. And then there was that sprained ankle.

Returning to the galley kitchen, she replaced the magnet on the refrigerator over the corner of the photo of Nick and herself in a carriage in Cozumel. The memory of that romantic cruise brought a smile to her lips, even though she had to lecture three times while on board the ship. But her fare was paid and Nick's was half price.

On the grocery list tucked in a white magnetized pocket on the white refrigerator next to the nameplate, *AMANA, FIRST EDITION*, Sam jotted Band-Aids.

Nick wandered into the kitchen behind her, rubbing his eyes. Points of curly dark hair stuck up around his head.

Sam turned toward him and snickered. "You look like the Statue of Liberty."

Nick bent to peck her on the cheek.

"Hi babe."

Sam suddenly remembered the green foam roller in her bangs and pulled it out. She stuffed the roller in the breast pocket of her nightshirt, fluffed the blonde strands and raked them back into the rest of her hair.

Nick pulled filters from the pine cupboard and patted one into the Braun coffee maker. Sam handed him the Dunkin' Donuts coffee that he ground from beans and kept in the refrigerator and set his moose mug on the counter.

His favorite mug. They had bought it at the Common Ground Fair in Windsor, Maine, about nine years ago. Under the shiny glaze, a black sketch of a moose's head reminded Nick of the wilderness he loved so much.

A hairline crack ran partway down from the lip. Sam didn't know what Nick would do if the cup broke. She'd been on a secret mission looking for one like it ever since he'd dropped it in the sink. Her search was fast becoming a search for the Holy Grail.

Nick made two cups for himself. Sam didn't like coffee.

"You're up early. Working on your column?" he asked.

"Yup. Do you want some breakfast?"

He leaned against the counter and pulled her into his arms. "No, thanks. I have Rotary this morning."

"Oh yeah. I always forget." She wrapped her arms around his waist and pressed her cheek against his bare chest. She liked the feel of his lean, hard body. He would be fifty this year and no rubber tire. No wonder he paraded around in his boxer shorts.

"You going to run tonight?"

"No. Weights and Nordic Track tonight. I run tomorrow."

He kissed the top of her head.

"Don't look too close," she admonished as she threw her head back. "I found two gray hairs last night."

She couldn't quite believe that she would be a half-century old in two years. *Where did the time go?* She thought back to the time her two little girls used to scatter plastic buckets and shovels over the sandbox in the back yard when the first hint of spring blew in. It was only yesterday.

"Well," he assured her, "they don't show."

That's why I love this man. She nuzzled his chest.

"How's the column coming?" he said.

She looked up at him. "Writer's block, at the moment."

"Writer's block? Take a walk." A crooked smile crept up his face as lambent light twinkled in his dark eyes.

Sam gave him the slant eye in return.

After a quick shower, Nick was off to work with his moose mug filled with a second cup of hazelnut coffee. Sam rinsed out the coffee maker, grabbed a blue Pyrex bowl, filled it with what she called 'nuts and twigs' cereal, and followed the woody trail back to her computer.

She stuffed a big spoonful of cereal into her mouth, set the bowl to her right on a tobacco-colored desk pad, and stared at the monitor, listening to the crunchy sounds inside her head.

Two hours later, a strange gurgling sound disturbed her concentration. Her stomach, rebelling against the long empty stretch. She squeezed her shoulder blades back and in toward each other.

A quick glance at the wall clock told her why. Picking up the empty Pyrex bowl, she padded back to the kitchen, vowing to stuff imaginary cotton into her ears against the siren call of the Ring Dings in the back of the vegetable bin.

Sam felt powerful as she grabbed an apple and a small wedge of cheese from the refrigerator. Losing weight was high priority now that spring was around the corner. She dreamed of lounging by the above-ground pool in the back yard in the lime green bathing suit she had bought on sale last fall. A svelte 130 pounds. That meant losing thirty pounds in two and a half months!

Back on the sun porch, she sank into the soft mauve and mint floral sofa cushions, crossed her ankles on the trestle coffee table Nick's father had made, and munched slowly on the Fuji. They were the best eating apples.

Sam loved this room, her office. Especially like this, mid-morning, with bright shafts of sunlight cutting through the bank of windows facing the sun. Dust motes drifted in the still air.

Selket lay coiled in her boot box on the bookcases that ran full length under the windows. The three months since the girls had moved out and Sam had picked the cat up at the SPCA had flown by.

Outside the windows, chickadees, goldfinches, and blue jays yammered around the scattered feeders in the wooded back yard. Their chirping glorified her morning.

"I am content. Yes, Sam, I am."

She stared unseeing, wiggling her toes, thinking about the column that had to go out in the afternoon mail.

Einstein said it, Sam mused, "God does not play dice with the world." There was order in the universe. Especially in her household.

She glanced at the scarred trestle table. Dust? Well, as Erma Bombeck once wrote, "Such dust you wouldn't find on the moon."

She looked out the window once again. There were one…two…three…six birds on the feeder. Six, the number of change in the home. Suddenly she felt uneasy.

And that's when the phone call came.

"Sam. I need to come over. Will you be there?" Charlie asked again.

Sam's voice sounded shaky inside her head. "Yes, I'll be here. I'm not going anywhere now, except to load my .38. I hope this creep doesn't know where we live." She slid the green polar fleece blanket off the back of the couch and bunched it against her chest. "And if he does come creeping around here, he'll get a bullet between the eyes."

"Yeah. Well, make sure Nick pulls him inside after you do it." He laughed but it didn't lighten her mood.

Sam spoke quietly. "By the way, Charlie, don't mention this to Nick or the girls or Mom. You know, about the note mentioning me. I don't want them upset unnecessarily."

"I'll keep it under wraps as long as possible, but you know Kent Butcher. He's got a nose on him like a bloodhound. Never could figure out how he finds out what he does. Kind of makes *Publick Occurrences* more interesting though."

"More like a tabloid, if you ask me."

"Seems Butcher's gotten even meaner since his wife left him two years ago. Don't know how she put up with him in the first place, her working all those hours and him spending all the money. Thinks he belongs on the cover of some fancy man's magazine or something."

Sam shuddered at the thought of Kent raving at her about the public's right to know.

"And then there's our unofficial town manager, Agatha," Charlie added. "She probably knew about it before it happened."

"Yes, there's always Agatha," Sam said softly.

"By the way, I heard Sadie moved in with Caroline over in Portsmouth. How do they like their new digs?"

Sam knew he was trying to lighten the conversation.

"Good." Her voice seemed to belong to someone else. "I feel better, now that they're living together. It's safer, and they share expenses. I'll see you in a few minutes, Charlie."

Sam stared vacantly at the phone for a long time, then flung it across the room into the wicker basket holding the girls' old stuffed animals.

Selket upset her cardboard nest as she bolted from the room.

The once comforting silence of her office now seemed threatening.

Sam draped the warm, lightweight blanket around her shoulders and hugged her legs to her chest. Fear telegraphed along her nerves.

How tenuous life is, she thought. *One moment can change everything.*

She pulled the blanket tighter around her knees hoping Stephen King was right. At a recent UNH lecture he had said never leave a hand or foot dangling over the edge of the bed, just pull up the covers and you're safe.

Even under the green fleece blanket, Sam didn't feel safe. Her eyes locked on the half-eaten apple. Would she be next? Or worse, her husband or daughters? Certainly someone was next, maybe a friend or a neighbor. After killing once, what was to stop him from killing again? The punishment for one murder was the same as for two, or six, or a dozen. He had nothing to lose.

The lump in her throat felt like a watermelon.

Would he stalk her? How do people deal with being stalked? Looking over their shoulders, starting at every ring of the phone, afraid to open the door, fearing the shadows of night. Well, it wasn't going to happen to her or her family. How dare that monster violate the sanctity of her home. She wouldn't live in fear. She'd go after the bastard first.

Sam snatched up the apple and the cheese, stomped to the kitchen, and ripped open one of the six Ring Ding packages ineptly hidden behind the organic butternut squash.

Chapter 2

Charlie unzipped his Red Sox baseball jacket, placed the matching cap on the table next to him, and with both hands, smoothed back his thinning hair. Then he picked up a thick white porcelain mug and slurped black coffee as he watched Sam scowl over a copy of the killer's message.

Sam looked up, casting ice blue eyes at the chief. "Jesus, Charlie! This is terrible. What are you doing about it?"

"Me and the State Police, you mean. You remember Grant Webber?"

"I should. He's your brother-in-law."

Upon meeting him for the first time, Sam had stuck out a friendly hand and said, "Hi, Grant."

"Officer Webber," he had replied, with a bone-crunching shake.

With his taut stomach and pumped chest, he looked like Road Runner. Sam expected one day the shiny buttons would pop off his spotless jacket and go beep-beep.

"We're doing about everything we can," Charlie continued, as he eyeballed the plate of chocolate chip cookies Sam had automatically placed on the trestle table. "Testing the paper and body for fibers, saliva. Checking out the type of paper, glue, where the letters might have come from, questioning Hammand's family and friends, anyone who might have seen him recently. And if we're lucky enough to find fingerprints, we'll send them through databases around the country. But you can help, Sam. This was directed at you."

He paused, then quickly added, "I don't mean 'at you,' like he's going to come after you, Sam. I mean he's trying to pull you into his sick game. Obviously that's where he gets his kicks. The cracker thinks he's smart, and he wants you to try and outwit him."

Charlie set down his coffee mug, shifted in the chair, and inhaling deeply, reached for a chocolate chip cookie with a hand the size of a baseball glove. He chuckled. "Love the smell of chocolate in the morning."

Sam caught the reference to the Duval character's love of napalm from the film *Apocalypse Now*, but she couldn't respond. She felt like she was wrapped in Saran, unable to move, barely breathing. *Is this how a mummy feels?* she wondered.

She stared at her hands cupped in her lap. Her stomach felt hollow, even after two Ring Dings. Talking face-to-face with Charlie about the murder and the note brought the reality of her fear home with a violent aftershock.

And she was upset with herself. At her waist, the band of her size large sweatpants was leaving a red ring the size of Saturn's. She tugged angrily at it.

"These cookies are great!" Charlie said, grabbing at a crumb that skittered down the front of his dark green work shirt and onto his lap.

Selket, food radar ever on alert, flumped down onto the carpet and rubbed against Charlie's brand-free pant leg.

Sam stared at Charlie Burrows, the friend she had shared her lunch with in grade school so he wouldn't go hungry. The years had thinned and faded his acorn-colored hair. His leathery skin was reminiscent of an old wallet whose tired edges reflected years of trustworthy service. Even though his eyes still twinkled, his gentle demeanor was belied by the ragged scar running down the left side of his face and onto his cheek. More than one roughneck had backed away from him in the face of trouble.

"Don't you give her any cookies, Charlie! She's fat enough," Sam admonished, then fell even more sullen at the thought of her own struggle with Ring Dings.

Charlie giggled at the twenty-three-pound orange tabby. "When you pick him up, do you lift with your legs?"

Charlie's soprano rills used to send Sam into convulsions in third grade and was responsible for the only dismissal in her school career, but nothing seemed funny this day.

"Her," Sam said for the umpteenth time. She didn't know why she bothered.

The cat, realizing she wasn't going to get any crumbs, heaved herself up onto the shelf and settled into her box.

Sam's attention was drawn back to the sheet of paper on the table before her. She was afraid to touch the copy, as if contact with the malignant message would suck her into an even more macabre world of horror. She lightly massaged her bandaged finger. A headache hovered at the fringes of her temples.

"He's obsessive," Charlie went on, punching a finger at the air. "Look at those penciled lines. Looks like the cracker measured them. Couldn't have one letter out of place."

Sam read the note for the fifth time.

13-14-24-22-3-9-9-8-14-25-9-3-12-25-5-20-9-20-13-19-5-18-12-14-15-14
CIVILIZATION IS THE KEY
DON'T RAIL AT THE FATES
RATHER FENCE WITH ME
SAVE VICTIM NUMBER 4 BY POSTING ANSWER
ON MCCUTTYS BULLETIN BOARD BY APRIL 1
CATCH ME IF YOU CAN SAM BLACKWELL

"Jesus, Charlie!" She rubbed her forehead hard. "Victim number four? It sounds like he's killed before. Do you think this guy's serious?" She desperately wanted him to say no.

"Don't know of any other homicides 'round here recently, at least not that would relate to this one. 'Course you never know how things tie in, Manchester and Boston being less than an hour from here. Could be someone passing through, but that don't seem likely, given the nutcase is waiting around for an answer at McCutty's."

Charlie took another bite and mumbled on through cookie chunks. "We have to assume he's local and he's serious. I hate to put this on you, Sam, but you see the problem."

He lifted a mitt to snare errant chocolate bits. "The answer lies in that rhyme, some kind of code, and he seems to think you can solve it. I have to agree."

He popped in the last cookie crumb. "You've studied codes for a long time. Got a goddamn library here on the subject." His hand swept right and bumped against Selket's box. Selket shot straight into the air like a jack-in-the-box and landed on the floor by Charlie's feet.

"Oops...sorry, old boy."

Sam eyes rolled ceilingward as Charlie grunted down toward polished size thirteen combat boots to scrub the tabby. "How old's this guy?"

"*She's* around ten. They weren't sure. She was a stray."

Totally oblivious of the pronoun change, Charlie said, "You got this guy at the SPCA, right? How come you didn't get a kitten?"

Selket arched into the vigorous rub, then, when Charlie fell back against the protesting rocker, she lumbered out of the room to find her food dish.

"I don't know." Sam looked out at a bright blue sky as if the answer lay out there beyond her grasp. "I was going to, then I saw this one, on the bottom tier, by herself. She was so thin, seemed lost. Like she hadn't eaten in a long time. No one wants the old ones."

Her mind drifted cloudlike as she watched Charlie replace the Timberland boot box on the bookcase and stuff her worn fuzzy pink bathrobe inside.

The Egyptians held these independent felines in high esteem so Sam had set out to buy a faux sheepskin oval in keeping with Selket's royal lineage. But the cat had turned up her damp nose at it, choosing the boot box instead. Didn't matter. She was happy.

Sam felt so remote, almost out-of-the-body. Here she was, thinking about shoeboxes and Egyptians, while Doug lay in the morgue, and the killer had challenged her to solve the code before he killed someone else. Probably someone she knew. A neighbor. Maybe her. Or, for another terrifying moment, she thought about Nicholas, her daughters and her mother, whereupon she crashed back into her well-grounded body.

Charlie settled back with another cookie. "We'll catch him. Don't you worry." His warm chocolate eyes surveyed her. "There isn't much that goes on in this town that I don't know about. And what I don't know, Brun will tell me."

Brunhilda and his four daughters were responsible for any sensitivity training that Charlie had learned.

Sam struggled to replace fear with an image of the irrepressible Brunhilda. "Well, she does know everyone. It's all those meetings she goes to."

"She's the meetinest woman I ever knew."

"The activity keeps her furnace burning on our long winter nights, Charlie, although I would think your Valkyrie maiden would be used to cold temperatures."

"If she stayed home long enough, I'd keep her warm."

"I'm sure you would," Sam said, and finally smiled. "You know, whenever I see her rushing about with that long pigtail flapping behind her, I hear strains of Wagner's Die Walküre."

"Yeah. Whatever. So what do you think, Sam? Any idea what kind of code this is?" Charlie's eye caressed a third cookie.

Sam looked once again at the chilling note. "Well," she felt a shiver run across her shoulders, "there's no number over 26, so maybe the numbers represent the letters of the alphabet. I don't know. I'm going to have to work on it." The ring of pain around her forehead tightened. "I need an aspirin."

She didn't want to think about the note. She had a column to finish, then Nick was going to meet her for lunch at the Gang Plank in Hampton to talk again about a trip to the southwest, just the two of them. After twenty years in the printing business, Nick wanted to take a month off. His hippie dream.

Sam wasn't sure. What would the kids do without her for a month? Caroline and Sadie called her the "Godmother," and they didn't mean the fairy godmother.

Embroiled in a killer's riddle was not part of her day's itinerary. But if she didn't solve the damned thing before April 1st, some other unsuspecting citizen of Georgetown would end up like poor Doug Hammand.

April Fool's Day. Twelve days away.

Under the insulated blinds at the top of one of the windows, a fly buzzed drowsily. The sound reminded Sam of an article she wrote about a befuddled spider and the fly that kept returning with the same message, over and over, waiting for the spider to catch on. Was she the spider and this madman the fly? Would he keep returning over and over with the same message?

This wasn't happening!

With her right thumb, she massaged the center of her left palm. Her mind tended to short circuit from one terminal to another these days. Premenopausal, she thought unhappily.

Charlie twisted in his chair; his shiny jacket hitched up under one arm. "I'm going to leave some photographs with you, Sam. Umm...I want to warn you, some of them are pretty graphic." He pulled an envelope from an inside pocket.

Sam faded against the flowered cushions. Ring Dings stirred in the volcanic depths of her stomach while her eyes followed the oversized envelope that Charlie slid across the trestle table toward her.

The chief of police slumped back, idly rubbing the pencil-thin scar by his left eye. Daggers of light flashed from his gold wedding band across the table and cut over the manila envelope.

They sat in a silence broken only by the sweet chirping of small birds in the back yard and the distant caw of a crow.

Finally Charlie spoke. "I'm sorry, Sam. Really. But, if you can look at them, you might see something that could help you with the note. If you can't, hey," he waved at the air, "I understand. Believe me."

Sam folded goosefleshed arms across her chest and worked to control the fear. She willed her internal pump to slow, the artificially flavored, partially hydrogenated chocolate lava rising in her chest to retreat.

Inside that deceptively plain envelope lay the final moments of a man's life—a man she knew. A man who had turned over a successful construction business to his daughter and gone on to become chief inspector of Coldbath Industries. He was a big supporter of Little League, a whittler. A pair of his beautiful loons sat on her mantle. Sam would always remember Doug Hammand's jack-o-lantern smile. Why did he deserve this?

Charlie finally succumbed, heaved himself up off the chair with a mighty grunt, zipped his jacket, capped his head, and grabbed a third cookie. He patted Sam on the shoulder.

"Give me a call if you have any ideas. Or if you need anything. Anything at all."

Sam nodded numbly.

Moments later she got a glass of water and popped two aspirins, then used the glass and a slip of paper to release the little buzzer outside.

No more death today, she said silently, as the fly circled up and away. She hoped it wouldn't return.

Chapter 3

The second set of historical facts every schoolchild in Georgetown committed to memory was that New Hampshire had become a colony in 1679, and some hundred years later, its independent natives overwhelmingly supported ratifying the Constitution. Little note was made of the date in between when, after a dispute over land grants in what is now Vermont, Ethan Allen and his Green Mountain Boys sent the proud New Hampshirites scurrying back home in disgrace. Georgetown residents remained stonily silent on the ignominious whipping wrought on their defeated ancestors with birch rods whittled from their own state tree.

However, first in the memory and hearts of every true Georgian was the year 1794, when William Hornblower Coldbath III made a discovery.

A sandy bog.

William's grandfather had been granted a tract of land through New Hampshire's first royal governor, Benning Wentworth. When the two elder Williams died and bequeathed land and fortune to their only male inheritor, the third William decided to survey the acreage. He had just crested the knob of a hill on the back forty acres when his palomino stumbled and sent him tumbling down through a thick stand of white pine. He landed face down in a sandy bog on an acre that his father and grandfather had deemed worthless.

But young William was a wily man who was known for his ingenuity, amongst other more carnal talents. As he lay in the spongy soil with a mouth full of sphagnum, he had an awakening.

Cranberries! The sandy bog would be ideal for growing *Vaccinium vitis-idaea* or mountain cranberries, also known as cowberries.

And he did just that. With the help of his ten sons, William's berries multiplied. The Coldbath men saw to the planting, and then the flooding of the bogs that destroyed insects as well as protecting vines from frosts and freezing weather. William's wife and two daughters made chutney from the cranberries that weren't traded or sold.

One auspicious day in 1798, Mrs. Coldbath carried two jars of her special chutney to her friend and neighbor, Mrs. Merryweather, who had suffered a broken foot when her prize cow, Maybelle, decided she'd had just about enough milking, thank you.

From the Merryweather's table, the second jar of Coldbath chutney crossed the Atlantic. Mrs. Merryweather was nothing if not quietly loyal to the crown and still in touch with her only brother, who groomed the king's stallions and was in love with chutney as well as the royal kitchen maid.

From there it was a mere skip and a jump to the table of King George III, who, once he had sampled Coldbath's Cowberry Chutney from the New World, would eat no other.

Word of the king's culinary approval spread, and soon the royal plates of Europe as well as the Presidential Spode were garnished with the tasty fruit.

William, of course, placed his signature on the label of his wife's chutney.

The fame of Coldbath Chutney grew down through the centuries and resulted in the thriving tourist town of Georgetown, which boasted a sparkling clean chutney plant and an autumnal Cowberry Festival held on the town green.

William's inheritors' begetting, however, had dwindled to the point that, today, the secret recipe lay in the capable but elderly maiden hands of his last progeny, Agatha Beatrice Coldbath.

Georgetown had a problem.

But Samantha had a bigger one at the moment.

She knew that Nick sensed something was bothering her during lunch at the Gang Plank, but his mind was preoccupied. His conversation had flipped between his plans for a southwest trip and the blues for this year's Coldbath Cowberry Chutney catalog sitting on his desk. Agatha wouldn't find even one mistake like she did last year, he had said, even if it were only a comma. Georgetown Printers had a reputation to uphold.

Sam left Hampton under a cloudless sky, crossed over Interstate 95, and raced west over Route 101 toward home. The local newspaper, *Publick Occurrences*, reported that this two-lane fifteen miles of Route 101 connecting Hampton Beach over Interstate 95 to Epping, where the road widened on its way to Manchester, would be under construction until the year 2001. Bridges would be completed first, thereby eliminating traffic lights that created miles of bottlenecked traffic.

The traffic on this route was especially unbearable and dangerous during the summer when vacationers from the forty-nine states and beyond swelled the body count in Hampton and its beach from twelve thousand to over one hundred thousand. The Hampton Beach opening of McDonalds was the second largest in the world, after Hong Kong. Sam often wondered aloud how evacuation would be possible if the neighboring Seabrook nuclear plant ever had an accident.

According to authorities, the continuation of Route 101 from Epping to Hampton Beach was long overdue. Markers counting the number of fatalities on this narrow two-lane stretch of road had finally come down, but Daylight Headlight Use signs still peppered the wayside.

Sam crossed over the Squamscott River and came to a stop at the last stationary traffic light, which was slated to disappear in the next few months. Her head felt tight as she sat drumming her fingers on the steering wheel.

Clustered around twenty-five foot walls of concrete forms, men in yellow hard hats and blue jeans talked, drank coffee, shoveled, poured cement. Sun glinted off Audley backloaders and trucks rumbling about in seeming chaos.

Someone knew what was going on. Sam wished she did.

She adjusted her dark Ray Bans as her eyes darted from the red light three cars ahead to her rearview mirror. Would she know if someone were following her? Not on this road, but up ahead, when she turned onto Pine Road, she would know. That short stretch of rumpled tar connecting to Middle Road saw few cars and occasional trucks. If someone did follow her, she'd stop at the end of Pine Road at the Thompson place.

Her heart felt as low as the gas gauge read. She'd have to remember to keep the tank full from now on. Just in case.

Oh God, she moaned. *What is happening to my world? Am I reduced to this?* Her body felt hollow, a shell carrying her about, moving of its own volition.

She ran a hand over the grainy cloth of the handbag on the bucket seat next to her. Faces of the children of the world gazed at her. She had bought the handmade purse at a fair last summer in York, Maine. Everyone remarked on the material—in line at Shop 'N Save, at Osco Drug, at the dentist's office. It worked because, in its roomy interior, she could stuff books, snacks, a water bottle, and now aspirin and another more potent item.

Her throat was parched. With her eyes glued to the traffic light, she rummaged inside the bag and felt for the bottle. Her hand lit on cold metal and recoiled.

Get used to it, she told herself. *You might have to use it.*

She pulled out a ten ounce Tropicana juice bottle now filled with water—she disliked drinking out of plastic bottles—positioned it between her thighs, and unscrewed the cap as the traffic light turned green.

As if the hounds of hell were on their heels, the cars ahead abruptly screeched forward. The driver in the silver Mercury behind her leaned on his horn as Sam fumbled with the water bottle.

She peered into the rearview mirror. White glare met her eyes. She couldn't see who was driving. The killer wouldn't blow his horn at her in the middle of the day with everyone watching, would he?

Sam attacked the gas pedal and her dependable Honda Accord lurched into warp speed, leaving the old Mercury chortling to catch up.

From habit born of the high mortality rate on this stretch of road, she hugged the white line on the right. Two miles later, signaling at the last moment, she slued left onto Pine Road. The Mercury continued west on 101.

As Sam watched her speedometer arc to twenty, then thirty, thirty-five, she cracked the window open to get some fresh air. She glanced into the side view and overhead mirrors. Perspiration broke out on her white-knuckled hands while the car bucked over potholes like an angry bull intent on unseating its rider. She glanced at the Band-Aid on her finger, as thoughts banged and thumped in her mind like a sneaker in the dryer.

Am I getting paranoid? It's broad daylight. Who would try anything now? Even on this less traveled road. This is ridiculous. He's not after me. She was not convinced.

She barely stopped at the T-intersection in front of the old Thompson homestead, didn't look to see if Scooter was seated in his wicker rocker on the porch, waving as he almost always did. She winged a right onto Middle Road and almost into the path of a dark blue Taurus. The driver shook his fist at her.

Sorry, she mouthed, threw her hands up quickly as an apology then gripped the wheel once again.

A moment later, a Vandalay Enterprises truck rumbled by in the opposite direction. Mmmmm, brrrrrrr, mmmmmm, brrrrrrr. She heard the Jake brake applied as the apple-red truck prepared for the hill.

The guy keeps his truck so clean I might hire him to come over and dust. Sam laughed too loud, startling herself.

As the crowd of white pines, drooping hemlocks, and burgeoning maples along the roadside thinned and the sky opened, her muscles began to unknot. The road gently wended past an open field where a handful of cows chewed brown grasses by a stream. Ahead on the right, a simple white-steepled church sparkled in the still cold late winter sun. Sam felt comforted by the pastoral setting. Only good things could happen here.

A weathered vegetable stand came into view. Behind it, and back from the road behind a row of ancient sugar maples, Peter and Anne Williams' old two-story frame farmhouse stood silent, almost lonely looking, its windows watching the road like a loyal hound dog waiting for its master's return. The Williams had gone to New York for his mother's funeral.

There would be another funeral service in a few days, Sam thought sullenly. She hoped there would be only one.

Back in the center of town, She slid her plum-colored Honda into her garage and pressed the remote on the visor. In the rearview mirror, she watched the statue of Old William Coldbath that dominated the center of the green disappear behind the lowering garage door. The door struck the cement floor with a clunk.

She was alone.

HE watched her. He loved to watch her.

The plum-colored Honda was six cars ahead. She had left the Gang Plank Restaurant and was heading west on Route 101, toward Georgetown and home, he assumed. When she turned quickly onto Pine Road, signaling at the last minute, he knew he was right. That sudden turn also told him she was scared. He was pleased. His plan was working.

As he sailed past Pine Road, he blew a kiss after her.

Chapter 4

The dim overhead light in Samantha's garage cast a pall over the rakes and shovels hanging neatly on the brown Pegboard Nick had installed when they first moved in—God, was it twenty-two years ago? Stacks of neatly tied newspapers sat at the foot of the Pegboard waiting for a trip to the recycling center. A black crowbar and two battered canoe paddles leaned into the corner between the two-by-fours. Overhead, an Old Towne canoe rested on the rafters.

Sam took a long drink of water from the Tropicana juice bottle, then dropped her head against the headrest. At least no one had followed her. She couldn't work herself into a frenzy and play into the psychopath's hands. He wasn't interested in her, except for the game he was playing. After a minute of deep breathing, she felt somewhat stitched back together.

As she stepped into the wallpapered back hallway, she caught a whiff of cat food and reminded herself to get a scented Plug-In for the outlet under the counter where the blue plastic dishes sat. She hoped to wean Selket off wet food and onto dry per the veterinarian's suggestion.

She stood stone still and listened. The house was quiet. Everything seemed all right. She draped the handle of her bag over the arm of the pine bench by the door and brushed a loose strand of hair back, reworking it into the yellow flowered scrunchie at her neck.

After a search of every nook and cranny of the house, during which she found Selket's yellow and white plastic ball with a bell inside and one of Nick's white Wigwam socks under their king-size bed, she made a quick trip to the bathroom for two aspirins. Then she slipped out of the mossy green jersey dress, into sweats, and plopped at her desk, spent.

An hour and a half later, the headache was history and the column, sealed in an envelope, waited on the hall counter. Work was speedier now that she had succumbed to a computer. The Internet, in spite of constant protests from Caroline and Sadie, was galaxies away.

If the truth were known, Sam sheltered a fantasy resulting from too many *Murder She Wrote* episodes, where she sat in a sunny kitchen, at a table covered with a blue gingham-checked cloth, manuscript pages stacked neatly to one side. Without error or hesitation, arched fingers tapped at round black keys on an old Underwood typewriter like her Aunt Miriam used to own. She was writing a mystery.

The reality was entirely different. Her words did not flow as they did from Jessica Fletcher's facile and fertile mind. Retyping was a nightmare, and page inserts were an anathema for editors. She knew. Her first two numerology books had come off a portable typewriter on an ironing board in front of the sofa. She was now addicted to her WordPerfect program.

Crumpled over sheets of paper, Sam worked on the ghastly code. Since there were no numbers over twenty-six, the numbers must represent the letters in the alphabet. But the solution couldn't be that simple, and it wasn't.

Using the number-letter code, she substituted A for 1, B for 2, C for 3, and so on. The numbers, resolved to the letters, read:

MNXVCIIHNYICLYETITMSERLNON

Samantha straightened up to stare at her neat, tight script. It didn't mean a thing to her.

She scratched the middle of her back with a wooden ruler, then seesawed her shoulders, absently wondering if the killer scratched his back with the ruler he used to draw those neat lines. What was going through his demented mind? What drove him to do such a terrible thing?

Her thoughts shifted to Doug. She imagined his lifeless rag doll body tossed in with the frozen fish.

Sorry. Don't need you any more. I'm through playing.

Sam had to quell her anger if she was going to concentrate. Somewhere hidden in those capital letters was the answer that could save the next victim's life.

She squinted at the line, willed it to speak to her.

After a good twenty minutes, her mind at *tabula rasa*, she glanced up at the clock. Time was ticking by and she was getting nowhere. She rippled her shoulders again and leaned back, yawning behind tented fingers.

Maybe the word 'civilization' was the key, just as the note said.

Tugging her beloved 2,059-page Random House Dictionary onto the desk pad and flipping through tissue-thin pages, she was reminded of how she'd carried, next to her five-year-old heart, the Children's Golden Book Encyclopedia with its brightly colored picture definitions. How she'd loved that book. She had taken it to bed each night and placed it carefully under her pillow hoping that when she woke she would know all those words.

Sam ran a finger under the word 'civilization.'

It was defined as: '1. an advanced state of human society, in which a high level of culture, science, industry, and government has been reached. 2. those people or nations that have reached such a state. 3. the type of culture, society, etc., of a specific place, time, or group: *Greek civilization*. 4. the act or process of civilizing or being civilized: *Rome's civilization of barbaric tribes was admirable....*'

Advanced state, people who are civilized, governments that are civilized. What does it mean to be civil?

She lowered her head, closed her eyes and rubbed the crease beginning to form between her brows. Like Nick's.

Her mind wandered. She had heard that, after so many years, married people begin to look alike. That was just fine with her as long as she got Nick's naturally curly hair.

She sniffed, leaned back, crossed her ankles on the wooden footrest and watched the dust strings on the paddle over her head stir every so slightly.

Living a civil life, a civil society.

Thoughts tumbled over synapses for another half-hour.

Drowsy, she closed her eyes for a few minutes, felt herself drifting away when the phone rang.

Sam jumped. She recalled the last time she answered the phone and it was Charlie with the news about Doug Hammand.

She let out a big sigh, pulled the elastic from her hair and onto her wrist, wincing as a lock got tangled. While the answering machine picked up the message, she massaged her head.

It was Kent Butcher. He pleaded. He begged. He cajoled.

Fat chance, Sam thought.

She pulled her hair back into the elastic and turned to Roget's Thesaurus that she kept to the left of the keyboard. Rifling through the index, she found the word 'civilization' with two subtitles: improvement 691.3 and society 642.3.

With a pen she printed CIVILIZATION at the top of a clean sheet of paper. Below it, heading two columns, the words improvement and society, were neatly underlined.

Under improvement, she listed: cultivation, culture, refinement, polish, civility, cultivation of the mind, acculturation, enculturation, socialization, enlightenment, education 475.4, 562.1-3.

Beneath society: culture, society, trait, culture, key trait, complex, culture-complex, trait-complex, culture area, culture center, folkways, mores, system of values, ethos, culture pattern, cultural change, cultural lag, culture conflict, acculturation, culture contact [Brit], cultural drift.

Chewing on her thumbnail, she stared at the two columns and thought about what the note said.

She sat motionless for a long time.

Suddenly, from out of nowhere, a ball of fur landed on top of her desk and sent papers flying and her blotter skating.

Sam threw her hands in the air as the papers fluttered to the floor. "Jumpin' Jiminy, Selket! You scared the bejesus out of me."

She bundled the mounds of flesh against her chest and kissed the old cat's head. The cat rewarded her with loud purrs and a lick of her hand.

"It's a conundrum, Selket," Sam murmured into the cat's thick neck fur. The cat purred louder, her claws kneading Sam's yellow sweatshirt.

"Ouch! Careful, sweetie."

She disengaged the long talons and reminded herself to trim Selket's nails. Setting the cat on the desk, she replaced the desk pad, restacked papers, and got up stiffly. Rubbing her temples, she began pacing the floor.

The sky was the color of morning glories, the afternoon sun a shimmering disk of gold. Nature was unaware of the death and mayhem that surrounded Sam, or at least, seemed blithely unconcerned.

The answering machine picked up another message from Kent Butcher. The first call had come from way up in Gorham. He was on his way back now and insisted on an interview. She turned down the volume.

It would seem the story hadn't leaked too badly so far, Sam thought, as she stretched down in an attempt to touch her toes. The tendons, or whatever the hell they were, pulled and screamed at the back of her calves, "I'll get you, and your little dog, too." She and Selket were going on a diet very soon.

Kent was the only reporter who had called, so he must have found out that her name was on the note—he had to have a crony in the police department—and with an exclusive dangling before his shark eyes, he wouldn't reveal what he knew to anyone. He'd be pounding on her door for an exclusive before nightfall. She wouldn't answer.

She found herself in the kitchen surveying the contents of the refrigerator. Yogurt, plastic container of peaches, bread, sliced cheese, raspberry spritzer, cream cheese, leftover beans from last night, Stonewall Red Pepper Jelly...that sounded good. She filled a tray and took it back to her desk. Selket watched entranced as Sam smeared cream cheese on the first cracker and topped it with an eyeball of pepper jelly.

Sam scanned the list again.

Government, civility, culture…

With a whole cracker in her mouth, she pushed herself upright in the swivel chair, closed her eyes, laid her palms face up, and forced herself to relax.

Let it go, let it flow…the cracker made crackly sounds inside her head…Why did I pick those three words out of all the words on this list?…crunch…government, civility, culture…images passed behind her lids…marching figures…

Sam had always thought everyone saw movies behind their eyelids. It wasn't until September of the second grade, when Mr. Gompers asked the class to tell what they had done that summer, that Sam realized she would never again talk to the outside world about her pictures.

She tried to relax.

Behind her eyes, the legions of dead marched on silent bony feet. Contrasting with the drab gray of their uniforms, the sky was a dazzling blue. Tufts of pink cotton-ball clouds squeezed bloody stars from their insides that rained down over the countryside.

The image, too terrible, sent a pulsating tremor through her. Her eyes snapped open. She pulled hard at the neck of her sweatshirt. Sweat beaded her forehead.

An army of dead? What could it mean? Not more bodies in Georgetown, please. At the root of her soul, a pain throbbed like a bad toothache.

All those years under the bed covers with a flashlight and puzzle book had to serve some purpose. She couldn't fail. Someone's life most certainly depended on her success.

She ran a finger nervously around the top of her glass, took another sip of ice water. Then she perused the sheets of paper spread over her desk. The 9 X 12 envelope lay to the side unopened.

Focus!

"Civilization is key…rail at the fates…"

What did it mean? Civilization and rail. What did they have in common?

With elbows planted on the desk, she buried her head in her hands. From the corner of her eye she could see the envelope. She rocked for a few minutes.

"Bite the bullet," she said, then cringed at the analogy.

With a trembling hand, she reached for the manila envelope and slowly untucked the flap. No visions of sugarplums dancing here, no more celebrations, holidays, Christmas wreaths or cowberry chutney. No more coffee klatches at the Bog Café. The genial hometown boy could never have imaged his final resting-place amongst frozen flounder in McCutty's Market.

What could his two sons and daughter be feeling now? It was bad enough to lose a loved one, but murder? Her mind could not wrap itself around the horror.

Not able to put her hand inside, she grasped the envelope by one corner, shook it. Five photographs slid out onto the tan desk pad. Face up. With a pencil's eraser, Sam carefully arranged the glossies side by side. She avoided a direct look.

She had read about strangle victims with their purple, swollen faces, features often twisted beyond recognition, bloody fluids seeping from the nose and mouth.

Pretend it's not real, she told herself, as unwilling eyes moved slowly over the first photograph.

It was grotesque. Not only had he been strangled, but he looked like he'd been filleted like the frozen fish around his lifeless body. A single incision ran from his neck to the bulging flesh at his belt line.

Hugging her chest and wishing she hadn't eaten that one cracker, she peered at the body splayed over the frozen food case. One leg seemed almost detached. It hung limply over the edge of the silver frame and twisted inward, back toward the case.

Focus on images.

A cowberry garland tight about his neck. A crushed yellow daffodil askew in the lapel slit. A single neat incision. A lifeless body nestled amongst the fish with their dead moon eyes and gaping mouths. A permanent record of the silent cries of the dead, the monochromatic scene seemed eerily colorful in the black hands of death.

Lost in a dream, Selket lay sprawled over the thesaurus on Sam's desk, twitching and snuffling. Sam's sad eyes watched her for a moment—with so much fat, the old girl probably didn't feel the book beneath her—then her eyes fell back on the photographs.

Doug Hammand was a whiskered plump little man with a happy smile. After the loss of his one and only wife eight years ago, he had turned his construction business over to his daughter, Patricia. Before work at the chutney plant, he had spent every breakfast and some lunches at the Bog Café, gossiping with cronies, teasing the waitresses, hailing acquaintances who dropped in for a jar of chutney or coffee to go. The days had become too short and the nights too long.

Sam teared up. At least now he was with Betty. With the tip of her forefinger, Sam lightly caressed the face in the photograph as tears spilled down her cheeks.

After a quick trip to the bathroom for a splash of cold water, she settled back at her desk.

Doug was wearing his one good suit, the suit he wore at his wife's funeral and the Cowberry Festival Parades in September. That was it. He was heard more than once referring to it as that damnable undertaker's suit. Surely he wouldn't have worn it without very good reason.

Sam would check the florist to see if Doug had bought a bouquet of daffodils recently but he could just as easily have picked a single daffodil most anywhere in town. Did the flower have anything to do with the solution?

Back to business.

Civilization is the key.

Sam clenched her hands and smarted when her bandaged finger rebelled. What was the answer?

She was hunched over her notes when the normally melodious chimes of the doorbell ran ragged over her nerves. Selket jumped from the desk and found her way to the Timberland box while Sam got up and draped the sweater from the back of her chair over the photographs on the desk. Arching her back, rubbing the knots in her shoulders, she hobbled into the breezeway on her left leg, which had fallen asleep, stopping to check the temperature.

In the kitchen, she hesitated briefly before the mirror on the brick wall to check her teeth, then limped toward the front door.

The Ridgeway grandfather clock in the living room chimed four times as she passed. Usually, like the tramp living by the railroad tracks who woke one night because the train didn't go through at the scheduled time, she didn't hear it. But now, every sound in her home seemed magnified.

No one used the front door. And it couldn't be Kent Butcher. No way he would have gotten here that quickly.

Through the door's sidelight, Sam spied her.

Agatha Coldbath pressed the buzzer resolutely then stood back, ramrod straight in her double-breasted wool Chesterfield coat, with a fine but worn black leather handbag securely under one arm.

Sam closed her eyes as she reached for the knob. She hoped the apparition would disappear before she opened them. She was not in the mood.

"I am most surprised at you, Samantha Blackwell!"

Agatha brushed past her and perched ninety-eight pounds on the edge of the green striped couch, the pocketbook clutched squarely on her knees.

As Sam quietly closed the door, her head dropped to her chest. "May I take your coat?"

"No, thank you, and please do not interrupt. I have something to say and do not need distractions."

Sam sank into the wing chair to Agatha's right as she eyeballed the dust kitties under the end table with some trepidation.

The old woman launched into her diatribe. "As President of Coldbath Industries and a member of the board of the prestigious Keep Our Berry Bogs Clean Committee, I would have expected more from you, Samantha Blackwell."

The good old KOBBCC, Sam mused, fingering the deep rose arm cover. But then Agatha would never stoop to use an acronym. She studiously fixed her attention on Agatha's sharp washed-blue eyes, above the white hairs that sprouted from her top lip.

"This state of affairs is totally unacceptable," Agatha announced. "You know our town's economy, not to mention my reputation, rests on my world renowned chutney. Why, the royal family to this day continues to import our chutney. It graces the dinner table of the White House. Our chutney has an impeccable history." Agatha was up to full steam. The little train that could. "You know that King George III was so delighted with my family's cowberry chutney that he would eat no other."

Sam worked hard at not reminding Agatha that his royal personage went quite mad the last nine years of his life.

"And now we have a dead body in McCutty's Market with a garland of *cowberries* about his neck. We cannot have a taint on our cowberries. What will happen to the town? What would William have said about such a sad state of affairs?"

Agatha shook her snuff-colored Mamie Eisenhower bangs. Real antique pearls peeked above the black velvet collar of her coat. Her monologue continued.

Sam wondered if the old woman knew that the dead body in McCutty's belonged to one of her employees. Maybe the death was related to the secret recipe of old William's chutney or more accurately, his wife's chutney recipe. Sam thought, somewhat gleefully, that William must be beside himself—heavens no, that would mean there were two of him—anyway, he'd be pretty mortified to find *his* sacred recipe in the hands of a female since he had regarded all women, including his wife, as convenient appendages. He had been given to signing his name in large script followed by the microscopic post, 'and wife.'

With thunder gathering on her brow, Miss Coldbath filled her thin chest with steam and prepared for the next chug.

"Would you like some tea, Agatha? And I have croissants from the Gang Plank."

Agatha hesitated, her thin colorless mouth set in a straight line. Pastries from the Gang Plank Bakery had the power to soothe the savage breast.

Agatha lifted her small chin and stared down her nose at Sam. "I don't suppose you have Earl Grey tea."

Luckily, Sam kept Earl Grey on hand for Caroline. Her oldest daughter's tastes ran to champagne. "As a matter of fact, I do. Milk and sugar?" Sam asked as she stood.

"Cream, please, with a twist of lemon."

How about a twist of lemon around the neck?

Sam immediately regretted the thought as a vision of Doug Hammand sporting a cowberry necklace loomed in her mind. "I only have milk but I think there's a lemon in the 'fridge somewhere."

She hated feeling like a grade schooler in front of this slip of a woman. What was it about her?

Through the kitchen window opening to the sun porch, Sam heard the answering machine on her desk pick up on the fourth ring. It was most likely Kent again. As in Clark Kent, she snorted, sure that he'd love the analogy. His superego could easily slip that red cape over his boxy shoulders. She envisioned him sliding into a phone booth, tearing off his silk turtleneck and cashmere sweater and leaping out again to save Metropolis. How many more red and blues were hanging in his closet, she wondered, smiling.

Sam reached into a bottom drawer for the lace place mat and matching napkins her grandmother had tatted. She laid it on a glass tray with the porcelain teapot and two floral English teacups Caroline had given her for Christmas three years ago.

What does Agatha know? Sam wondered. *And why is she here? Does she know my name is on the note?*

By the time the aging lemon was sliced, Earl Grey tea bags in the pot, and the cream pitcher filled with milk, the teakettle was whistling. Sam poured the boiling water, gathered the croissants, two small plates, silverware, and a jar of cowberry chutney, along with her wits, for surely she would need them, and returned to the living room. The tempting fare was deposited on a Queen Anne style coffee table before her uninvited guest.

"I heard about the incident at McCutty's," Sam said as she handed Agatha a napkin and plate.

Agatha's coat and black purse now lay neatly on the couch beside her. She wore a dark purple print dress with a shirred bodice. The clean smell of aloe soap clung to her.

"The tea will have to steep a few minutes," Sam said, dropping into the wing chair and hoping Agatha hadn't noticed the dust kitties.

"Incident? I should say it is more than an incident, Samantha! Douglas Hammand was strangled with a cowberry garland," she said indignantly, while casting an approving eye at the chutney. "What I want to know is what are you going to do about it?"

"Me? Why me?" *God. She knows.*

"Because, Samantha Blackwell, you were specifically named by the..." she struggled for the word "...by the person who composed the note. And it is your duty as an upstanding citizen of Georgetown to see to it that he does not strike again. Do you not understand that we cannot let one more day go by with this horrible deed hanging over our heads? Why, William Hornblower would be turning in his grave if he knew what was happening in his town."

Incredulity shouldn't have spread over Sam's face, but it did. "How did you know my name was on the note?"

Unconcealed disdain was evident when one wispy brow curled upward. No one questioned Agatha Beatrice Coldbath. "Please answer my original question, Samantha. What are you doing about this despicable mess?" Agatha dropped a generous scoop of chutney on her open croissant. Inherited right of royalty brooked no disobedience.

Sam couldn't help herself. In Walter Mitty fashion, she fantasized about applying a hammerlock to that scrawny neck, thus saving the town from future tyrannical tirades.

"I'm working on it, Agatha. Believe me. I want to solve this as much as you do."

"That is hardly possible," Agatha retorted between dainty bites. She dabbed at her thin lips with the lace napkin. "Douglas was an employee."

Catching an almost imperceptible hitch in the frail woman's voice, Sam replied softly, "Yes, I know."

"And he was a wonderful employee. I could always depend on him if a jar fell from the conveyor belt or one worker dawdled with another. And his taste buds were almost as good as mine. He knew immediately if a batch of our chutney was the least bit off its superior flavor."

"Yes," Sam said. "Doug was efficient and well organized. As well as talented. Did you know he whittled beautiful loons? In fact, he did those on the mantle." She pointed at the exquisitely carved mated birds resting between wooden candlesticks over the center of the fireplace, and suddenly fell sullen. "His large hands did such intricate work."

She stared at the teapot. At the purple and yellow pansies.

"Yes, he was talented," Agatha said. "But his hobby never interfered with his work, I have to say that."

Drawn from the soft, petaled faces, Sam observed Agatha busying herself with another dollop of chutney on the second half of the croissant.

She asked slowly, "Do you know why Doug was dressed up, wearing his only suit? I've never seen him in it except at weddings and funerals.

He isn't the type to dress up without a reason. Or, he *wasn't* the type." Sam was having trouble with tenses. She rubbed her bandaged finger.

Agatha's lips tightened. "I cannot imagine why he was wearing his suit. It is rather odd about the flower in his lapel."

Sam was beyond wondering where the woman got her information. "Yes, you're right. That daffodil. Sort of makes you think he had a date or something."

She waited, but Agatha merely nodded. Sam wondered if Doug had stuck the daffodil in his lapel to impress a woman or if the killer had placed it there as a message. She leaned forward. "Shall I pour your tea?"

She poured one for herself too.

After staring pointedly at the lemon, then the milk, Agatha took her tea straight.

"I do not know what I am going to do without Douglas. You realize he was chief inspector of chutney. No jar left the factory without his perusal. I could count on him to do the job right. He did not take sick leave like most of my employees who do not know the value of hard work and the satisfaction of receiving a decent paycheck."

Sam doubted the verity of the latter statement, but commiserated with Agatha on the slack attitude of today's workers. Nick was always complaining about it.

"Was Doug seeing anyone that you know of? Or did he mention anything to you or perhaps a coworker about an appointment last night?"

Wrinkles stacked on Agatha's brow. After a moment, the old woman spoke. "No and no, not that I can remember."

If Agatha had been asked six questions, she would have given six answers, in order, and no sentence would contain a grammatical contraction.

Sam said, "Did he seem anxious or upset when you last talked with him?" A fine sheen of sweat, caused by the afternoon sun that beat hot through the west window, covered Sam's face. She stood, closed the blind, then fixed herself a croissant with, under Agatha's watchful eye, a larger than normal spoonful of chutney.

"No. In fact, he seemed quite chipper," Agatha said. "He left at precisely 5:04 yesterday. That was most unlike him. He had punched out only once before 5:15 in the nine years he worked for me. Please. Sit down, Samantha."

Sam's hand hung suspended between plate and mouth. "You mean in nine years he only left once before 5:15?"

Agatha looked up at her. "That is what I said. You must listen, Samantha. He punched out early only once, and that was the day his wife died. He took three days then, with pay, of course. Now please, sit down!" Ms. Coldbath always managed to sit level with or above those around her.

Sam dutifully obeyed and sunk into the chair once again.

Douglas got awards for perfect attendance in grade school and Sunday school. He was never tardy. Sam remembered him standing before the fifth grade class in his white shirt, bow tie and Buster Brown shoes, hair slicked back. He recited the poem, "A Minute," that tiny little minute that he wouldn't abuse because…"eternity is in it."

Sam reached over for a cloth napkin and dabbed her face.

Yes, Doug was always punctual. He wouldn't have left the chutney plant before 5:15 unless it was very important. Incredibly, not even eleven minutes early. And Agatha would know for, surely, she scrutinized the company's time cards each night.

Sam set her plate aside, crossed her knees and leaned her chin on her fist.

Doug was wearing a yellow daffodil in his lapel when he died. A man like Doug wouldn't tuck a flower in his lapel to meet another man. He had to be meeting a woman. A special woman. Someone he wanted to impress. He was lonely. That was why he spent so much time at the Bog Café. A lonely man. Wife dead for eight years. Suddenly he has the opportunity to date a woman. Someone he was so anxious to meet that he would have left his job eleven minutes early so he could get home and change into his one 'undertaker's' suit. Maybe he plucks a daffodil from the Town Square on his way to meet her. Tucks it into his lapel. Crooks his neck to smell it and smiles. He's happy. Maybe he won't be lonely any more...

"Samantha! Stop daydreaming, girl."

Sam blinked.

Agatha wiped her hands thoroughly on the lace napkin, folded it, and placed it neatly beside her plate. She rose to full stature, slipped on her Chesterfield, and buttoned it deftly, despite her arthritic hands. The black handbag was then wedged securely under her left arm.

"As I was saying, I must go along now. I have called an emergency meeting of my department heads for tonight. I want to report to them that you are doing your utmost to finalize this distasteful situation. May I give them that assurance?"

Unused to dissent, she turned on her solid black heels and marched toward the front door. Before exiting, she turned. "I will expect a full report on my desk by the end of the week. Also, if you wish, I have the name of a very good housekeeper."

The door shut with purpose.

Sam muttered, "Agatha has left the building."

Chapter 5

Nicholas Wentworth Bennett tapped a slender finger on the pine table. After his three mile run and weight workout in the basement, he had showered and come to the table in blue jeans and a neatly tucked-in wildlife tee shirt.

He and Sam finished a quickly prepared supper of gardenburgers, garlic and herb couscous, and baked cream corn. Sam was slicing a warm cowberry walnut loaf bread for dessert. She handed him a plate and cut another piece for herself.

"I love the smell of this bread, don't you, honey?" Sam slathered on more butter than she meant to, then slid the glass dish toward him.

On clear days, the morning sun spilled through the small panes of the bay window into the dining room and over Wallace Nutting photographs and rich brown wainscoting. In the evening, like tonight, the light from dead stars twinkled against the dark canopy of forever.

Sam gazed out, recalling her childish wonderment at the vastness of it. Where it began, where it ended. How could there be no end? She was eleven then. The questions still fascinated her. A dog bayed in the distance.

"'Tis a night of 'cloudless climes and starry skies,'" she said at the window.

Nick was not to be dissuaded. "Samantha?" A questioning inflection at the end of her name brooked no escape. "You hardly ate lunch and you picked at your supper, although that's a generous slice of bread you cut for yourself. Comfort food?"

In Georgetown, as in much of rural New Hampshire, the evening meal was 'supper,' unless you had guests and got out the good china and cloth napkins. Maybe candles, if you really wanted to impress. A born and bred Georgian, Sam wouldn't change the custom for all the chutney in the world.

"You saw the paper," she said, toying with her fork.

"Everyone in town's seen the paper. Doug Hammand's death is all over the front page. I also saw the reporters in town. I'm sure it will be on the news tonight. But it doesn't take a genius to know you're involved in this more than you should be.

"When I pulled into the drive tonight, Kent Butcher screeched to a halt out front and bounded out of his Miata. I told him to stay off our property or I'd call the police. He yelled something about the public's right to know, but slid back into his car anyway and took off. But he'll be back. You can be sure of that. He's probably hiding in the bushes under this window right now with an eavesdropping device."

"I know. I was wondering why he didn't show up."

"The question is, Sam, why did he show up here in the first place? What's going on? How are you involved in Doug's death?" Nick's fingers laced firmly around his moose mug. When he couldn't find his mug in the cupboard, he'd often resort to pulling it from the dishwasher and rinsing it himself. "I'm waiting, Sam." The worried crease between his dark brows deepened.

Sam took a hippo bite.

Charlie had given her permission to tell Nick in her own good time, with an oath of secrecy, until the full-blown story got out.

Now Agatha Coldbath and Kent Butcher knew. It was just a matter of time before every citizen in Georgetown found out. The town's grapevine had a life of its own. Given the nature of this news—a dead body, a riddle, a cowberry necklace and a daffodil, the killer's challenge to a numerologist—the tabloids and national newspapers would surely be on the scent. She'd better tell Nick now, in her own way, rather than have him hear distorted accounts on the evening news or read some reporter's take on it in the newspaper.

Licking butter from a forefinger, Sam rose sullenly, went to the sun porch, took the phone off the hook, and returned with papers in hand.

Nick listened silently, with growing disbelief, as Sam related the details of Charlie's visit. Avoiding a direct look at the glossies, she laid out the photographs, then showed Nick a copy of the note. She went on to tell him of Kent Butcher's string of telephone calls, Agatha's amazing detective work in ferreting out her name on the note, and the old woman's laconic demand that Sam turn in a report.

Sam skipped the part about the housekeeping slam.

Chances were, Sam added, neither Agatha nor Kent would reveal any information publicly until it behooved them to do so.

After seeing the photographs, Nick's bread lay half-eaten on his plate, but it was reading the note that nearly lurched his meal back onto the supper table.

"My God!" He slumped back against the captain's chair. "I can see why you've lost your appetite." He was silent a moment, then said, "And I'm surprised Charlie left those photographs with you. You shouldn't have to look at something like that."

Nick's face remained impassive, but the furrow between his dark eyes was now trench-like. It was that worried look that had attracted Sam to him in the beginning. Being the handsomest man in the world was a plus. After twenty-three years of marriage, she recognized his quiet anger.

"Don't blame Charlie. It's his job. He told me I didn't have to look at the photos if I didn't want to."

"I know. I'm just worried."

His face softened as he leaned forward to take her hand. Caressing her etched wedding band, he said, "You know, Sam, this has nothing to do with you. This nutcase has a sick mind and wants to play games. I know you feel you have to play, but you must remember, no matter what happens, it's not your fault."

Somehow comforted, Sam looked down at his tapered fingers, the white half-moons on his nails, indicative of good circulation, the result of a daily exercise regimen. She noted her solid pink nails.

Nick looked hard at her. "If, God forbid, he does strike again, it has nothing to do with you. You must remember that." He gathered the photographs and stuffed them back in the envelope.

"Yes, I know." Her voice faltered. "But...he *is* going to do it again. I *have* to solve that code."

"Even if you do solve it, there's no guarantee that he won't kill again. You know that, sweetheart. People like this don't keep promises." He pulled back and clasped the arms of the chair. "And I'm afraid you're going to have to steel yourself for an invasion of the media. Butcher is onto something, or he wouldn't have been barreling down our street. I swear to God the man's psychic. He's always in the middle of the fray. If only he weren't so..."

"Self-serving and malicious?" Sam finished for him.

Nick nodded. "Do you have any ideas about these numbers?"

"No!" she answered heatedly.

"It's all right, Sam, calm down," he pleaded, rubbing his forehead with his middle three fingers. "Let's talk about something else."

"How can I talk about something else?" she retorted. "Someone's life is on the line. I have been wracking my brain trying to think of a reason, any reason, why someone would want to kill Doug. Do you suppose it's over the chutney recipe? It's got to be worth millions, and Agatha is the only one who knows it. Do you suppose Doug had access to the spice cupboard where she keeps all the ingredients? Maybe the killer thought Doug either knew the recipe or could get into that cupboard, and when Doug wouldn't or couldn't answer his demands, he strangled him in a rage."

"That's a lot of supposes, Sam." But Nick was thinking.

"Then," Sam said, "there's Benjamin King. He's always after Agatha, trying to get her recipe or buy Coldbath Industries."

Benjamin Hines King III, the Cranberry King, according to his advertisements, had been after the Coldbath cowberry chutney recipe for years. It was bad enough he accosted Agatha at every stop and stoop, but, to top it off, he had committed the unpardonable sin of being born in Vermont. The fact that he now lived in Massachusetts only furthered his perfidy.

Sam asked, "Have you ever been in the herb cupboard?"

She was sure Nick would have told her if he had, but sometimes husbands forget to tell their wives unimportant things like someone blew up the town hall or they were at war with Vermont.

Nick replied, "No one goes in there but Agatha, and she has the only key."

Sam thought about the windowless cupboard located centrally in the chutney plant and accessed through one solid wood door. "That's true, but someone could have made a duplicate."

"Oh, I'm sure that would have been easy," Nick responded a bit sarcastically. Then, with a half grin, "She wears that key around her neck and probably swallows it at night."

Sam laughed outright at the image of Agatha climbing onto a four-poster bed, drawing closed heavy velvet drapes, and smoothing great-great-grandmother's comforter just so before pulling *the key* from under a Victorian nightdress buttoned securely at the neck.

"Swallowing that key," Sam chuckled, "would take practice, but I doubt there is any task that daunts Miss Coldbath. Can't you just picture Agatha adjusting her hairnet before laying back rigidly on a firm but functional pillow?"

Nick's mouth spread into a smile. "How she would retrieve said key in the morning poses an interesting question."

They both smiled, then fell silent.

Finally, Sam spoke up. "You know, Nick, Agatha is getting on in age. I wonder who the recipe will be handed down to, if anyone. The loss of that recipe could destroy this town, not only financially, but psychologically."

"That true."

Nick tapped the table.

Sam knew he was thinking about all the businesses that were tied, directly or indirectly, to cowberry chutney. Many townspeople ordered printed materials from Georgetown Printers.

Sam looked slyly at her husband. "You know, at Agatha's indeterminate age, decades past menopause, it's unlikely she's going to produce an heir, even given modern insemination advances."

Nick laughed around a mouthful of cowberry bread.

They sat in silence once again. Finally, Sam rose, picked up the envelope and notes, returned them to the sun porch and rejoined her husband at the table.

"I'm sorry I've been so crabby, Nick. This thing is really getting to me."

"It's okay, sweetheart. Who wouldn't be, given the circumstances?"

A sudden hammering at the door startled them. Nick jumped up, putting a restraining hand on Sam's shoulder. "I'll take care of this."

A moment later Caroline and Sadie burst into the breezeway.

"Dad. Did you hear the news?" Caroline asked breathlessly. She followed her father into the kitchen.

Sadie bounded in front of her older sister. "We've been calling for the past hour. The line's been busy." She tripped over Selket who tried to wind between her legs. Apologizing, Sadie scooped up the cat and planted a kiss on her broad orange face before releasing her.

"I was having a conversation with your father," Sam said as the girls bundled into the dining area. She rubbed the hollow at the base of her throat. "I took the phone off the hook so we wouldn't be interrupted."

Nick said, "Sit down and have some cowberry bread."

Sam placed two more plates on the table.

Caroline cocked her head. "You've never taken the phone off the hook for an hour before, mom. What's going on?"

Sam looked levelly at her oldest daughter. "Sit down, Caroline, please."

Caroline was dark and slim like her father, dressed in black silk pants, and a cream-colored blouse with a jeweled velvet band at her throat. She smelled of Chanel #5.

Sam sliced two pieces of bread and placed them on the plates. She handed one to Sadie who had plopped in *her* chair with her back to the bay window. Sam smiled inwardly. Old habits died hard. She placed the other plate on Caroline's place mat.

"Please." She patted the table. Sam could see Caroline working hard at being patient as she slipped into her chair.

"Yeah, mom. What if we needed you and couldn't get through?" Sadie said. She slumped against the back of her chair, metallic black cats dangling from her ears just below her blunt-cut blonde hair. Her long, slender fingers twisted the hem of her jean jacket. Three inches taller than her sister and a bare one hundred fifteen pounds, Sadie had once considered modeling.

"Sam." Nick took his seat. "We've got to tell them."

"Tell us what?" Caroline swung toward her father.

Sadie's eyes got full, her fingers fell silent.

"There's nothing wrong with us, we're fine," Sam assured her daughters. "It's just that…"

"Just that what?" Caroline demanded.

Sam began slowly, her tale interrupted only by the occasional baying of a lone dog somewhere out there under the sliver of moon that moved pane by pane past the family home. Budding fingers of a forsythia bush scratched at the window in a light gust of wind. The Ridgeway ticked away the minutes, its quarter-hour chimes so familiar no one heard them.

Sam had just finished when Caroline screamed and pointed out the window. Nick was on his feet before she could speak.

"There's someone out there. I saw a shadow moving," she gasped, a white-knuckled grip on the arms of her chair.

Sadie leaped up, knocked her chair over, and scrambled toward her mother.

Sam was already on her feet. With one arm, she cradled Sadie behind her and with the other, reached for Caroline's hand.

"Sam. Where's the gun?" Nick whispered hoarsely.

"In the back hall, in my handbag."

"Call 911."

A shaft of moonlight caught in the treetops and spilled jagged patterns on the crescent lawn between the Bennett-Blackwell home and a thick stand of pines bordering their property.

Charlie stood looking out at the yard, then turned and walked over to the fireplace. "You been doing any gardenin' round that window, Sam?"

He had arrived moments after she hung up the telephone, as if, Sam thought, he'd been waiting for something like this to happen. He lifted tired eyes above his thick coffee mug.

"Why?" Sam sat on the living room couch flanked by her daughters, whose hands she held in an iron grip. Selket nestled into the sofa cushion behind her head. Nick, drinking black coffee, stood next to Charlie by the fireplace, silent, watching his women.

When Caroline screamed, Nick told Charlie he had raced to the breezeway for the gun in Sam's purse. He slipped out the back door of the sun porch and eased along the back of the house. Sam had seen the snags where his tee shirt caught on the rough shingles. Nick said every cell in his body had been on alert as he knelt and peered around the corner through the forsythia branches. He had waited a few minutes in silence, listening, the hair on the back of his neck bristling. But he saw no one and heard nothing but the dog barking in the distance and the wind brushing against the bushes under the bay window.

Charlie Burrows shifted his weight to his other foot, placed his mug on the mantle beside Doug Hammand's loons, and unzipped his Red Sox jacket. "Could I talk to you alone, Nick?" Charlie said, casting his eyes toward the kitchen.

"Charlie!" Sam's eyes bored through him. "You're not going anywhere. The girls already know the story, so anything that's going to be said is going to be said in front of the four of us. We're a family. We're in this together and we need to know what's going on."

"All right, all right." Charlie waved his spread fingers before him in an attempt at appeasement. "I found broken twigs under the window. Fresh breaks. Leaves mashed into the ground. They wouldn't be mashed down like that after the dry spell we've had unless something heavy was on them. Coulda been a large animal." He stuck big hands in his pockets. "Are you sure you saw someone out there, Caroline?"

"Charlie!" Sam cried.

The chief pulled a hand out of his pocket, held it up to quiet her. "Please Sam."

"So someone was outside our window?" Nick said.

"Someone or something, Nick," Charlie answered, with an eye toward Sam. "Course it could be a kid foolin' around. We've had some break-ins, petty stuff. Walkmans, CDs, little jewelry, money. But they never hit until the place is empty. No one's been hurt," he assured them. "So maybe this joker was just casing the place."

He paused, then rubbed a forefinger over the childhood scar along the side of his face. Every time he did that, Sam's heart melted. How painful it must have been, physically and psychologically, for the little boy she had befriended. Charges were never brought. Just another case of a home "accident."

Selket plopped down from the back of the couch and forced herself into Sam's lap.

"I swear that cat looks like Jabba the Hutt," Charlie chuckled.

"Look, mom," Caroline said. She released her hand from her mother's iron fist and turned eyes the color of blackberries toward her. "I know what I saw. But Charlie may be right. It's most likely some kid looking for money. There has been a string of burglaries the last few months. I read about it in *Publick Occurrences*."

Fear is relative, Sam thought, as she stroked the cat. The need to embrace the burglar theory was palpable.

"Perhaps," Nick replied, rolling his moose cup between cold hands. "At any rate, we're having an alarm installed first thing tomorrow. And I want you girls to put a dead bolt on your apartment door immediately. In fact, I have one in the cellar. Mom and I will follow you home and install it tonight."

"We already have one, dad," Sadie said against her mother's shoulder. "Mom insisted when we moved to Portsmouth."

"Should we tell grandma?" Caroline asked.

"No!" Sam spoke more harshly than she meant to, then went on in a softer tone. "I haven't decided yet if we should tell her. Please. Let me take care of that."

"I'm calling Jimi Duncan tonight," Nick said. "We'll have an alarm installed here before the sun goes down tomorrow."

Chapter 6

Sam spent a sleepless night.

A ring of fire encircled her home, its smoke billowing into a blood red sky. The girls and Nick screamed from inside the house, but she was mesmerized by the telephone poles lining the street—only they weren't telephone poles, but huge numbers with connecting cowberry lines. Coming at her, a skeletal Douglas Hammand headed an army of marching bony soldiers who grinned from sockets in their skulls. The army of dead surrounded her, pounding spears on the frosty ground, chanting her name.

She awoke with a start. Hot prickles mushroomed from an interior heat and suffused her face, arms, and chest. She threw the covers off, took a hot shower, put a green foam roller in her bangs, and went to her desk where Nick found her hours later.

He put his hands on her shoulders, bent down, and kissed her neck. "Hi, babe. Are you all right? You tossed most of the night."

Sam looked up into his wonderful face framed by thick curly locks. She told him repeatedly that in their next life she was confiscating his hair. To make matters better, Nick had even white teeth and almond-shaped eyes the color of blackbirds. Caroline had those eyes. After twenty-four years of marriage, Nick's eyes still held her captive.

"I'm fine. Thanks. There's a storm coming," she said in response to a twinging ankle.

"Want some hot chocolate?" Nick asked.

He went into the kitchen and returned with a glazed mug brimming with whipped cream and placed it in front of her. Grinning through pearly teeth, he shook his head. "You've outdone yourself this time, Sam."

"What?" She rolled her chair back and stood to massage her rump.

"Purple plaid sweat pants, a torn Cozumel tee shirt, and a lime green polar fleece shirt. Your outfit goes especially well with that green roller in your hair."

Sam fought the urge to grab for the roller. Instead, she faced her husband, arms akimbo. "And?"

"I hope you're not leaving the house."

Sam cocked one eyebrow at him and plunked down at her desk. She picked up the cup and stared unseeing at the computer screen while gingerly sipping hot chocolate.

Nick went off to the bedroom.

Sam put the cup down, yanked the roller out of her hair, stuck it in her sweats, fluffed her bangs, and scowled at the monitor.

From the bedroom, she could hear Nick pulling open bureau drawers. He finally reappeared, holding up his environmentally correct forest green tee shirt.

"How about this one?"

She turned. "This one what?"

"How about wearing this tee shirt?"

Sam fingered the bottom. "Nope. I like the lightweight ones." She turned back toward her monitor.

Within minutes, he returned with a cranberry Georgetown Printers tee. "What about this?"

A cursory glance. "Too heavy."

He left again and called from the bedroom. "I have tee shirts in the basement, you know."

Sam stifled a laugh. Nicholas Wentworth Bennet was nothing if not persistent.

Nick didn't want to go to work, but Sam insisted, especially after his critique of her apparel. The killer wasn't after her; he couldn't play this game by himself. She knew how to handle her gun—hours at the Country Brook shooting range had taught her well—and she had a license to carry the weapon. Besides, she reminded him, the police station was right around the corner. Foregoing his morning run, Nick left for work and called a half-hour later. Jimi Duncan would be there before noon.

Sam didn't confide that the moment Nick was gone, Kent Butcher leaned on their buzzer. She had eyeballed the reporter through the breezeway's glass storm door, told him to talk to the authorities, and firmly shut the inside door.

Sam set the phone back in its cradle.

A pewter sky filled her sun porch windows, and small birds circled the big feeder. A blackbird swooped down and scattered his lesser brethren into the still damp air. Caroline and Sadie had called to see if she was all right; her mother had called to talk about Doug Hammand. Sam couldn't shake the image of the marching dead.

Selket lay across papers on her desk, stretched out like an overweight Olympic diver in midair flight. As Sam lightly stroked the cat's stomach, Selket arched more, and purred in that deep and rumbly roll.

I should take a walk, Sam told herself, *clear my head. But Jimi's coming, I don't want to miss him, and maybe I shouldn't be too public right now.*

A flush crept up her chest and over her face. She flapped her sweatshirt front. At the thought of remaining more secluded than normal, she said out loud, "No way, Jose." Exercise, once a formidable foe, now became a raison d'être. She would walk wherever she wanted and whenever she felt like it. This cipher would not dictate her lifestyle. In fact, her personal year cycle seven dictated that she take care of her health, think, and perfect those things she already knew.

Like the mystery she had begun so long ago. She would start taking walks down Tumble Brook Road, the heavily wooded development down the road a piece. If she included the Loop, the jaunt was only one and one-half miles. Nick ran it often, twice around. She'd walk and think and jot down ideas for her book. So there.

On her desk in a neat pile beside the telephone lay the envelope Charlie had left with her yesterday, along with the notes she had made. As the pressure mounted and the need to save the next victim from this demented psychopath began to torment her once again, Sam chewed on her top lip.

Suddenly she had the peculiar feeling she was being watched, felt almost as if she could feel someone's aura pressing against her back, a dark, deadly thing. She whipped around expecting to find the killer looming over her, but the room was empty, bathed in a sepulchral silence.

A quick glance outside. The thick pines gave up no intruder. Could someone have slipped into the house during the night and hidden in the hall closet waiting for Nick to leave? She told herself she was being ridiculous. She was overwrought because of the murder, the note, and the glossy photographs of Douglas Hammand.

But still, she slipped into the back hall, took the revolver from her handbag, and proceeded to check every closet, and look under every bed and behind every piece of furniture where even the smallest assassin could fold himself. She locked the door to the basement and slipped the .38 into her pocket.

She had been at her desk for a good half-hour when the phone vibrated at her elbow. Kent's voice scratched through the answering machine. "Samantha, please. I need just a moment of your time. Call me." He left his number.

Sam knew he was on his car phone; he'd been sitting in his shiny red Mazda Miata a few doors down from her house since Nick left. It was a public street. There was nothing she could do about it.

Then the breezeway doorbell rang.

It couldn't be Kent, unless he happened to be standing on the stoop with his cell phone to his ear, which wouldn't surprise her. She hoped to find Jimi with the alarm.

Through the small panes, a lanky man smiled at her out of a scruffy beard. Jimi Hendrix Duncan was a thirty-something eccentric bachelor who knew more about alarms than the guardians of Fort Knox.

As Sam opened the storm, Jimi said, "Hi…ah, Mrs. Blackwell."

Samantha had kept her maiden name after marrying Nicholas Bennett, who was a very distant twig on the family tree of the first New Hampshire governor Benning Wentworth, although Nick's branch had fallen off long ago. After twenty-three years of marriage, Georgians were still at sixes and sevens over how to address Sam. Ms. still meant manuscript, even to the librarians.

Jimi adjusted the blue print bandanna tied over his head.

Suddenly, a disembodied hand reached out from behind the arbor vitae against the house and grasped the metal edge of the door. Kent Butcher pulled himself onto the step, shoving Duncan aside.

"Hey, man. Watch it," Jimi said, unnerved. Catching himself before he fell off the brick stoop, he stepped back and down. He tightened his grasp on a black notebook under his arm and adjusted his rimless glasses with the middle finger of his right hand.

"Samantha," Kent said in dulcet tone. "You know you're going to talk to me sooner or later. It might as well be sooner."

Sam's eyes narrowed. Kent thought he was smiling, but the lipless opening made him look more like a shark smelling that one drop of blood.

"How about it?" He whipped out a leather notepad and Mont Blanc pen. "Just one comment."

Sam glared while Kent oozed on. Butcher had the short, square figure of a man built like a hockey player, with the same aggressive attitude. The paradox was that his silken voice had the power to seduce, the kind of voice that Rudolph Valentino would have killed for. That smoldering silent film star's high squeaky tones finished him when talkies came in. Just as Sam was about to finish with this interloper.

"Kent Butcher!" Sam worked hard at not screaming, then looked to see if anyone on foot had heard. The coast was clear. Swinging blazing blue eyes back at the object of her scorn, she continued, "If you set foot on my property one more time, I swear I'll call the police and have you arrested for trespassing, harassment, and any other thing I can think up in the meantime."

"All right, all right," he retorted, hands up. He backed down off the steps. "Don't have a cow. I'll talk to you later."

"When hell freezes over," Sam mumbled under her breath. She felt herself flushing again.

"Sorry, Jimi. I'm a little wrought up over Doug Hammand's death. Come on in."

Appearing bewildered, Jimi Duncan followed Sam into the house and through the kitchen to the table by the bay window. He settled his lean frame into one of the captain's chairs, opened the peeling black notebook and started riffling through plastic-covered pages.

"Would you like something to drink?" Sam said.

"No, thanks. All set," Jimi said, without looking up.

"Well, if you don't mind, I'm going to have a cup of tea. Sure you won't join me? I have herbal. And some chocolate chip cookies?"

"In that case..." He looked up, smiled, and adjusted his John Lennon specs again.

"When did you hear about Doug?" Sam called from the kitchen. She knew by now it was a question of when and not if.

"At the Bog Café."

"I'll bet Chris and Julie were pretty upset. He used to joke with them all the time, teased them if his coffee wasn't on the counter when he walked in."

"Yeah."

Sam thought Jimi's voice sounded oddly distant.

She brought in cups, tea bags, paper napkins, and a plate of cookies. Five cookies.

Suddenly she remembered a Rotary banquet where she had overheard a restaurateur telling a friend that he didn't know why, but if the price of a meal didn't end in a five, it didn't sell. He had tried a new dish and priced it at six dollars, and it bombed. But when he raised the price of the same meal to $6.95, it sold like hot cakes.

Sam knew why. Five stimulated the appetite, inspired communion, and increased sexual excitement.

She placed the plate of cookies on the table.

"I hope Orange Mandarin is okay. The hot water will be ready in a minute."

Jimi nodded and reached for a cookie. Sam noticed his long knobby fingers—the sign of an intellectual, if her book on hand analysis had any verity—and the nails chewed to the quick. She winced inwardly, then slipped into her chair and lifted her eyes toward his.

"I remember the last time I saw Doug," she said blandly, awaiting the slightest nuance from Jimi. When none was forthcoming, she glanced out the window in response to a thumping ankle. The sky was leaden. Definitely snow. Branches whipped in a sudden burst of wind. "At the League of New Hampshire Craftsmen Fair," she went on, shifting her eyes back on Jimi, "at the Junior High School over in Hampton. He was selling his loons. I heard he donated half his sales that day to the Georgetown Little League."

Jimi's knee jiggled nervously under the table as he finished off the cookie. He didn't say a word.

Sam noticed the nervous knee movement, then suddenly remembered. Jimi probably hated Doug Hammand because of Patricia. Pat and Jimi were high school sweethearts, that is, until Doug put a stop to it. Douglas Hammand didn't want his daughter associating with druggies.

Sam had always thought Doug had been uncharacteristically unfair and unreasonable. Just because Jimi's parents were flower children who died unpleasantly didn't make Jimi a drug addict. As far as Sam knew, Jimi had never touched the stuff. His behavior sort of fit the unwritten rule: kids invariably do the opposite of what their parents do.

But Doug didn't see it that way. There had been talk that Doug and Jimi had it out in front of the high school one day while Patricia watched and sobbed and clutched her schoolbooks. Doug must have put the fear of damnation into her because, as far as anyone knew, she never looked at Jimi again.

Sam had to ask. "When did you see Doug last?"

"Ah...I don't remember exactly." He paused to finish chewing the second cookie. "I think the kettle's whistling."

"So it is."

Sam returned, poured hot water into the cups, and set the teakettle on a Good Luck Kitchen Witch trivet on the table. She rested her chin in one hand while absently stirring the tea. This was the chair Caroline had been sitting in last night when she saw someone outside the bay window. Fear caught in her throat again.

"Good cookies." Jimi reached for another.

Sam cleared her throat. "Oh, thanks."

She wondered if Jimi Duncan could have killed Doug. But why would he wait, what, ten years now? Still, some people harbor hatred for decades until some little thing sets them off. Even if Jimi didn't kill Doug, he might have seen something.

"Who would want to do such a terrible thing?" Sam said.

Jimi's eyes drifted toward her.

"Would you mind, ma'am?" When addressing Samantha Blackwell, ma'am seemed the safest appellation for those of faint heart. "I've got a busy schedule. Your husband wants this installed today, so you need to pick out the kind of alarm you'd like." He turned the open notebook toward her.

"Of course. Sorry."

But she wondered why he was so nervous. A passing thought of the Boston strangler, the serial killer, who turned out to be the locksmith who installed bolts on the apartment doors of the women he murdered, was not what she wanted to think of at this moment.

Sam hurriedly decided on an electronic field that set off the sound of barking dogs. Certainly, angry Dobermans would curdle the blood of the most hardened criminal. Unless, of course, it was Jimi Duncan. The thought unnerved her.

Sam watched Jimi head out to his van and pull a pack of cigarettes from his jacket. He leaned against the bright flowered side panel, shivered, and lit up. Dragging the smoke deep into his lungs, he blew it out through his nose and watched the ring rise above his head until a windburst twisted it invisible.

Sam also wondered about Kent Butcher.

She scowled through the storm door. Kent's Miata was empty. He was probably stuffed into a phone booth nearby, waiting. Would he have killed to get an exclusive? She wouldn't put it past him. An exclusive interview with the numerologist mentioned on a death note would make salacious copy for *USA Today*, the newspaper Butcher had set his sights on. He'd be a star. He might even win a Pulitzer. They'd make a movie about him.

Her attention was drawn back as Jimi stubbed out the butt with his Nike. She wondered if Jimi seemed nervous because he had coded messages on his mind, or were the jitters because he needed a cigarette?

It couldn't be him, she thought. *I've known him forever.*

Suddenly, Sam felt bad for Jimi. Her father had died of emphysema after dragging an oxygen tank behind him for two years. Jimi could be headed for a similar fate.

Chapter 7

Light snow fell from a gray sky.

The back porch railing, the measure of snowfall in the Bennett-Blackwell household, supported about three inches, Sam figured, by the time she looked up from her desk. The thermometer read thirty degrees. A plump mourning dove waddled through the powdery snow and picked at seeds that had fallen from the big house feeder above. A wire suet cage, which hung suspended from the small maple planted last summer, was the object of two feisty sparrows' attention. From her perch, Selket watched intently.

Sam had worked on the code all morning and needed some air. The alarm system was up and running. She and Nick had tested it last night, then called the girls to tell them about the installation. Caroline and Sadie didn't need to be confronted with angry Dobermans, even if the dogs were phantoms. Her mother's phone had rung and rung. Elizabeth was out again. Sam would touch base with her later.

After supper the previous evening, Nick and Sam had followed their normal routine. They watched Channel 9 news, which covered Doug Hammand's murder in as full and lurid detail as allowed (more would be upcoming as information was available), then Peter Jennings for national news, and at 7:00 P.M., curled in Nick's lap on the couch, a *Seinfeld* rerun.

Laughter is indeed the best medicine, Sam thought, at the memory of Kramer trying to extricate himself from a pair of tight jeans. They had laughed until their stomachs hurt. Sam then watched Jeopardy while Nick donned his shiny purple sweat suit, orange reflector vest, and spotless white New Balance sneakers with black toes, and went out for a three mile run.

Sam felt renewed this morning.

Reluctantly, she changed out of her nightshirt and into gray sweats. After stuffing a piece of paper into the pocket of her yellow polar fleece jacket and tugging on a pair of Australian Uggs, boots that Nick said lived up to their name, she grabbed Nick's spaghetti-stained shirt, set the alarm, and headed out.

By now she'd had enough snow, but this was New England. She remembered one year when they had a huge snowstorm on April 20th. A shudder passed through her as the cold began to seep into her bones.

God! April 1st is the deadline. April Fool's Day.

She thought of the Fool in the Tarot, that young innocent who blithely steps off into the abyss, unaware of the life experiences into which he is falling. Was she the Fool? What was she falling into?

An old business card, on the back of which Nick had printed 'GAS, OIL CHANGE' and which she kept in her console, was stuck in the slot in front of the speedometer as a reminder to the next driver. First stop, gas.

She would pick up a few groceries at Shop 'N Save in Hampton—the prices were good there—then come back to Georgetown to the cleaners and the florist and maybe McCutty's market. The crime scene should be cleaned up by now, and perhaps a look around would lend some clues.

The roads were good; plows had been out early. Sam filled up at Tiny's Tank-up, just past the green, and headed out of town, driving by pastures that lay soft and quiet under a collecting blanket of white. The tree line was smudged in the distance. This storm would probably drop only six inches and some would be disappointed, Sam thought. The hardy New Hampshire folk took ten to twenty inches of snow in booted stride.

A TV commentator once said, "There is something heroic about living in New England in the winter time," and many Georgians figured themselves among that illustrious group, Ethan Allen and his boys not withstanding. April was a few days away, she reminded herself again, somewhat buoyed by the thought, and the snow would melt quickly.

She shivered again and reached down to feel air from the heater. Lukewarm. She punched the floor vent button on the dash and turned the heat dial on red. Her hands were freezing on the steering wheel.

Why didn't she wear gloves? In her perennial race out the back door, she invariably forgot something.

In rhythm with the monotonous thump of the windshield wipers, the words from the killer's rhyme ran back and forth in her head.

Civilization, rail at fates, fence with me, civilization, rail, fence.

Her breath hung like ghostly tendrils in the chilled air before dissipating into nothingness. She absently patted the handbag to her right.

After a quick trip through the aisles of Shop 'N Save during which she would be eternally reminded of the horrifying film, *The Stepford Wives*, and a stop at the post office for stamps, she headed back home to Georgetown and the town green where she lived.

Black Skillet Lane flowed around the rectangular common and ended where it started. No one was quite sure where that was. In Georgetown, all roads led to Black Skillet Lane. On the east and west sides of the green, mounded with snow, sat old but well-tended Cape Cods, stately Victorian homes—some converted into businesses, and a few newer structures put up before the town fathers decided there would be no future development. Quaint electrified gaslights had been installed twenty years ago in keeping with old photographs. The town would retain its heritage.

Sam glanced at the Second Puritan Church, gracing the north end of the green, frosted white, and right off a Christmas card. It was presided over by Pastor Hannibal Loveless, who would conduct funeral services for Doug Hammand, since the family attended his church. Sam had once read that a killer could never resist attending funeral services for his victim. She would be alert.

On the south end of the common, dominating the town, sat the Coldbath estate.

Three hundred and sixty-five days of the year, three hundred and sixty-six on leap year, cowberry wreaths hung from every lamppost, fence, and any vertical structure legally acceptable and unmoving. Garlands graced the gazebo in the center of the green, the merry red strands festooned 'round every door and window. There were tourists to consider.

Samantha and Nicolas resided in a more contemporary Cape Cod, built in 1948, next door to A Loosen'd Spirit, her mother's bed and breakfast.

Sam slid the Honda into her garage, hit the remote button, and pulled plastic grocery bags from the back seat as the door lowered.

With the groceries stored away, she headed on foot across the common toward the cleaners, which sat between Hornblower Stationers and a pale mauve Victorian home currently leasing space to a law firm and a CPA. She pounded the snow off her boots on a large rubber mat inside the door of Clean As A Hound's Tooth cleaners.

Sam crinkled her nose. The faint, noxious smell of chemicals had taken residence in the building years ago. A wicker basket filled with gummy bears sat on the white speckled counter next to a bell and a tented hand-lettered note that read: PLEASE RING FOR SERVICE. Rows of plastic-covered clothes disappeared into the bowels of the building.

A wide lizard smile greeted her. "Hello, Miss Samantha. Nick's shirt, I take it?'

"Yes, Clarence," she said, and handed the shirt over. "You know how he loves spaghetti, and I just can't get those tomato stains out. And this is one of his favorite shirts."

"Ah, yes." He rumpled it looking for the stain. "L. L. Bean. The man likes quality."

"I guess that's why he married me." Sam laughed.

"I would have to agree with him there," he replied. His huge watery eyes took her in.

Sam liked the old guy. A thought fluttered through her tired mind. He was probably only sixty. Time was when she considered that ancient.

Clarence tagged the shirt and dropped it into a cloth-lined bin to his right. "And how are you today?"

Clarence Tuttle wore a starched white shirt with sharp creases down the front. He always wore a starched white shirt, and it always had sharp creases down the front. He wrote out a slip with a crooked pen from Handson Chiropractic Clinic and passed the pink slip to her.

"I'm fine." Sam wished it were true. "I should be asking how you're doing. I'm really sorry about your troubles."

Clarence's wife, Harriet, had run off with Harold, who previously owned the dry cleaning establishment, leaving poor Clarence with nothing but a note and one over-starched shirt. Out of retribution or boredom, no one was sure which, Clarence had sold his house, bought the bankrupt business, moved upstairs, and renamed the place, 'Clean As A Hound's Tooth.'

Clarence's eyelids fell to half-mast. "Ah, yes. Well, that's life." He sighed and wet his flat lips. "They're in Florida, you know. My sister lives in Orlando and says the two of them are living in an apartment, running out of money. Seems Harold's trying to get a job at Disney World. Harriet always loved Disney World. 'Course, if he does, they can get in free. Harold has relatives down there, you know." Although they were alone, he whispered behind his hand, "Some think he's mob connected, but who knows for sure. At least, that's what I heard."

"Really." It was all Sam could think of to say.

Clarence's dry cleaning establishment was a huge success. Knowing where their loyalties lay, the townspeople forsook the new Quickie Clean franchise in Exeter and flocked to Clean As A Hound's Tooth. They weren't in all that much of a hurry anyway and besides, rumor was rampant about Harriet and Harold, and Clarence was only too willing to relate the latest tidbits with, of course, considerable aplomb. He seemed to enjoy the attention and appreciate his wife's decision more each day.

He leaned closer, the flakes from his dry skin drifting toward the counter. "Wasn't that awful about poor Douglas? You know, he never came in much except with that suit of his, maybe once a year. 'Course when Betty was alive, she was in more often. She was very particular. I just don't know."

He looked sad but, since he had the floor, he continued.

"What's this world coming to? You know, in a small town like ours." He straightened and punctuated his statement by sweeping the town green with big wet eyes. "Did you see the police cars out there yesterday morning?"

"My office is in the back of the house, Clarence. I seldom know what's going on out front."

"Well," he settled into a long winter's tale, "people were emptying out of buildings, standing around watching. Charlie and Lenny and the State Police—I guess Charlie's brother-in-law, Grant, is in charge of the investigation—well, they were stringing that yellow strip like you see on television around McCutty's Market like it was a scene from *NYPD Blue*. Reporters, television vans. I've never seen anything like it." His baldhead shook from side to side.

Sam marveled at his flaky skin. She wondered if lizards, like snakes, shed their skins. She wished she could shed the last few days and start over.

"I was told it happened late Monday night," Sam said. "Did you hear or see anything unusual?" Sam knew exactly when it happened, but gave Clarence the opening.

"You know," he licked his lips again, the light back in his eyes. "I've been going over that in my mind ever since this tragic event. I closed regular time, 4:30, then went upstairs to my apartment like I always do, washed up, made coffee, and turned on the 5:00 news. You know, I can see right out over the town green from my chair next to the window."

That's why I'm asking, Sam thought.

McCutty's Market was a few doors up the street from Clarence's business, on the same side, and across the street from Sam's home. Even so, she would never have seen the goings-on from the back windows in her home, plus the heavy pines and hemlocks around her house muffled any sounds that might seep through. Beethoven, Brahms, and Presley camouflaged the rest. She might just as well be living on a distant planet, and that's the way she liked it.

Clarence rubbed a corner of his eye, and a flake of skin fluttered to the speckled counter.

"How do you sleep with the light from the lampposts shining through your windows?" Sam asked, silently blessing harsh cleaning chemicals.

"Oh, I like it really. Never did like sleeping in the dark. A childhood thing, you know."

So the shades were up.

The strap from her handbag slipped off her shoulder. Sam tugged it back up. It was heavier than usual, and she was beginning to feel it.

"I didn't see anyone after 9:00 o'clock," he went on. "But, you know, I was watching TV and went to bed at the regular time, 11:30, so…I don't know."

Respectable Georgians were snug in bed by 11:30. Although, once, a light was spotted on the bottom floor in the Coldbath mansion at the south end of the green at 2:45 in the morning. Clarence knew because a spicy chili supper had resulted in an upset stomach and a trip to the bathroom for Pepto Bismol at said time.

Speculation had run rampant the next day as customers received more than plastic-wrapped shirts and suits. Citizens might understand a light on the upper floor of the Coldbath mansion, but the *first* floor? Their stolid natures, plus a dash of fear of the feisty octogenarian who resided therein, disallowed questioning the source, but did little to dampen the fervor by which the news rippled out from Clean As A Hound's Tooth.

Clarence rubbed his chin as if he were searching for something. Flakes sifted down like the snow outside. "I've already talked to Charlie and Grant. Seems them fellows have questioned everyone 'round the green."

Clarence might be *old* but he certainly was not at the stage where his memory was failing. He could have seen something, even if he didn't realize it was important.

"So you didn't notice anything unusual."

"Not really," he answered slowly. "But…if I do think of anything, anything at all, I'll be sure to let you know."

Sam knew he would.

Chapter 8

Samantha Blackwell checked with Florence at Berry's Bouquets. Doug had not been in there since his wife's death eight years ago.

Clutching her handbag against her chest, she crunched over the footpath between the snow-capped privet hedge surrounding the green and headed for her mother's inn across the way. Big flakes caught on her lashes and clung to her hair. The gray sky leaned against the earth, and the air was chilled and soft.

People moved more silently than usual, bundled in their down jackets and thick boots, trudging over snow-covered sidewalks. A heavy man climbed over a small drift to clean his car windshield. Watching a youngster before her, a mother kept her second, more recalcitrant, child firmly in hand. Neighbor eyed neighbor, their taciturn greetings now monosyllabic.

It seemed surreal.

Sam felt insular. Had one of them killed Doug Hammand? How well did they really know each other? What really went on behind closed doors?

A van rolled by, its tires muffled in the deepening snow. Sam turned. It was Jimi Duncan. He waved. She returned the wave, suppressing thoughts about the Boston Strangler.

At the center of the green, the statue of William Hornblower Coldbath posed in frozen glory, one hand on a hip, the other proffering a cowberry wreath. His long coat flapped in a breeze that had long ago ceased to blow. Sam would never pass the granite figure without wondering why the sculptor hadn't carved a miniature Mrs. Coldbath peeking out from behind the folds of the great man's coat. Four granite benches sat equidistant around the statue for those weary of foot to sit and admire the larger-than-life hero who had founded the town.

She did not stop.

Sleigh bells jingled on the cranberry-colored door of A Loosen'd Spirit as she stepped inside the inn her parents had run together until her father's death from emphysema eighteen years ago. Elizabeth Blackwell ran it now, with the aid of Caroline and Sadie, who most likely would take it over one day.

Sam stamped her feet again and brushed snow from her hair. She hated wearing hats, and would never have thought to put one on anyway in her habitual rush out the back door.

The inn's wide, dark-paneled hall was warm and smelled of cinnamon.

"Hi, mom," Sam called as she found her way past the oval tea table with a scenic panel. A Waterford crystal vase stood full to bursting with fresh flowers.

In the living room, she dropped into one of two overstuffed chairs flanking the fireplace. She lowered her bag onto the old Chinese rug. Logs on the fireplace crackled, releasing yellow blue-edged flames and tiny sparks in the thermal draft. The warm embrace of memories drained some of the tension from her body.

The room was familiar and comforting, with fine but worn English furniture set in conversational clusters around the large "breakfast" room, as her mother called it. Behind Sam, a bright bouquet of irises, daisies, and Queen Anne's lace in a Chinese vase sat at the corner of the mahogany partner's desk that had belonged to her father. Fresh flowers from Berry Bouquet were delivered every Monday.

From the wall of bookcases at the back of the room, which led to her living quarters, Elizabeth Blackwell emerged and bustled toward her only child. She patted Sam's knee, then seated herself and smoothed the skirt of her rose wool suit. At the look on her daughter's face, one penciled eyebrow went up. She leaned forward.

"What is it, dear? You've heard the news about poor Douglas? Of course you have. My goodness. I've been thinking about getting a dog. Did you hear about Florence's dog, Sergeant? He got loose the other night and she had a devil of a time finding him. Poor dear. She was so distraught. Do you think the girls should get a dog? They told me they put a lock on their door at your insistence. That was smart of you." Elizabeth Blackwell dabbed at a white beehive hairdo resistant to the most insistent wind.

Sam stared into the fire and didn't speak.

Elizabeth waited a moment, then said, "You look tired, dear. What is it?"

"Oh, nothing." Sam curled her legs beneath her and smiled wanly at her mother.

"We can talk," Elizabeth said. Her voice registered concern. "All the guests are out right now."

Sam looked into the flames once more.

Elizabeth cocked her head, folded her hands and waited.

A prolonged silence ensued. Sam knew her mother could out wait her.

"I'm just tired, mom."

Her mother's pale blue eyes locked on her.

Sam could not hold her look. Heat from the fireplace soaked into the left side of her body; sparks snapped and rose in showers up the chimney. She lay her head back and absently twisted her wedding band, hypnotized by the dancing orange and yellow flames. She heaved a sigh. "Where are the girls?"

"Sadie's picking up cleaning supplies and Caroline went to the mall. She had an idea for the headboard in the Hannah Coldbath room. It needs a little touch of something."

A bit of a smile crinkled Sam's eyes. Her mother, an early feminist, wasn't about to let old Mrs. Coldbath go unrecognized. There was no William Coldbath room.

"I'll make some tea," Elizabeth added.

It was an old trick and it always worked. Sam was still perfecting the technique.

She watched her mother walk away and trail a veined hand over the corner of the partner's desk she and Robert had bought at an antique shop so many years ago. The sudden realization that her mother didn't stand as tall or smile as wide as she used to hit her hard.

Sam sunk back into the chair. How could she dump this on her mother, this fear she carried like a black shroud since the moment she had read those evil words? That fear now permeated her every thought, her every breath. The sky was not as blue, the birds' songs less joyful. This monster had stolen her life. She put her hands over her face and cried.

"I'm stronger than you think, Samantha. You should have told me this sooner instead of waiting until you had worked yourself into such a tizzy."

Sam wiped her face with the pink tissues her mother had whipped out of the desk drawer when she had returned with two cups of tea and found her only child in tears. She would never get over how amazing her mother was. Sam sipped at her tea, then placed the cup carefully on the glass-covered cherry table to her right.

Earl Grey. How like my mother Caroline is.

"What am I going to do, mom? I can't seem to get my mind relaxed enough to work this thing out."

Elizabeth set her teacup on the brass drum table beside her, leaned back, and folded her small hands. Her size five shoes barely touched the floor. Her look was far away. "Do you remember how your father used to put those puzzle magazines in your Christmas stocking every year? You were so excited. It was as if there were no other presents for you."

Sam's eyes welled again.

"I used to check on you late at night…to be sure you were still breathing," she said in response to Sam's quizzical look. "Most nights you were under that red patchwork quilt with your books, do you remember that?"

"I didn't know you knew about that," Sam said, taken aback. "You never said anything."

Her mother smiled at her. "I knew how much you loved doing puzzles. And how much fun you were having under that old quilt, like it was a secret clubhouse that only you had permission to enter. How could I have said anything?"

"I love you, mom," Sam whispered.

"Yes, well, I love you too, dear. Now," she hoisted herself up, her shoes now off the floor. "What are we going to do about this note? You say it said, 'civilization is the key.' What was next?"

"'Civilization is the key, don't rail at the fates, rather fence with me.'"

"You worked out the numbers I take it."

"Yes, it resolved to a row of letters." Sam fished the crumpled piece of paper out of her jacket pocket and handed it to her mother.

The stacks of wrinkles that gathered on Elizabeth's brow accentuated the aquiline English nose that she had given to her daughter. "I see what you mean. Well then, the answer to these letters lies in the riddle. Let's look at the nouns. Civilization, key, fates, fence. Is there any connection amongst those words?"

"I wonder if it has anything to do with armies." Sam told her mother about her dream of the marching dead.

"Certainly the words civilization and fates would fit in with armies, and war determines the fate of many," Elizabeth said. "You may be on the right track, dear."

They talked and sipped tea, and Sam left feeling better.

Moving slowly down the walkway between the iron-piked fences bordering the inn's lawn, Sam kicked at the deepening snow. She couldn't face the crime scene at McCutty's Market. Maybe later. Right now, all she wanted was to get into her plaid nightshirt, wrap herself in the polar fleece blanket, and with a cup of hot tea, look out at the birds in the back yard.

Her mother's words echoed in her mind—armies and war, right track. She moved as if in a dream, oblivious to the cold and the flakes that fell against her face. Snow-capped picket fences glided by. One part of her brain began counting the pickets.

Then, a movement to her right caused her to hesitate.

Stopping abruptly on the sidewalk, Sam exclaimed, "My God, that's it! I know it is."

She looked up to find herself across the street from her home in front of McCutty's Market, and an old farmer with red earflaps pulled down tight who appeared to wonder what 'it' was but was of no mind to ask. Some things just were. Georgetown residents lived with the forces of nature and Samantha Blackwell.

Sam pirouetted on her Uggs and raced across the green to her sun porch. She fell to her knees and scooted along the floor in front of the bookcases. Her hand touched each volume as she moved.

"It's here somewhere. Damn! Where is it?"

Fifteen minutes later, her coat and boots still on, she held up a piece of paper triumphantly.

"Charlie," She practically screamed into the phone. "Get over her quick. I solved it!"

Chapter 9

HE grinned.

Samantha Blackwell was a beautiful woman, not emaciated like those Twiggy model types but full-bodied, Rubenesque. He liked that word—Rubenesque. He had read an article in Glamour Magazine about the history of women's beauty through the ages. And Sam was Rubenesque. It pleased him that she had gained the extra pounds. She was more of a woman now.

And he knew that when she understood how much he loved her and what he was doing to impress her, she would abandon her meaningless lifestyle and join with him to discover new worlds. But first he had to detach her from all that was familiar, erase her past as if it never existed, leave her with no defenses, trembling, afraid, reduced to helpless fear. Then, when she was truly free, she would come to him. He would embrace her as a lover, a friend, an intellectual equal. And she would be so grateful, so full of love for him because of his sacrifice. He would be her hero.

He waited under a heavy sky in the parking lot at Fox Run Shopping Mall, a one-story, tentacled, concrete block complex with acres of blacktop like so many others throughout the country. It stood testament to the insatiable appetites of the American public. Advertising, television, and the movies had created a monster with so unquenchable a thirst it could not be slaked. If you didn't possess a closet full of designer clothes and enjoy a social life rivaling that of royalty, if your schedule was not filled with monumental decision-making meetings at which you presided equipped with Gucci briefcases, Armani suits, and Rolexes, if you didn't have socially approved high goals in life, then you were a failure, your life was empty and devoid of substance.

But he was happy. He had a goal.

His breath came out in frosty puffs as he surveyed the area through the patch of frost-free glass where his sleeve had wiped the windshield clean. Night plows had left mountains of snow at out-of-the-way corners. He could hear the muffled slosh of tires as cars drove by slowly through snow turned to dirty slush by Firestones and Michelins and Timberland boots and Reeboks.

Shoppers continued to scuff and trudge to and from the wide glass entrance doors in their jackets and coats, some of the apparel open at the neck. The teenagers self-consciously wore only cotton sport jerseys. They were New Englanders, and it wasn't that cold, just in the thirties.

His car sat at a discreet distance from Caroline's old black Dodge Dart. She had been in the mall forty-five minutes. A layer of snow batting had frosted her car, the windshield a blanket of pure white, pure like his love for her mother.

A shiver ran through him. It was chilly but he didn't want to turn on the motor. No telltale trails of exhaust coming from his car to draw attention to him.

He examined the backs of his hands, satisfied that he had removed all hair follicles last night while watching TV. Suddenly chilled, he blew on his fingers, rubbed the knuckles of one hand on the palm of the other, then reversed the process. The snow was letting up; it would spend itself by midafternoon.

Caroline and Sadie. He preferred to do them both at once, less suspicious that way. Maybe a car accident. But for now, he would watch their movements, get familiar with their routine, then lay out his plan.

Suddenly sobered by a ragged thought, he thrust his manicured hands under his armpits. Icicle fingers of loneliness stabbed at his insides, leaving gaping holes through which he felt the burning hatred stir, and bubble, turning to toil and trouble.

He had to keep a lid on it. He laughed out loud, a deep guttural sound that caught in his throat.

If only they knew who he was. The laughter trailed away.
If only he *knew who he was.*
His eyes blanked for many minutes as he chanted the old nursery rhyme, One a penny, two a penny...over and over.

Chapter 10

"Jesus H. Christ, Sam! He's after Henry Lincoln."

Charlie Burrows wiped a big paw over his leathery face while staring at Sam's quickly scribbled note in his other hand. "What'd Henry ever do to anybody? He's as honest as the day is long. Brun went back to him with a dead rosebush we'd had for a year, and he replaced it without so much as a blink." He dropped into a chair opposite Samantha on the sun porch. "How the hell did you figure this out?"

"A number of things, Charlie." Sam trembled under the green blanket then an odd smile manifested on her face. "Forgive the pun."

His brows twisted up.

"Pun, you know," she said. "Number of things, like numbers on the note?"

"Yeah, whatever." He scratched at his acorn-colored hair, which was thinning by the day.

"I told you about my dream, about Doug marching at the head of an army of dead soldiers?"

Charlie nodded impatiently.

"And those lists I made from the thesaurus, the words kept running through my mind. Then I talked to mom around noon today. She mentioned the word 'war.' I thought—war, soldiers, civilization—then I mentally rummaged through the words I had written, like people and nations, and when I was walking home from mom's and saw her fence, and then other fences, civil war popped into my mind. I don't know why.

"But anyway, I remembered something about a code used during the Civil War here in America. And then it hit me: the Rail Fence Code."

"What the hell is the Rail Fence Code?"

"I'm going to show you, just hold your horses." Sam was alert but her nerves were shredded.

Charlie leaned dangerously forward on the edge of the rocker and frowned.

Caught in a Bizzaro world of pleasure and horror, Sam tossed the blanket from her shoulders and hunched over the trestle table.

"He gave us the clues." Her finger traced the words she had copied neatly on a separate sheet of paper on a small clipboard kept at hand for making notes when the muses struck. "He wrote: Don't *rail* at the fates, rather *fence* with me. Rail Fence Code."

"I can see that. I reiterate, what is a Rail Fence Code?"

Sam hesitated, trying to stem her surprise.

Charlie reddened. "Brun's word for the week."

"Good word. Now look, Charlie," Sam said. "This is how it works."

Charlie moved over to drop two hundred and twenty pounds on the protesting sofa beside her. He still clutched the hastily written note Sam had given him when he arrived.

Sam was now ten years old and under the old patchwork quilt. "To decipher the code, resolve the numbers into the letters of the alphabet using this number-letter code. She handed him a 3 X 5 card with the code so he could follow:

A=1	J=10	S=19
B=2	K=11	T=20
C=3	L=12	U=21
D=4	M=13	V=22
E=5	N=14	W=23
F=6	O=15	X=24
G=7	P=16	Y=25
H=8	Q=17	Z=26
I=9	R=18	

With the gray Saga ballpoint pen she favored, Sam carefully printed the corresponding letter above each number on the original message:

M N X V C I I H N Y I C L Y E T I T M S E R L N O N
13-14-24-22-3-9-9-8-14-25-9-3-12-25-5-20-9-20-13-19-5-18-12-14-15-14

Charlie shook his head slowly. "Why did the nutcase go to all this trouble? Why not just come out and write the damned message?"

"He obviously likes the challenge," Sam said. "Now, cut the string of letters in half. Place the first thirteen letters, from M to the L, above the second thirteen letters, but a little to the left like this…" She demonstrated for Charlie.

M   N   X   V   C   I   I   H   N   Y   I   C   L
  Y   E   T   I   T   M   S   E   R   L   N   O   N

"…so the letters above and below are off balance, and voila!"

Charlie squinted and leaned closer.

He needs bifocals, Sam thought, saddened by the thought of their aging. "See. It looks like a rail fence. Now if you slide the top row of letters down into the bottom row, you come up with: MY NEXT VICTIM IS HENRY LINCOLN."

"Wow. This guy's no dummy." Swept up in his own processing, Charlie went on. "Do you suppose this nutcracker targeted Henry Lincoln because of his last name, Lincoln being President during the Civil War?"

A haze blanked his eyes as if he were trying to envision a deranged creature hunched in a shrouded corner pasting letters on a piece of generic paper. "Imagine if he planned to kill a man because his last name matched a Civil War code he was using." He shook his head and scowled. Crooked lines formed on his ruddy forehead, rippling one end of his facial scar like a piece of wet spaghetti. "This cracker's colder than a well digger's lunch."

Charlie rose slowly and moved to stare out the window. "How do you suppose this warped creature knew about this fence code?"

Sam looked past him.

Snow had tapered to pinpoints and now wafted down like dandruff from Mother Nature's shaken locks. A deep layer of snow covered the roof of the glass-sided wooden birdhouse; under it, a gaggle of mourning doves pecked through the snow. One flew up to a pine limb and sent snow fluttering to the ground. Sam visualized the lone dove she had seen that morning calling her friends. 'Hey, come on over to Sam's yard. The bird feeder's full.'

"I don't know how he knew," she said, feeling peculiarly empty now that the euphoria of deciphering the code had waned. She pulled the blanket back around her, her hands and feet felt icy. She thought about turning up the thermostat, but that wouldn't warm the terrible cold that gnawed at her bones. The game wasn't over yet.

Sam went on. "Obviously he's—and we're assuming it's a he—he's well read. No misspellings on the note." Her eyes scanned the scrap of paper. "The poem shows thought. He's probably read books on codes, most likely my books too, since I'm named at the bottom."

Charlie turned back toward her. "I'll check with Water Street Bookstore, RiverRun, Stroudwater, all the bookstores in the area. See how many of your books have been sold recently. Also, books on codes and the Civil War. The libraries too. Somebody might remember someone or something that could help."

"What happens now, Charlie?"

He turned back to the window and got quiet for many minutes.

Then in that dead calm voice Sam knew came from a past he would never talk about, he said, "This son of a bitch isn't going to stop now. Problem is, he could get angry when he finds out you solved his riddle. There's no telling what he'll do. And there's no knowing who'll be next. But we'll get him."

He feared for her, Sam knew that. And it frightened her even more.

"And by the way," he finally said, turning back toward her, seemingly struggling to break out of his dark mood, "I talked with Grant. He doesn't mind my being involved in this case, figuring you'd be more comfortable talking to me, but he'll be talking with you too."

"Thanks, Charlie. I appreciate that."

Silences between them were never uncomfortable. They went back too far.

Then Sam asked the question she feared the most. "So, do you really think there will be an attempt on someone else?"

Charlie didn't have to answer. "The next step," he said, turning once more toward the back yard as if the birds, like the dove carrying the stick to Noah's Ark, would send a signal that solid land was ahead, "is to post your answer at McCutty's."

She shuddered. "What are people going to say when they read, 'My next victim is Henry Lincoln'?"

"I don't know, Sam.' Charlie swung around, ran fingers through his hair. "We just have to hope no one reads the bulletin board except the cracker. It's covered with hundreds of business cards. Who looks at that sort of thing anyway?"

"Kent Butcher."

"Yeah." Charlie snuffled heavily and rubbed his rubber club nose, the result of more than one school fistfight and, Sam suspected, poundings from his long dead father. "He'll see it all right. We've got a snowball's chance in hell of keeping this out of the papers, then there's TV. Right now I've got to contact Grant, tell him what you figured out. And we'll have to alert Henry Lincoln. Chances are this maniac won't touch Henry now that he knows you figured this out. We'll be watching, but you never know.

"I'll tell you one thing for sure. We're going to videotape McCutty's, the doorways, the back room, the closets, and the god damn john." An angry red crept up his face. "Anyone who steps foot in that place will have their puss on camera for the whole world to see."

"Who could have done it, Charlie?"

"I don't know. What we do know is the cowberry wreath Doug was strangled with came from a lamppost down by Stony Pond. So, either he was strangled down there and dragged to McCutty's, which isn't that far through that stand of trees behind the market, or the killer somehow lured Doug into McCutty's, which seems kinda strange. How would they get in, and why wouldn't Doug think that was a strange meeting place? But if that was the plan, the killer coulda taken the wreath down beforehand to use as a murder weapon. We just don't know right now."

Sam pulled the blanket tighter against her chest. "If he were dragged into the market from the pond, wouldn't it take someone pretty strong to pull his dead weight?"

"You'd think so, but there was a case where a one hundred pound woman lifted the back end of a car to free her son who was pinned underneath. When the adrenaline's pumping, people do amazing things."

"Any suspects, Charlie?"

"Well, Doug did leave a life insurance policy, $200,000. Pat's the beneficiary. Seems he changed his will 'bout the time his wife died. I guess by then he figured them boys of his wasn't going to amount to a hill of beans."

"Uh huh. I suppose that would be enough of a motive for some people."

"Yeah. And problem is, Pat doesn't have an alibi. Said she went to bed early that night."

"What about Bobby?"

"Claims he didn't get home until 2:00 A. M. His buddies verify he was drinking with them at the Pigpen out on Wattles Road." Charlie was referring to Iggy's Den, a dive on the edge of town.

Sam wrinkled her nose. "An appropriate name for that place."

Iggy's Den had the dubious distinction of being mentioned every week in the police log in *Publick Occurrences*.

"So, Bobby wouldn't know where Pat was that night?"

"Right." Charlie scrubbed his face with both hands. "But we have to wait for forensics, see if we can come up with fibers, DNA, or anything before we have a strong enough case for arresting anyone. By the way, he did die of strangulation. The incision must have been an afterthought or some kind of signature."

Even under the fleecy blanket, Sam was beginning to understand the true meaning of chilled to the bone. Banishing Charlie's last sentence from her mind, she tried to imagine Pat killing her own father. "Where was the other brother, Michael?"

"Claims he was out with a woman. Won't give her name. Says the lady's married to someone pretty influential."

"That I can believe."

"Maybe so. But if we find any traces leading back to him, he'll have to give her up, unless he wants his pretty ass in prison. Not a nice place for a good-looking guy."

"I find it hard to believe that Pat, or Michael, or even Bobby, would put my name on that note. Why? We've never had any problems. I don't know them that well."

She wondered if Charlie remembered the fight between Doug and Jimi Duncan. But she didn't want to implicate Jimi just because he fell in love with Doug's daughter and now installed protective systems like the Boston Strangler once did. That didn't make Jimi Duncan a killer.

Plates felt warm in Sam's hand as she unloaded the dishwasher. Charlie's warning, that the perpetrator could get mad, had played hard in her head since he left. It was logical. The killer would somehow see the note posted on McCutty's bulletin board, get frustrated that he *or she* had lost round one, or round four it would seem from what he had written—then what would he do?

Sam knew. There would be another body and another note. How could anyone stop him when they didn't know who he was or where he would strike next? That's when she decided to make a silken tofu chocolate pie.

Charlie had left a half-hour ago. Sam called the family—not to tell them about the solution to the riddle, she didn't want to talk about that at the moment—but to invite them to dinner. She did ten virtuous minutes on the ski machine in the basement, showered, wrapped herself in a thick robe, and went to her galley kitchen, where she felt snug surrounded by soft hues of old pine.

A wide wallpaper border—apples, cherries, and grapes on an ancient Italian wall—ran parallel to the soft cream-colored countertop. Behind her, and opposite the windows opening onto the sun porch, a small airtight wood stove sat on a hearth against a brick wall that divided the kitchen from the living room. Some chilly winter nights, Nick would roll and loop newspaper to start a fire. Heat, radiating from the wood stove, warmed more than the body, somehow stirring memories of friendships and small bits of wisdom. The stove also came in handy during nor'easters when the power was down.

Sam needed to embrace the simple satisfaction of cooking.

She slipped an Elvis tape into the boombox on top of the television in the living room, turned the oven on to 425 degrees and washed her hands. From the cupboard above the stove, she took down the wooden recipe box with a rooster painted on the front. From behind the P divider, she pulled out the smudged 3 X 5 piecrust recipe card. She tucked it into the groove on the cardholder that Sadie had given to her on Mother's Day fifteen year ago—a tiny kitchen table with apples, rolling pin, and red striped bowl glued to its top. Since the recipe had been committed to memory long ago, the card wasn't necessary; nevertheless, it always ended up in the tiny kitchen table.

Sam smiled thinking of Sadie, the family historian, faithfully recording events in her diary. At the end of her daughter's life, she'd have volumes to rival the Durants' history of the world.

The best piecrust recipe in the world had come from a woman's magazine over twenty years ago touting the merits of some brand of cooking oil Sam had long forgotten. The chocolate pie called for a single crust.

She measured one cup of flour with a plastic one-cup measurer. Jitterbugging to "Jail House Rock," she tossed in a dash of salt, a quarter cup of oil, and an eighth cup of milk without spilling a drop. At this stage, she always remembered her mother's warning not to work the dough too much. Makes it tough.

The doughy mixture was placed between two sheets of waxed paper and worked. Sam took pride in the almost perfect circle she and her wooden rolling pin could create after twenty-three years of marriage.

That done, she lifted off the top layer of waxed paper, crumpled and tossed it into the stainless steel sink to her right, then picked up the corners of the waxed paper beneath the crust and turned it nicely into a greased pie plate. She fluted the edges with her thumbs.

No mess, no fuss. The rolling pin stays clean. The crust was foolproof and deliciously flaky.

The red light on the oven was off. Holding her head back from the escaping heat, she opened the door, slipped the pie plate into the oven and set the timer for ten minutes.

As she pulled the tofu package from the vegetable bin, her hand brushed the Ring Dings package. Ignoring the call, she slit the cellophane top of the white plastic container with a knife, drained the water, and spooned the slippery jell into her new Cuisinart—the paddle in her old blender had seized in the midst of the last pie venture—and hit the blend button.

Early on, she learned that noses turned up at the mention of tofu, so it was with smug satisfaction she accepted raves for her silky chocolate pie. There were now two secret recipes in Georgetown.

And the best thing about the pie was she didn't feel guilty eating it, well, only half-guilty. Tofu was good for you.

Picking up the words to "You Ain't Nothing But A Hound Dog," she poured a heaping cup of chocolate bits into a pan within a pan—her homemade double boiler—and stirred with a wooden spoon while the chocolate melted. Sam could feel saliva trickle inside the corners of her throat as she breathed in the smell of melting chocolate. Nibbling the few bits that had inadvertently fallen on the counter top was no sin. After all, she had done ten minutes on the Nordic Track.

With a white rubber spatula, she scraped most of the chocolate into the Cuisinart and blended again. The piecrust was almost done.

Sam watched her reflection in the big mirror attached to the brick wall. With her hands extended high above her head, she bumped and gyrated, spun and twisted, feeling proud that she was adding another few minutes of exercise to her day. Maybe she'd lose a few pounds.

The buzzer on the stove went off. She slid mitted hands into the oven and set the steaming piecrust on the witch trivet. She scooped the tofu-chocolate mixture into the pie shell with the rubber spatula and stuck the pie in the refrigerator. Later, a spurt of whipped cream from the can would top the yummiest chocolate pie ever created.

It can't get much simpler than this, she thought with satisfaction.

This was her kind of recipe. Two ingredients…well, four, if you counted the piecrust. Sam had refined her culinary talents to creations with less than five ingredients.

Rather than waste any of the brown gold, she licked the wooden spoon and the white spatula, both sides, and unscrewed the bottom of the Cuisinart to finger out the residue that hid beneath the little silver blade.

After licking her fingers clean, she rinsed her hands and wiped them on the dishtowel hanging from the refrigerator door. Dinner would be at 6:30.

With a package of Ring Dings and Patricia Cornwell's paperback, *Cause of Death*, Sam flopped on the sun porch couch, and after Selket had crept up to her chin and kneaded her chest until she cried out, "All right already!" she and Selket settled down to eat and read.

Chapter 11

Sam still didn't tell her family. She wanted one simple evening at the dinner table to restore some normalcy to her life.

It was 'dinner.' She had lit two candles and set out the lace tablecloth she had bought on the transport boat into Cozumel. Her mother, who never came empty handed, bustled in with a box of dark chocolate mint truffles from the Chocolatier in Exeter, and the girls arrived fifteen minutes later, breathless and rosy-cheeked from the cold, discussing Caroline's latest date.

The snow had stopped; trees and lawn shone silver in a wedge of moonlight. They dined by candlelight over fresh pasta primavera, hot Italian bread, and a Romaine lettuce salad with shredded carrots and slivered almonds, and finished with scrumptious silken chocolate pie topped with whipped cream.

The evening had regenerated her.

"Charlie. What's happening?" Sam paced through the house the next morning with the portable phone to her ear. At breakfast, she had told Nick about deciphering the code.

"Huh? What time is it?" She could hear something thud, then, "Damn."

"It's quarter to nine. Did I wake you?" Absently, she cradled the phone between her shoulder and ear and unrolled the green sponge from her bangs that she had stuck back in after Nick left.

"Got to get up anyway." Rustling sounds accompanied grunts. "I contacted Grant after we talked yesterday."

Sam stuffed the roller in her sweats and leaned against the kitchen counter, eyeing the refrigerator while Charlie yawned loudly. "Yes, I know. He was here for an hour yesterday."

Charlie said, "We set up surveillance cameras at McCutty's during the night and posted your answer on the bulletin board. Didn't get out of there until 5:00 this morning. But in plenty of time before Mike opened at 6:30."

"Oh, God." Cold crept through her body. "What if he was watching?" One arm hugged her chest. She started pacing again and found herself on the sun porch.

"Most likely you solved his clever little message long before he expected you to. Anyway, we had the area canvassed. Went through the back in dark clothes. No one saw us, Sam."

Hopefully no one but Clarence.

"Not to worry," he was going on. "We've got a team watching those cameras 'round the clock. When he shows his slimy little face, we'll catch him."

"What should I do?"

She could hear him sigh. "There's nothing any of us can do now but wait and watch. And I mean that, Sam. Don't you go poking around. This cracker's killed once, maybe three times if what he said on his note is more than a god-damn fairy tale, so he's got nothing to lose."

"What about Henry Lincoln?"

"We talked with him and his wife. They were pretty upset. We advised Henry to close the garden center until this thing blows over. They packed up and left first thing this morning for their daughter's place in Utah. We sent a cop with them to the airport in Manchester. They weren't followed. We'll keep in touch with them."

Sam felt relieved as she looked out the sun porch windows. The Lincolns were devoted to the community and everyone loved them.

"What about the press?" She squinted at the L. L. Bean thermometer outside, fifty-eight degrees. New Englanders took seismic temperature changes with considerable aplomb. She remembered one steamy summer when an approaching storm caused the temperature in Concord to drop twenty-one degrees in four minutes.

She watched snow thud down off tree limbs sending snarls of birds into the air. Tiny grass patches peeked up through puddles of shimmering water. She noticed the bird feeders were getting low.

"Better prepare for the worst," Charlie warned. "The crime scene tape's been down two days so the market's been open to the public, and Butcher's been in McCutty's every day snooping around, asking questions. If he sees that note we tacked up this morning, then he'll be on you like flies on shit."

Sam pulled at the neck of her sweatshirt. "He knows my name is on the original note or he wouldn't be hounding me, Charlie. God only knows what he'll write if he sees this note, and I don't talk to him. Tomorrow's paper could be a doozy."

"Yeah."

"Well, I'm not talking to him and that's that. I'll never forgive him for stamping on Caroline's locket and laughing in her face while she picked up the pieces. It was her eleventh birthday present from Nick and I."

"How long ago was that, Sam?" He sounded amused, but Sam knew he was only trying to make light of the comment for her benefit. He, more than most, knew that childhood pain clung like a wet tee shirt on a cold winter night.

"Doesn't matter," she responded. "Butcher was a mean kid then and he's a mean adult now. Some things don't change."

"You don't have to talk to him if you don't want to. He'll write what he wants to anyway."

"What are people going to think when they see 'My next victim is Henry Lincoln?' scrawled on McCutty's bulletin board?" The words felt thick in her mouth.

"We're hoping no one notices, including Butcher. That board is crammed with so many business cards and notices no one ever looks at it. Least, that's been my experience."

Sam knew he was right. She never looked at them. Sensory overload. But she plunged on. "Yes, but that board sits right next to the cash register. Anyone standing there can see it."

"Yeah. But you know the old mystery trick. Hide the clue in the most obvious place and no one will see it."

"Except that someone will. The killer will see it." She hated saying that word.

"Right. And we want him to. And when he does, we'll know it. We've got experts working on this. They're watching every person who passes through that doorway. Every eye movement, twinge, lift of the brow, curl of the mouth will be noted. These nut cases always give themselves away."

Sam sprawled on the couch, feet up on the cushioned back. She pressed a knuckle into her forehead. "God, Charlie! I just remembered. I haven't even called Doug's family."

"You've been pretty busy, Sam."

"That's not an excuse. I'll make a dish and take it over to Pat's tonight," she said, mostly to herself. Then, "When do you think they'll release Doug's body?"

"Have no idea. I gotta go, Sam. Gotta get to work, and Brun's yelling about breakfast getting cold. That's if I can fight my way through all this pantyhose. You'd think the girls could hang this stuff on those fold-up things."

Sam could hear swishing noises. "You mean a clothes rack?"

"Whatever."

"You better be careful if you're swatting at those nylons, Charlie." She couldn't stop herself from smiling at the image of Charlie in his shorts, phone in hand, slashing through a nylon jungle. "You'll be in deep doo-doo if one of your women finds a run in her stockings."

"Jesus!" After another string of invectives, she could hear him grunting again. Probably bent over, carefully straightening things.

"Let me know as soon as you hear about Doug. Okay, Charlie?" Charlie grunted again, then shook the frog free from his throat. "Right now," Sam said, "I'm going to call mom and the girls. Then I think I'd better talk to Agatha before she sends out her swat team to get me. This report will be verbal."

He laughed. "Better you than me."

Sam chuckled at his high-pitched giggle.

Minutes later, she filled the bird feeders, put in a load of laundry, and prepared for her one and two o'clock numerology readings.

Agatha now occupied the house that the first William had commissioned master builder and carver, Samuel McIntire, to construct in 1798. The Coldbath mansion, a square brick Federal town house with four corner chimneys, was set back from the road behind a curving drive and was noted for its "imposing but balanced and restrained façade."

Much like its present owner, Sam thought, as she pulled up on the pebbled drive edged with mounds of fast-melting snow.

Warm sun polished the brass knocker on the Williamsburg green front door, which two together probably cost more than her Honda, and glinted off the fourteen shuttered windows on the three-story face. There were probably another three dozen such windows around the remaining sides of the home. Someday she was going to count them. How much newspaper and Windex Agatha used to clean these acres of glass, she could only imagine, wincing at the thought of the distasteful task. Sam sported skinned knuckles every spring before she and Nick had even finished with her eight sun porch windows, and they had no mullions.

As she hesitated and girded her loins for battle, the door flew open.

"You are late. Come in, come in," Agatha motioned.

If only she were my age, Sam growled to herself as she stepped inside and onto a gray marble floor.

Agatha reset the alarm and marched off into the sitting room to the right of the spacious foyer.

Sam hesitated, wondering about her wet boots. Ahead lay a large pale blue Persian carpet over polished parquet floors. Beyond the thick rug, magnificent wide stairs rose to split at the second story. The risers were white, the treads a polished oak. A lustrous white railing girdled the upper level.

Flanking the vast hall on gleaming mahogany tables were English porcelain vases filled with fresh flowers. Sam whispered the word vases with a long 'a.' There wasn't a speck of dust anywhere.

She slipped off her boots.

As she started after Agatha, explaining to deaf ears that it was only a few minutes after 4:00 and their appointment was for 4:00, she looked up and stopped in mid-sentence. Her breath caught in her throat.

A bar of light through the semi-elliptical fan light over the front door set the crystal chandelier high above on fire. Thousands of prisms threw shards of gold-white light against the blue silk walls.

It was as if a spiritual light flowed into her. Sam couldn't breathe, for breath would disturb the moment. The Creator had moved the sun just for her. She whispered, "Thank you."

"For heaven's sake, Samantha," a thin but commanding voice called from her right, "are you coming in or not? Some of us have things to do. Must I remind you that 'idle hands are the devil's workshop'?"

Still elevated by the mystical moment, Sam padded in on not-so-little wool feet and sat on a fabric-covered William Morris chair. Her spirit drifted dreamily toward Monet's stunning Haystack hanging over the marble fireplace. From a spread in Home Beautiful, she recalled that Monet had called them grain stacks. The room smelled of aloe.

Her eyes refocused on the mistress of the mansion.

Agatha looked Sam down, hesitated at her feet, then up. Although she appeared to be in deep thought, she paused only momentarily.

"What have you got to report?" Her gnarled hands rested on the cherry arms of her chair; the forefinger of her right hand tapped at the wood.

Suddenly, like a schoolgirl before the principal's piercing eye, Sam felt naked. She was guilty. Had to be. Of something.

She met the old woman's eyes. "Actually, I've been quite busy these past few days, Agatha," she retorted with lifted chin. She could feel the prickles starting.

"I would certainly hope so, with what has been happening in our town."

Agatha was dressed in soft gray wool with an antique cameo at her neck and looked almost pretty, even with the hairy lip. She would have been quite a catch, Sam thought, as heat crept up her neck. She wondered how many suitors had tried. Beauty and all that money. But if Agatha was a handful now, one could only imagine what hell on wheels she had been at twenty-one.

"You know about the note, I take it?" asked Sam. She wanted to grab the ubiquitous *Old Farmer's Almanac* off the table and fan her face. The magazine seemed incongruous in that setting.

"Yes. Your name was on it, Samantha. This person is challenging you." It was a statement.

How could her face feel so hot, and her hands and feet feel so cold? "I'm afraid so," Sam agreed. "At any rate, I deciphered his message."

"And when did this happen?"

"A few hours ago."

"And what did the message say?"

Since Agatha was unofficial town manager, it was a given that she be told. The woman was stubborn, demanding, and obsessive, an exasperated Sam would frequently tell her husband—qualities of her own, Nick had tactfully suggested once—but Sam knew that an Iron Maiden could not extract a secret from the old maiden's thin, clenched lips.

She said, "The message read: Henry Lincoln is my next victim."

Agatha's brow dipped as she gazed at the cold fireplace. Sam's eyes followed. Brass andirons glowed in the waning afternoon light. A matching set of tools sat to the right.

"Oh, dear. I had hoped that was not true." Her voice wavered, then she turned hard eyes on Samantha. "What is being done?"

The heat subsided, leaving a bead of sweat across Sam's forehead near her hairline.

"The Lincolns have left town for parts unknown," she fibbed. Agatha probably knew exactly where they'd gone, but Sam exulted a bit in the remote possibility she might have knowledge the old woman didn't. "Charlie and his team have set up surveillance cameras in McCutty's. The answer is posted on the bulletin board by the door. Charlie seems confident they will catch him soon."

"I see." Agatha examined her. "Would you like tea?"

She rose and motioned behind her toward a silver tea set on a Louis XVI sideboard with bronze mounts made in the 19th century. Next to the tea service set a black-and-white photograph of two young girls in a silver frame.

"No, thank you. I would like to stay, but I have another errand to run." Sam wanted to wipe her forehead before trickles started down her face.

Agatha sat back down. She looked at laced fingers in her lap, then began smoothing her dress repeatedly.

Sam couldn't believe the woman was actually fidgeting. Had the stars left the heavens? Would the moon collide with the sun? What was happening to the sleepy little hamlet of Georgetown?

"I have not told anyone this, Samantha. And I do hope you will not speak of it unless and until I give you permission to do so."

"Of course, Agatha." Sam was nonplussed.

"I received an anonymous call from a man. He wants to meet with me." She looked almost stricken, then shifted her bony shoulders slightly and cleared her throat.

Sam forgot her manners. "Who? About what?"

"It is a private matter. All I can tell you is that it is a matter of the utmost importance. I want you to know that I plan to meet him. And if anything happens to me, anything at all, you are to tell Chief Burrows that I have left a sealed letter with my attorney stating the exact time and location of the meeting, and other details about the telephone conversation that I recalled."

"But...but..." Sam slid precariously close to the edge of the Morris chair. "What do you mean? Nothing's going to happen to you. Have you been threatened?"

Ms. Coldbath waved a hand in the air like the Queen of Hearts when she blithely ordered, 'Off with their heads.'

"Enough, Samantha! That is all I will say. Now, even though you dwell on subject matter that I cannot say I approve of, and you do not attend church regularly, and heaven knows you could use a good seamstress," she gave her another disdainful once over, "I know you are moderately intelligent and can be trusted to keep a secret. That is all."

One bead of sweat broke loose and trickled down to the corner of Sam's eye.

"But..."

Samantha was summarily dismissed.

Chapter 12

Patricia Hammand lived in the family's two-story frame house with an unkempt yard and rampant hedges. She was the youngest of three, the son her father always wanted, and had taken over his construction business when he retired after his wife died.

Hammand & Sons, the dream, had become the nightmare when his two sons were lured by the profligate lives of a gambler and an accomplished drunk respectively. By then, the expense of changing lettering on trucks, signs, and letterheads seemed a foolish waste of money. And no Georgian worth his salt would ever considered doing so if such a circumstance had ever come up before now. Which it hadn't.

Sam pulled into the Hammand driveway. She knew that beneath the fast-melting blanket of snow, the grounds had deteriorated since Betty died. Betty Hammand had been an avid gardener. The yard had been a showplace of daffodils and crocuses in early spring, followed by drifts of soft color—-old-fashioned satiny white Ocean Pearls; pink, deep rose, and white Early Summer Lace Baby's Breath; and magenta Purple Queen. Summer brought zinnias, dahlias, and Blue Boy cornflowers.

In addition, Betty's simple but spotless summer table had been graced with early snap peas, varieties of lettuce, summer squash, carrots, tomatoes, cucumbers, watermelon, and Sam's all-time favorite, asparagus. For winter, potatoes and butternut squash were stored in the root cellar. The tall wiry woman never sat still.

An exhausted Pat greeted Sam at the door. "Samantha. Come on in." She held the door wide.

The place smelled like an ashtray.

Sam grabbed her gumption, stepped inside, and wiped her boots on the braided rug by the back door. She handed Pat a cheesy green bean and tomato casserole in a Corning Ware dish.

"I'm sorry to bother you so close to supper, but I thought you might be able to use this tonight. It's still warm but you might want to heat it up."

Sam had rushed home from Agatha's, thrown the dish together and tossed the damp laundry into the dryer while the casserole heated. It was a quarter to six by the time she arrived at the Hammands'.

"You don't know how much I appreciate this, Sam, and I'll be sure you get your dish back."

Pat took the casserole and set it on the tired counter behind her, then raked fingers through her short tousled chestnut hair. "The town's been so good, calling, sending flowers, everyone stopping by to remember pop."

Sam wondered where all the flowers were.

The kitchen was old. Layers of grease clung to the yellowing ceiling and the windows needed a good scrubbing. The counter looked wet, like it had just been wiped down, Sam thought. Square wooden canisters, whose painted decorations were now past identification, sat beside a matching breadbox. Dishes lay in fresh soap bubbles in the sink. There were no signs of supper. By the looks of things, Pat had just got home and hastily cleaned up after one or both of her lazy brothers.

Sam crossed over Armstrong's most popular red brick inlaid pattern, which was wearing thin by the sink and doorways, and took the seat offered on one of the mismatched painted chairs at the drop-leaf table. A yellow hard hat and portable phone lay next to an old wooden lamp on the gouged surface.

"Can I get you something?" Pat's face was drawn. There were dark circles under her eyes. She wore tan boots, dirty jeans, and a gray tee shirt revealing strong arms with defined muscles. She was quite pretty, Sam thought.

"No, no, thanks. You must have just gotten home."

Pat turned a chair, straddled it, and rested her arms and chin on the back. "Yeah. And I'm really tired. Pop's services are on Saturday but I still have to keep the business running. I've got so much to do. I appreciate the dish. Otherwise, we'd be eating cold cereal, I'm afraid."

With a tweak of envy at the high cheekbones and clean curves of youth, Sam reached out to squeeze her strong hand. "Do you want to talk?"

"No. I'm trying not to think about it. In fact, I've put all the cards and flowers in the dining room and shut the door." She indicated the direction with a toss of her sweat-dried locks. "I appreciate the thoughts but they make me sad. I just can't have them out where I'm constantly reminded. The church ladies are coming over tomorrow after the service to set up in there so they'll arrange the flowers, I'm sure."

Sam wondered if the abundance of bouquets and sympathy cards were causing a feeling of déjà vu, reminding Pat of her mother's funeral.

A voice from the other room bellowed. "Do I smell food?" Bobby Hammand, with a Bud in one hand and cigarette in the other, belched his way into the kitchen.

Spying the casserole, he growled, "'Bout time. I'm hungry."

Thirty-something and beginning to bald, Bobby Hammand looked more like fifty, Sam thought with some smugness because she felt she didn't. He lifted the cover of the casserole, and jabbed in a thick finger, which he proceeded to suck. Sam could only imagine where that finger had been.

"Not bad," he pronounced. "Don't like green beans all that much but it's not bad." Grimy blue jeans did not cover his background essentials. Sam looked away.

"If you don't like it," Pat shot at him, "eat the dog food!"

"What's the matter with you, huh? Got a hair across your ass?"

After her brother left the room mumbling he couldn't wait much longer, Pat apologized.

"Don't worry about it." Sam said. "Is there anything I can do for you?"

"No, thanks. I'm fine." Pat rotated the hard hat with both hands. A knuckle on her right hand looked like it had been run over by a lawn mower.

"Has Charlie talked with you?" Sam knew he had but she wanted to gauge Pat's reaction.

"Why?" Pat's hands froze. Her hazel eyes were defiant. "Why would he talk to me?"

Sam didn't show her surprise. "He might figure you'd know something about where your father was going that night. Doug did leave work a few minutes early that day. Agatha said he had rarely done that in the past."

"What else did the town crier say?" Pat retorted. "I suppose everyone knows all the little details of pop's death." She stared morosely at the hard hat.

The rickety chair creaked as Sam sat back. "News travels fast in a small town." *'The news, like squirrels, ran,'* Sam thought.

Her nerves felt like hungry squirrels were overrunning them. She was tired and hungry and angry and she hated the smell of cigarettes. She wanted to go home. She didn't want to talk to this young woman who had lost her mother eight years ago, and now her father, so grossly murdered. And *he* was still out there. He would read the note at McCutty's and then what?

Sam couldn't look directly at Pat. Was it possible that she and Jimi murdered Doug? Or maybe Jimi did it, figuring Pat would come around if her father were out of the way. Sam didn't like the way her mind was working. She was suspicious of everyone. How she wanted life to be like it was, how long ago was that?

She gazed at the far wall. The squat refrigerator was most likely filled with cases of Budweiser—in the can, more macho—and the bright new freezer that sat next to it stuffed with TV dinners. Pat didn't have time to cook and probably wouldn't anyway, and Bobby was too busy with beer, belching, and ball games to be of any use.

She wondered where Michael was. Surely he would have torn himself away from Foxwood long enough to come home for his father's funeral.

Pat broke the silence. "I already talked to Charlie and his brother-in-law," she said sullenly.

"Agatha's concerned about you too." Sam couldn't believe she was defending the old bat. "And it's Charlie's job to talk to everyone in the family. Besides that, he's a friend. He wanted to offer his condolences."

"You're right. I'm sorry." Pat's eyes were glued to the hard hat. "Nothing is going right these days. Pop's death, the bills…"

Standing, she went to the porcelain sink, poured water into a jelly glass from the windowsill, and drank it down in four gulps. She wiped her lips with the back of her hand.

"Your father must have left life insurance," Sam said gently.

Pat gazed past the red checkered curtains at their Golden Retriever, Champ, chasing fluttering dead leaves in the fenced back yard. "Yeah, he did, some. It's not that. It's, you know. This and that."

Sam surmised that 'this' was supporting Bobby, and 'that' was keeping the dark suits and white ties away from Doug's second disappointment, Michael. And perhaps the unspoken 'other thing' was Jimi Duncan.

Pat turned to face Sam. "I can't imagine where pop was going Monday night. He was usually in bed by 9:00."

Like everyone else in town, Sam thought. Unless there was a free slide show, a library reading group, or a town meeting. Although summertime might keep the citizens of Georgetown up till the eleven o'clock news was over.

"I was beat that night after digging the Potswell foundation," Pat said. "We hit granite and had to get a blasting permit. I think I fell into bed at 8:30."

Was she reinforcing her alibi? If so, it wasn't very imaginative. Unless, of course, there had been more than one body in her bed. But there had been no talk. As far as anyone knew, Patricia Hammand had no boyfriends and wasn't interested.

The portable phone rang. Pat answered it, and asked to be excused. Sam responded, "I'll just stretch a little."

Pat left the room.

With hands clasped behind her back like she had been taught as a little girl on shopping trips with her mother, Sam began visually poking around.

On a painted yellow hutch next to the living room doorway sat the only touch of femininity in the stark kitchen, a bouquet of daffodils. Fading yellow faces poked out of a dark blue glass vase. Arranged artistically. Pat was creative.

Lots of people loved daffodils, Sam mused, why wouldn't Pat stop and pick a few on her way in? They grew profusely beside her back stoop and along the side of the house. Maybe Doug had stopped by and picked one for his lapel.

Dust lay in a thick gray blanket over the hutch. Sam felt exonerated. She resisted an impulse to finger her name in the inch-deep stuff in front of a row of German beer steins. She liked order in her home, but dust…well, she could commiserate. If it weren't for Sadie's bi-weekly visits with dust cloth and vacuum, Sam would have been forced to find a way to plead, cajole, or blackmail Nick into doing it.

She wandered over to the cluttered oak roll-top desk. Above it and behind an old radio, on faded berry-sprig wallpaper, hung a Currier & Ives calendar. A January winter scene. People bundled into an old sleigh pulling up before a two-story farmhouse.

Scribbled on yellow Post-its were stuck haphazardly to the top edge of the desk's cubbyholes.

Holding her breath over a dirty amber glass ashtray, Sam bent slightly to examine the pigeonholed back stuffed with papers, extra checkbooks, hand stamps, an opened roll of peppermint LifeSavers, paper clips, and elastics.

Nothing incriminating.

She turned away, took another quick breath and bent closer for a look at the Benning Oil calendar anchored under the edge of the desk pad. Its big white squares were filled with right-slanted script. Presumably Patricia's handwriting. Potswell, dump fee, Eggerts 9:00, Fray 2:30. Sam winced at the thought of her last dental appointment.

When her eyes lit on the Hammand and Sons envelopes tucked in the back of the desk under the cubbyholes, her blood pressure rose as her thoughts slammed back twenty-three years. The day Caroline was born, the middle-aged nurse in crisp white had directed Sam to fill out the birth certificate form. After a heated discussion about the propriety of taking the man's name, the tight-lipped nurse had stared bug-eyed at Sam's neat and deliberately clear handwriting: Caroline Bennett-Blackwell.

"You could at least put your husband's name last," was the nurse's final comment.

That was when Sam had let loose at the nurse's retreating back that she had carried Caroline for nine months, had gone through thirteen hours of labor, and wasn't about to change her daughter's name. And, furthermore, she'd be damn sure that no one walked Caroline down the wedding aisle to give her away because you can only give away what you own and no one would own her.

Motherhood did strange things to a woman, Sam clucked. Elizabeth Blackwell never realized what she had done when she'd taught her child to be independent.

Still, Samantha felt for Pat. Patricia must have been made to feel some guilt by her conservative family, even if only subconsciously, for being 'a girl.' Was the guilt great enough to push her over the edge, prompting her to kill her own father? Or to encourage Jimi to do it for her?

Maybe Doug was a "street angel and home devil." A tyrant at home who drove his sons to wasted lives and his daughter to pick up the pieces to fulfill her father's dynastic dreams. Could the loss of Jimi, her father's thwarted dreams, the weight of her mother's death, business debt, supporting and protecting her brothers, have filled Patricia

Hammand with so much rage that something broke inside? And like Humpty Dumpty, she couldn't put herself back together again?

Or maybe the mother's demand for perfection twisted the mind of her daughter. Betty had been the daughter of a strict Calvinist preacher, and the stories told about her early childhood were not pretty. Was the disrepair into which the property had fallen a statement of defiance toward Betty or just the result of too much work and not enough time?

Sam recalled a scene from the film *Network,* where a the actor, Peter Finch, stuck his head out an apartment window and screamed, "I'm mad as hell, and I'm not taking it anymore."

Did Pat sweep aside her red gingham curtains and yell at Champ that she wasn't going to take it anymore? She was certainly strong enough to strangle her father and drag his dead body from Stony Pond into McCutty's Market.

But if she had, how would she have gotten into the locked market, and why would she risk being caught? Why not just kill him and run?

Of course, Michael could have done it, might even have helped one of his siblings, hoping to inherit enough money to satisfy his indebtedness to the guys in black and white. Sam wondered if the mob still dressed that way, right out of *Guys and Dolls.*

And that sloth, Bobby. She would have disgusting dreams about that finger.

As Charlie said, the police always look to the relatives first.

Sam crouched down to peek under the cubbyholes into the back of the desk. In the right corner, on a stack of opened envelopes, lay one from Pierce Investigative Services. Addressed to Patricia Hammand. Well! What did Pat want with a private investigator? Sam's mind rummaged for a logical explanation for that one and could find none.

With her eyes glued to the return address, she was unaware she was breathing in stale cigarette smells.

Did she dare?

In the name of criminal investigation?

No. She couldn't. She believed in an individual's right to privacy. In her home, mail was opened only by the person to whom it was addressed. Still…

The sound of footsteps delivered her from her moral dilemma. She scurried back to her seat, and when Patricia reappeared, Sam was sitting with knees crossed and foot jiggling. She was humming nervously, "Waitin' for the Train to Come In."

Her mother's song.

I have to change my tune, she told herself.

Chapter 13

Saturday was almost balmy.

And even if it weren't a weekend, Sam thought, the good Georgians would have poured into the Second Puritan Church to honor their friend and neighbor, Douglas Hammand.

Snow was lumped around the edges of the green, melting into puddles Sir Walter Raleigh would have admired, but the sidewalks and lawns were clear. The air, wiped clean by the storm two days before, presented the kind of spring day that begged for a rake and trowel.

Sam never ceased to marvel at Mother Nature's capriciousness, although the old gal seemed especially fond of her New England children, offering them the joy of watching the red mercury rise and fall like a roller coaster. The unpredictable weather gave the taciturn Georgians something to talk about publicly. And they did so, with restrained glee.

"Not much of a storm. Them weather forecasters can't seem to get it right."

"Heard tell it was gonna be real hot startin' Monday, though you never can tell."

"Yup. Well, last year this time we had that flood that near took my barn with it."

And so the conversations went, rising up the wide church steps along with their speakers.

Inside, the church had that cool smell of massed flowers. The polished walnut casket sat in front of the pulpit, surrounded by baskets of carnations, baby's breath, and gladioli. A large white cross hung on the wall behind. Sun streamed in through the east bank of tall, plain windows, laying sections of the congregation in rectangles of defined light.

Ostentation was the hallmark of everything the Puritans had left behind, and hundreds of years had not altered their view.

Sam, sitting in the last pew on wood worn smooth by thousands of pious if uncomfortable derrieres, wondered why people waited until their loved ones were gone before giving them flowers. But of course, the blossoms were comfort for the living, not the dead.

Her mother, the girls, and Nick had slid into the pew ahead of her, and the women had busily arranged hair and folds before generally settling down for the upcoming ceremony.

Sam had donned her one simple black dress, a pair of low heels and the soft Evan Picone raincoat that Nick had bought her at Christmas in a fruitless attempt at improving fashion awareness in his wife.

Nick, smartly immaculate in a herringbone charcoal Brooks Brothers suit, light gray shirt with a white button-down collar, and red and black striped tie, smiled sideways at her. She knew he approved of the way she looked. He would love to come home to find Donna Reed in heels, dirndl skirt, and earrings, hair perfectly coiffured, chocolate chip cookies steaming on the counter, and scrubbed children sitting at the dinner table with folded hands, awaiting the master of the house. He was entitled to his fantasies, and she loved him for trying.

Sam scanned the congregation while keeping a watchful eye on the couples and families streaming down the center aisle in the simple white church. The pews were filling quickly.

Sam thought she even spied a few Episcopalians.

The Hammands sat in the first pew on the right. Pat dabbed at her eyes with tissues, Bobby's balding head hung low, Michael stared straight ahead, unmoving. Morning sun through the side arched window shone on his slicked hair, turning it almost golden.

Strategically seated by the aisle, Sam watched as Agatha moved past, under escort and wearing the long black ancestral veil inherited from previous generations of Coldbath women. Soft murmuring increased slightly, row by row, as all heads turned due right and left, depending on which side of the church the mourners sat. Agatha was seated beside Patricia.

It seemed a curious seating arrangement after what Pat had said in her kitchen just yesterday, but then, Sam concluded, Pat's remark was made in the heat of the moment. She had been upset. Her father had worked for Agatha for a number of years and Pat knew on which side of her bread the chutney was spread.

Had Agatha had her meeting with the stranger on the phone? Sam wondered. And if so, what was it all about? Why the extracted promise not to tell anyone unless something untoward happened to her? Agatha was not a shrinking violet. Maybe something a bit more substantial, a quaking aspen perhaps, she thought wickedly. She hated to admit she was worried about the old biddy.

The loud whisper she heard from Clarence Tuttle to Chris Byrnes and Julie Walker seated in front of Sam interrupted her thoughts. It seemed Benjamin King III, the Cranberry King, had been delivered to the church steps in a gleaming black Mercedes CL 600 Coupe. The two women were duly impressed, they related, since their meager salaries at the Bog Café precluded more than secondhand vintage transportation, and they had never even sat in a Mercedes.

Sam elbowed Nick and nodded toward the conversation. Nick gave her a scowl.

Sam couldn't believe the gall of King as he paraded down the aisle in a black pinstriped suit that Nick said probably cost a thousand dollars—and Nick would know—to seat himself in the first row on the left, opposite the Hammand family and Agatha, and beside the lovely Emmaline, wife of Reverend Hannibal Loveless. King probably thought he'd catch the old woman in a weak moment, Sam thought unkindly again. Then, realizing where she was, she quickly recanted on both ruminations, just in case.

Three rows ahead of the Bog duo, Charlie was ensconced amongst Brunhilda and his four blonde daughters. McCutty and his family sat behind the Hammands, as did Florence Livermore, Elizabeth's Thursday night bridge partner. Elizabeth gave her a tiny wave. Florence beamed. Florence was especially pleased since the array of baskets in the church and most of the bouquets delivered to the Hammand home had come from her shop, Berry's Bouquets.

Sam was surprised that Florence's German shepherd wasn't sitting next to her in the pew. They were inseparable.

Jimi Duncan sat by himself amongst the Episcopalians to the right rear of the church, but then, he had always been a rebel.

The Selectmen, Conservation Commission members, and merchants from around the green had come to pay their respects, as had the Little League, their coaches, and the League of New Hampshire Craftsmen. There were a few strangers in their midst, most likely reporters or out-of-town relatives of the natives, curious about the whole affair.

A hush descended as Reverend Hannibal Loveless swept in from a side door like a great black crow, swooped up onto the dais, and grabbed the pulpit edge with taloned fingers. He peered over reading spectacles at the congregation. Emmaline stirred softly, like a dove ruffling her feathers, before settling down into calm repose.

"She is lovely," Nick whispered to Sam, when he noticed her watching the minister's wife.

Sam was thinking that Emmaline and the gangly preacher, with a nose like a tomahawk and a rather prominent wart situated at the crease where his right nostril flared, seemed mismatched. She recalled Jill Ireland's haughty response when the media referred to Jill and her husband, Charles Bronson, as Beauty and the Beast. The actress had said, "I don't think I'm so beastly." Surely, one of the great comebacks in recorded history.

She chuckled. Nick scowled at her again. "It's a funeral, Sam."

Sam grimaced and cast about for a reaction to her seemingly inappropriate behavior, but everyone seemed intent on the Reverend. Reaching into her bottomless purse, Sam pulled out two small patent leather pocketbooks with tarnished chains. She leaned across Nick and handed them to Caroline, whispering, "Give Sadie hers."

Caroline looked down, then back at her mother, her eyes suddenly wet, while Nick shook his head.

When the girls were very young, Sam had taken them to the 5&10 cent store to pick out their own handbags. Caroline chose black, and Sadie, after much pacing and indecision, decided on yellow. The bags were used for special occasions like church services, weddings, and funerals. Sam would fill them with surprises and pull them out of her own handbag just before a service began. They had proven to be wonderful baby sitters. People remarked about the well-behaved little Bennett-Blackwell girls.

Sadie took the yellow bag from her sister, then frowned and scoped the congregation, but she had no need to worry. All eyes were on Reverend Loveless, who was shuffling papers at the pulpit. Sadie whispered hoarsely, "Mom!"

But Sam knew she was pleased. Elizabeth looked straight ahead, hands clasped properly in the lap of her powder blue suit set off by a suitable black silk scarf cascading down her chest. She looked worlds away, but Sam knew she hadn't missed a trick.

Sadie pulled her coat over the little bag and opened it quietly. Her head stayed erect but her eyes rolled down. In her purse were a few M&M's in plastic wrap, a small yellow pencil, a slip of paper with a hand-drawn maze, a pair of candy lips, a tiny Peter Rabbit book, an old hanky Sam had embroidered for her long ago, and a black plastic square containing white-lettered pieces that moved to make words.

Tears spilled down Sadie's now lowered and greatly embarrassed face. Caroline was busy delicately dabbing her meticulously applied makeup, a paint job that gave the effect that she had none on. Caroline didn't think to offer her sister a tissue so Sadie grabbed one from Caroline's adult purse.

Although he had spoken only two lines, Reverend Hannibal Loveless was slightly surprised but mightily pleased to see the effects his oration had on the two young people in the back pew. He took heart. What had begun haltingly, flapping across pews and brushing against arched windows, now lifted on soaring wings toward the mighty God of his fathers.

Sam wondered about Hannibal Loveless. There were rumors that he had left his last parish in Trumbullton Corners after two homicides, one of the bodies discovered by him in the basement of his church. No one had mentioned it publicly, though, like Dickinson's squirrels, the news ran over wires and back fences.

However, by consensus, according to Sam's mother, the Thursday Bridge Club ladies had decided he couldn't have been involved. Look at that nice wife of his. Fortunately, the bridge ladies did not know that the English teacher, the former Miss Emmaline Parker, enjoyed a hobby reading palm prints advertised in classified ads under an assumed name—M. Lines—if Sam remembered correctly. A clever play on the name Emmaline. The minister's wife picked up her clandestine mail in a post office box in a nearby town. Traveling in different circles than most, Sam knew, but she wouldn't disillusion the Thursday Bridge Club for the world. And besides, she kind of liked the idea. Maybe she'd have her palm read one day.

Still, Sam pondered about the preacher. Men of the cloth weren't immune from the *sins* of the flesh, though they were wont to pontificate greatly on that subject, and some had been known to harbor dark passions held in check only by their fiery words of denial. Shakespeare had said it best, "Me thinks thou dost protest too much."

One had only to recall the protestations against prostitution by Jimmy Swaggart, who was later exposed as a taster of those sinful pleasures. And there was Jim Bakker. And Jim Jones. What was it about the name Jimmy?

Her eyes swung toward Jimi Duncan sitting amidst the Episcopalians. Jimi's fine brown hair, tied back with rawhide lacing, trailed down his back and disappeared behind the pew. Today was one of the few times she had seen him without his bandanna. He wore a long tweed coat over his jeans. Sam could see his profile, brows drawn down, mouth tight. He was staring straight ahead. Was he looking at Patricia? Did he yearn to comfort the woman he loved?

Because of his profession, as well as the odd jobs he performed as a handy-man—he had repaired many a back step in the small town—Jimi knew the layouts of many homes in Georgetown. Could he have been the one Charlie talked about who was breaking into homes? Had he been the prowler outside her bay window the other night when the girls stopped by? Or worse?

Sam shuddered. The question that chewed around the edges of her mind was why would anyone she knew involve her.

Something rustled behind her. She turned to see Madsen Chills slouched against the back wall by the doorway. She nodded, but he didn't notice. His face was slack, his eyes blank.

Sam turned to face front, the mother's eyes in the back of her head wide open. She folded her arms as if to ward off some evil spell.

Strange old duck. Living out there in the woods by himself. No one knew anything about Madsen Chills. He'd showed up in town one day, thirty odd years ago, bought ten acres of woods on the outskirts of town, and started picking trash wherever he could find it. He seemed so vacant at times. Sam wondered if he were on the leading edge of Alzheimer's.

Could he have been involved? Did he even know Doug? She'd have to ask Clarence or Brunhilda if there was any history between the two.

Sam felt a heat surge and struggled to slip off her raincoat. Nick offered a hand.

"Are you all right?" he whispered.

"Yes. Just hot." She dabbed at her sweaty forehead with the back of her hand.

The girls leaned forward to check on their mother. She smiled okay and wondered if she was.

"I'd like to hike Chocorua next Sunday, if you think you'll be okay," Nick whispered in her ear.

Sam smiled her approval. Every two weeks Nick needed a dose of wilderness to regenerate his outdoor cells. In high school, he'd wanted to be a forest ranger. He swore he would never sit behind a desk forty hours a week, which, as fate often directs, was exactly what he did.

The ceremony was blessedly short by request of the family, and the gathering seemed relieved to move out into the brilliant sunshine while the casket was slipped out a side door to the waiting hearse.

Reverend Loveless had invited the congregation to join the family at graveside for the final tribute, then return to the Hammand home where the women of the Friends and Neighbors Committee were already preparing a little something. This meant, of course, every casserole recipe that had been handed down through generations of Georgians, plus salads, steaming crusty breads, baked beans, pies filled with berries and puddings and meringues. And, of course, an array of Coldbath Cowberry Chutney. The wise women of the church knew the soul of the living would rest easier in the body when comforted by good food.

Hannibal stood by the church doors as each person passed through, thanking, murmuring, placing a consoling hand on a shoulder.

Sam looked around for Madsen Chills, but he seemed to have disappeared as soon as the service ended. Again, she wondered why he had come to Doug's service. Maybe he was curious. Or crazy.

At curb side, waiting for Nick to bring the car around, Samantha, Elizabeth, and the girls watched as Benjamin King flap-stepped over to Agatha, who had just lifted the veil from her tired face. Her eyes were ringed red, but her lips held firmly.

"Agatha! How are you doing?" He didn't wait for an answer, but took her frail elbow and steered her away from a surprised Pat and her two brothers. "I have an even better deal for you," he said into her ear, speaking loudly as if deafness were a prerequisite of growing old.

"Sir!" Agatha pulled away with amazing force and stared at the bloated man with a hatred Sam had never seen in the old woman's eyes. "Do not put your hand on me again. How could you speak of such things when a good man lies dead in this church?"

Murmurings ceased. The milling crowd flash froze.

"Listen!" he said quietly, but with a steely voice, "I've made you offers no sane person could refuse."

Sam scowled, watching intently, even as part of her was thinking that King's thick, short-cropped gray hair, which grew in a widow's peak close to his eyebrows, gave him the air of a pompous penguin.

"Are you questioning my state of mind, Mr. King?" Agatha demanded to know.

"What I'm saying is that you're not going to live forever. Why not enjoy the fruits of your labor now rather than leaving them for someone else to enjoy?"

A collective gasp rose from the stunned bystanders.

If Agatha's stare had been a spit fork, King would have been trussed and rotating over fiery coals by now, regardless of the holy ground on which they both stood.

"Is that a threat, sir?"

"Call it what you want, little lady." He shook a pudgy flipper in her face. Light glinted from somewhere. "But I'm going to get your chutney plant one way or another."

Sam had had enough. She stormed over to plant herself in front of Agatha.

Somewhere in the back of her mind, Sam knew that Caroline, fearing an undignified public display, and Sadie, afraid of what her friends would think, were appalled at the donnybrook their mother was surely about to engage in. Sam's mother, the unflappable Elizabeth Blackwell, was surely pleased.

"Listen, you big bag of wind," Sam said in a low constrained voice, her hands clenched by her sides, "you'd better get in your fancy Mercedes and high-tail it out of here before Old William there rises up in righteous anger. And, believe me, I'll gladly lend him a hand."

A flashbulb went off.

Sam blinked but held steady. She'd deal with Butcher later.

Undistracted by publicity-seeking hounds, Benjamin Hines King III, stared in disbelief at Samantha and hesitated, as if deciding whether to attack two women on the steps of the Second Puritan Church during a funeral service or to retreat. He opted for the latter and waddled backwards toward his shiny car. A fashion-correct chauffeur held the back door open.

Flash!

King lowered himself into the Mercedes, pulling black Florsheim's in after him. The young chauffeur shut the door and nodded at Sam, who thought she detected a twinkle in his eye.

As the Mercedes began to pull away, the smoky back window rolled down. King stuck his head through and said, "I'm going to get your business, old woman, believe me."

Sam started for the car. The window quickly rolled up and the Mercedes sped away. Sam turned back to find the crowd clapping, albeit sedately. Coldbath Cowberry Chutney, and by extension, Agatha Coldbath, were sacred berries in Georgetown.

"That was not necessary, Samantha," Agatha sternly scolded her. She adjusted the glistening pearls at her neck. "I can take care of myself."

Sam felt the flush start again. "I'm sure you can, Agatha," she said between clenched teeth. She wondered if she'd ever learn.

Charlie Burrows stood behind Agatha. Sam thought he must have sent his wife and daughters to the car when trouble was afoot. He was not clapping, and he had that look on his face Sam recalled from grade school after he told her his father had been found dead in the woods, an accidental shooting.

Sam tossed her head at him, turned on her black pumps, and headed toward a puzzled Nick, who had just stepped out of his white Toyota Four Runner.

"What's going on, Samantha?"

"Nothing!"

Caroline and Sadie scattered while Sam and her mother climbed into the truck. Nick, Sam, and her mother took off under the delighted eyes of many who knew a juicy story when they witnessed one.

Except for Agatha's long mourning veil, a passerby might have thought flashbulbs popped in celebration as the white truck pulled away from the church holding the bride and groom with mother-in-law hanging on in the back seat. Black was a fashionable color for weddings today.

HE liked her spunk. But when she was his, he'd teach her to know her place.

She looked so beautiful, sitting there in the last pew. How he wanted to stroke her smooth cheeks, kiss those full lips. Possess her as only two true intellectuals knew how.

He hoped she was going to the reception. He liked being near her.

Pleased that his plan was on schedule, he told himself to be patient. It was only a matter of time.

Chapter 14

"Of course we're going to stop at the Hammands," Sam said in the Four Runner after they had left the church. "Why do you ask?" She pulled down the visor to check her lipstick and caught a glimpse of her mother in the back seat. Elizabeth was smiling like the Cheshire cat.

"You hate these things," Nick explained.

"Since when?"

"Since every other time there's been a funeral. You can hardly wait to get home and into your sweats."

"You exaggerate."

"The pot calling the kettle black," Nick mumbled under his breath, eyes straight ahead. The trio stopped at the Inn for an hour while Elizabeth checked on a few guests, which also allowed time for the graveside ceremonies to end. Then they headed for the Hammand home.

Reverend Hannibal Loveless stood inside the Hammand's front door welcoming mourners into the cramped dark hallway. He wore a simple black suit, shiny at the knees. His neck arched out of his white collar like a vulture's, but his hand was warm and his smile genuine.

Emmaline hung back a step and waited for amenities to be exchanged. Then, with a sweet smile and a nod, she accepted their outerwear and hung the coats on the brass-colored hooks that lined the narrow hall toward the kitchen.

Sam, Nick, and Elizabeth were then bustled from the gangly arms of Reverend Loveless into the plump, open arms of the Friends and Neighbors Committee women and released only after each had a china plate, fork, and napkin in hand, and had given assurances that they brought their appetites.

The girls had arrived minutes before and were waiting for them.

The dining room was tall and square as in most Victorian homes of modest architecture. The wallpaper, a design of pale green fronds on a beige background, had peeled loose over the long front windows from what appeared to be water seepage. Over the big claw-foot oak table, in which two extra leaves had been inserted to hold the casseroles and pies and breads, hung a dull brass electrified candelabra. Six oak chairs and a dozen metal folding chairs lined the walls. A cloth-covered card table holding cheese and crackers stood by the arched doorway. Flowers were everywhere.

Nick, with Sadie on his tail, joined the rhumba line around the dining room table and dug into the feast with unabashed enthusiasm. On any given day, Sadie's caloric intake would stuff an elephant, yet she never gained an ounce, Sam thought enviously.

Through slices of space, Caroline, with pursed amethyst lips and a connoisseur's eye, surveyed a table heavy with dishes of every size and hue. Elizabeth, who spotted Doris with two of her bridge partners, looped her arm through Caroline's before Caroline could attempt a landing in the food queue and skittled them both off to converse with the bridge ladies.

Sam was left to her own devices. A little snooping was in order. She surveyed the room.

In front of windows framed by yellowing lace curtains and looking out onto the street, Agatha stood next to a drawn Pat Hammand. Selectman and conservation board members encircled the women. An unconscious gathering of power.

Off to the left, Bobby Hammand was jabbing a thick finger at Jimi Duncan, probably debating whether the Red Sox had a shot at the World Series this year. Sam couldn't imagine his little gray cells activated by much more than sports, food, and passive criticism. But stranger things had happened.

Could he be presenting a false persona? Did a sharp mind lurk behind that slovenly facade? A regular Jekyll and Hyde? Sam thought of the bean dip finger. *No, it wasn't possible.*

Bobby seemed to be wearing the same grimy jeans, but at least the rumpled gray wool jacket covered his backside.

Sam worked her way toward the far side of the room where Clarence Tuttle was still talking with Julie Walker and Chris Byrnes. Chris wore a stylish buff-colored pantsuit that Caroline had pointed out to Sam before Elizabeth whisked her off.

Passing the card table, which was draped with a worn map of Germany tablecloth, Sam grabbed a few slices of smoked cheddar cheese and a sesame cracker. She imagined the faded cloth had been brought back by one of the Committee ladies' sons after his two-year army stint, back when enlistment was mandatory.

Brunhilda and two of her four daughters beamed at Sam as she passed. She'd have to ask Brun about Madsen Chills. Charlie looked at Sam without expression. She wondered what he was going to say to her later.

The room felt stiflingly hot with the smells of food, flowers, perfumes, and after-shaves and the thermostat set at seventy-five. Sam had noticed the Honeywell dial on the wall by the doorway. The Friends and Neighbors touch, no doubt. Those dedicated ladies were surely warm-hearted but their blood flowed icy.

Sam threaded through the "what a shames" and "he was so youngs" and past the barely whispered "imagine a murder in our town," until she reached the little knot of people.

'Hi Clarence, Julie, Chris," Sam said, nodding at each. "It was nice of you all to attend Doug's service."

"Miss Samantha." Clarence shifted a punch glass to his other hand and shook hers with a chilled right. "What a nice turnout, don't you think?" His wet trout eyes slid around the room, punctuating his statement. "Doug would have been pleased to see all his friends here."

And at least one enemy? Sam wondered. "Yes, he would have. How are you Chris, Julie?"

"Just dandy, Samantha," Julie twittered from her robin's egg blue granny dress. "Well, I mean, you know," airborne ringed fingers fluttered as if looking for a place to roost. "I'm fine, but I sure will miss Doug. He was so much fun."

Julie was refreshingly happy, if you were riding high, or disgustingly chipper when you were in a black funk. A teased nest of mousy brown hair raised her height a good three inches, to the bottom of Sam's chin.

"And you, Chris?" Sam smiled up at the tall woman.

Chris looked directly into Sam's eyes and said warmly. "I'm just fine, Samantha. But, like Julie said, I will miss Doug."

Sam envied Chris' deep turquoise eyes and wondered why she didn't get contacts and lose the clown glasses. Her eyes would have been stunning with the right shade of eye color and a little less black liner. Sam wasn't a fashion plate but she knew how it worked. As it was, Chris, with her bangs and shoulder-length dark shiny hair, looked like a myopic Cleopatra.

"I remember the last time I saw him," Sam said, hoping to entice responses, "at the market. He was squeezing the melons."

"He liked to squeeze," Julie tittered.

"Really?" *Squeeze what?*

"He was always pinching my cheek and telling me how cute I was. Not that it's true," Julie faltered, "but he was like that. Full of compliments. Isn't that right, Chris?"

"Yes. He had an eye for the girls." Chris nodded and her gold triangular earrings swayed.

"But he was never fresh. He just liked to flirt a little," Julie said.

Chris drew herself in and smiled with scarlet lips.

Sam thought Chris seemed less forgiving than Julie of Doug's little flirtations, if that's all they were. But Doug was a man, after all, and had needs. His wife had been dead for many years. Who knew what went through his mind. Harmless flirtations, maybe, but then again, maybe he'd ticked off some woman enough to cause her to finish him off. When he was murdered, he was wearing his one good suit and that flower in his lapel. He wasn't meeting the boys for coffee at the Bog. That much was certain. But then, she couldn't imagine a woman strangling Doug Hammand before filleting him like the fish amongst which he was found. In spite of the warm room, Sam shivered.

"Samantha!"

Sam turned to find Michael Hammand slipping through the crowd behind her.

"Michael. It's been a long time." Sam extended her hand. "I'm so sorry about your dad."

Michael Hammand looked like a blonde Mel Gibson and smelled like surrender. The man was dangerous.

Michael took her hand in both of his and moved in. Like any two blocks in the Great Pyramid, not a slip of paper would have fit between them. "Thank you. I appreciate your being here."

Finally, he edged out a bit and into the little circle. "And you, Mr. Tuttle, and Julie and Chris. Thank you. I know dad would be pleased."

Clarence nodded vigorously; flakes fell.

Michael returned his attention to Sam. His long lashes swept up and down her torso. She felt positively naked. "You're looking lovely, Samantha."

Thank God for little black dresses.

Samantha found herself as flustered as a teenager on her first date. What was wrong with her anyway? Did Michael Hammand affect all women this way? Of course he did. Just look at him.

"Thank you," she said with studied casualness. "You look as if you've kept yourself very fit."

Too fit. Too gorgeous. Thankfully I'm madly in love with my husband.

When she could tear her eyes off him, she noticed Julie Walker, her tiny mouth open like a baby bird, and Chris Byrnes, Sphinx-like, both observing the middle Hammand child. Sam couldn't tell if they were star struck or jealous of his attention to her. All she knew was that something was wrong. The creepy-crawlies skittled down her back.

She turned back to her admirer. "When did you get into town, Michael?"

"I came as soon as I got the call from Pat, arrived home Tuesday afternoon. It's pretty awful. Losing a parent is bad enough but…like this…" He shook his head, a frown wrinkled across his clear tan forehead.

Was it an act or did that perfect face register pain?

"How are Pat and Bobby doing?" Clarence asked between sips of his punch.

"Well, you know Bobby. He doesn't say much about his feelings. And Pat has always been headstrong. She wouldn't let down in front of anyone."

"Oops." Clarence held out his drink as it sloshed dangerously close to spilling. Selectman Ralph Munch clapped an apologetic hand on Clarence's shoulder. "Sorry, Clarence. It's pretty crowded in here."

"No apology needed, Mr. Ralph."

Sam turned her attention back to Michael again. "Rather than headstrong, I would say your sister is a strong person."

"Yes, I admire that in a woman." Michael looked pointedly at Sam. Sam's left eyebrow lifted imperceptibly.

"Some men find that unattractive in a woman. It's a threat to their masculinity."

He tipped his head toward her. A golden lock fell deliciously over his forehead. "That's only if they're insecure to begin with."

It was that 'little boy lost' look that got women, Sam thought.

"Well, I like strong men," Julie chirped.

"You like all men, Julie." Chris laughed, deep and throaty, then threw Michael a dark look. "How are things going at Foxwood? Are you winning?"

"I always win." Michael's mouth smiled, but his eyes went flat. There was a palpable pause. Then he said, in a strangely offhand manner, "If you'll excuse me, I should circulate."

"He's a hunk," Julie commented to Chris, her eyes glued to Michael's retreating back.

"A hunk of what?" Clarence wanted to know.

"It's just an expression," Chris offered. "It means he's very handsome." With a free hand, she smoothed her thick black hair. "If you like that type."

Just then Sam heard his voice. She'd know it anywhere. Her head snapped left toward the hall where, through the moving throngs, she caught a glimpse of *him* talking with Reverend Loveless. The minister maneuvered Kent Butcher toward the back of the hall.

Sam quelled an urge to part the throngs and bring a plague down on the newsman's head. If Kent Butcher had brought his camera into the Hammand household...she sighed. She couldn't make another scene.

Sam excused herself and squeezed toward the hallway, catching snatches of conversation here and there. Nothing meaningful to her investigation.

As she passed under the arched doorway, she spied Hannibal and Kent Butcher at the far end of the gloomy hallway, their heads together in an animated exchange.

Sam jumped. Out of the half shadows, Emmaline Loveless rose from the hall steps like Botticelli's Venus emerging from the half shell.

"Samantha. Is everything all right?"

"Oh, yes, Emmaline. Thank you." She looked past Emmaline's shoulder at Hannibal who was gesticulating energetically. What were they talking about?

"It's terrible about poor Douglas. I just can't get over it," Emmaline said.

Sam suddenly felt drained and weepy. She bit at her lower lip.

Emmaline placed a slender arm around Sam's shoulder and led her through the living room, away from the noisy dining area, and past more bouquets of flowers, into the unoccupied kitchen. Bags and pans and boxes lined the counter, hutch, and pine table. Dirty plates and silver sat piled neatly in the sink awaiting the hands of the church ladies. Even amidst the mess, lingering warm smells made the room feel cozy and inviting.

"Sit down and talk with me, Samantha. The few times I've seen you about town these past days, you've looked so worried. Were you that close to Douglas?"

Sam plunked down on a chair and fought the fear that rumbled in subterranean chambers. "No, not really. It's just the horror of it all, I guess." She looked into Emmaline's soft gray eyes. "Actually, it's more than that."

Emmaline's skin was the color of creamy alabaster. One eyebrow sat slightly higher than the other, giving her face an off balance but strangely ethereal effect, as if the Creator's hand had slipped when painting her features but He liked the effect so well, He wouldn't change it.

'He' would be Hannibal's version, Sam thought. *'She' is more appropriate because the pronoun includes 'he' in the spelling.* She drew herself in tight. This wasn't the time for linguistic equality.

How can my mind bounce around like this? Focus. Sam looked at Emmaline.

Emmaline's face bore traces of old pain that had settled into feathery lines around her eyes. There were small brackets at the corners of her full sensual lips, lips that men must find alluring but inaccessible, Sam thought. Emmaline Loveless could have had any man she wanted, yet she chose Hannibal. Life was not always easy for a beautiful woman and therein might lay the reason for her choice. Especially a woman like Emmaline, so supple, so fluid, someone who, like water, seemed to flow into and take form within the edges of her moments.

Sam leaned forward and blew on her cold fists. She looked down at Patricia Hammand's scratchy pine table covered with the outer wrappings of the kindnesses of neighbors, and said, "I'm more involved than you know."

Emmaline nodded and reached for Sam's hand just as Sam had done yesterday with Patricia Hammand at this very table.

Just then Ethel Peters burst through the door. "Oh, hello. I'm sorry. I don't mean to interrupt. I need more mayonnaise." She waved a smudged dish at them and pulled open the refrigerator door.

"That's perfectly all right, Ethel," Emmaline said, rising in one fluid motion. "May I help with something?"

"No, no, thank you." Ethel hastily spooned mayonnaise into the glass dish, dropped the spoon in the sink and, with a wide hip, pushed her way through the swinging door, calling back to her, "We've got everything under control."

Observing Emmaline's posture, Sam sensed that a tightly coiled discipline lay beneath her surface, a strength one would find in the hard body of a ballerina after years of grueling training.

"These women are remarkable," Emmaline said as she lowered herself into the chair. Her eyes lingered a moment on the door, then swung back to Sam. "Samantha. I don't want to pry but if you need to talk, I will listen. I'm a good listener."

More than pretty good, Sam thought. She had probably helped more people through the classifieds than her husband had through the Good Book.

"Sometime," Sam said quietly, "I'd like to have my palm read."

Emmaline's crooked eyebrow rose. Her lips formed a little 'oh.'

"It's okay, Emmaline. I know about your hobby." At Emmaline's worried look, Sam added quickly, "As far as I know, no one else in town has any idea. If they did, Brunhilda, Agatha, and the bridge club ladies would have been the first to know. I've never mentioned it to my family. There are some things that are private.

"Tell you what. How would you like an exchange? I'll give you a numerology reading in exchange for a palm reading. Would that be fair?"

Emmaline laughed. "Samantha. You are a woman of surprises."

"You're no slouch yourself, Emmaline. And please, call me Sam."

"Sam, it is. And yes, I would love to exchange readings. You name the time and the place, discreetly, of course. My husband's reputation, you know."

Minutes later, a composed Sam found Nick and Sadie cramped in a corner on metal chairs, balancing plates on their knees, and probably on their second round of food, she thought. Normally she felt good when her family ate heartily, but today her mind was otherwise engaged.

"Can you believe it?" Sam whispered in Nick's ear. "Kent Butcher is here. What a nerve. Have you seen him?" She popped her head above the murmuring crowd for a quick scan, then bent down to her husband's ear. "He was in the hall talking with Reverend Loveless. The Reverend didn't look too happy."

"Sam." Nick looked up through narrowed eyes. "Don't even think about it."

"Think about what?"

"You know exactly what I mean."

"Mom?" Sadie said, with her fork suspended between her plate and mouth. She looked stricken. "What are you going to do?"

"Nothing, honey."

"Honest?"

"Yes. Honest."

And she didn't.

Chapter 15

Sunday breakfast at the Bog Café had become a weekly ritual after the girls had moved out. And even though the events of the past week had drained her, a normal routine was what Sam needed desperately. Besides, what better place to latch onto the latest gossip.

The Bog Café was a converted diner with a knotty pine addition. It served surprisingly good food. Dress was sub-casual, which was fine with Sam. She fit right in.

An array of pick-ups and panel trucks lined the front of the Café this morning, Charlie's rusting bronze '89 Ford Fairlane, the town's squad car, amongst them. Charlie had been battling the town for years for a newer model, but 'waste not, want not' was invisibly stamped on the foreheads of the town council. The squad car would disintegrate into a pile of rusty bolts and wires before they would approve that kind of intemperate spending.

Sam had suggested Charlie buy Christine from Stephen King. Repairs would then be unnecessary. Not having read the book of the same name, Charlie hadn't seen the humor in her remark and had let Sam know in so many words that the condition of his squad car was no laughing matter. How would the town fathers feel if they had an emergency and he couldn't get there because the transmission fell out? Which, he was sure, was imminent. Given the current state of affairs in Georgetown, a new squad car might magically materialize.

At eight o'clock Sunday morning, Nick and Samantha took their place in line at the Bog Café. Nick was still in his jogging suit, his face flushed from his morning run.

Julie Walker dashed over and assured them the wait would be about ten minutes. She was dressed in jeans and a short-sleeve, blue-striped tee shirt. A fine sheen of perspiration covered her face. Sam wondered if Julie ever combed the teased nest on her head. Did she ever get mad? And how could someone be so cheerful all the time?

Jimi Duncan stood at the head of the queue. Sam, who could smell the cigarettes on his clothing, acknowledged him with a smile while Nick spoke around the couple in front of them. "Hey, Jimi. Thanks for coming so promptly the other day."

Shuffling his feet, he replied, "No problem, Nick. I appreciate the prompt payment." His self-conscious grin revealed a little gap between his front teeth. Looking at Sam, his eyes faltered a moment, then he quickly turned face front.

Was it Sam's imagination or was everyone looking at her, even if askance? She knew she had made a spectacle of herself yesterday on the church steps with Benjamin King. And now that the heat of the moment had passed, she was embarrassed. But the emotion had had a life of its own and just bubbled up out of her, as if some other force had taken over.

Why did she do things like that?

She fiddled with the zipper on her navy UNH sweatshirt as she thought of Caroline on the school grounds, standing by helplessly while her pretty locket was stomped to pieces by Kent Butcher. That's why. She hated bullies, anyone who preyed on the weak and vulnerable. It was as good an excuse as any.

Sam knew everyone had a story—she'd heard enough of them during client sessions—but that didn't give people the license to push old ladies around. She dreaded picking up the next issue of *Publick Occurrences*. Squaring her shoulders a bit too defiantly, she thought, *So I'm weird. They'll just have to live with it.*

"What are you going to have for breakfast?" she asked Nick, eyeballing the white board. "The apple raspberry pancakes look good."

"Mmm. Maybe." Nick shifted and rolled his head from side to side in a gentle stretching exercise.

Sam's eye caught Charlie hunched over the counter pulling on a cup of coffee at the same time he spied her in the mirror on the wall before him. He nodded imperceptibly, his lips tight. They had to talk soon. She'd listen to him rail at her about making a scene in front of the church, bringing attention to herself when there was a killer loose with her name on his lips. Then she'd offer him a plate of chocolate chip cookies and he'd be happy.

Sam didn't feel she could voice her suspicions to Charlie about Jimi Duncan and Patricia Hammand or tell him about Pat's mysterious letter from Pierce Investigation Services until she had more evidence. It wasn't fair to incriminate innocent people.

Sam bit her lower lip and shifted her attention back to her husband.

Normally Nick didn't like to wait but he loved the Café where he could shoot the bull with the old timers who reminded him of his grandfather. Gramp had been full of old colloquialisms and country humor that he dispensed between puffs on a 7-20-4. After two or three puffs he'd stub out the end of the stogie and tuck it in the bib pocket of his overhauls for later use. One cigar would last him four days.

Sam kidded Nick about how, when talking with Homer Parsons, Seth Biddle, and their ilk, Nick's speech slipped unconsciously into *aint's* and *ayup's*.

A part or her wished she could be more like her husband, and her mother, and be seen by the community as normal. Why couldn't she hobnob with the neighbors, join local clubs and let incidents like yesterday's pass? She was tired of tilting at windmills.

Samantha leaned against her husband's shoulder and stared blankly across the room at the row of plaid backs and ball caps hunched over the counter. On one of the red plastic-covered stools, a young boy, with a cap on backwards, sat next to a man, probably his father. The boy's little white Nikes swung happily as he munched. The man bent and said something in his ear and the boy turned a sugarcoated face up at him and laughed. The shoelace dangling from the little boy's sneaker tugged at Sam's heartstrings.

Next to the white board with the morning's menu, warm greasy smells wafted from the kitchen through an open window cut through the wall behind the counter. Putty, a huge man with thick jowls, and his helper Eddie, a pimply teenager, had a rhythm all their own as one ladled apple raspberry pancake batter and the other slapped bacon onto the steaming grill to sizzle. From a battered radio on top of the plate and mug shelf, the sound of Garth Brooks mingled with the occasional cling of the cash register and a cacophony of old and young voices.

Then, Jimi ambled off. Nick and Sam moved up. One more to go.

Sam arched her neck to see where Jimi went. He had dropped into a high-backed booth next to Patricia Hammand's, with his back to her. Pat stared straight across her table at the man opposite her. Pat's breakfast companion was partially hidden but the feathered haircut and sparkling ring on the clean slender hand that held a coffee mug suggested the 'he' was Michael. This was confirmed, in Sam's mind, by the fact that Julie had been hovering over the Hammand table like a hummingbird.

Sam slipped an arm around Nick's waist.

Pat hadn't moved a muscle after Jimi went by, and Jimi hadn't looked down at her. The fact that, after all these years, they couldn't even acknowledge one another gave rise to the suspicion that they still cared or maybe were secretly involved. Was Georgetown turning into Peyton Place?

The couple in front of Nick and Sam was seated.

Julie noticed a few coffee mugs waving her way and left the Hammand table, hopping from one booth to another, then across the room, weaving between tables, pot in hand.

That's when Sam spied Kent Butcher in a back booth by the restroom door. He was with another man she didn't recognize. She shook her head slowly, imagining the headline with his byline in the next edition of *Publick Occurrences*. Knowing his proclivity for sensationalism, he'd probably sent copies to the *Boston Globe* and *USA Today* as well.

Chris Byrnes crossed the room to take his order. Sam's eyes swung from Kent to Chris, whose gold earrings in the shape of an 's' swung with each step. Chris wore a long-sleeved white shirt and pressed jeans. Always immaculate.

Chris Byrnes leaned against the edge of Kent Butcher's table, and with the pencil in her right hand, wet the nub between scarlet lips.

Kent reached up, pulled her hand into his and kissed it. Sam could then see Kent's mouth moving as he cradled Chris' hand. How she wished she could hear what the 'mild mannered reporter' was saying. Probably hitting on Chris. Would Chris go out with a man like Kent? Sam hated to admit how charming Kent Butcher could be in a slimy sort of way. And he did throw money around to impress his women friends.

Kent kissed Chris' hand once again.

Chris shifted slightly, straightened her shoulders and withdrew her hand. She smiled at Kent, took his order and walked away. Kent watched the back of her jeans undulate with each step.

Sailing behind the counter, Chris speared the order slip on a tall nail on the shelf of the kitchen window and thumped the silver bell.

"Order," she yelled over the din.

Sam blinked. The voice didn't fit the image.

Chris picked up an order then turned and moved away as smoothly as a barge on the Nile, serene and unruffled, her face mysteriously sexy under the black bangs and gold glasses.

Sam watch the row of ballcaps turn in a rolling wave as she glided past the counter juggling three plates stacked on her right arm and a coffee pot in her left hand. Was there a more pronounced swing to those slim hips as she sailed before that row of eyes?

Sam's attention then shifted to Bobby Hammand who had just rumbled out of the rest room, hitching up his jeans. Her nose wrinkled. She knew where that finger had been and she felt like gagging.

As he passed a table of four, Bobby gave a high five to a particularly greasy looking guy with wispy hair, then he mumbled something to Jimi in passing before he lowered himself into the booth next to his sister.

No love lost there, Sam thought. She wondered what they had been talking about at the Hammand house after the funeral. They weren't the same type and didn't travel in the same circles. Maybe Bobby didn't want Jimi near his sister. If Jimi and Pat got together, their union could rob Bobby of his meal ticket. He might even have to move out of the house; maybe he'd lose part of his inheritance. Sam wondered about the will.

She scanned the knotty pine addition lined with booths. A table in the center was about to open. She preferred a booth but would take anything at this point. Her stomach was rumbling in spite of Bobby Hammand's finger.

A young mother with limp hair and a harried look was stuffing her daughter's arm into a pink sweater while admonishing two boys who were batting at each other on the other side of the table. While the boys wrestled toward the door, the mother perused her tab and carefully counted out a number of bills, scowled a moment with her mouth twisted to one side, then added another bill. With her daughter in hand, she avoided a collision with Julie and the coffee pot and hustled past Sam and Nick out the door after her sons.

"Boy, am I glad those days are over," Nick whispered into Sam's ear as they made their way past the counter toward the now cleaned and wiped table.

"Hi Pat, Doug, Michael." Nick stop to make the rounds, friendly, charming but reserved, conscious of their recent loss. Nick was one of those tactful types who did pretty much as he pleased and got away with it. He could fire employees and have them thank him for it.

A sea of eyes washed over Sam. Prickly heat climbed out from her chest. She smiled at the Hammands, slipped an arm around Nick and tugged at the back of his jacket.

By the time they were seated, two tables from the mournful group, Sam was sweating. She pulled a thin napkin from the black metal dispenser in the middle of the table and dabbed at her forehead.

"Is it hot in here?"

"Are you all right, Sam?" Nick looked concerned. "Your face is glistening."

"I'm fine," she snapped. "It's just hot in here."

Nick raised his eyebrows and sat back. He picked up a sticky laminated single sheet that served as a menu.

Suddenly, someone yelled. There was a thump and a crash. Dishes clattered to the floor and smashed. Everyone swung in the direction of the commotion.

Bobby Hammand was on his feet. Eggs, muffins and hot coffee splattered over the rocking table and off the edges. Bobby pulled Jimi from the booth by his Mick Jagger tee shirt. Pat screamed, scrambled out of the booth, and grabbed at her jeans in a futile attempt to pull the steaming denim away from her legs. Michael slipped out of the way just in time to avoid the boiling coffee flow.

"You son of a bitch," Bobby bellowed and pulled a beefy arm back to take a swing at Jimi. With both hands, Jimi grabbed the wrist at his throat, drew his knee back and sent a swift hard jab into Bobby's groin.

Bobby let out a primal scream, sank to his knees and groaned. Then he fell on his side to the floor. He clutched at his genitals and drew his knees to his chest in a fetal curl, whimpering.

By now, Charlie and a few others had come to the rescue. They had Jimi by his arms and were pulling him away from the moaning heap on the floor.

"Take it easy, take it easy," Charlie said in a calm, low voice as Jimi struggled to free himself.

Putty stormed out of the kitchen with a baseball bat in his hands. He'd been robbed only once. "Don't you guys go breaking up my restaurant," he roared, swishing the bat above their heads. Charlie was suddenly by his side, casting Putty a withering glance.

The restaurant was as silent as a first date. Only Garth Brooks yodeled on.

Sam wasn't sure if it was the two hundred and fifty pounds of meat behind Putty's Louisville slugger or Charlie's scowling scarred face that decided the issue. But she would have bet on the latter.

Customers stepped back discreetly.

Michael bent over Bobby, who was still groaning with his hands between his thighs. Patricia had run to the ladies room and hadn't yet emerged.

"What happened?" Sam whispered across the table to Nick.

"I have no idea." Nick strained to look around the dispersing bodies.

While Michael helped Bobby into the booth, Jimi tossed money on his table and left.

A subdued buzz filled the room as patrons filtered back to their tables and generally settled down to breakfast. The good citizens of Georgetown had had a week that would go down in the annals of local history, perhaps even surpassing old William's discovery of the bog.

And Kent Butcher had another a good story. But without pictures, Sam thought smugly. Butcher had raced to his car for his camera but didn't get back in time for any shots.

Sam was beginning to feel like she had wandered into an alternative world, a mirror image of her own. Like the imaginary planet on the other side of the sun that was identical to earth but everything was reversed, as in a looking glass. She'd have to check the wart on Reverend Loveless' nose to be sure it was still on the right side.

"Well, that was something," Nick said softly and leaned both elbows on the table. "But Bobby started it. I saw him jump and pull Jimi from his booth." Nick twisted his neck toward the ladies' room. "Do you suppose Patricia's okay? Maybe you ought to go check on her. She might have got burnt."

"You're right." And besides, Sam was curious. "I'll be right back." Her fingers walked across Nick's shoulder as she left the table.

Inside the two-stall bathroom, Sam could hear the rustle of fabric and Patricia sniffling behind a closed door. There was no one else in the room.

"Pat, it's Samantha Blackwell. Are you all right?"

"I'm fine." A rip, then the crinkle of toilet tissue.

"Did you get burnt?"

"No."

"Do you need a fresh change of clothes?"

"No."

Sam leaned on her hands against the stained white porcelain sink. It felt cold under her palms. She was running out of ideas. "Are you sure?"

"Yes."

Silence.

Sam tilted her head. Pat's boots were at a right angle to the toilet. She was standing.

"Pat. What happened out there?"

Sam waited a full minute then the stall door flew open and banged against the door of the next stall. Patricia's face was tear streaked, her eyes puffy, her cheeks red blotches. The front of her jeans was dark and wet.

"Men! We have to cater to their needs from the cradle to the grave!" She glowered at Sam and raced from the rest room.

Sam turned slowly and looked, unseeing, at her reflection in the spotted mirror. Pat was mad.

Mad enough?

"'Hell hath no fury' like an angry woman," Sam said to no one in particular as she washed her hands and patted her flushed face with cold water.

Nick was wide-eyed as Sam returned to their table. "What happened? I was ready to come in after you. Pat tore out of here like the devil was after her."

Sam sat down and looked into her husband's dark eyes. "Perhaps you're right, my darling," she said distractedly, "perhaps you're right."

Chapter 16

HE was amused.

The military night-vision goggles he had bought illegally cast a greenish tint over the scene played out beneath him. In the dark closet, through a small square he had cut in the floor for this very purpose, he watched, grinning, as his victim lay sprawled on his back on the dirt trying to move. The bastard would never bother him again.

In the basement, the man woke in inky blackness.

A cold terror seized him. Had he died? Was this Hell? Was the church right after all? He tried to swallow, but his tongue wouldn't work. If this were the nether region, where were the flames? The heat? The Man?

He felt a shiver but, because he couldn't move, it worked internally, starting at his jaw line, moving down through his shoulders. Why couldn't he move? He felt the cold bile of panic rising in his chest.

Breathe in deep through the nose, exhale through the mouth.

Breathe in.

Exhale.

When he finally had himself under control, knowing that panic was the last thing to succumb to if he wanted to get out of wherever the hell he was, he decided to use his senses. Not his eyesight in this pitch-black hole, but his sense of smell and touch.

The air around him felt damp and smelled musty. Not at all what he imaged hell to be. He wiggled a finger, slowly.

Dirt.

He was lying in the dirt and his head hurt. He could hear a distant drum beat. He tried to rub his temples, but his arms felt like crowbars.

God, no! I'm paralyzed!

Then it all flooded back into his consciousness. He had been with her. That's where he had been. He remembered they had been drinking white wine, something cheap he had picked up at the supermarket. The floozy wouldn't know the difference. They had been listening to someone named Ottman Lee…something, he thought. Someone she liked. He had planned to get her into bed before the night was over and show her what a real man was like.

But something had happened…and he was laying here in the dark in the dirt. And his head.

Oh!

When the wave of pain ebbed, he listened. No sound. Just the drum.

Maybe this *was* purgatory, that gray area in between the promised land of Heaven and the scorching terror of Hell. Maybe he'd get another chance. That's what purgatory was for, wasn't it? The place for second chances?

A board somewhere above him groaned.

He blinked. *If this is purgatory*, he thought, groping for strength, *it has a second story.*

He had to move. He had to try. First the toes.

Yes!

Feeling was seeping back into his body. He flexed his hands, then shakily wiggled his elbows and thought hysterically about making a dirt angel like he and his brother used to do. Only that was a snow angel. He'd never heard of a dirt angel.

Get a grip!

Slowly, an inch at a time, he lifted his right arm above him. Just space. *Empty space*, he thought almost hysterically. Thank God he wasn't buried in a casket!

Very carefully he rolled over onto his side and pushed up into a sitting position. His head again. He held it gently between his palms and rocked for interminable minutes. Finally, the pain subsided.

Good.

Now. He had to find out where he was. He needed a bearing. Anything. Slowly, he turned his head first to one side then to the other, his eyes searching a blackness the color of the Devil's own heart.

Crazily he thought of his mother's recitation, learned from her French mother, while preparing coffee each morning for his dad:

'Black as the devil,
Hot as hell,
Pure as an angel,
Sweet as love.'

His dad would laugh derisively, saying it was the only recipe she could make. Every morning his father's scornful laugh echoed through their ramshackle house. Every morning, that is, until that morning his laughter died in his devil's cup of poison. His mother had smirked all through her trial while her fresh bruises were healing. Her broken collarbone and wrist had healed years before. His father had taken great care to pound only where soft tissue would cushion the blows. His mother got ten years, then had taken Demon Rum to her bosom and died in an alleyway in Boston during a nor'easter.

Stop it! the man told himself. Dredging up old history wasn't going to help. He couldn't let his mind wander. He had to calm himself, to look for something, a shadow, a point of light. But strain as he might, he saw only blackness and couldn't find even the tiniest glimmer of hope.

There was another smell above the musty odor in the...room, it must be a room he was in. A smell like old potatoes. He knew that smell because he used to fetch potatoes for his mother from the basement where they were stored for the winter.

That's it!

He was in a basement, in some kind of storage area or root cellar. Most likely a root cellar, which would account for the lack of windows.

Rolling his shoulders and stretching a bit from side to side, he began to feel more like his old self.

Cautiously, he moved from a sitting position to all fours, and began feeling ahead on the dirt. If he moved forward slowly, he'd come to some kind of obstruction eventually.

So the man crept, one palm in front of the other, six inches at a time, feeling gingerly before moving forward each time. Then his hand fell on something slender and cold. Shaky fingers ran over the cool bumpy cylinder. A nail. Like a ten-penny with a head. Probably rusty. Old. But it might come in handy. He stuck it in the secret pocket inside his safari jacket.

He thought about yelling for help and was about to when something told him to be quiet, be very quiet. In his condition, he couldn't defend himself. And whoever caused the squeak on the floorboard above him may not be all that friendly.

Maybe he would call for help later when the effects of whatever the bitch had slipped into his drink wore off. It had to have been a Mickey Finn. When he got his hands on her, he'd make sure she never did this to anyone again.

He wished the drum would stop. It's incessant pounding was driving him mad.

Another five palm lengths and his hand hit wood. Shelves. He raised himself slowly, holding onto an upright two-by-four.

God damn it!

A sliver of wood broke the skin on the fleshy side of his right palm. He felt for it. Thankfully it was a big sucker, and he yanked it out.

With his free hand, more carefully now, he felt along the shelves. Glass jars. All different sizes. Covered with something granular and powdery. Probably dust and debris filtering down from above.

He inched along like a blind man, with one hand on the shelf to steady himself, and the other waving from side to side in front of his face. He stopped to feel on the shelves again. More glass jars with lids.

He shook one. Liquid. It was a root cellar. No wonder it was so dark. But there had to be a door.

He didn't know how long it took him to discover that the room he had awakened in was not more that ten-by-ten, by his estimate. On the fourth wall he found the door, and his spirits soared. Patting it down like a cop frisking a drug dealer, he discovered it was one of those new steel doors. No way he could break it down.

He slumped to the floor, his back against the cold steel.

He was tired and thirsty. He couldn't drink from any of the glass jars, God only knew what was in them. He wouldn't put it past the bitch to have stuffed her neighbor into a wood chipper and canned the purée.

He clenched his eyes tight. He had watch *Fargo* too many times.

Think...

Think.

Was it his imagination or was the air getting thinner? He seemed to be breathing harder.

The nail. He could try to pick the lock. They did it all the time on television shows and in the movies.

The minutes ticked by as he poked and prodded and finally stabbed in desperation until the nail broke in his hand. He flung the stub across the lampblack room and sank to the floor as tears welled up in his eyes and began dribbling down his cheeks. Maybe no one would ever find him. He'd be one of those missing persons, case unsolved.

Then it hit him. He slapped his forehead.

What a dummy!

There had to be a light in here somewhere. She'd need a light to find whatever the hell she had stored here.

He began feeling up and down the wood paneling next to the doorframe and sure enough, a toggle switch. He flipped it on.

Light, wonderful light!

He blinked against the harshness and covered his face until his eyes adjusted to the brightness. It was only a single, dim watt bulb hanging from a white porcelain base but it looked like the most glorious sunset he'd ever seen.

Squinting, he examined his hand. Wasn't bad. His eyes swept the room. Shelves, canned good, boxes. Then he looked up at the ceiling. He couldn't reach the ceiling, but even if he could, it appeared to be nailed tight with heavy wooden boards that he couldn't possibly break through, not with the tools at hand.

He scanned the room again. Dirt floor, shelves lining three sides, the fourth, shorter wall containing the steel door. No way out.

But the shelves might yield something that he could use to free himself or at least arm himself. Some kind of weapon.

One wall of shelves held the expected pickled beets, pickles, tomatoes and carrots, relishes of some kind. A thick layer of undisturbed dust covered everything. No telling how long this stuff had been down here. At the end of the shelves, he found a bin of rotting potatoes, white worms oozing over the blackened skins. The symbols of death curdled his blood.

He backed away.

Pinpoints of light flickered before his eyes like dimming firefly batteries and the drum pounded on, boom…boom…boom…rhythmical and persistent. But he pressed on, moving toward the shelves opposite the doorway.

Along with banana boxes, cardboard cartons, and green corrugated cardboard filing-cabinet drawers, there were broken picture frames, some rusted metal shower rings, and a beige telephone base with the cord dangling, no hand piece. *Yeah, like I could ring up someone for help.* A glass punch bowl, odd ceramic plates.

Nothing.

He tried to remember back when he read *The Swiss Family Robinson*. What did they do to survive? But he wasn't on a deserted island with the sun and beach and trees. He was locked in a filthy root cellar with no windows and no way out.

Since he had nothing else to do, he might as well go through the contents of the boxes. Maybe he'd find something. And it would keep his mind occupied while he thought.

The man pulled the first banana box off the shelf. It fell with a soft thud onto the dirt floor. He settled beside it and began pulling out old issues of *Life* magazine, then two packs of greeting cards wrapped in elastic bands, the kind that come in the mail almost daily from omnipresent charities. He even found a year's worth of the *TV Guide*. Why would anyone save the *TV Guide*? Except for George's father on the *Seinfeld* comedy. He snickered softly, grateful for the momentary respite.

HE could take a break.

The bastard had fallen asleep, probably would be out for an hour, and he had to pee. So he closed the trap door and left the closet not knowing it was the biggest mistake he would ever make.

The man jerked. He must have fallen asleep because he was startled to find himself slumped over an open box. He felt weak and heady but fought to calm the panic rising in his chest.

Concentrate.

He reached a shaking hand into the open box and pulled out the next item, a small flowered book. The kind you see in stationery stores. Like a diary. The clasp was broken. He ran his finger over the initials, then began to read.

Slowly at first, then with heart-thumping speed.

My God!

He turned the pages. Faster and faster! Reading a story he could not believe.

So that's who she was.

If only he could get out of this filthy prison with this book. It would change his life. He had the story of a lifetime. He'd be above the fold on the major newspapers across America. He might even win a Pulitzer Prize.

Thank God he had worn his safari jacket. He tucked the small book in the jacket's secret pocket, zipped it, and patted his chest a few times.

He was so tired. So very tired. And he wished the incessant drumming would stop. He had to rest his eyes.

He slipped into a deep sleep, thinking, *Yes. My life is about to change.*

It was the last thought he had.

Minutes later, as the medicinal smelling odor piped into the root cellar, he got his wish. The drumbeat ceased.

Chapter 17

A week had passed uneventfully, if one could call having one's picture plastered over the front page of the *Occurrence* uneventful. Butcher got some good shots in front of the Second Puritan Church, she had to give him that. King shaking his fat finger at a recoiling Agatha, the horrified Reverend Loveless plastered against the church clapboards, Sam poised over King like a hooded cobra over a plump mouse, her arced mouth ready to strike. Sam was surprised Butcher hadn't painted white fangs on her face.

Most certainly out of retribution for her refusal to talk to him, the Kent she knew and loved, the Kent unable to leap over even small buildings in many bounds, had selected the worst shot of her.

She was horrified.

Kent had seen the note posted at McCutty's and had somehow managed to get a copy of the killer's riddle. By the middle of the week, the story screamed from the front page of the national tabloids: NUMEROLOGIST SAVES LINCOLN.

Like it was Abraham, Sam had told her husband over supper Thursday night, close to tears. She was clutching the tabloid she had picked up earlier in the day at the supermarket where too many people were trying not to stare at her. Not as 'salacious' as Clinton's impeachment hearings, but close to it.

There was her face, taken from the back of her book jacket, a copy of the riddle and the solution, and details about her life that even she didn't know. The papers speculated about who murdered the well-loved Doug Hammand. He had become a saint. The story had even been found worthy of second page news in the *Boston Globe* and *USA Today*.

Sam had played the answering machine each evening to screen messages, a long process as the calls piled up. She liked publicity as well as the next person, well, maybe not. She wanted her work to be known, but she valued her privacy. She wasn't about to give interviews to *Hard Copy*, *Star* and the *National Enquirer*.

God. Even Jerry Springer and Geraldo had called.

And hundreds of potential clients requesting a session with Samantha Blackwell. Please call back at your earliest convenience. Collect.

Henceforth, she would be known as the numerologist who solved the death riddle. She canceled her readings, refused to answer requests coming through her phone, and thought about getting an unlisted number. Charlie had threatened the reporters and TV people with bodily harm if they invaded her space. She expected to find a DO NOT CROSS yellow police line around her home before long.

Sam knew the squirrels were running all week. And probably would do so far into the next millennium. Besides being a national public spectacle, she had to contend with her hometown. Next to Doug Hammand's murder, her role in solving the riddle was the biggest news since Old William had discovered the sandy bog. On top of that, she absolutely hated the story in the following issue of *Publick Occurrences*. Above Butcher's byline, a two inch block headline screamed the question that had made her nauseous—IS BEN FUTURE KING OF COWBERRIES?

Cute.

"Only Roy Rogers holds that title, you nincompoop!" she shouted out when she read it, startling Nick who had just dropped the paper on the counter after scooping it up off the front step. Sam would have liked Roy even if he weren't born on her birthday. Same day, not year, she would hasten to add whenever his name came up.

Sam contemplated dumping five hundred copies of *Publick Occurrences* on Butcher's front step so he could wallpaper his entire apartment, if he hadn't already done so.

Where he was anyway? Like she should be worried about him, but she hadn't heard from or seen the not so 'mild mannered reporter from the Daily Planet' in over four days. Something strange was going on. And it made her more nervous than if he had been hounding her.

Sam breathed deeply, attempting to unknot her muscles. It was Sunday morning and she was warm and snug under the quilt next to the man she loved. There had been no sign of the 'cracker,' as Charlie called the killer, since the police posted that note on McCutty's bulletin board. Maybe he was through. Maybe he had moved. Maybe he'd died. She liked the last resolution best.

She wondered about the fight between Jimi Duncan and Bobby Hammand. Until last Sunday, she couldn't have imagined Bobby having the energy or the gumption to kill his father. But after the furious eruption at the Café, she wasn't so sure. He had been livid.

And there was Jimi. What did she really know about him? He'd always been reclusive. His parents had been hippies, both dead now, one from a drug overdose, the other from AIDS, probably from sharing needles. Shuffled from one relative to another—what kind of an upbringing could he possibly have had?

Sam knew enough about palmistry to know that his long knobby fingers indicated the mind of an intellectual. He was organized and efficient, but he had a hard time looking you in the eye. And now he knew the layout of their house. She shook off those thoughts as she tried to imagine the little boy and the horrors he must have seen.

Nick was snoring gently beside her. Her heart swelled with love when she thought how lucky she was to have him. And the people who loved her. Her dead father and her mother who had provided a warm supportive home. And now she had Nick and her two daughters.

She reached behind her and lightly placed her palm on his warm bare back and felt safe. How could anything bad happen with Nick beside her? She curled up on her left side and looked out the east window.

The sheer curtains stirred, the morning sun a red line seeping through the trees. The old adage ran through her mind: "Red sun at night, sailor's delight. Red sun in the morning, sailor's take warning."

She pushed it aside. This was a new day. In fact, it was April 1st, April Fool's Day. What's in a name? Just the sound of the word 'April' renewed her spirits.

After three days of 'gathering' as she called it, this was her day to get started on the weekly column. Recent events had interrupted her writing schedule and she desperately needed to get back to it. Routine. Order. Control.

She vowed that today she would turn over the well-worn new leaf. She would get up, go to the bathroom, get dressed, comb and pull back her hair, get an apple from the refrigerator, and plant herself in front of the computer. Sometime during the day, she would take a walk. This would be her routine from now on.

An hour later she sat at her computer in her nightshirt. The idea had come to her on the john. This week's column. On names.

Column 5-5, April 8
I've Got Your Number
By Sam Blackwell

"What's in a name? That which we call a rose
By any other name would smell as sweet."
But there's the rub, you see. How could we have named the rose any differently? Language reflects the consciousness of a people. The words we choose to identify our perceptions reflect our innate understanding of those perceptions.
I'm reluctant to take umbrage with Shakespeare, but as a numerologist, I have learned that changing the name of any *thing* alters that thing in our consciousness.

Think back to your childhood and the names your mother called you. Just the good ones, okay? Mom, in a flowered apron, opens the screen door. The loving call. "Sandy. Come on, honey. Supper's ready." Five minutes later, the slightly frustrated call. "Sandra. Are you coming?"
Two minutes pass and bring with it: "Sandra Coby! Get in here!" Finally, the 'you've had it, you're grounded, go to jail' declaration. "Sandra Louise Coby!"
Yes, you're the same person but the conscious relationship between you and your mother changes according to how she addresses you. Because of her selection, you know the state of her conscious mind and that knowledge modifies your consciousness and perhaps your behavior.
You are your name...

Sam glanced out the window at the thermometer. Forty-one degrees. She shivered at the chill on the sun porch, her fingers felt cold on the keyboard, but the baseboard, crackling with incoming heat, reassured her. Soon the green fleece blanket over her knees would be tossed back on the couch, Nick would be up bringing her a steaming mug of watered-down Nestle's Rich Chocolate—diluting made her feel less guilty—peaked with Hood's Instant Whipped Cream from the can—but it was just as good. After Nick had showered and shaved, they'd go to the Bog for breakfast. Then Nick would be off to the mountains for his nature injection and she had the whole day to work on her column. She just knew her life was back on track.

Samantha blew on a fist and stared at the monitor while listening to the halting, languid voice of Robert J. Lertzemer. His voice issued from the radio on the small bookcase behind her. Her peripheral vision picked up sparrows and a flash of red. She turned quickly to see a red cardinal perched on a wavering branch of the small maple, its soft red breast puffed up with unconscious pride. Mesmerized by the bird and the music, Sam's mind wandered through philosophical minefields.

What does it know?

How does it know?

Is it aware of itself as separate from the group mind?

Does it fear?

At the word fear, she'd had enough. She tossed the blanket onto the couch as a flush spread over her body. Fresh air would do her good. Maybe she'd lose a few pounds in the process.

Because of the media attention, Sam hadn't been out of the house for days. Nick had told her that things might be dying down since he hadn't noticed any strange cars around the common when he'd arrived home last night other than touristy-looking couples and families, and no dark figures lurking behind Old William's statue. The last comment was meant to elicit a smile. Perhaps interest in her really was waning. Dared she hope?

It was 6:15 and Nick was still snoring. Sam slipped into her gray sweats, wrote Nick a quick note, and stuck it in the mouth of the brown plastic frog on the back hall counter. Breakfast at the Bog would taste even better after a brisk walk.

She pulled on a pair of old black Reeboks whose Velcro had seen better days, and tucked a pencil and notepad in the pocket of her hooded sweatshirt, along with the key to the breezeway door. After resetting the alarm, she slipped out into the cool morning air.

The sun was a red half disk rising behind the trees and casting long shadows in front of her and across the green. The birds had risen with it, chirping noisily. *How they must love spring,* Sam thought, stopping for a moment to take it in. But for nature's songs, there was a stillness, a time for centering.

She flinched as a lone car zoomed by, but, thankfully, there were no reporters in sight. Maybe they didn't like early Sunday mornings.

According to last night's weather report, the temperature would climb into the sixties today. You wouldn't know it by the thermometer on the garage wall facing west across the common. It read thirty-nine. Like a true New Englander, Sam not only liked to talk about the weather, but she kept track of it diligently, listening to the morning and nightly forecasts.

Stretching her arms over her head felt good. She arched her back like Nick told her to before bending toward her toes. Three quarters of the way down her hamstrings screamed uncle.

Enough of that.

Ignoring the strangely uneasy feeling stirring in her gut, she squared her shoulders and proclaimed, "Yes, it's going to be a good day. I might even try a little jogging."

Perennially optimistic, she sprang down the driveway and turned left onto Black Skillet Lane, avoiding a look at McCutty's Market. Instead, she waved at old William posturing in the center of the green.

Her mother's house was still dark as Sam bounded by, but Elizabeth would be up any minute to prepare the morning feast with help from Caroline. Then Sadie would arrive to clean.

Soon winded, Sam eased into a fast walk, swinging her arms like a Russian soldier. It felt good. She'd have to do this every day.

Tumble Brook Road had grown, almost overnight, into a row of expensive turreted three-story homes. Through the thick stands of birch and spruce, each house sported a different twist, but they all had that cookie cutter look, even if the cookie cutter was stainless steel.

A mile later, Sam wheeled onto the final loop of that road, imaginatively called the Loop. It used to be the main road to town but was bypassed by Tumble Brook Road. The impenetrable woods on either side of the Loop would have muted sounds from the main road, if there had been any sound this morning, but most people in the 'new section,' as the townspeople called it, liked to sleep in.

With the combination of the sun gathering strength and the effort of the walk, a sheen of sweat broke out over her face. She slid off her hood and wiped a sleeve across her forehead. Comfortably warm and proud of herself, she vowed to do this every day.

The early morning silence—broken only by the sound of her sneakers padding over the hot top as she moved in and out of shadows cast by tall pine, hemlock, and a few gray birches standing in fields long abandoned—became a spiritual litany. The mossy-covered crumbling stone walls that wove through the thick woods stood as altars to those intrepid farmers who cleared their fields in order to plant crops in communion with nature and used the stones as boundary markers. Their time worn commandment—waste not, want not—was the inexorable law of Nature.

New Hampshire is rightly called the granite state, Sam thought as she swung her arms, and stretched her legs into long strides. Its people were hardheaded, stubborn, determined, and fiercely independent, much like the stones the farmers struggled to pull from their fields. When Sam was little, she believed that the omnipresent stones grew out of the earth like tomatoes. She had grown to love the old stone walls and was glad there were laws to prevent their looting.

Inhaling the smell of sunshine and chuckling to herself, she recalled Garrison Keillor saying that New Hampshire had a reputation for being cranky.

Right on!

And she loved it. Why would anyone want to live anywhere else?

Her thoughts drifted back to the walls as she strode over the hot top. The Chinese also honored stones. They saw the life force as the dragon, and the stones as the bones of the dragon. Sam could imagine the meandering walls as the spine of that sleeping life force.

An occasional rustle in the dead leaves gave notice of furry little critters scrambling for their life-giving breakfast. Birds rustled through the treetops, singing. It was Nature's world, except for the crushed beer cans, candy wrappers, and other kinds of used wrappers littering the roadside.

Sam smiled and stepped up her pace. Even though an ancient foray into Weight Watcher's had taught her that it wasn't the method but the distance you covered that mattered, she felt the need for an aerobic push.

Up ahead and around the corner, through a break in the trees, she caught a glint of red.

Looks like a car, she thought. She hoped it wasn't teenagers who had fallen asleep after a Saturday night binge. It had been known to happen on this road given the evidence.

She broke into a jog and rounded the bend.

What she saw stopped her dead in her tracks. She bent, panting, and put her hands on her knees. She was unable to take her eyes off the car. A red Miata. Kent Butcher's red Miata.

And he was sitting in the front seat!

Furious at him for laying in wait for her, she stormed over to the driver's side and was about to pound on the window when she saw his face.

Dead white!

At his throat lay a cowberry necklace.

And between the folds of his open jacket, she could see a single incision starting at his neck and disappearing down behind the folds of the safari jacket toward his waist.

Sam froze.

All her nerve endings went on alert but she couldn't move. Her stomach fell three stories. She was going to be sick.

Deep breathing.

Her chest heaved.

Keep breathing, she told herself, *keep breathing.*

She did, as the words rolled around in her head: Kent Butcher is dead. Kent Butcher was murdered just like Doug Hammand.

She tried to swallow but her throat was dry. Her top lip stuck on her teeth. She pushed it up with her tongue and took another long deep breath, and let it out slowly.

She had to do something.

What?

Check for danger, she told herself.

Sam looked around quickly. No human sounds, no human movement. She was sure she was alone.

Her first impulse was to run, but she forced herself to look back at the Miata. The door locks were up, so someone could have easily gotten into the car with him. There was no sign of a struggle, except that his jacket was unzipped and rumpled around his motionless chest.

She bent a little closer and peered into the front seat, terrified of what might be there.

And it was!

Pinned to Kent's safari jacket. Another coded message.

At the bottom it read: SAM THIS ONE IS FOR YOU.

HE waved a hand, then gave up.

Clouds of mosquitoes had ganged up on him as he watched and waited from deep within the woods while the rising sun filtered through the heavy forest and pointed slanted yellow fingers into tiny pools of gold on the woody floor.

Let them bite.

He forced himself to remain motionless. No sound would give him away. He could be very patient.

He watched through a telescopic lens, brushing away the whining insects obstructing his line of vision. A rivulet of sweat trickled down his back between his shoulder blades. His feet felt damp in his combat boots. Camouflage was a hot but necessary evil.

She had outwitted him the first time. He remembered how the fury of her victory sent him into a black fugue. When he had come out of it, he found he had taken a black magic marker and drawn a skull and crossbones around her face on the book jacket, drawn X's around the four corners, and with his Exacto knife, had stabbed the cover repeatedly.

Suddenly he was back at the kitchen table where he watched the shredded pieces in the ashtray curl into purple-yellow smoke. He didn't remembered lighting them either, but he found a box of wooden matches by his hand.

The whining of a mosquito around his head...Did he leave the back door open...?

He was sorry he burned her picture. He'd have to buy another book so he could look at her each night and kiss her picture before he tucked the book away in his portable desk and slid it under his bed.

The whining was louder...incessant...interrupting his thoughts...

He blinked. And blinked again. He wasn't in his kitchen anymore.

As his head cleared, he realized he was in the woods off the Loop, enshrouded by thick pines, birches and brambles, watching Samantha round the bend and approach the Miata. Through the telescopic lens he observed the expression on her face when she bent slightly to peer into the car and the shock when she saw the body...and the note. He watched her hesitate, then race off toward Tumble Brook Road.

And he smiled.

He had everything under control. Even Caroline, Sam's oldest daughter. Though Caroline didn't know it yet. Beautiful as Sam's daughters were, he wasn't interested in either of them. He wanted Samantha.

The sun on the leafy canopy overhead was heating the woods into a sauna. And the police would be arriving soon.

He had to get out of there.

Chapter 18

The next thing Sam knew, she was on the ground and Nick was hovering over her. She reached up slowly and touched the back of her neck. Charlie's jacket was under her head.

"Sam, Sam! Honey. Are you all right?"

"What happened?" She rubbed a shaky hand over her face and tried to orient herself. And then it came flooding back.

After she found Butcher, she had raced to the end of the Loop and down the first driveway she found, pounded on the door of the palatial home and yelled, "Call the police. There's been a murder."

A voice from inside had yelled back, "I'm calling the police," as if *she* were the criminal. No one let her in. Sam had seen the heavy drapes at a front Palladium window rustle.

She remembered stumbling back to the end of the privet-lined drive to perch on a boulder. Shivering, arms hugging her chest, cut off from the multistoried home by thick woods, she had waited. What seemed an hour was only eight minutes. Charlie's bronze cruiser came barreling around the corner on two wheels.

She had tried to speak, but all she could do was wave a shaky finger toward the Loop. Charlie had scooped her trembling body into the car and left ten feet of rubber.

"You got out of the cruiser," Charlie said, as he and Nick helped her to her feet, "followed me to the Miata, took one look at Butcher and keeled over."

Nick grabbed Sam as she started to sway. "Take it easy, babe."

"Kent. Kent Butcher. In his car." She pointed at the Miata, six feet from where she had fallen.

"We know, Sam. Never mind that," Charlie said. "Everything's under control. Are you sure you're all right?" He scrutinized her as if she were a bug under a microscope, while his rubbery face twisted into a Walter Matthau look alike. "Were you attacked?"

"No. I guess I fainted." Red crept up her cheeks as she stared at the car, numbly brushing at the back of her sweats. Pine needles and gravel fell to the hot top.

"Thank God," Nick said. "When you didn't come back, I got worried, especially with the reporters hounding you all week and a madman on the loose. I was about to come looking for you when Charlie called. The thoughts I had…" His voice trailed off as he peered into Sam's face. "Are you sure no one attacked you, hit you on the head?" He ran a hand over Sam's hair.

"No, Nick. I fainted, that's all." She was disgusted with herself. She tried to will away the flush of embarrassment as she said, "Did you see the note?"

"What note?" Nick's face suddenly blanched. "Don't tell me there's another note."

"Yes." She shuddered as she watched Charlie circling the Miata, stopping to bend down and examine the ground.

"What did it say?"

"I don't know. All I can remember is the last line." Her face twisted as she looked up into Nick's face, at the furrow deepening between his eyes. Tears started to well. "It said, 'Sam this one is for you.'"

"Christ, Sam." He swept her into his arms, where she began to sob uncontrollably.

"Kent's dead because of me. And all those horrible things I said about him…" She buried her face deeper into her husband's gray wool sweater. "How can I ever forgive myself?"

Nick pulled her closer and stroked her hair. He kept murmuring, "It's okay, Sam. It's okay"

"All week I was cursing him," she blubbered, "and he was dead, murdered by that, that…"

"Your cursing didn't kill him, Sam," Nick said softly but sternly. "Remember that. This nutcase has his own agenda."

Minutes later, an ambulance careened around the corner and screeched to a halt, spraying gravel and leaves in its wake. Charlie directed the two medics toward Sam who had just barely managed to pull herself together.

"Charlie! You didn't call the ambulance on my account," she said, flushing once again. "I'm not hurt, I just fainted."

"Nothin' to be embarrassed about," he said quietly, taking her arm. "I know big burly guys who faint when they have their blood taken. And that ain't nothin' like what you've been through." He gave her a lopsided grin, then turned toward the medics.

"Seems she's okay, fellas. Just fainted after finding this dead body. Can't blame her none. Appreciate your looking her over for me though."

"I'm fine, Charlie. Please!"

"Sam!" he snarled, and turned to glare into her startled face. "You let them look you over, you hear."

He stormed over to the squad car, pulled the phone from the dash, bellowed into the speaker. "Lenny, call Grant. And make it quick. We've got ourselves another one."

While the photographs were taken, the note bagged and tagged, and the crime scene marked with yellow police tape, Sam was given a clean bill of health by the two medics. She then gave the police a detailed account of what had happened.

Nick stood by waiting, scowling, hands shoved deep into his pockets. When the authorities were through with his wife, he bundled her into the car and headed home.

Charlie said he'd be over later.

Sam cringed. She knew why.

What was happening?

Was she Lao Tze's man dreaming he was a butterfly, or the butterfly dreaming it was the man? Was this madness real or would she awake in bed beside her husband, throw her arms around his warm body, and tell him about the horrible dreams she just had? Murder was unfathomable enough to comprehend, but, because in some twisted way she felt partially responsible for the deaths, the heinous act was even more crushing.

Sam spent much of Sunday in bed in a fog. Nick, her mother and the girls had crept in and out of her room "on little cat feet," as if she were a victim on the critical list in ICU. Selket snuggled against her side until Sam's restlessness drove the feline to perch on the night table to stand guard over her mistress with emerald eyes.

At intervals, Sam lay on her back staring at the blank white ceiling.

Tabula rasa. She wished she could erase the painful memories from her brain and become as blank and empty as the rectangle above her.

Then images crept onto her ceiling screen. A glistening flounder, raising Doug Hammand's lifeless body by one ankle for a fisherman's photograph. *Look at the one that didn't get away.*

The flounder fin transmogrified into a long taloned finger, jabbing in her direction. Uncle Sam wants you! Only it was the killer who wanted her. And he was loose in her town, a maniac with a sick fixation.

She rolled and thrashed until the blankets twisted around her like strings 'round a hapless marionette. Behind the pillows in which she buried her head, disembodied hands jerked at heavy hemp ropes attached to the arms and legs of a limp puppet in a blood-red safari jacket.

Finally, exhausted and hollow, she saw the fear, and it bore her face. The mystique of power fell from the killer's persona. He was just a man. A demented one, but fallible. She would gather her wits and get inside his head. Become him. Think like he did. In the knowing lay victory.

Her ankle twinged. A storm was coming.

Sam would not be afraid any more.

Chapter 19

It was Monday morning and rain beat at the sun porch windows. Nick refused to go to work and was reading the newspaper in the living room. Still in her nightshirt, Sam couldn't face the weeks ahead with clients, so she gave in and cleared her calendar for the next month, then flopped on the couch. Like Scarlett, she would think about her column tomorrow. Right now, she had to analyze the past few weeks and put the events in some kind of order. Mental housecleaning.

Rain drummed the roof, attacking the glass panes obliquely. The woods, like Longfellow's forest primeval, lashed each other in some ancient mystical battle. As the storm outside her windows churned, Samantha lay poised in an eye of calm. Life imitates art.

Finally, she went to her desk and picked up the copy of the original note that Charlie had left with her.

3 by 9
FATHER SON HOLY GHOST
BUT WHERES MOTHER?

9 5 7 8 3 4 4 1 2 5 3 5 2 7 1 5

SAVE VICTIMS 5 AND 6
POST ANSWER MCCUTTYS BY APRIL 15

Just like the first note, the letters had been cut out of a magazine and glued onto a sheet of plain white paper. The numbers, dots, and hash marks, however, had been made with a pen. Sam wondered if the ink could be traced. Chances were it came from a generic ballpoint.

Her eyes moved over the copy of the magazine cutouts.

Father, Son, and Holy Ghost is the trinity; three times nine equals twenty-seven. So we have 3, 9, 27 and the trinity. But no mother.

Sam had often asked the same question: Where's Mother in the trinity? Did *he* have the same problem? How bizarre if he, or she, were a woman's libber. He had killed two men that Sam knew about. A shudder rumbled through her. She shook it off. What would the question about mother say about him? He had a strong mother? An abused or abusive mother? An absent mother?

She pulled a piece of scrap paper from a blue stationery box where she kept discarded drafts of her columns, and with a Saga ballpoint, began doodling on the back, drawing number 3s and little triangles. Then, on the points of one large upright triangle, she skewered the male trinity members.

Idly, she sketched a downward pointing triangle, the ancient symbol for Yoni, the Great Mother, and scrawled the names Maiden, Mother, Crone around the perimeter. She outlined it with a heart.

Her handwriting was going to hell in a handbasket. No wonder. Her arms felt leaden.

She was staring at the primitive art when Nick poked his head around the corner. "Would you like a cup of hot chocolate, honey?"

Sam looked up at him and smiled. "That sounds good."

Encouraged, he walked up behind her and began kneading her shoulders. Tingles ran up her neck and across her shoulders as she said, "Oh, that feels good."

"Any progress?"

"Not really. I was on the couch for a while, just thinking."

"For an hour and a half."

"You're kidding! I didn't realize I had been there that long. Oh." He hit a sore spot.

"You want me to stop?"

"No. I need it bad."

"I can think of another way to relax you."

She smiled and shrugged her shoulder to press her cheek against his hand. "I'll just bet you can."

He swung her chair around, knelt in front of her, encircled her waist with his arms and, with a soft moan, buried his head in her lap. "I love you."

"And I, you." She burrowed her fingers in his thick hair.

They remained in that position, and listened to each other breathing.

Finally, Nick stood, eyes damp. "Enough of that mush. Hot chocolate coming up. Diluted with a dollop of cream."

She laughed. "That's why I keep coming to this restaurant. You always remember."

As she watched him leave the room, she wiped at her eyes. *It's getting so bad, we cry over birthday cards.*

Sam sat for a moment with her hand looped over the neck of her nightshirt. She looked out at the puddles forming in the back yard. The snow was gone, most likely until next winter. She was glad. She longed to plant morning glories by the pool fence, feel the heat of the sun on her body, and watch green shoots break through the awakening earth. The resurrection of life. That's what Easter was about.

Nick returned with her favorite mug, one she had bought from the potter at the Common Ground Fair at the same time Nick had picked up his moose mug, and set in on the trestle table. The ceramic design looked like cream cheese brownies.

"So, talk to me." Nick lay back in the rocker, fingers curled around his moose mug, his long legs, crossed at the ankles, stretched out before him.

Sam sat Lotus style on the couch and reached for her cup. "Well, there's Doug Hammand wearing his one good suit. When did you ever see him in that except for the Cowberry Festival Parade? And he wore that daffodil in his lapel."

"You think a woman killed Doug? And Butcher?"

"Maybe. But would a woman be strong enough? Strangulation isn't usually a woman's method of elimination. And the knife wounds…"

"It isn't necessarily physical strength that makes the difference," Nick said. "Remember that movie, was it *Game of Death*, where Bruce Lee decimated Kareem Abdul Jabar in a martial arts bout? Kareem had to be a foot and a half taller than Lee. Even though it was a movie scene, I'm sure, in real life, Lee would have been the victor."

Sam had to agree. Even Charlie acknowledged that, under stress, people possessed amazing strength.

On the other hand. "Of course, if a woman rendered her paramour helpless, like with a drug, she'd have no problem strangling him."

Nick shook his head. "I can't see Doug agreeing to meet a lover at the frozen fish section in McCutty's Market in the dark after the market had closed."

"Maybe they met out back and Doug was dragged in."

"But someone had to have a key. Mike keeps that place locked tighter than a drum ever since someone started pilfering the meat counter a few years ago."

Sam put her cup down and scratched her right cheek. Her eyes drifted toward the weeping sky. Slowly, she unfolded her legs and rubbed at her knees. "Butcher wouldn't have been a problem in that sense. Maybe he had a romantic tryst on the Loop. It seems to be the place of choice given all the Trojan wrappers littering the side of the road. How hard would it have been for some sweet thing to slip him a Mickey?"

Nick nodded wordlessly, then finished off his coffee. After a moment, he said, "I hate to think it, but it does seem like the killer is someone here in town." Sam knew he was worried. Someone they knew was a killer.

She hesitated.

"What?" Nick asked.

"I don't know. It's just that I'm beginning to suspect everyone. Jimi Duncan, for instance. Sometimes I think he knows too much about everyone's business. He's never been married, never talks about his past. And he seemed mighty nervous the day he was here to install our alarm system. When I brought up Doug's death, seemed like he changed the subject too quickly. Acted nervous." She tapped her fingers against her front teeth.

That's when the doorbell rang.

Nick leaped up. "Stay here, Sam."

What now? she thought.

She could hear Nick's muffled voice welcoming someone into the living room.

It was the front door. Not a regular visitor.

"Sam," Nick whispered through the kitchen window. "It's Emmaline Loveless. What shall I tell her?"

Samantha jumped up. "Show her to the sun porch. I'll be back in a flash."

Minutes later, in clean sweats, hair freshly combed and pulled back, and a dab of blush and poppy lipstick, Sam greeted the surprise visitor.

Standing behind Emmaline and holding her dripping black raincoat, Nick's eyebrows tented, then he made a discreet withdrawal.

"Samantha." Soft furrows formed on her brow. "I hope I'm not intruding. I don't usually barge in this like without calling first."

"Don't be silly, Emmaline." Sam motioned her to the stuffed rocker and dropped onto the couch. "This is a pleasant surprise. What brings you out on such a wet day?"

"I was running errands." Drops glistened on her cheeks and chestnut hair. She tucked a loose strand behind a shell-like ear.

"Can I get you a drink? Hot chocolate?"

"That would be nice, thanks."

"Honey?" Sam called.

A voice from the hall. "Coming right up."

Stifling a snicker, Sam glanced at Emmaline, whose mouth was compressed but laugh lines crinkled at the corner of her eyes.

"So much for privacy. Maybe I should send *him* on an errand."

There was a pause, then Emmaline said, "He's worried about you."

"I know. He's not the type to eavesdrop."

They waited until Nick brought their cups. He cleared his throat twice, then excused himself. He was going to the office for a few hours and told Sam that she should call him when Emmaline left. His voice was pleasant but Sam knew he meant she'd better do it.

Emmaline leaned back, graceful fingers lightly wrapped around the glazed mug, and smiled down at it. "Whipped cream, too."

"He does it right." Sam folded her ankles on the trestle table and sipped gingerly at the steaming liquid. She came up with a white mustache, like the 'Got Milk' ad.

A corner of Emmaline's mouth tilted.

Sam chuckled and grabbed a napkin. "I'll never grow up."

Emmaline placed her cup on the table beside her, grasped the arms of the rocker and looked around. "This is a wonderful room."

"Thank you. I love it out here." With the crumpled napkin against her lips, Sam fixed a look on her visitor. Then she said, "What's bothering you, Emmaline? I'd like to think this is a social call, but I have a feeling there's another reason you're here."

"Yes, well..." Emmaline recrossed her legs, tugged her skirt over her knees, and realigned the satin band on her taupe sweater set. A small gold butterfly pin set with colored stones was pinned to her left shoulder. "This must have been a hard week for you with all the publicity, your photograph in the paper, and that story..." She frowned, her anger barely suppressed. "I'm surprised they didn't make mention of the style of your underwear."

Sam's eyes snapped wide. Emmaline's hand flew to her mouth. They stared at each other for a moment, then burst into laughter. Sam barely got her mug on the table before she doubled over. Tears streamed down their faces.

This explosion of laughter was like the time Sam had read Nick a passage from a Dr. Seuss book about the southwest-facing crane. They couldn't stop laughing, and every time they looked at each other, they went into peals that left their stomachs knotted.

Sam dashed to her bedside table and returned with a box of tissues. After wiping and blowing their noses, they settled back with sighs.

"I needed that," Sam said.

Emmaline nodded. "So did I."

"It would seem, Mrs. Emmaline Loveless, there's more to you than meets the eye. Not that what meets the eye isn't more than enough," she added hastily. Sam had had a serious case of hoof and mouth disease since she first learned to talk. Like Sagittarius with the arrow, her statements often bullseyed, leaving the victim mortally wounded, and Sam at a loss to explain the reaction. She cocked an eyebrow at Emmaline. "You've got a bit of the devil in you."

"You've found me out. I beg you, don't tell the preacher."

Sam threw her hands up. "Please, don't start. My stomach muscles can't take it. Now," she countered devilishly, "unless you're here to convert me to the ways of the Lord, which I can tell you right now isn't going to be easy since I'm more inclined toward the Lady, what's really on your mind?"

"I think I may have information about the death of Mr. Butcher and perhaps, by extension, Mr. Hammand."

"What!" Sam gulped, then grimaced at her response but it had slipped out before she had time to think about it. "I'm sorry. What do you mean, you have information?"

"It's about Kent Butcher really. And I didn't know who to talk to. Then I thought of you. We had such a warm rapport in Patricia's kitchen, at least *I* felt it."

Sam nodded.

"And we're sort of in the same type of profession, even though mine is hidden from the eyes of the public."

Sam was getting impatient.

"Emmaline, please. Tell me."

"You promise it won't go any further?"

"Well, yes, if that's what you want. But you realize if what you know can help with the investigation of these crimes, then you should tell the police."

"But there's my husband to consider. He had a hard enough time accepting my palmistry. I don't know what to do." Her eyes welled. She grabbed another tissue from the box on the trestle table.

"Emmaline. Look at me. Take a deep breath and start at the beginning."

Emmaline's gray eyes drifted toward Sam. She hesitated, as if pondering her next move. "I know you can be trusted." She shifted in her chair, then sighed. "Kent Butcher was doing an exposé on small towns. He found out things about my husband." Her voice cracked. She cleared her throat. "Things about his past that would destroy his career, everything he's worked so hard to build.

"My husband is a good, decent man. I know he comes across rather strange, he isn't the handsomest of men," Sam thought of that hawk nose and jerky marionette body, "and I know those people who judge a person by their looks wonder why I married him. But they don't know the sweet, tender, almost childlike side of this man. He doesn't deserve this kind of treatment."

"Everyone has a few bones, if not a skeleton, in their closet, Emmaline," Sam said, wondering if she should, right then and there, get out her numerology charts and give the distraught woman a reading.

Instead, she asked, "Do you mind telling me your birthday, just the month and day, not the year?" The addendum was automatic. From experience, she knew most women were reluctant to reveal their age.

How many times had she told female clients that women have been programmed to believe their only value was their youth, ergo their attractiveness to the male of the species. There were 'plain Janes' but no 'plain Johns.' Unless you were describing a white toilet. That usually got a snicker but this didn't seem the appropriate moment for a joke.

"No, I don't mind," Emmaline said with a little smile. "My birthday is July 6th."

Sam did a few quick calculations in her head. "You see, Emmaline, like the seasons of the year, our life cycles repeat every nine years. Not the same events, of course, but the same types of experiences. So, tell me what was happening to you about nine years ago."

"Well," Emmaline's lips pursed. Small furrows appeared on her smooth forehead. "Let's see. That was…oh yes! That's when I met Hannibal." She beamed. Her face took on the glow of one who is in love rather than one who loves. "I couldn't believe I had found such a man. And it happened so quickly. If it hadn't been for him…" Her voice trailed away.

"Did the events of that year change your life?"

Emmaline tilted her head. "Yes. They certainly did." She paused, thinking, then swallowed hard. "Oh, my goodness! I don't believe it."

Sam had heard that expression thousands of time. She waited.

"Nine years ago," Emmaline said, "my manuscript had been accepted by Bridgeton Publishing."

Sam was impressed. "You're kidding. I didn't know you wrote a book. What kind?"

"It was a novel about intrigue in an Ivy League school. It did pretty well but it's out of print now."

Sam said, "I'll contact a bookstore I know in Vermont that does book searches. They can get out-of-print editions."

"Thank you for that. Anyway, what I was going to say is that my manuscript had been accepted and I was thrilled. That's when it happened."

"It?"

"Edward Bridgeton, the grandson of the publisher, had the final say. He propositioned me in his office. Either I have a one-time fling with him or the book wouldn't get published. I couldn't believe what I was hearing. I was desperate. There was my mother, bills. So much depended on that advance.

"I had spent two weeks every summer at a bed and breakfast at the seacoast down Maine. That's where I met Hannibal." She smiled.

Then her shoulders rose and fell slowly. "Edward was honeymooning at the same inn. He met me on the back deck early one morning and demanded I meet him in a secluded cove and he'd bring a book contract.

"I can't believe I even considered his proposal. Of course, I refused. And then…then he was murdered."

"Oh, my God!" Sam would never hear that word again without sweeps of fear.

"With Edward gone," Emmaline continued, "the editors who loved my book went ahead with the publishing."

"So," Sam urged, "you see some similarity between the events of that year and now?"

"Yes. You see, recently I was propositioned again." Her head fell to her chest. Sam watched her twist her fingers. "Why does this happen to me? I don't think I do anything to encourage male intimacy. I love my husband and I'm not interested in anyone else."

"You're a beautiful woman, Emmaline. Men would be naturally drawn to you. Now, if I may ask, who propositioned you?"

Emmaline hesitated only a second. "Kent Butcher."

The words slammed against Sam's ears. "Oh, Emmaline."

"Yes. I know. And now he's dead. Murdered. And I'm so afraid. First, for my husband. And then for me. Will the police think I did it?"

"Why would they?"

"I was involved in the investigation of Edward Bridgeton's death. The police found the killer but still…. Kent Butcher was going to reveal some sordid information about my husband's past, things that happened when he was young, things that could ruin him. He said if I…if I…"

"Yes, I know the rest."

"I've thought about this for days. Any number of people might have had reason to kill Mr. Butcher because of those exposés he was writing. I don't know how Mr. Hammand was involved."

"Unless," Sam interjected, "Butcher killed Doug for some reason we don't know, then someone killed Butcher."

"But why?" Emmaline rubbed her left cheek. Her fine features had collapsed, leaving her face gaunt and haunted.

Sam thought about Agatha and the anonymous phone call. Could that have been Butcher? And who was pasting her name at the bottom of the death notes?

"That's the problem, Emmaline. I don't know why. I don't know anything at this point."

Chapter 20

After Emmaline left, Sam first called Nick as she had promised, then rang up the girls. It was a last minute decision, but she could always count on them for lunch. She needed to get out of the house, and even with the rain, the fresh air had a way of clearing her head.

Lunch with Sadie and Caroline was always a happy break in her day. She vowed to keep her hoof on the floor.

They were to meet at the Gang Plank in Hampton for pizza, which somehow always seemed a treat. Sam was hoping Sadie's trip to the mall that morning with her friend, Medra, had produced nothing more than yearnings. Her youngest daughter got aroused just looking at credit cards.

Sam shook rain from her coat and met the girls in front of the bakery in the foyer of the restaurant. The Drool Room. Over the years, thousands of delighted eyes had canvassed the glassed cases wherein resided thick creamy eclairs, Kahlua brownies, Napoleons, chocolate mousse cups, carrot and chocolate raspberry cakes, and Parisienne loaf breads, muffins, and cinnamon nut twists. More than one belly bulge was attributed to its wares.

The women asked for a booth in non-smoking, where, once seated, Sam set about aligning her silverware and napkin. Under the amused eyes of her children, she reached across the dark pine table and aligned theirs as well.

"How are you doing, with the notes and all?" Sadie asked. She had wrapped an arm around her mother's waist as they walked through the dining room.

"Fine." She wasn't, but Sam didn't want to talk about it. And when Sam pulled her lips tight, her daughters knew that further conversation on the subject was an exercise in futility.

A young waitress wearing a navy blue skirt and spotless white blouse in keeping with the nautical theme of the restaurant sailed over to take their order.

"What are you going to have, mom?" Sadie asked.

As Sam looked up—and under the curious sidelong glance of the buxom waitress—Caroline and Sadie unobtrusively slid their napkins to the center of the table and misaligned their silver.

"Mmmm…I think I'll have a vegetarian pizza and a Coke," Sam said.

"Big surprise," Sadie laughed. "Want to split a pepperoni pizza, Carrie?"

"Please don't call me that," Caroline frowned, "and yes, that sounds good. Do you have Earl Gray tea?"

The waitress hesitated. "Probably. I'll check."

"If not, I'll have water." Sadie ordered Mountain Dew.

When Sam looked back, ready to add a finishing touch to the girls' silver, her daughters broke out laughing.

"You're obsessive, mom," Caroline said.

"Yes, I know." Sam shook her head at her own foibles. "Speaking of obsession, remember what Emerson said, 'No matter the graceful distance of miles between the dinner table and the slaughter house, there is complicity.'"

"Mom!" Sadie cried.

Caroline sat in stoic silence, lips pursed.

Sam looked down at her place mat. "Sorry, sorry. It's just that meat's not good for you."

"We've heard it for a thousand years, mom. Let it go."

Sam realigned her silver once more, then tried out an appeasing smile at Caroline. "So, you've been out twice now with some guy. What's he like?"

Sadie piped in. "He's cute, if you like short, dark, and kind of handsome."

"Everybody's short next to you," Caroline retorted down her nose, then turned to her mother. "He's about five foot ten, three inches taller than I am."

"How'd you meet him?"

"I almost ran into him in Shaw's parking lot. I was backing out and he came from out of nowhere with a shopping cart and I almost hit him."

"What's his name?" Sam asked.

"George Allensby. He was shopping for his mother, who's some kind of an invalid. We got to talking and he asked if we could meet for a drink sometime."

The waitress returned with their drinks. They sat back and waited for her to leave.

"I wasn't about to meet a stranger alone…"

As Caroline blinked, her dark fringe of bangs caught in her eyelashes. Sam fought the urge to pin them back. Sam had been a teenager once—how long ago was that?—and realized that style always comes before comfort when you're young.

"Oh, right!" Sadie laughed.

Caroline cast her a withering look.

Sam wondered what her daughters did that she would never know about.

"Anyway," Caroline stirred her tea, holding the tea tag in her left hand, her little finger arched daintily, "we decided to meet at the Brewery in Portsmouth. You know how busy that place is, and Sadie went with me."

"That was wise." Sam nodded approval at Sadie.

Sam sipped at her ice-cold Coke. As she looked down into the dark amber liquid, she recalled the early years of her marriage when she went to bed with a stack of books, a giant Mr. Goodbar, and a tall glass of Coca-Cola, and read under a book light long into the night. She wondered how she'd slept with all that caffeine in her system. Now the candy bars were history, replaced by daily forages in the refrigerator for Ring Dings, but she had only an occasional glass of Coke. As if that were absolution.

"When was your first date?"

"Saturday night." Sadie answered for her sister. "The place was packed. And I never left her side, mom."

Caroline just shook her head.

Sam leaned over her Coke toward Caroline. "I hope you're going to check him out before you get too serious."

"Mother!" Caroline retorted. "I'm not a child."

Sadie giggled and, behind her hand, whispered conspiratorially, "Mom, I'll lift his prints off his glass next time and you can send them to the FBI."

Not a bad idea, thought Sam. "You can't be too careful, especially with what's been going on in Georgetown."

"Mother, I know you're worried, and you've been through a lot, but I'm twenty three-years old. I don't need a baby sitter. You've got to cut the umbilical cord."

"Yeah," Sadie interrupted. "My older sister."

"By two years, and don't you forget it."

"Well, sometimes you *do* need a babysitter."

"Let's not get into that."

Sadie wrapped her beautiful long fingers around her glass of Mountain Dew and leaned back against the high wooden booth. She grinned at her mother while Caroline stumbled over the evening's events, all the while throwing daggers at Sadie, daring her to interrupt again.

They all sat back as the waitress delivered pizzas from under her voluminous bosom. "Is there anything else I can get for you?"

They shook their heads no.

"Okay. Enjoy."

Sam cut steaming slices and slid them onto small white porcelain plates for her daughters.

"You want to cut my pizza into little pieces for me, mom?" Sadie asked amused.

"Sorry, honey. Old habits die hard. So, what happened then?"

"We talked, had a few beers. Caroline had to have Old Brown Dog, of course. Then he left and we left, and that was it."

"What did you talk about?"

"All kinds of things, you know," Sadie said.

"He knows about your books." Caroline offered as she sliced a neat triangle of pizza.

A pain roiled in Sam's stomach. "Really?"

Ordinarily, she enjoyed the recognition. Writing was not like acting or playing an instrument where you got applause when you were done. Sam spent many hours alone at the keyboard, sometimes wondering if anyone was out there, and if so, whether they cared. But now, what with two homicides, Attn: Samantha Blackwell, she had more attention that she bargained for. And she was getting paranoid.

"Yeah. Seems we talked more about you than anything else." Sadie piped in.

"We did not!"

"Yes, we did."

Sam didn't like even a hint of trouble in the family. "You didn't give him your phone number or anything?"

"Mom. Please."

"You have to be careful, Caroline." Sam was beginning to suspect everyone, including her readers. The killer could be a deranged fan. Stars were stalked all the time. Not that she was that well known but...she had to get a grip.

"She didn't give him our number, mom," Sadie assured her. "But he can't be all that bad. Shopping for his invalid mother and all."

"What's wrong with his mother?"

"I don't know," Caroline said. "Funny though." She paused.

"What's funny?" Sam asked.

Caroline looked down at her pepperoni pizza. "He calls his mother Gracie."

Chapter 21

Lunch with her daughters was always nourishing, even now, with murder and mayhem rampant in her town. She left the restaurant a bit concerned about Caroline's new friend but also with a new sense of resolve. She'd put a lid on the paranoia.

The rain had let up and the air smelled damp and sweet.

And the gas tank was low.

Sam swung into Tiny's Tank-Up. The cracked macadam led to a two-bay garage with a glassed-in office to the right. Stalks of last year's geraniums poked out of a narrow, dark-stained box affair to the right of the door. The pelting rain had spattered dirt onto the window and left trails of soil down the cement foundation.

On the inside of the plate glass window, under a hand-lettered sign offering lubrication and an oil change for $19.95 and next to a sign proclaiming the merits of Penzoil, hung a faded poster of last year's Cowberry Cranberry Festival. Justly exhibited on the far wall over the cash register hung the more sumptuous merits of a biker babe.

Sam turned off the ignition as a mound of greasy denim emerged from one of the bays and wiped black hands on a dirty rag. Yards of blue undulated with each step. "What'll it be, Sam?"

"Fill it up, Tiny, with regular."

Tiny pulled at a lever and pushed the nozzle into the gas tank. "Too bad about Doug."

"It's just terrible."

He grunted, which in itself was an effort, for Tiny wasn't much for making unnecessary noises. "Heard he bought it at Stony Pond out back of McCutty's," he said adjusting the toothpick dangling from his thick lips for better clarity.

"Yes. Seems someone dragged him inside the market after they killed him." She watched the numbers spin on the pump, wishing they would stop so she could get on with her chores and not think about Doug. But then, Tiny might know something.

She was distracted when Madsen Chills' 1977 pea green Ford Pinto station wagon sputtered and jerked to a stop on the other side of the pumps, leaving a trail of rust and billowing smoke.

The back of the car was crammed with bulging black trash bags, cans and bottles, crumpled cardboard boxes, and yellow, blue, and green plastic laundry baskets in descending stages of disrepair. Into the baskets were stuffed clothes, broken pots, bottles, books, and sundry other articles so jumbled they defied identification.

"Whoa. Stop there, Mr. Chills," Tiny yelled above the clatter as the car lurched forward another foot. "Hose won't reach much further."

Sam wondered how the man got his rust bucket inspected. Probably through sheer meanness.

Madsen stuck his pointed nose out the car window and bellowed, "$2.50. Just $2.50, and don't you go over one cent like you did last time 'cuz I won't pay you."

"That happened at least ten years ago, Mr. Chills," Tiny commented meekly.

Madsen's eyes went blank for a moment, then he drew down wispy eyebrows. "Don't make no matter. Cheatin's cheatin."

He flung his door open and grabbed onto the doorframe to pull his gaunt bones out of the vehicle. He wore a black knee-length raincoat over high-water brown and tan checked bell-bottom trousers, magenta knee socks, and soiled Nikes with tears along the soles. A Merrimac Lumber ball cap pulled down over his scraggy white hair and a pair of pistachio green sunglasses completed the ensemble.

Sam would have bet, if she were a betting woman, which she wasn't, that the entire outfit had been extracted from the Salvation Army receptacle next to the Seacoast Artists Association in the North Hampton

Mall. Trousers of the same ilk as those worn every day by Chills had been seen extruding from that bin on more than one occasion, and there couldn't be a matching pair left on the entire eastern seaboard, if indeed in the civilized world.

Thank God the numbers have stopped spinning, Sam thought, but now Tiny couldn't attend to her needs because he didn't dare let go of the handle of the nozzle that was pumping $2.50 worth of regular gas into Madsen Chills' Pinto. She tapped her fingers on the steering wheel and watched cars roll by the station.

Tiny replaced the nozzle and said, "Right on the button, Mr. Chills. That'll be two dollars and fifty cents." Even Tiny found the smell of stale sweat and unwashed linens a bit too much as he reeled back on his run-down heels.

"I know how much it is, you young whippersnapper, just hold your hosses." With that, Madsen Chills stooped toward his car, released a lever, and pulled the driver's seat forward, causing a child's plastic beach pail to spill its contents.

Through a wedge of space, Samantha could see the bottom of the sand-coated bucket he'd probably picked up at Stony Pond. Chills was out there every decent weather day with his metal detector, foraging for treasures lost beneath the grains of sand. In between, he picked through trashcans left at curbside followed by trips to the dump, in case he'd missed anything. Madsen Chills gave recycling a new meaning.

Chills cursed at the spilled contents, angrily stuffed the items back into the bucket, and held it with one hand while he rummaged behind and under the seat with the other. Not finding what he was looking for, he stuck the bucket in the corner of a yellow laundry basket. Then he returned the seat to its original position, flipped the console open, and poked around with a long dirty fingernail. He speared a piece of torn paper that he examined before sticking it in his coat pocket.

"Need some help there, Mr. Chills?" Tiny ventured.

"Mind your own business. I'll find your blasted money."

Kneeling on the front seat with his plaid rear axle poking through the split in his raincoat, he reached under the passenger's seat where he extracted a healthy wad of bills wrapped in a wide red elastic band. With the bills firmly clenched in a fist, he backed out of the car and carefully pulled one twenty-dollar bill from the roll.

As Tiny disappeared into the station to get change, his assistant Danny came out of the washroom, spied the old man, and sauntered over. "Fill 'er up, sir?" He reached for the nozzle.

Madsen spun on the youngster, his skin stretched tight over large yellow teeth. "I'm waiting for my change," he snarled.

Danny backed away, palms up. "Okay. Just asking."

"I've got it, Danny," said Tiny, waving the young boy away. "Here you go, Mr. Chills. Have a good day."

"Yeah, right." With that, Madsen Chills creaked down into his mechanical marvel and chugged away in a cloud of colorful prose and blue-black smoke.

Tiny shook his jowls. "That man's meaner than a junkyard dog."

Sam commiserated while Tiny capped off her tank, wiped a spot from her windshield with the dirty sleeve of his jacket, and took her money.

Something was bothering Sam about Madsen and his trash-filled Pinto. Never mind. It would come to her later.

Chapter 22

"Just a minute, please."

Nick mouthed the name 'Agatha' as he handed Sam the phone.

"Samantha. I hope I am not disturbing you. I wanted to give you a few days to recuperate from the experience of finding Mr. Butcher."

Sam's head was buzzing from working on the second death note. It was Tuesday morning and she still had her column to finish. "Umm…thank you." She leaned on an elbow and rubbed her forehead.

"I would like to speak with you. Would you be so kind as to come by today?"

Sam looked up at Nick. "Today?"

Nick was watching her with a quizzical expression. In response, Sam shrugged, her eyes widened in that clueless look.

"Would another time be more convenient?" Agatha asked.

"No, no. Today is fine. What time?"

"Would 4:00 o'clock fit into your schedule? We can have tea."

Suddenly, Sam remembered Agatha's mysterious telephone call. "That'll be fine. I'll see you at 4:00." She laid down the phone slowly.

Nick stuck his hands in his pockets, then hesitated. "What was that all about?"

"Hmmm?"

"Sam." He shifted his weight. "What does Agatha want?"

"I have an audience with her royal personage."

He was quiet a moment. Then, "What for?"

"Well, I think I know, but if you don't mind, honey, I'll tell you about it when I get back."

The furrow appeared between his brows. "That's…" he looked at his watch. "…seven and a half hours from now."

"I know." She swiveled in her chair toward Nick and crossed her knees. "Look at it this way. You're a mountain man. You study nature and you know that an animal's survival depends on its patience."

He laughed. "You're a fine one to talk about patience."

Narrowed eyes and tight lips told him he had a snowball's chance in hell of finding out before the appointed time.

High tea was more like it.

Sam stared at the sweat beads on the bulbous silver teapot sitting on Agatha Coldbath's mahogany coffee table. *'I'm a little teapot, short and stout, here is my...'* Sam couldn't remember the rest of it.

She had to eat something. She couldn't insult the queen.

"This is so unexpected, Agatha. It looks wonderful."

"I do enjoy high tea," the old dowager said. "It is a shame that people today seldom practice these civilized rituals. Would you like Earl Gray tea or white wine?"

"Tea, thank you." *And the lemon better be fresh.*

"Please help yourself to anything else you would like."

Agatha handed Sam a Waterford crystal dish.

Sam wished she hadn't worn sweat pants.

Forsaking the crackers and cheese, orange and apple slices, and scones with the ubiquitous Coldbath chutney, Sam picked up a few triangular finger sandwiches——there were eight of them—which she hoped contained ingredients that had never born a face. She placed them on her plate. She might have a miniature frosted teacake later. Maybe two. They were small and there were ten of those. And perhaps an orange slice.

She didn't get a chance to count the orange wedges before Agatha said, while pouring steaming hot water into the graceful floral cups, "I appreciate your coming on such short notice, Samantha."

Sam had made sure she arrived two minutes before 4:00. She held the tiny sandwich between two fingers, her pinky finger extended. It looked so elegant when Caroline did it.

"That's not a problem, Agatha. These sandwiches look tasty." *What's in them?*

"Thank you. My mother made cucumber and watercress sandwiches like these for me on hot summer days. I still enjoy them immensely."

Thank goodness nothing in the sandwich had parents.

Sam took a small bite. It was cool and watery. Her taste buds curled along with her toes.

"Aren't you going to have something?" Sam asked.

Agatha leaned back with her teacup. "I'm not hungry, dear. My mother always said I ate like a bird."

Dear? Red flags went up.

Suddenly flustered, Sam said, "Birds eat their own weight in food every day."

Brilliant! She mentally kicked herself. *Why do I always say the wrong things in front of her?*

"Really?" Agatha looked hard at Sam. "That is interesting." She took a small sip of tea, set the cup back in its saucer, and placed it on the highly polished table between them.

"Maybe," Sam added, "it's because birds are so small that people think they don't eat much. Sadie, my youngest, is thin as a rail, yet she eats everything in sight."

"She's an attractive young woman." A flicker passed over Agatha's wrinkled face as she glanced at the silver-framed photograph on the sideboard.

"Thank you," Sam said, wondering what was going through her host's mind. "I think so, but then, I'm prejudiced."

"Mothers should think so. That is their duty."

Sam thought that was a strange way to put it, but in a way, Agatha was right. If you have children, it is your duty to love and nurture them and to think they're the cat's meow.

Sam sipped at her tea and looked up at Monet's Haystack over the mantle. Strange there were no family pictures—or rather, portraits—in the room, other than that one on the sideboard. Sam knew there was serious family history in the Coldbath family and she knew she shouldn't pry.

But it tumbled out before she knew it. "What was your mother like?"

Under a long strand of pearls, Agatha's chest stopped lifting as if the air had been sucked out of the room. Her whiskered lip twitched only once.

The sun's golden rectangle through the tall draped window cut diagonally from Agatha's left shoulder across her right hand and onto the thick Persian rug beneath her feet. Her pale hands, one in shadow, one in the light, lay on the arms of the chair, death-pose still.

Sam was aghast. She'd stepped into the lion's den many times in her life, sometimes unknowingly, but this time she padded in with an arrogance that made her ashamed. She knew how private this frail old woman was, and now she'd torn at the depths of Agatha's past as if those relationships were a piece of raw meat to chew up and devour.

"I'm so sorry, Agatha." Sam leaned toward her and placed her cup on the table. "I didn't mean to pry." She could feel the tears starting. She clenched her jaws. "Umm…what did you want to see me about?" Her face was getting hot.

Agatha let out a wisp of air. She spoke haltingly. "I called because I have something to tell you. I do not think it is something that the police need to know yet. We do not want to impede their investigation."

We? Exoneration?

"It is about that telephone call we discussed the last time you were here. Do you remember?"

"Yes, yes. I certainly do." Sam wished she had a fan.

"I am sure the call was from Mr. Butcher."

Sam sat in stunned silence. She couldn't react any more. She was wrung out. Her emotions had been yanked about like a yo-yo, wound up, stretched to the limit, and left hanging. Round the world. Seesaw. When was this convoluted nightmare going to end?

"Butcher," she said softly.

"I am almost positive it was Mr. Butcher. When I heard he was, uh, he was gone, I thought it best if I discussed the telephone conversation with you before I spoke with the authorities. I would like to see if your opinion matches mine."

Something chomped at Sam's stomach. "Please, go on."

Agatha placed her hands, one on each knee, precisely even. "I was at my desk in the study going over the previous day's figures when the phone rang. It was 2:35 in the afternoon. A man said he had salacious information that would change my life. Unless I wanted this information published in the newspapers and broadcast on the nightly news, I was to meet him at the old logging road off Tumble Brook Road at one o'clock in the morning this past Wednesday. He said he would give me four days to collect the money he requested, and it was to be in small bills. I was to come alone. He said he would know if I contacted the authorities."

Agatha wasn't the type of woman to meet a strange man in the middle of the night. *Maybe in her younger days.* Sam shook off that thought. "Did this man give you any indication about what kind of information he had?"

"He gave me enough that I knew it was important I meet with him. That is why I left detailed instructions in a sealed envelope with my lawyer, as I told you."

"So, did you go?"

"Yes. I arrived at twelve-thirty and waited until three in the morning. He never came. So I went home."

"And now you think, because the man didn't show up, that it must have been Butcher?"

"Yes. I was almost positive it was he in the beginning. Then, when I heard about his demise, I was sure of it."

Kind of hard to keep appointments when you're dead, Sam thought. "And you have no idea what he was offering you?"

A passing cloud cast dark shadows over Agatha. Her thin shoulders fell forward. "All I can tell you is that I did not get the information I wanted."

Nothing was said for minutes.

Agatha seemed to gather herself when she spoke next. "But that is not why I asked you here today. I would like your opinion on whether I should discuss this with Chief Burrows and his kind. Do you think it would make a difference in the apprehension of the perpetrator?"

Sam's mind was twirling. "Did you see anyone while you were waiting for this man? Any strange cars or people on foot?"

"No."

"Did anyone besides me know about the call or about your going to meet this man?"

"No."

"You know that was a dangerous thing to do, Agatha. You could have been hurt." *Or worse.* Sam was surprised that the thought carved a hollow in her stomach.

Sam rubbed her top lip, staring down at the feast before her. Smells—pungent, fruity. Colors—reds and oranges, the silver of the tea pot, delicate trails of pink on the dark chocolate frosting on the teacakes. High tea. The civilized world of the English.

"As you can see, I am just fine," Agatha said sharply. "Now, have you had any success with the note found on Mr. Butcher?"

Sam shook her head. Her mouth hitched to the right as she looked down at her laced fingers. *That damnable note. What about mother?*

"I know you will do your best, Samantha."

Sam looked over at her. "Do you think that whatever Butcher was going to tell you had something to do with his death and perhaps that of Doug Hammand?"

"That is the problem, Samantha. I do not know."

"Then perhaps you should let the authorities decide."

A clock in the hallway bonged five times. Agatha stared out the window to her left. The cloud had passed. "I was afraid you would say that."

Chapter 23

Sam was at sixes and sevens. To clear her head, she decided to walk around the town green before heading home.

The rain had washed away the final traces of snow yesterday and the grass was greening. In a protected pocket in front of Hornblower Stationers, perky yellow daffodils swayed in little gusts of wind. Sam loved their buttery faces and vowed, this year, to plant some bulbs in her back yard by the pool.

The setting sun threw long shadows through trees whose branch tips bulged with new growth and under Sam's sneakers as she padded softly in and out of the waning light and past the buildings on the west side of the green. The evening breezes cooled her cheeks and played with the wisps of hair that had fallen loose from her braid. She could hear the soft sounds of a woman calling her child in from play.

Up ahead, a few cars were parked in front of McCutty's Market. Townspeople picking up last minute items for supper. Two women gabbed over the roofs of their station wagons while their kids bounced in the back seats. Shops were closed, although figures bustled behind the long windows at the CPA's office that had been a beehive of activity for months, late into the evening. The April 15th deadline loomed.

This was her home and she loved it. She'd be damned if she'd let the 'cracker' terrorize her town. She breathed in the sweet spring smells and sounds, hoping for some clarity.

Kent Butcher was dead, he who had propositioned Emmaline Loveless and perhaps tried to extort money from Agatha Coldbath. Did the same person kill both Butcher and Doug Hammand? Both dead men were connected to Agatha. Butcher was preparing exposés, certainly a good enough reason for some to send him to his maker. Then there was Pat's letter from Pierce Investigations. What could she possibly need a P.I. for?

Sam thought about Sunday at the Bog Café, the fight between Jimi and Bobby Hammand. And there was something else that morning that didn't quite fit, something she'd seen…

"Miss Samantha."

Sam jumped, her hand at her throat. She looked around. Nobody.

"Up here," the voice said.

Sam craned her neck to see Clarence poking his head out an upstairs window over Clean As A Hound's Tooth Cleaners.

His clientele, who received more than starched shirts and spot-free frocks on their weekly visits, gleefully appreciated Clarence Tuttle's position in the catbird's seat overlooking the center of town.

"Oh, Clarence. You scared the life out of me."

"I'm so sorry, Miss Samantha. I wouldn't frighten you for the world."

"I know. It's not you, Clarence. I'm just jumpy."

"Well, it's no wonder. Why don't you come up and sit a spell?"

Sam was getting a crick in her neck. "Well, just for a moment. I have to get home and get supper ready."

She trudged up the wooden stairs along the side of the two-story clapboard building to the landing where Clarence stood in his apartment with the inside door pulled open toward him. He beckoned through the vacant top half of the metal storm door. "Come in, come in. This is a pleasure."

Sam's body momentarily tilted away from the pungent odor of chemical cleansers that assaulted her nose.

Resigned to taking short breaths and holding, she gathered her courage, pulled open the storm door, and stepped in. "Thank you for the invite but you're probably busy."

"Oh, no," he replied. "I have plenty of time."

Her worst fear but she pressed on. "I'd love to visit longer but I have only a minute"—with a slight shiver, she thought of Doug Hammand and his poem—"and then I have to dash. Can't keep a good man waiting, you know." She didn't want to arrive at her supper table with a buzz on.

Clarence closed the red striped seersucker bathrobe he wore over his undershirt and slacks and tied the belt. He apologized. "I was washing up. Come, sit down."

He shuffled across the floor, his loose moccasins flapping over the worn linoleum, favoring his right hip which he had broken years ago, and pulled out a fifties style tubular chair with duct tape crisscrossing the green plastic seat.

Sam took in the room with a quick sweep. A small television flickered in the far corner of the room. Facing it sat a mud brown sofa, the kind that hid one of those mattresses with a bar right across the middle of your back. A cuckoo clock hung on the fake wood paneling.

As she started toward the table, a movement caught her eye. Camouflaged in the folds of an orange and brown afghan tossed over the back of the sofa lay the meanest looking cat she'd ever seen. Its canary yellow eyes watched her. Waiting.

Sam crept toward the kitchen table as quietly as a mouse. *No, wrong analogy*, she thought. She kept one eye on the orange cat, the other on the door.

"I've been thinking," Clarence was saying, "about the terrible events of these past weeks, trying to recall something about the night Doug died. You know, something that could help find the killer."

Sam slid into the offered chair and placed folded hands on the maroon oilcloth. "Have you thought of anything?"

"Would you like coffee or tea?"

"No thanks. I just came from Agatha's. We had tea." *That's an understatement.* She smiled ruefully. All those delicious-looking treats wasted. Well, not wasted. Most likely, tightly Saran-wrapped and nestled in Agatha's freezer.

"Indeedy. I hope Miss Agatha is well?" he asked expectantly.

Sam sighed. "Yes, she's fine. You were saying something about the night Doug died."

"Ah, yes. Would you mind if I got myself a cup of coffee?"

He worked his way to the counter treading over a serrated patch of yellow and green linoleum before the sink that stood witness to many years of foot traffic. A bottle of body cream nestled on a windowsill infested with African Violets.

"What kind of cream is that, Clarence?" Whatever it was, she didn't want any.

Clarence glanced at the windowsill as he pulled a bank issue mug from the cupboard. "It's a generic brand," he said, pouring coffee from a metal pot on the stove. "I get it for a good price."

Not good enough, Sam thought. She wondered if he actually used the cream because there were more flakes on Clarence's face than there were residing in Washington, D.C.

"It's really creamy. Would you like to try some?"

"No, no. Thanks, Clarence."

The cuckoo bird boinged out of its wooden chalet and squeaked once. Sam flinched. The fat cat uttered a low guttural growl in Sam's direction.

Sam heard a crackling noise as she started to lift her hands from the oilcloth. She cleared her throat as she yanked discreetly, then fiddled with her well-bound braid. She arced an eye toward Attack Cat. Was it her imagination or was he growing before her eyes?

"I don't know, Miss Samantha." Clarence set the chipped mug on the table, sat down, and ran a pointed tongue over his lips. "I have been over and over that night in my mind. And the only thing I can remember is a dog barking."

"A dog?"

"You probably wouldn't have heard it, you know. Because it came from out back, down by Stony Pond."

"Does that mean you don't usually hear a dog barking at night?"

"Yes, that's correct. We have a leash law here in town, as you know. This dog must have broken loose. It howled pitifully for a long time then stopped suddenly."

Sam wondered if it was Florence's dog. "Did you tell the police about this, Clarence?"

His large watery eyes slid from her face to the television. "No, I'm afraid I didn't. I didn't think of it until just a few minutes ago."

He leaned back and rubbed the stubble on his chin. "Actually, when I saw you coming down the sidewalk, the incident suddenly popped into my head. But, you know, it's probably nothing."

"Chances are you're right, Clarence. Still, anything out of the ordinary that happened that night should be reported."

News danced in his eyes. "So, you think I should tell Mr. Burrows?"

"Definitely."

He seemed mightily pleased.

The cuckoo poked its head out again, squawked twice laryngitically. Clarence seemed unaware of the painful repetitive performance of the imprisoned bird. On cue, every fifteen minutes, for life.

Sam glanced at the clock. "It's five-thirty, Clarence. I do need to get home. I enjoyed our visit."

She rose.

Attack Cat rose.

Adrenaline pumped large into her veins. Fight or flight? Sam chose the latter.

Sam had cleared the dishes off the supper table. Moonlight spilled over the back of Sadie's empty chair as Nick, holding the sheets of scrap paper almost at arm's length, scowled at Sam's doodles.

"Do you need reading glasses, Nick?" she asked.

"I may," he said distractedly. The furrow between his brows deepened as his fingers repeatedly traced the outline of his lips. "Geeze, Sam. I haven't got a clue."

She pulled a chair next to him. "Let's do word association, okay?"

"What's that?"

"You know. I say a word and you tell me the first image that pops into your mind."

Nick chuckled. "Like that Rorschach joke."

"What joke is that?" Sam asked, a bit irritated. This wasn't the time for jokes.

"You know the one where the psychiatrist asks his patient to give a one word response to different ink blots and the guy says sex to every picture. And when the psychiatrist suggests the patient is obsessed with sex, the guy says, 'Hey, you're the one with the dirty pictures.'"

Sam's face became stony as she rocked slightly in her chair. She wasn't at the end of her rope, she was about to let go.

"I can see where this conversation is going. I need your help, Nick."

"I know, honey. I'm sorry. I want to help." He got serious and relaxed against the chair. "Shoot."

"Clear your mind."

"That's not hard."

"Nick!"

"Sorry." He took a deep breath and closed his eyes.

Sam waited a moment then said, "Three."

"Company."

"Nine."

"Dressed to the nines."

Sam smiled in spite of herself.

"Twenty-seven."

"One past the alphabet."

"Hmmm. That's interesting."

Nick's eyes snapped open. "What? Did I say something helpful?"

"You just may have, my darling."

Sam gathered her notes, kissed the top of Nick's head and disappeared into her office.

Chapter 24

Sam knew she was on the verge of getting it. With her middle finger, she pressed hard at her third eye, the pituitary gland between the eyes that controlled the major functions in her body. Maybe it would jump-start her thinking.

"That's an interesting pose. Are you competing with Rodin's Thinker?"

"Hmm? Oh, Emmaline." Sam gave her a sideways grin. "Hi. Actually, I was thinking."

It was mid-morning and Sam had run to the grocery store for jelly beans, Cadbury vanilla cream eggs—Sadie's favorite—and a bag of plastic grass for the Easter baskets she kept for the family from year to year. She had already picked up solid chocolate Easter bunnies and cream mints at the Chocolatier in Exeter.

Ring Dings were second on her grocery list.

"From the looks of your cart," Emmaline said, "you must have little ones coming for Easter." The minister's wife was dressed in a creamy white slack suit with gold buttons. She wore gold bracelets on her wrists.

"You'd think so, wouldn't you," Sam grinned and pushed a strand of hair out of her face. It fell back. "Would you believe they're for Nick, my mom and the girls? I can't seem to let an occasion go by without over-doing it."

Emmaline's laugh tinkled out like silver bells. "You are a woman of extremes. I heard about the time you walked through a restaurant to give a lecture dressed in long red underwear, complete with horns and a tail."

Sam was secretly amused. "Are people still talking about that?"

Emmaline's bracelets made a clinging sound as she reached for a large jar of Skippy crunchy peanut butter. "I think the town rather enjoys you. 'Better the devil you know than the devil you don't know.'"

Stifling the giggles, Sam bent her head over her cart as a large young woman pushed by, her top-heavy grocery cart threatening collapse. A small boy crouched on the bottom rack, dragging his sneakers on the tile floor. Two more little ones tugged at her stretch pants, begging for a ride on the mechanical horse outside the store.

Emmaline had her back to Sam, engrossed in the ingredient label on the Skippy jar. Her shoulders shook slightly.

When the mother had passed, Sam said, "Alrighty then," in a poor imitation of Jim Carrey's Ace Ventura, Pet Detective, "now that we're back in control. What brings you out today?"

Emmaline put the peanut butter jar in her cart and turned back to Sam. "I'm picking up a few items for an Easter buffet. Hannibal and I would love to have you and Nicholas stop by after church. The invitation holds even if you don't attend services." She cocked her head to one side, the crooked eyebrow askew. "Samantha. How are you doing? You've been through so much these past few weeks."

"I'm stuck on the second riddle."

"Oh. The note found on Mr. Butcher?"

"Yeah." Sam tugged at the waist of her sweat pants. "It's like I know the answer. I can almost say it but it's suspended just beyond my lips."

"I've had that happen, too."

They moved down the aisle together.

Sam stopped at the crackers. She cleared her throat. "Do you mind if I ask you something personal?"

"What is it?"

Sam looked up and down the aisle then spoke softly. "I saw your husband and Kent Butcher in what seemed a heated argument at Pat's house after the funeral."

Emmaline stiffened. "You don't think Hannibal had anything to do with Mr. Butcher's death?"

"No, of course not," Sam said, putting a hand on Emmaline's arm. "I was just wondering if he knew about the phone call Butcher made to you, if he knew Butcher was propositioning you?"

"I'm sure he didn't."

Sam wasn't so sure. She had heard stories about Hannibal's dark past, but like the child's game of gossip, the tales were most likely embellished by the time they got back to the beginning of the circle. Perhaps Hannibal did know about the phone call. Perhaps his anger boiled to the point of murderous jealousy and rage. His black cloth did not exonerate him from the passions of the flesh, given witness to by all those Jimmys. She wondered if his middle name was James.

"Hannibal prevented Mr. Butcher from disturbing the gathering," Emmaline said. "Can you believe that man actually wanted to take photographs of the bereaved?" She pulled herself into a graceful pose, erect, like a ballerina who flows with the melody but whose muscles burn with tension. "He was a man without principle."

"I agree," Sam said. "And I'm sorry if I upset you. Truly. I'm just trying to figure out what's going on."

Emmaline's gray eyes grew soft again. "I know, Samantha. I don't mean to be defensive about my husband. It's just that I know people make fun of him, his looks. He is such a wonderful, warm human being. It's too bad we can't look beyond the outer trappings and see the real person beneath."

To lighten the mood, Sam almost said 'warts and all,' then realized the remark would have been taken wrong. For once, she kept her hoof on the ground. Nick kept telling Sam she had the uncanny ability to verbally hit the sorest spot in her victim's psyche.

Back home, Emmaline's words rolled around in Sam's head like ball bearings, clinking against each other, going nowhere. She wasn't looking deep enough, wasn't looking "beyond the outer trappings to see the real person beneath." What was she missing?

After five hours at her desk, Sam flopped on the sun porch couch with her notes and a pen in hand, and pulled the fleece blanket over her legs. She closed her eyes to think.

Some time later, the phone jarred her out of a deep sleep. She felt numb. She lay there, blinking, as the answering machine picked up.

"Samantha," a man's voice said, "This is Benjamin King III. I want to apologize for our little misunderstanding in front of the church at Hammand's funeral. Can I make it up to you? How about dinner? Your choice of time and place?"

Sam threw off the blanket, was on her feet and reaching for the phone. "Please call me at..."

"Hello." Dizzy, she dropped into her chair, trying to think. What did the man really want? She cleared her throat. "This is Samantha."

"Samantha! This is..."

She rubbed her left eye. "Yes, I know who it is."

She wanted to tell the Penguin to stuff a fish in it but she was curious. Maybe he was the killer. Could Agatha have been mistaken? Maybe King, and not Kent Butcher, was the anonymous voice behind the phone call. Sam spoke slowly. "Exactly what is it you want, Mr. King?"

She was trying to think. Surely Agatha would have known his voice. But King could have gotten someone else to call for him. Like his son. Even if Agatha thought it was Kent Butcher on the phone, in stressful situations, one's senses weren't always accurate.

"Just a friendly dinner. Let an old man assuage his conscience and buy you a dinner."

There was a long pause as Sam's mind raced. Maybe King killed Doug trying to get access to the Coldbath spice cupboard and then boffed Butcher because the reporter found out. If she refused King's invitation, she might never find out what he wanted.

She'd meet him and take along a little insurance. She couldn't cross the Massachusetts state line with a handgun so the meeting would have to be close to home. Portsmouth. And it had to be discreet. The Cosmo was on a back street. Studs was there and they served great dinners.

"All right," she said slowly, running a forefinger over the calendar on her desk. "Let me see. It so happens I'm free this evening. Do you know Portsmouth?"

They agreed to meet at 7:00 P.M. She had two hours.

Fortunately Nick had called earlier and said he wouldn't be home for dinner. He was on a blitz to finish the chutney catalogs, and that usually meant midnight.

Sam rationalized that it made no sense to tell him about her evening tryst with the cranberry king. Nick would just insist she stay as far away from King as she could, especially after the debacle on the church steps. He would tell her she was already more involved than she should be, there was no need to go looking for trouble.

And he was right. Except—King wanted something, and Sam needed to know what it was.

She thought about calling Charlie, but he had already chewed her out for the Sunday display. And besides, what could she tell him? That King wanted to buy her a dinner to apologize? That didn't make the man a suspect.

She tried to convince herself she wasn't worried. She'd have company. Small, black, and deadly. And for back-up, there was the bartender at the Cosmo.

Sam arrived at the restaurant thirty minutes early. She wanted to talk with Studs and be in position when the king arrived.

The evening was pleasantly cool. The sun had dropped behind the three-story parking garage behind the restaurant, and the Cosmo parking lot lay in deepening shadows. It would be inky black when she returned to her Honda. She'd ask Studs to walk her out.

She slipped the gun into the pocket of her raincoat and stepped out of the car. An ambulance siren wailed in the distance. It rattled her insides, as if it were a harbinger of death. Swallowing hard, she passed it off as the repercussion of hearing too many ambulances recently.

With one hand clutching her handbag and the other in her coat pocket wrapped around the .38, she glanced around nervously. Most likely the other three cars parked at the far end of the parking lot were employees. She let go of the gun, pulled out the car keys, locked the door, slipped the keys back into her pocket, and grasped the cold steel once again before stepping quickly to the restaurant door.

Sam peered through the frosted glass of the heavy oak doors before pushing into the restaurant. Through the balustered partition separating her from the bar on the other side, she could see Studs joking with a waitperson, wiping out whiskey glasses with a white towel, and with a practiced hand, setting them on a shelf behind him.

She went in.

The place was empty of customers. Nodding at Studs, she went directly to the ladies room. Why did she always have to empty her bladder when she was nervous? She took care of business, then washed her hands and splashed cold water on her face, patted it dry with a paper towel, and stared at her reflection in the gilt-framed mirror.

She was safe here, in a public restaurant with people she knew. She practiced deep breathing. Then, she put her hands into her raincoat pockets and shouldered the door open, stepping into the small hallway that led to the bar.

At the polished mahogany bar, a slender man crouched over a drink.

Sam thought he must have come in while she was in the ladies' room. There had been no other cars in the lot except those belonging to, she assumed, Studs, the waitperson and the hostess, the cars she had seen at the far end of the lot where service people parked.

The man at the bar was dressed in chinos and a short sleeved, light blue shirt. Above his left wrist was a good-sized bandage.

Studs spied Samantha and opened his mouth to greet her. Sam shook her head.

Studs closed his mouth. He was a discreet man, which is why so many people poured out their hearts while he poured their drinks.

The man at the counter glanced into the large mirror behind the bar, appeared to have seen Sam, and quickly lowered his face.

She felt uneasy, a single woman in a bar at night, but she forced herself to concentrate on the mission ahead. As she motioned at the bartender with a tilt of her head, Studs gave one nod.

The hostess obliged Sam with a seat at the far end of the dining area then took her drink order. A minute late, Studs ambled over.

"What's up, Sam?"

"I'm meeting a man here in half an hour," she half whispered.

He grinned and tweaked the end of a full handlebar mustache. Studs was medium height, with light blonde hair. If he'd been wearing a cowboy hat, he would have looked like Yosemite Sam. "I'll never tell, little lady."

"No, Studs," she said, trying to hide her exasperation. "It's not like that. I'm meeting Benjamin King. You know, the guy who calls himself the cranberry king?"

"Oh yeah, I know the guy. Hear you two had a fight at the O.K. corral."

She looked down, smoothed the crisp white linen tablecloth and began straightening her silver. "Never mind about that."

A flush crept up her cheeks. The light was dim; she hoped he didn't notice. She waited a moment then looked up at him. "Listen, Studs, I need a favor."

"Sure thing, ma'am." Aw shucks had to be next.

So Sam told him what she had rehearsed. She was helping Charlie with the investigation—she had told herself earlier that she really was, deciphering the notes and all, so it wasn't really a lie—and that King might know something. He wasn't a suspect or anything, but since she was new at this detecting business, she could use a little backup. In case King got rough. And she knew she could count on Stud's discretion.

"Sure enough. And if he lays a hand on you, little lady, I'll kick his ass from here to Sunday. Don't you worry."

She knew he would.

As Studs made his way back to the bar, Sam slipped the raincoat off her shoulders and let it slide behind her back, making sure the right-hand pocket was easily accessible. The waitperson brought her Coke and she sat back to wait.

She wrapped her fingers around the icy glass and tried to relax. Her eyes rolled around the room.

The man at the bar looked vaguely familiar. But since he didn't speak when he saw her reflection in the mirror, she thought she had mistaken him for someone else. She wasn't about to approach a stranger with the worn pick-up line, "Do I know you?"

She sipped Coke through a straw, then ran a finger over the rivulets of water snaking down the side of the glass. But there was something about him...

The seating of an elderly, white-haired couple distracted her. The man's navy blue jacket strained at mid-button as he pulled out the chair for the woman. She dropped a large black pocketbook on the floor beside her chair and arranged her ample bottom on the small chair seat. The waitperson greeted them as old friends.

Sam stirred her Coke idly. She watched the couple give their drink order, then hold hands across the table. The man's shoes were worn down at the back of their heels and his suit was shiny at the knees. Her satchel bag looked like vinyl and was peeling around the tarnished studs that fastened to the handle. Sam imagined they would eat every last morsel of their dinner, leave exactly fifteen percent, and return next month.

Studs appeared, pulling the towel off his shoulder, "What time's your date?"

Sam scowled up at him. "It's not a date, Studs. I told you that."

"I know. I didn't mean it that way."

Immediately relenting, her voice softened. "Sorry. I'm a little uptight. He's due to arrive at 7:00. What time is it anyway?"

Studs glanced at his wrist. "Five of."

"Studs." Sam's eyes waffled toward the bar. "Who's that guy? He looks so familiar."

Studs glanced back, shrugged. "Don't know. First time he's been in. Hasn't said a word other than to order his drink. Why?"

"He looks familiar."

"Want me to ask?"

"No, no. He probably just looks like someone I know."

At precisely 7:00, the Penguin waddled in. Another party had been seated, but Studs had alerted the hostess to seat patrons far enough from Sam to ensure privacy. The hostess delivered Benjamin Hines King III to Sam's table.

"Sam!" He reached out a fleshy white hand and took hers. "Thank you so much for agreeing to see me."

His handshake was surprisingly strong for an overweight old bird, Sam thought, as she hastily slid her hand back into the raincoat pocket.

When her trembling fingers touched the cold metal, she recoiled. What was she doing? Was she mad? She wasn't about to kill anyone. Not even this slug. She willed her heart to slow down before she had a heart attack.

King ran a hand over a paisley silk tie and starched white shirt, tucking the tie further inside his jacket. In the flicker of the tapered candles on their table, King's large, square diamond cuff links sparkled. Sam was sure they were diamonds. He wore a Masonic ring on a stubby finger.

"What would you like to drink?" King snapped his fingers in the air.

The waitperson, an athletic young woman with brown hair neatly pulled back into a bun, had taken away Sam's Coke glass minutes earlier. She appeared instantly at King's side.

"Bring us the wine list."

Since it wasn't Benjamin King's habit to look at waitstaff, he didn't notice that the young woman, who stood slightly to his rear, had the wine lists in hand.

"Right here, sir."

She opened the maroon book with its gold tassel and laid the long folded cardboard in front of him, then handed one to Sam.

"Ah...let's see."

He rubbed his first chin. Without waiting for a response from Sam, he ordered a bottle of Opus One, Vintage 91. He handed the menu over his shoulder and waited for an appreciative response from Sam. When there was none forthcoming, he rubbed his hands like Scrooge preparing to count his pounds.

"It certainly is a nice evening. Feels like spring. Makes me feel young again." Candlelight danced in his small dark eyes. "I thought it would take me longer to drive here but I made it in forty-five minutes."

"You are a punctual man, Mr. King."

Killed anybody lately? Sam smiled. Like a black widow spider, she hoped.

"Yes. Punctuality is a virtue, my father used to say."

Hmm. Maybe there was a key to the man through his heritage. "Is your father still in the cranberry business?"

"He was until the day he died," King said proudly. "Never took a day off. Ran the place like a drill sergeant. Died when he was eighty-seven. Then I took over, just as he had from his father."

"So it was your grandfather who started the business?"

King nodded. "Yes. On two hundred dollars borrowed from his best friend."

Certainly a better investment than the stock market, Sam thought. A recent article in *New England Highlights* listed King Cranberries as the fifth wealthiest company in the six states. Coldbath Cowberry Chutney was third.

That must stick in his craw.

They were interrupted when the waitperson brought the wine. King inspected the label, waited while the cork was drawn from the bottle and a small amount poured into his glass. He sniffed, tasted, pronounced it passable. The waitperson filled Sam's glass, then King's, and King sent the young woman on her way with a wave.

The Penguin raised his glass in a toast. "Here's to a pleasant evening, Samantha."

Sam nodded, raised her glass, then took a sip of the red liquid. It slid down much too easily. As it flowed through her body, she felt the familiar limpness wash over her; she had never been very good at this. She glanced over at the bar that now seated a half dozen buzzing customers. Studs was busily mixing drinks.

"How is the wine?" King's long upper lip curled into a smile.

Sam wondered if penguins hatched from eggs. "The wine is very good." She'd sip slowly. Then, in a deliberately offhand manner, she said, "You must have admired your father."

"Yes, I did." He downed the wine in three swallows, then picked up the bottle for a refill.

She watched with interest. *Perhaps he isn't a wine connoisseur after all.*

Benjamin King filled his glass again and took a mouthful. "He was a great man. No one can fill his shoes." Momentarily lost in some memory, he stared into his wineglass. Liver spots mottled the top of his baldhead.

Sam said, "I'm sure he would have wanted you to fill your own shoes, not his."

King looked up, almost pitifully. "But you don't understand." Another swig left a small trail of blood red liquid trickling from the corner of his mouth. "He had standards. Very high standards." His voice rose. "My father was a man of principles, unflinching in his discipline. I've never known such a disciplined man."

Maybe it was the way King's flesh tightened around his eyes when he spoke the word 'father' that gave him away. She could see the man struggling between love and hate, those two demons on the same side of the line. She wondered if the opposite emotion or lack of it—indifference—was desirable in some cases. Something inside her felt pity for the little boy trying to fill his father's shoes.

She didn't know what she would do if King started blubbering here in the restaurant. Besides, his anguish was not the issue now. Someone's life was on the line. She had to change the subject.

She let go of the gun in her pocket and folded her hands in her lap. "I'm sure your father was just what you say he was. Now, Mr. King, your invitation had a purpose. What is it you want to talk with me about?"

He blinked a few times. She could see the flab around his jaw muscles constrict. "Yes, well, Samantha. You're very good friends with Agatha Coldbath."

Just what she thought. "Not good friends, Mr. King. We are acquaintances."

"But she respects you."

Given Agatha's comments about Sam's limited intelligence and the offer of a decent dressmaker and housekeeper, Sam found that laughable. "Now, how would you know that?"

"Word gets around."

That's the problem, she thought. *That's what lands us in a 'sea of troubles.'*

"If that's the case, Mr. King, then you must have gotten *the word* that I won't help you anymore than Agatha will." Sam's voice had turned venomous.

Oblivious, King poured a third glass of wine, then waved the bottle towards her. She shook her head.

"Now, Samantha. Be reasonable." He downed the wine. "I'm willing to 'make you an offer you can't refuse.'" He grinned stupidly.

Ice dripped from Sam's words. "And what might that be, Mr. King?"

"I'm willing to give you a healthy percentage of all future sales if you convince Agatha to sell Coldbath Industries to me."

The waitress started toward their table to take their order. Sam raised a palm. The woman backed away.

"You've got to be kidding!" Her skin prickled. The heat was rising along with her temper. "Do you think that money can buy you anything you want, Mr. King? Well, it can't. If you think for one moment that I would, if I could, influence Agatha to sell her business to the likes of you, then you're sadly mistaken."

Both her palms were on the table. She started to rise and lean over the table toward him.

Studs watched, towel motionless in his hands.

"Please, Samantha," he pleaded. "You don't understand. I have to have that plant. You don't know. You just don't know."

He started to whimper softly.

Sam hovered above her chair, totally confused about the emotions that played across her mind.

"You see," he said, "if I don't get that plant, my father..."

She inched back into her seat, glanced toward Studs and smiled quickly, signaling that she was okay, then looked back at the bird across the table. "Mr. King. Your father is dead."

King's head fell forward on his chest. His chin folds spread to each side like Silly Putty as the tears started down his flaccid cheeks. "Not to me. I was with him when he died. He made me promise I would get Coldbath Industries. If I don't, he'll thrash me within an inch of my life." He stopped, wiped his cheek roughly with the back of his hand. "I mean, he would have."

King loosened his silk tie, picked the napkin off his lap and bunched it high on his cheeks as he pretended to wipe his mouth. When he was done, he smoothed the napkin on his lap, then clutched the stem of the wineglass as if for support. His voice was very low.

"It started when I was ten years old. Every summer my father sent me to this run-down hunting cabin deep in the woods for two weeks. The cabin had a small generator that ran a propane stove and refrigerator. He left me with food, but no phone and no access to civilization. He said it would make a man out of me.

"I was terrified. Especially at night."

Only his lips moved, the rest of him frozen by the fear of old demons hunkering behind his tiny eyes.

"It was so black in the woods. I could hear animals howling outside. I didn't know what I would do if one attacked me. Hurt me. I spent the two weeks inside the cabin. I never ventured outside of those four walls even once."

He poured himself another glass of wine and gulped half of it.

"But when my father came to pick me up, I would tell him how brave I had been. The adventures I had investigating the trails he had designated. I wanted him to be proud of me. I didn't want him to know I was a coward. I didn't want him to know I had failed."

Sam had heard stories in her career but this was up there with the worst. Her heart ached for the little boy cowering in the lonely cabin, fearful of every sound, waiting for the monster every child believes in, to tear through the door and rend his tender flesh. She visualized the capital letters on the note.

BUT WHERES MOTHER?

"What about your mother?"

King looked at Sam as if wires had sprung from her brain. "What could my mother do?"

Sam was almost speechless to think a father could do such a thing to his son and that the mother was too terrified to stop it. She was about to commiserate when King lunged and grabbed her wrist so tight it hurt.

"So you see, Samantha." His eyes spit fire. "I have to have that chutney plant and you're going to help me get it. Or else."

Sam tried to pull her arm free.

"Or else what, Mr. King?" Studs suddenly appeared beside their table with both arms poised at his sides as if to quick draw.

Sam wrenched her arm away, rubbed her wrist, and examined the red marks left by King's fingers.

King looked blankly at Studs for a moment, then turned abruptly, knocking over his wineglass. He watched numbly as the bloody liquid spread over the white linen.

Sam stared at it. A red Rorschach ink blot.

A hush fell over the restaurant. All heads focused pointedly on dinner plates and liquor glasses as eyes slid obliquely in the direction of the portly man and middle-aged woman.

"I'm afraid you're going to have to leave, Mr. King," Studs said in a measured tone.

"I beg your pardon." King sneered at Studs. "Since when does a bartender tell me what to do?"

"Since now, pal." Studs grabbed King by the nape of the neck and pulled him through the dining room toward the exit. As he pushed him through the door, he said, "And don't plan on tying on the oat bucket here anytime soon."

Sam watched the scene as if it played in slow motion. She didn't think she could feel anymore drained than she did at that moment.

Her eyes fell on the stain on the tablecloth as King's pathetic story went into reruns. Sam thought about the mother that had psychologically abandoned him. Had 'she' been left out of the King trinity of grandfather, father, and son? Had she been abused too?

The line on the note wheeled in her brain.

BUT WHERES MOTHER?

Sam begrudgingly paid the bill, thanked Studs for his help and asked him to walk her to her car.

She arrived home hungry and spent and decided to check the answering machine before she made a sandwich. She stroked Selket's back as she pressed the play button.

It was the third message. What she heard was a parent's worst nightmare.

"Sam! Where are you?" It was Nick's voice, shaky and barely audible. "Come to the Portsmouth Hospital as soon as you get this! The girls have been in an accident!"

Chapter 25

Sam couldn't remember driving to the hospital.

The shell that carried her parked the car, asked at the emergency room desk, and walked the sterile corridors to the ICU where she found Nick and her mother listening intently to a young doctor in a white jacket with a stethoscope hanging around her neck.

They're alive, she thought numbly. Her legs moved her mechanically toward the threesome. Nick saw her first.

He met her, pulled her close. "Sam. It's not so bad, honey. Sadie has some serious bruises but she's okay"

He didn't mention Caroline, Sam thought.

A voice she didn't recognize asked, "Caroline?"

"Caroline's alive."

Sam's heart pounded in her ears. "But?"

"She's in a coma."

"Oh God, no!"

Elizabeth came over unsteadily and reached for Sam's hand. Sam had seen that same pain when her father died.

She looked up at Nick and whispered. "What did that doctor say to you?"

She stared at Nick's Adam's apple as it moved up, then down. "Caroline has a good chance of coming out of it."

"When?"

"They don't know. It could be tonight or next week."

"Or ten years from now." Sam was on the edge of madness, clinging to the end of that rope.

Nick held her firmly at arms length. "Look at me, Sam. You've got to get hold of yourself. Caroline needs us now. She needs us to be strong."

Sam just nodded, quick jerky movements, the tears storming down her cheeks. "What…happened?"

"The doctor said we can see Sadie in a minute," Elizabeth said, patting her shoulder repetitiously, "so let's sit down and wait."

Nick led Sam to a row of plastic chairs. The three of them huddled, holding hands, as Nick explained what he knew.

"I'm sorry about the message on the answering machine, Sam. I didn't know what had happened when I called. Roger Sargo called me at work. He happened to be driving by on Route 101 when he saw the girls' car off in a ditch. He saw stretchers being carried into the ambulance. The police told him the ambulance was coming here to the Portsmouth Hospital. He knew from Rotary that I was working late on Agatha's catalog, so he called me at work. He said he didn't want to leave a message on the answering machine at home."

Sam kept nodding. Elizabeth squeezed her hand. "It's going to be all right, Samantha, you just wait and see." Elizabeth had pulled an endless stream of tissues from her bag.

"Mr. and Mrs…ah…" the doctor examined the chart in her hand, "Bennett-Blackwell." The doctor smiled thinly. The three of them stood. "You can come in and see Sadie now."

Sam flew into the room. Sadie was sitting on the edge of a metal table dressed in a light blue johnny, her long legs barely touching the floor. Her eyes were black, she had a large purple bruise on her forehead, and her right knee was bandaged.

"Mom?" Sadie put out her arms and Sam enfolded her as if she were a newborn.

"It's okay, baby. It's okay" She kissed Sadie's cheek and pulled her head gently into her shoulder. Sam looked at the white string at the back of Sadie's johnny. It was untied. She wanted to tie the white string.

Elizabeth stood behind her granddaughter, one hand braced against the cold metal table, the other gently stroking Sadie's cropped blonde hair.

Sadie looked up at her father. "Dad."

Nick choked, his eyes filled with tears. He put his arms around his wife and daughter. No one said anything for a while.

Finally, Sadie asked. "Caroline?"

"She's going to be okay" Sam couldn't tell her now. "What happened?"

"Mom, it was awful. I was driving. It wasn't my fault. Some guy in a big car was following us. Right on our tail. I was headed for the next store, any place where there were people, and he started bumping the back of the car. He hit it so hard I lost control and…and…"

"Did you see who it was, what kind of car it was?"

"No, it was too dark." Sadie started to sob.

"Shhh…shhhh…" Sam held her and repeated the sound over and over into her ear.

She knew who did this. Her eyes became slits behind Sadie's head as Sam sent a telepathic message. I'm coming for you, you bastard…and 'hell's coming with me.'

At 1:00 A.M., the four of them crept into Caroline's room. She lay motionless against the white pillows, her black hair spread around her face like dark ocean waves. If it weren't for the gash on the right side of her forehead near her hairline and the tubes stuck in her arms and running to blinking machines, she could have been asleep.

Sadie burst into tears. "It was my fault. It was my fault. Oh my God…" She buried her face in her hands.

Nick sat Sadie in a tan molded plastic chair and knelt before her. "Look at me, Sadie." He pulled her hands from her face and held them tightly. "It's not your fault. You didn't deliberately drive the car off the road. The driver of the other car did that. And we're going to find out who it was. And Caroline's going to be fine."

Elizabeth pulled more tissues from her handbag, the action reminding Sam of the endless string of silk handkerchiefs a magician pulls from his sleeve. Sam needed magic now. She needed to wave a wand over the still body of her firstborn child and say, awake, my sleeping beauty. But she didn't have that kind of magic. She could only pray.

Sam took Caroline's hand in both her own. "We're here, honey. We'll always be here. You rest because, when you wake up, we're going on the biggest shopping spree you ever had. And all name brands. I'll even dress up for the occasion."

Nick had taken Sadie out of the room. Elizabeth walked up behind Sam and slipped an arm around her. "She's going to be fine, Samantha. The doctor told you she has no internal injuries. Just that bump on her head."

"I know, mom. It's a blessing she was wearing her seat belt or she might have gone through the window and cut that beautiful face." She sucked in a deep belly breath like they had taught her in Lamaze classes so long ago to ease the pain.

Elizabeth looped her bag handle over her arm, slid a putty-colored chair behind Sam, and motioned for her to sit. Then she walked to the other side of the metal bed to sit on Caroline's right side. Her knuckles were white on the tortoise shell handle of her bag.

They sat in silence for a long time.

Then the door opened a crack. "Honey? Charlie's here. Do you want to talk to him?"

Sam blinked hard and nodded. "I'll be right out. Mom?"

"I'll stay with her."

Sam stepped out into the corridor. A muted cacophony of sounds mingled somewhere in the back of her mind, the elevator bell dinging, a buzzer signaling something, the swishing of a nurse rushing by on silent feet, the low murmuring of voices—one on the phone, sounds that spoke of hushed desperation.

"Sam. I came as soon as I heard. What's the latest?" Charlie stood before her, his arms hung rigidly by his side. His shirt was buttoned wrong, the empty bottom buttonhole crumpled over his belt.

"I told him Sadie is fine," Nick said. Sadie lifted her blackened eyes to Charlie in weak confirmation.

Charlie gently squeezed Sadie's shoulder. "What about Caroline? How's she doing?"

Sam's heart flapped like a caged wild thing. "She's still in a coma."

"Jesus!"

Charlie turned and paced toward the elevator then back again to face his childhood friend. "If it's the last thing I ever do, Sam, I'm going to find out who did this. I promise you."

Sam couldn't speak. She looked at the blank walls and the white ceiling and the tiled floor.

"Grant knows this is high priority," Charlie said. "He's got extra men on it, and Lenny and I will work day and night 'till we find this cracker. And then I'll crush the little bastard in my hands like a Saltine."

Sam knew he was remembering the abuse his little sister took from their father, that faraway time when he was too small to protect her. "You think it's the same guy, don't you, Charlie?"

"Yeah, Sam. I do."

Nick stepped over. "Charlie. I want a police guard at Caroline's door twenty-four hours a day. It doesn't matter what it costs."

"You've got it, Nick."

"Sadie. You're staying with mom and I. Sam, one of us will be at the house at all times with Sadie until this thing is over."

Like a soft cotton sheet drifting down over her, a strange calm enveloped Sam. Somehow she just knew, in her heart of hearts, that Caroline was going to be fine.

And she had things to do.

Chapter 26

Caroline came out of the coma at 4:00 A.M., with Sam and Nick by her side. They kissed and cried and laughed. Then Sadie hobbled in with Elizabeth behind her carrying coffee and hot chocolate on a brown tray from the cafeteria, and they cried some more.

At 5:30, with assurances from the doctor that Caroline was fine and would probably be home in a few days, Sam, Sadie, and Elizabeth left the hospital. Nick stayed behind with the uniformed police officer.

At home, Sam and Elizabeth fussed over Sadie, tucking her on the living room couch under an old afghan against fluffed pillows, her blue childhood teddy bear from the basket on the sun porch resting by her side. Selket climbed onto Sadie's pillow and spent a good three minutes kneading the needlepoint cover until she settled down to purr.

Sam had read once that the vibration of a cat's purring has healing properties and that cats instinctively lay next to the body part that is ailing. She believed it.

On the coffee table within reaching distance lay the cordless phone, the TV Guide, a pile of videos, the remotes to the TV and VCR, and a can of Mountain Dew. Elizabeth settled into the stuffed recliner next to the sofa to watch over her granddaughter. Five minutes later, she was asleep.

Sam checked the house alarm, then went to the porch with the .38 tucked in a small holster under her blousy red plaid shirt. She had some thinking to do.

She wadded up the green fleece blanket—green, the color of healing—tucked it under her head and folded her hands over her chest. Her body felt like it had been run through the old wringer washing machine that she had used years ago for the girls' diapers. Every ounce of her energy squeezed out between those two hard wooden rollers.

Her hand moved to the gun. A finger traced the outline of the holster.

Caroline and Sadie were safe and in one piece, but she would never take life for granted again.

Her eyes moved to her feet where the sun cut a warm triangle over her ragg socks. It was always that seam on the right sock that rubbed against her last two toes. She ruffled those toes, then sat up and yanked the socks off, and tossed them on the floor. Even her socks felt restrictive, but soon, with warm weather coming, she'd be padding around the house barefoot. Nick had told her often she had a serious case of claustrophobia down to and including her feet, but she claimed it was a freedom thing. The only thing she hated more than schedules and tight clothes was sitting in the dentist's chair.

With the low murmur of the television as a backdrop, Sam lay back against the blanket and closed her eyes to see. Things waited in the recesses of her mind, waited for an opening.

She soon fell into rhythmic breathing.

Let the images come.

In the shadows of the Cosmo parking lot, she had heard the siren. That must have been the ambulance going to pick up the girls. And that guy at the bar with the bandage on his arm. He looked so familiar.

Behind her lids she saw the Cosmo sign hovering above Hornblower's Stationery, the curly 'C' pulsating, separating itself from the other letters and bounding over tree tops and buildings, landing on the roof of Madsen Chills' station wagon. The 'C' blurred, the second 'C' sliding to the right, like in double vision.

The phone rang. Sam sprang to answer it before the first ring ended. She didn't want the ringing to disturb Sadie.

"Samantha. This is Benjamin King. I heard about the accident your daughters were in. I'm calling to see if there's anything I can do."

Sam ground her teeth. Give him the benefit of a doubt. "Thank you. No."

"Are you sure?"

He hasn't asked how they are. "Yes, I'm sure."

"I hope your daughters have health insurance, Samantha. Hospital stays can be so expensive."

So this is where the conversation was going.

"My health insurance is none of your business, Mr. King."

"Of course, Samantha. But I remember how many tens of thousands of dollars it cost when my father was ill. Surely you could use some help?"

"Are you thinking of putting on a bake sale for us, Mr. King?"

He chortled, as if a squid had caught in his throat. Flightless, clumsy on land, penguins were excellent swimmers. Sam wondered if King could swim with a pair of cement shoes.

"Of course not, my dear. But I do have another solution."

Here it comes.

"My proposal still stands. If you can convince Agatha to sell me Coldbath Industries, there will be a check waiting for you in the sum of five hundred thousand dollars."

Money. He's offering me money when I almost lost my children.

Sam closed her eyes, thought of a dozen exquisitely painful things she could do to the man. The Bell of Death had a nice ring to it. The Hot Box was a possibility. Drawing and quartering was another option, albeit rather messy.

Instead, slowly and deliberately, she hung the phone. Pure hate boiled in her veins.

The man could have done it. He could have hired someone to drive the girls off the road so we would need money to pay the hospital bills.

Her eyes welled.

"Mom?"

Sam jumped up and wiped her eyes as she ran to the living room. "What is it, honey?"

"Could you get some ice in a glass for my drink? I didn't want to wake Gramma."

Elizabeth's head lay to one side. A light rumbling sound rolled from her open mouth.

"Sure thing, baby."

Sam returned with the glass of ice and a blanket. She then covered her mother with the green fleece blanket from the sun porch. Sadie poured the remaining Mountain Dew into the glass.

"When do you think Caroline will be home?" she asked her mother.

Sam folded her arms and leaned against the dividing wall between the kitchen and the living room. "The doctor said probably this weekend. They're doing last minute tests, but she's fine."

"Who do you think did this, mom?"

Sam didn't want to tell Sadie that she thought it was Doug Hammand and Kent Butcher's killer who had run them off the road. "Probably some drunk fooling around when he saw two young girls. Then he got scared when he saw your car go off the road and he took off."

Distress clung to Sadie's every word. "Well, why did dad want a policeman outside Caroline's door? And why are you wearing that gun strapped around your waist?"

Sam's hand involuntarily shot to her waist.

"I'm not stupid, mom."

Sam sighed. "I know you're not, honey. It's just that I don't want you worried over this thing."

"You think the person who killed Mr. Hammand and Mr. Butcher drove us off the road, don't you?"

Fear crept into Sam's stomach on sharp ripping claws. "I don't know. The driver could have been a drunk."

Sadie tightened her grip on the blue teddy bear as Selket started kneading the pillow next to Sadie' head again. "Right. When pigs fly."

"Sadie…"

"Listen, mom. The police are outside Caroline's hospital room. Dad insisted we both stay with you for a while. There's a killer loose in

Georgetown, and you're dressed like Wyatt Earp. You both act like he's after us. What am I supposed to think?"

"He's not after you!" It came out loud and angry.

Elizabeth started, lifted her head and blinked a few times. "What's wrong?"

"Nothing," Sam said. "Everything is fine. Go back to sleep, mom. You must be exhausted."

Elizabeth closed her eyes and drifted off.

Sam crossed the room and knelt beside her daughter. "I'm sorry I yelled. You've had a rough night." She stroked Sadie's arm. "We don't know for sure if the driver is the man responsible for the deaths of Doug and Kent Butcher. We hope he isn't. But dad and I want to take every precaution to ensure your safety."

Sadie started to cry. "I know. You're right. I'm just scared."

Sam took Sadie in her arms. "Of course you are, baby. You have every right to be. And so am I." Sam tried to laugh. "Just think of the stories you'll be able to tell your grandchildren."

Sadie lay back against the pillows and wiped her cheeks with the back of her hands. She tried to smile. "These last two days will make interesting reading in my diary."

Elizabeth had gone home and Sadie was asleep in the spare bedroom.

"She arrived at 6:45 this morning, full of vim and vinegar," Nick said as he sipped at his Cabernet Sauvignon.

The lights were off in the Bennett-Blackwell household, the room softly lit by a string of tiny lights around the perimeter of the ceiling.

"You're kidding? Agatha?" Sam set her wineglass on the coffee table.

"None other. And you should have seen her standing in the hospital hallway belting out orders to Andy Goodman. He was the cop on duty."

Sam laughed softly, relieved to be able to find something humorous in the past few weeks, and nestled into the corner of the couch, pulling the afghan over her knees. The wine was working its magic. "It must have been a sight."

"It *was* comical. Andy didn't quite know how to take it. I think he was incensed that a woman was telling him what to do, but terrified she might deck him with that black bag of hers. So he slunk back against the wall and folded his arms, apparently deciding 'discretion was the better part of valor.'"

"It was nice of Agatha to take over so you could come home this evening for a few hours."

"She insisted. Said she wasn't leaving until Caroline came home."

"I guess I'll never figure that woman out."

Selket chugged across the Chinese design rug and, with considerable effort, jumped onto the couch. She settled at Sam's feet.

"I don't know how Selket gets up onto the couch carrying all that weight," Sam said.

Speaking of weight, I haven't had a Ring Ding in days. Wonder how they taste with wine.

Nick set his glass on the end table and leaned back in the recliner. "Did you notice Selket doesn't sit? She lowers herself and retracts her legs like something out of Star Wars."

Sam chuckled in spite of the reference to extra pounds. "So, Caroline is feeling better."

"You should know, Sam. You called the hospital six times today."

"So?"

"So nothing." He rubbed his forehead and sighed. "She's fine. She'll be home Saturday."

"Good. And she's staying here until this thing is resolved."

"Yes. That surprised me. Neither of the girls argued about that arrangement."

"They're scared."

"I know."

The waning moonlight undulated across the couch as Sam moved her knees under the afghan. They sipped in silence.

Finally Sam said, "King called this morning."

"What does his majesty want now?"

"He offered me five hundred thousand dollars for the hospital bills if I convince Agatha to sell Coldbath Industries to him."

It took a moment to sink in. Nick's jaw muscles clenched, his eyes narrowed. "The bastard!"

Another stretch of silence.

Sam slumped into the cushions. "I haven't worked on the code since the accident."

Nick swallowed, then said, "How could you, honey?"

"I know. But I've got to get back to it. You don't suppose victims five and six were meant to be Sadie and Caroline?"

Nick didn't answer. He stared across the room at the fireplace and the mantle where Doug Hammand's loons rested.

"After we got home this morning," Sam continued, "I was laying on the sun porch couch, sort of meditating, and I saw the Cosmo sign."

"That wasn't very smart, Sam, meeting King like that at night in a back street restaurant."

"Please, Nick. We've been over that. Just listen."

He threw his hands up.

"I was laying on the couch and I kept seeing the 'C' in the Cosmo sign bouncing around and doubling itself."

"You mean like C.C.?"

Sam's eyes drifted out the window. Could that be what she saw?

She looked back at Nick, then leaped off the couch. Her wineglass fell to the rug, the red liquid spreading out over the fibers.

"Oh, God. I'm sorry. Nick, would you clean that up, please?" she called, as she careened around the corner to the sun porch. "I've got to call Charlie."

Chapter 27

Sam slid down in the front seat of the cruiser.

After spilling the wine last night, she had tried to reach Charlie. Brun said he'd been called out on a domestic dispute and might be late. Sam wasn't about to call Grant on a maybe. Charlie called her at 6:30 the next morning.

"Put that gun down before I arrest you for assaulting an officer," Charlie yelled toward the cluster of shacks, a hand against his holster.

A blue jay telegraphed alarm.

The gun disappeared back through the shack window.

"Get yourself out here, Chills, I want to talk to you."

The splintered door creaked open a sliver. Madsen Chills stuck his pointed nose out. "What you want, Burrows? I ain't done nothing. I already told you."

"We'll see about that. Put the gun down and come on out."

The door shut. Charlie waited, puffing.

Sam pulled herself into a sitting position in the front seat of the cruiser and took a deep breath. She had forgotten how dark and thick these woods were, even at 8:00 in the morning. The place smelled of week-old wet socks at the bottom of a laundry basket.

A minute later, Chills shuffled warily onto the porch, clutching a stained raincoat around his wasted frame.

"I can get a search warrant mighty quick if I need to. So you'd be better off to cooperate," said Charlie.

"Coperate 'bout what? I ain't done nothing." Sam could almost hear his old bones rattling.

"I want to look in the back of your station wagon." Charlie thrust a heavy jaw toward the cone-shaped pile of brush that hid the rusting Pinto.

Sam knew Charlie didn't relish the thought of his polished combat boots sloshing through the small pond in which the car seemed to float.

"Why?" Chills panicked. "There ain't nothing in there but junk. And it's mine. I found it all."

"Look," Charlie said, so softly that Sam barely heard his voice. "I'm not going to take any of your stuff. I just want to look, okay? I promise."

"Okay...if you promise. Wait here."

Chills disappeared inside the dark hut and returned with a heavily laden key ring. He shuffled over to the puddle and waded through the morass, seemingly unaware of the muddy water rising above his ripped Nikes.

"Well, are you coming?" he sneered back at Charlie who stood at the edge of the small pond. Sam could see Charlie contemplating the lengths to which he was willing to go.

Finally, he took off his Red Sox ball cap and ran his fingers through his hair, recapped and growled, "Yeah, I'm coming."

"Can't trust no one," Madsen muttered, eyeing the chief to let him know he was not among the exempt. He unlocked the passenger door and stepped back.

Sam slipped out of the car and went to stand at the edge of the puddle.

Charlie motioned Chills around to the other side of the car, then yanked a flashlight from his back pocket. He told Sam later that the car smelled like sour milk and sweat. As Charlie knelt on the seat, it squawked in protest under his weight. Slowly, he swung the light over the mass of debris in the back.

After a minute, Charlie pushed himself back end first out of the car, grunting during the maneuver. Sam knew he had to lose some weight and it worried her.

Then she saw it!

Charlie waved a plastic bag in Sam's direction. It held the book she had seen in the back of Chills' car that day when she had stopped for gas at Tiny's Tank-up. The little flowered book that looked like a diary, the book with the initials C.C. on the cover.

"We need to talk," Charlie said to Chills. "You want to do it here or down at the station?"

"Here, here," the old man gasped. "I ain't done nothing."

"Let's get out of this mud hole. We'll talk on the porch."

Chills slowly locked his car and trudged back to the house where he crumpled onto the sagging steps.

Charlie followed, took a moment to catch his breath, scowled at his boots, then addressed the old man. "Look, Madsen, I can't believe you had anything to do with Hammand or Butcher's death but…you had this book in the back of your car." Charlie waved the small book in Madsen's face.

Sam crept up behind Charlie.

"I did?" Chills looked blankly at the book, then at Charlie.

"Yes, you did. Now, Madsen. Tell me exactly when and where you found this book."

Madsen jaw hung slack as he watched a line of ants filing in and out of a hill next to his wet sneakers.

"Madsen! The book!"

Chills checked back in. "Yeah. He didn't need it any more."

"Who didn't need it, Madsen?"

"You know. That reporter fella."

"You mean Kent Butcher?"

"Yeah, that's him."

Sam gasped. What was Kent Butcher doing with a book that could possibly have belonged to Cora Coldbath?

Charlie gave her a scathing look then turned back to Chills. "Did Butcher give you the book?"

"No, he had gone with the angels." Madsen flapped bony arms at the air. Keys clicked in the soft silence.

"Whadya mean, 'gone with the angels'?"

"You know, he was dead."

Charlie rubbed his mouth with the palm of his hand. "Where did you find him dead, Madsen?"

"Sittin' in his fancy car on the Loop. He didn't need it no more, so I took it."

Charlie stuck the plastic wrapped book under Madsen's nose. "Exactly where did you find this book, Chills?"

Chills hugged the keys against his concave chest. "Inside his jacket. Like he had a secret compartment or something."

Goose bumps gathered at the nape of Sam's neck as she thought about Madsen going through the pockets of a dead man. He probably didn't even think twice about it. Butcher was dead. He didn't need it. Madsen could use it.

Charlie tucked the book under his left arm and whipped a note pad from his jacket. He spoke with restraint, "Madsen, tell me exactly what happened."

Chills pinched wispy brows and spoke as if Charlie were wearing earplugs.

When Chills was done, Charlie said, "Listen. I know I told you I wouldn't take anything, but I'm going to need this book. It's evidence. I'll see you get it back if no one else claims it, okay?"

Chills looked up with rheumy eyes, pleading. "That's all you going to take?"

"Yes, that's all."

"Cause that stuff is all mine. Yes, it is."

Charlie's boots squished as he lumbered to his car and radioed Lenny at the station to call Grant and then get his ass down there with a pair of dry boots.

Charlie turned to Sam. "God only knows what's in this book."

Chapter 28

"They're going over the diary now with a fine tooth comb," Charlie told Sam on the sun porch. "I asked them to run off a copy for you. Should get that in a day or two. It belonged to Agatha's sister, Cora, like you thought. We talked with Agatha. Seems she had a sister who ran off when she was fifteen. Long before I came to town."

Sam's mind flashed to the silver-framed photograph of the two little girls in Agatha's living room. Sam sighed sadly. Agatha and Cora.

It was Friday night. Nick was at the hospital and Elizabeth was in the front room with Sadie and a room full of flowers from friends and neighbors, watching the video *A Fish Called Wanda*. The skin around Sadie's eyes was still black and blue, but tinges of yellow were seeping through. Her knee was healing nicely. Caroline would be home tomorrow. Sam could hardly wait.

"How do you suppose Kent Butcher got that diary?"

"Don't know, Sam. Got any of those chocolate cookies?"

Sam returned to the sun porch with an iced glass of Mountain Dew, two small plates, and a serving dish heaped with chocolate chip cookies, frosted brownies, and cheese twists, some of the many offerings from the Friends and Neighbors Committee ladies.

"I appreciate you keeping a man at Caroline's hospital door, Charlie."

Charlie hovered over the platter like a dragonfly over a bog before spearing three cheese twists and four cookies, which he piled on his plate. "Actually, Grant pulled the Statie off after Agatha insisted on hiring her own hardware. Heard he's an ex-FBI man."

"You're not serious."

"Sure am," he mumbled.

Sam let out a little puff of air. "She's a conundrum."

Charlie gulped a cookie chunk. "Watch your mouth, Sam!"

"Hmm?" After a moment, she caught on. "Conundrum, Charlie, not condom. Conundrum's a puzzle."

He chuckled. "I'll have to tell Brun about that one." Charlie stretched his legs, crossed his ankles, and took a few swallows of Mountain Dew. "I stopped by the hospital before coming here. Caroline looks good." He tipped his head toward the living room." And Sadie seems up to her spunky old self." He had popped in to see Sadie before following Sam to the sun porch.

"Thank God."

"Amen to that." Sam knew he was thinking of his own daughters. "Brun sends her best. You know she had to go home for a few weeks. Her mom broke a hip."

Sam nodded. "I'm sorry. Seems like that happens frequently to older people."

A comfortable silence hung between them.

Then she said, "Everyone's been so thoughtful, calling, sending flowers, casseroles, and all these desserts. People really do care." The outpouring of affection had touched her from her neighbors.

Charlie compressed his lips in acknowledgment.

Sam yawned and scratched the back of her neck with both hands.

Then Charlie asked, "Any more thoughts on Butcher's note?"

She sighed and pulled at the neck of her gray sweatshirt. After a moment, she waved a forefinger before her lips.

"It's right here, Charlie. I can feel it." She curled her fingers into a fist and tapped them against her mouth, then said, "You know, there's a couple of things that are bothering me, but I'm not sure they mean anything."

Charlie was into the loud crunching stage but he managed to say, "Tell me."

Sam snatched a cookie off the tray quickly, as if that would lessen the caloric intake. She leaned back into the sofa and crossed her ankles on the trestle table, nibbling at the edge of the cookie.

"Well, first, when I met King at Cosmo the other night, I saw this guy at the bar. He looked familiar, but I can't place him. It keeps nagging at me." She nibbled again.

"What did he look like?"

"Slender, dark hair, maybe tall, I don't know. He was sitting. But he acted funny. I know he saw me in the mirror over the bar but instead of speaking, he dropped his head, almost as if he were trying to hide."

"Did you ask Studs about him?"

"He doesn't know him. And another thing—-the guy had a bandage on his left arm."

Sam noticed she had nibbled around the outer edge of the cookie like Caroline used to when she was still in the high chair.

"So?"

"Well, Clarence told me that he heard a dog barking for quite a while down by Stony Pond the night Doug was killed. Then the barking stopped abruptly, as if the animal had been hurt." She finished off the middle of the cookie.

Charlie scooped up a third cheese twist, tapping a glistening boot while he waited.

After the last swallow, Sam wiped her hands on her napkin and said, "Florence didn't find Sergeant until the next morning. You don't suppose the dog Clarence heard was Sergeant? Maybe he was out there the same time the killer was and when the killer tried to quiet him, the dog bit him."

Charlie was interested. "And you think this guy in the bar the other night might be the one the dog bit because of the bandage on his arm? He might be the killer?"

"I know it's far-fetched." Sam drummed the fingers of both hands on her thighs, slowly and rhythmically. "Somehow this scenario ties in with something else. I just can't get my finger on it."

Charlie rubbed a paw over his rubbery nose. "It's not enough to go to the Staties with, but I'll keep it in mind."

They talked a while longer, then she asked, "Want something else, Charlie?"

"Nope. I'll just take a few cookies with me." His plate was empty, so he grabbed half a dozen from the platter.

Charlie stood and zipped his jacket.

"I'll get you a plastic bag for the desserts." Sam stacked their two dishes and picked them up in her left hand, balanced the cookie plate on the inside of her arm, and had started to reach for Charlie's empty glass with her right hand when she exclaimed, "Oh, my God!" The dishes fell from her hands. "I know who did it!"

Charlie sat back down in the rocker slowly. "Say what?"

Elizabeth called from the front room. "Is everything all right out there?" Sam's mother wouldn't leave Sadie unattended for one second.

"Yes, mom. Just dropped some dishes. Go back to your movie."

Sam picked the dishes off the rug. Luckily none of them had broken, but the desserts were history. "I'm almost sure I know who did it."

"Okay." The word was stretched out.

Sam piled the pastries on the platter and set the dish on the trestle table. She sat on the edge of the couch wiping her hands on a napkin then leaned toward Charlie, folded her arms on her knees, and explained.

When she was done, Charlie was shocked. Just as the town would be shocked when they found out. If she were right, all the newspapers would carry this story above the fold. *If.*

"Jesus, Sam. Living a double life isn't grounds for an arrest for murder, no matter how bizarre that life is." He pulled at his nose. "How are we going to prove it?"

Sam liked his choice of pronoun.

"We both know how to solve problems, Charlie. We need a plan."

With his forefinger, Charlie slowly traced the scar by his left eye. "It'd better be a good plan because the evidence we've got now isn't enough to convict a man. Grant would laugh in our faces."

She angled her head. "Charlie, would you pick up that brownie by your feet?"

He looked down between his boots.

"No." She directed. "It's to your left, under the chair."

Charlie leaned and grunted. "There's frosting on the rug."

"I'll clean the rug when you leave."

Charlie looked longingly at the brownie in his hand. "You sure you can't salvage some of these things?"

"Not unless you want cat hairs in your food."

"I can pick them off."

"Brunhilda better get home fast," Sam chortled.

With the back of her fingers, she slid the plate with the rest of the fallen desserts toward him. "Take what you want." She stood. "I'll get you a bag."

Charlie squinted at the gooey brownie between his fingers. He picked off a cat hair and shook it at the air. It stuck to his finger. Ignoring the napkin on the table beside him, he wiped his fingers on the right side of his pant leg.

Why do men always do that, Sam wondered.

"We'd better come up with a damned good plan," Charlie said. He licked a finger. "Grant won't cotton to you taking over his investigation. Especially if you're right."

Chapter 29

"I'd better be right," Sam said to herself.

She was trembling. She wasn't sure if it was from the cold—it was nippy, the thermometer read forty-two degrees—or the anticipation of confronting a killer. She looked into the rear view mirror, a habit she had gotten into of late.

Caroline would be home at suppertime and Sam needed to pick up a few things at the grocery store. Nick was tending to Sadie; Elizabeth had gone home to relieve her friends from inn keeping duties.

This time of year, the sun climbed higher in the sky. It never was directly overhead in Georgetown, given the forty-three degree latitude.

As she wound through the greening countryside with the sun glinting off her windshield, she recalled how years ago, in response to her girls' argument about the position of the sun, she had stuck a long knitting needle through a Styrofoam ball. With a blue magic marker, she drew an equator around the widest circumference of the earth-ball. Above and below the equator, in red magic marker, she drew two more lines representing the Tropic of Cancer and the Tropic of Capricorn.

She had then taken the shade off a table lamp, angled the earth by holding the tips of the knitting needle obliquely, and slowly walked around the lamp, showing how the light from the lamp moved over the equator. She explained that because of the permanent tip of the earth, the sun's rays moved in a serpentine fashion over the equator—twenty-two and a half degrees north to the Tropic of Capricorn, then twenty-two and a half degrees south to the Tropic of Cancer.

If the earth weren't permanently angled toward the sun, there would be no seasons. And without the seasons, there would be no life as we know it on this planet. Therefore, in Georgetown, at forty-three degrees of latitude, the sun was never directly overhead. "Show and tell" was Sam's strength.

Just like now. She and Charlie would "show" the killer that the cracker couldn't terrorize their town. And she had a few choice words to "tell" him as well.

Their plan was elegant. She would make the call, the video would be in place, and the killer's words would be all the proof they needed. But she'd have to be careful.

Charlie balked at the plan at first, but Sam insisted. It had been her daughters the psychopath tried to kill. She knew that resonated with Charlie.

After turning into the wide expanse of hot top before the squares of glass and brick that composed Shop 'N Save, she slid the Honda into a spot under a young maple, one of many planted in even rows in a landscaper's sterile attempt at beautification. "Nature abhors a straight line," she said for the umpteenth time since the place had gone up. It was her mantra with the trees.

She locked the car and squinted. The noon sun sliced off glass and metal and blurred the edges of her vision. She shielded her eyes and scoped the parking lot. The lot was about half full of vehicles. Most people had done their shopping Thursday and Friday, payday for most. An older woman seemed to be looking for her car. A man was holding open the door of his midnight blue Four Runner for two little boys in caps and some kind of uniforms.

Sam hurried toward the entrance, stepped under the overhang, and blinked her eyes. Nests of shopping carts were wedged to her right. She tugged one out, swung it around, pulled a scrap of paper from her sweat pant's pocket, and talking to her grocery list, headed through the automatic doors.

"Sugar, King Arthur unbleached flour, Plug-Ins for Selket, Oreos—Nick loves his Oreos and we're almost out—Courtlands—maybe I'll make an apple pie for Caroline—, Simple Green, carrots, The Country

Hen eggs." These eggs were produced by free ranging hens and fed certified organic feed free of antibiotics. She wasn't about to support egg farms that kept their frustrated hens in cages in long buildings their entire lives. She felt it was cruel, and the eggs were unhealthy.

She serpentined through the supermarket aisles, picking up the required items along with odds and ends she had forgotten until seeing them on the shelves, and greeting townspeople and clerks with a quick smile and a friendly greeting. A young woman's voice came over the intercom and interrupted the Muzak. "Fresh asparagus is on sale in the vegetable section. Buy one bunch, get the second bunch for half price. Thank you for shopping at Shop 'N Save. Have a good day."

Sam loved asparagus and her one sorry attempt at planting a bed in the back yard had failed. She had read about an asparagus garden in England that had been producing for one hundred years. Maybe she'd pick up some for tonight.

Tonight. She forced herself not to think about what she and Charlie were doing tonight.

Turning into the notions aisle, she spied Patricia Hammand standing before the greeting card display. She was glowing.

Sam called to her.

Pat looked over her shoulder. "Oh, hi Samantha." She replaced a daughter card into the acrylic slot.

Sam noticed. She pulled her cart closer. "You look particularly radiant today, Pat."

"I feel wonderful, like I have a new lease on life. I just talked with my daughter."

"Your what?" Sam was glad she was holding onto the handle of the shopping cart. "Your daughter?"

"Yes." Pat turned full face toward Sam. "I might as well tell you because everyone else is going to know. And I want to shout it to the world."

"Well, shout away."

Gold and green flecks danced in Pat's brown eyes. The light creases running from her nose to the corners of her mouth spread and deepened as she smiled broadly. The words tumbled out. "I have a daughter. She's twelve years old. And I'm going to see her in two weeks."

For once in her life, Sam wasn't sure what to say but she made a stab at it. "Wow! That's wonderful, Pat. I didn't know you had a child."

"Clorissa was born the August after I turned sixteen. My parents sent me off to stay with an aunt. I wasn't married, you see. And my parents, well…"

"Oh, Pat. I'm so happy for you." She hugged the surprised woman, then took a step back and smiled at her. "No wonder you're so excited. Daughters are a wonderful thing to have. I know." Sam thought of her two precious children. "And times have changed, Pat. Even in Georgetown. Single women have children all the time now."

Pat thrust her hands into the pockets of her jeans. "Thanks, Sam. It's not about what people think about me. I couldn't pursue this when dad was alive. He…" She sucked the inside of her cheeks then her mouth relaxed. "He had his ways and some of them were hard."

Sam commiserated with Pat. She could only imagine the endless years of struggle with pain and guilt, the intense desire to find the only child who came from her womb. Ironically, Doug's death had freed her.

"How did you find your daughter?"

One corner of Pat's mouth twisted up into an impish lopsided grin, reminding Sam of a little girl with her hand caught in the cookie jar. "I hired a private investigator."

"*Amazing.*" One mystery solved—the letter from Pierce Investigations that Sam had seen on Pat's desk.

"It took four months and three weeks, and it was worth every penny. She was adopted right after she was born."

"What about the adoptive parents?" Sam didn't dare ask about the real father.

"They're really nice. She's a minister and he's a family counselor. Clorissa always knew she was adopted, so when they asked her if she wanted to see me, the answer was yes." Pat was nearly levitating.

Sam left Patricia Hammand poring over daughter cards at the display rack and levitated herself out of the store. The thrill she felt for Pat's good fortune couldn't alleviate the fear gnawing at her insides like rats in a hot box.

Sam unlocked her car, climbed inside, and locked herself in. She never noticed the beat-up Chevy that followed her at a respectable distance most of the way home.

HE had suspected they were up to something. She and Charlie had been tight since the accident. And when he got her telephone call on the phone he had installed the day after his mother died, his suspicions were confirmed.

He wanted to believe that she wanted him. But women were all the same. Even his Samantha, so it would seem. But maybe he could convince her to change her ways. Maybe she was different. Even so, she would bear close watching the rest of the day. He didn't want any more surprises.

Chapter 30

Caroline wisped through the door into Sam's open arms.

"Welcome home, sweetheart," Sam whispered into her daughter's ear, then led her gently to the living room where Sadie was laid out in the recliner rocker with the afghan over her legs.

"How's my older sister?" Sadie asked, a hint of the old rivalry back in her blue eyes.

"Don't start," Caroline said shakily, but she was smiling. "It's so good to be home."

Sam lowered Caroline onto the couch. She winced inside as she got a close look at the gash on Caroline's forehead. It was scabbing over and the doctor said there would be just a fine line of a scar, barely noticeable. But it would always remind Sam.

Nick brought two king-sized pillows from their bed and Elizabeth had the green fleece blanket clutched against her chest, waiting her turn. It wasn't until Caroline was settled amongst the pillows and cushions, tucked in tight, and insisting that she didn't want anything more that Sam noticed Agatha Coldbath. Agatha was standing by the dividing wall in her Chesterfield coat, grasping the black pocketbook with both hands in front of her like a chipmunk with an acorn.

Sam went to her. "Agatha. I haven't had the chance to thank you for stationing a man outside Caroline's hospital room. Please. Come in and sit down."

Nick took her coat and Agatha positioned herself in the rose brocade chair to the right and behind Caroline's head. With military correctness, she set the pocketbook on the floor beside her.

Caroline twisted her head and rolled her eyes up to see Agatha. "Thank you, Miss Coldbath. Mom told me what you did."

"You are welcome." Agatha straightened the creamy pearls at her throat, then set her hands on the arms of the chair, her fingers spaced evenly. There was a pronounced knob on her right forefinger. Sam wondered if it hurt.

"Can I get you something?" she asked.

"No, thank you." Agatha's hairy lip barely moved.

Probably the stale lemon, Sam thought. She vowed to keep fresh lemons on hand from that time forward.

The day was ebbing. Dark shadows fingered across the lawn and reached through the living room windows. Sam switched on both lamps and made a mental note to set the clocks ahead that night before she left on her secret tryst. Daylight Savings Time. 'Spring ahead, fall behind.' Simple acts that stitched her life together.

Suddenly, thoughts of what she would do this night slammed against her brain. Clawed feet ran around her stomach like a frightened rodent in a revolving cage. She inhaled deeply through her nose, exhaled slowly through her mouth. She had to keep calm. Next week, the news would be shouted from every Middlesex village and farm, and she wanted to be there to hear it. She did have to buy those lemons for Agatha's Earl Gray tea, after all.

She tried to involve Agatha in the family conversations but the old woman seemed content to sit and watch, if that stoic look on her face could be called contentment. Sam never knew what Agatha felt because the old woman's face remained as immobile as those on Mt. Rushmore. Maybe a twitch of the brow, a slight deepening of the lines around her mouth, movements that only the most observant would notice. And most people dared not look long into that face lest they be turned to stone.

It was dark when Agatha rose. Everyone except Caroline and Sadie rose with her. They all gave her a heartfelt thank-you for all that she had done. Agatha nodded once, marched to the back door, and was gone.

Nick went to the kitchen to rustle up beans and hot dogs—NotDogs for Sam—and Sam went to her bedroom closet and pulled out the four Easter baskets.

The baskets for Elizabeth and Caroline were of naturally woven fibers stuffed with straw. Inside were Chocolatier solid chocolate bunnies and truffles and eggs wrapped in purple, aqua, and yellow foil.

Sadie's basket was wooden, with ducks and bunnies on little poles around the edge that spun when ticked with a finger. On top of the green grass were the chocolate bunny, Lindt chocolate balls, green, red, yellow, and black jellybeans, and her Cadbury Cream Eggs.

Nick liked the old plastic Easter basket he and Sam had the first year they were married. Sam put one of everything in Nick's basket.

When she was done, she called out to Nick to go into the living room. Donning a pair of bunny ears and tail, with two baskets looped over each arm, she hopped into the living room to the delighted applause of her family. She did this every year; they applauded every year.

True to the warning—life is uncertain, eat dessert first—they each sampled the baskets before the beans.

Shortly after supper, Elizabeth took her leave.

It was then that Sam noticed Agatha's bag on the floor beside the brocade chair in the living room. She glanced at the clock on the television. 7:30. She wasn't leaving until 9:00.

"Agatha left her bag. I'll run it over to her and be right back. You girls stay right where you are, and dad and I will set you up in the twin beds in the spare bedroom when I get back."

"It's pretty dark out there, Sam," Nick said over his shoulder as his wife passed through the kitchen. He was stacking dishes into the dishwasher.

"I'll take the car," Sam called from the back hall. "Agatha will be upset when she realizes she left her bag. You know how some women are about their pocketbooks, especially older women. Her place is just at the end of the common." She grabbed the car keys from her pocketbook. "I won't be long." She was out the door before Nick could object again.

The lights in the living room of the Coldbath mansion were on when Sam pulled up in front. The rest of the house was dark. The driveway was dark. And the front steps were very dark.

Sam felt uneasy as she stepped out of the car and ran to the front door. She rang the bell, flattened her back against the door and peered into the deepening blackness. The waning moon offered little light under the cloud cover that had moved in. Then Sam heard a rustle in the mass of rhododendrons and arbor vitae that filled the semi-circle between the front door and the street.

Maybe this wasn't such a good idea.

She held the ignition key tightly in her right hand, point out, just in case. And Agatha's bag in her left.

Not much of a weapon. But if this key doesn't do the trick, there's always the black bag.

Suddenly Sam had a crazy vision of Agatha whacking the cop at the hospital over the head. She started giggling. And trembling.

Without thinking, she had left her own handbag, containing the gun, hanging on the bench in the back hall. She was just going to Agatha's and back home. Less than ten minutes.

She thought about the telephone call. She had given her name over the phone. Told him to meet her at McCutty's at 10:00 tonight. She had a diary that he would find interesting. A diary that his mother had written. A diary that incriminated him in the deaths of four people.

But what if he had decided to come early, was watching her house, saw her leave, followed her, and was now out there in the bushes with a cowberry necklace in his hands?

She couldn't swallow. Her mouth was too dry. Her left hand felt clammy on Agatha's black bag.

Hurry up, Agatha. For God's sake, hurry.

As she pressed her back into the wooden door, she could feel the ridges of the Christian cross through her sweatshirt, against her flesh. She was about to be crucified. She knew it!

Just as she had decided to make a mad dash back to her car, the front door opened and Samantha fell ass over teakettle into the foyer.

Agatha sprung sideways. "For heaven's sakes, girl. What is going on?"

Sam picked herself and the pocketbook up off the floor.

"I, I..."

The phone rang.

"Please," Agatha said, with a shake of her gray locks. "Take a seat in the living room."

Sam shut the door as Agatha went to answer the phone. Tugging her sweatshirt down and pulling her chin up along with her dignity, she went to the living room and sat on the Morris chair.

I have to get a grip if tonight is going to work. I can't be jumping at every little night critter rustling in the bushes.

Agatha returned minutes later and sat opposite her. "Now, Samantha. It has been quite a while. To what do I owe the pleasure of this visit?"

An attempt at humor? This is a first.

Sam picked the pocketbook off the floor and thrust it at Agatha. "You forgot your bag."

"Oh, my. How did I do that?" She took it, laid it in her lap, and smoothed the soft surface. "It is my favorite bag. Thank you, Samantha. I would have worried all..."

"You won't have to worry much longer, you old biddy."

Sam and Agatha flinched in tandem. In the hall archway stood the killer, and she had a gun in one hand and a cowberry necklace in the other.

Sam leapt to her feet and backed against the side of the marble fireplace. "Ah...what, what are you doing here?"

Agatha hadn't moved. Her eyes, tiny orbs in a sky of white, swung from the intruder to Sam, then focused back on the intruder, a puzzled look on her face.

The killer took a step into the room. "I know, dear heart. We had a meeting tonight at McCutty's, but you see, I know how smart you are. You were trying to lure me into a trap, weren't you?"

Her eyes were thick with liner, her cheeks rouged. A white bandage was wrapped around her left forearm.

"No," Sam said, her voice an octave higher than normal. "No. I wanted to talk with you, you know, about the diary."

"Ah, yes. The diary. Well, that will have to wait until later, until after we finish our business here." Her voice was low and round and full of intention. She lowered her head slightly and stared at Agatha. Her smile was terrifying.

Heeeeere's Johnny, Sam thought crazily, drawing out the word in her mind.

She had been prepared all along and tonight dashed out of the house and left the gun in her purse at home. How stupid could she be?

But wait a minute. The woman said "we."

Sam didn't like the way the killer was looking at Agatha and jiggling the cowberry wreath in her left hand. Somewhere in Sam's mind a spot of clarity opened.

The killer had one wreath.

She's going to kill Agatha but not me for some reason.

"But," Sam said above the pounding of the waves in her chest, "*we* don't have to do this. We can just leave and have our talk and things will be fine."

She wanted to scream, to attack and savagely destroy this bastard who had run her girls off the road and nearly killed them, but her legs weren't going to hold her up much longer. Her fear beat palpably and filled the room with suffocating wings. She tried to breathe. Her chest hurt with the strain.

But she couldn't let the woman feel it. She had to do something to distract her.

Sam said, "Your notes were very clever. I still haven't figured out the second one." She wondered if her voice felt as tremulous outside as it did inside.

The woman grinned like a child. "You think so? I worked very hard on them."

"Yes, I can see that you did." Sam could feel the fireplace poker behind her hand. "And they were very neat."

The skin on the killer's face slackened. "I didn't go outside the lines, did you notice that?"

"I certainly did. You were very precise."

"I did it for you, you know."

It was too much. Spots danced before Sam's eyes, she felt herself swaying. She forced herself to take hold of the mantle. "Oh."

The killer's tongue flickered across her painted lips. "Now we can go away together, you and I."

With that, Chris Byrnes tore his black Cleopatra wig from his head and tossed it aside.

A shudder shook Sam's body.

Muddy images sloshed through her mind. Chris belting out orders at the Bog. Chris and Julie at the church services for Doug Hammand. And at the Hammand home. The uneasiness Sam felt in that knot of people, Clarence, Julie, Michael, and Chris. All along it was Chris. All that time she, he, was just feet away from her. Sometimes inches. God! He even held her hand.

Sam had to keep him talking while she thought of something to do. "That would be wonderful, Chris." She took a wobbly step toward him. "Why don't we leave now?"

He roared. "Stop right there!"

Once again, Sam backed up against the fireplace, her heart frozen.

Chris threw his head back and laughed, a strangled evil sound that echoed the insanity that was enveloping him.

"Chris," she said, her voice now sounding surprisingly calm in her ears, "why don't we talk about it? You're an intelligent man. Surely you must have your reasons. Everyone will understand."

"No one could possibly understand," he cried. The gun trembled in his hand. "Men slobbering over me. Disgusting hairy hands pinching my ass. The leers. Doug Hammand found out the hard way."

Sam's throat was as dry as the Arizona desert. "What did Doug do to you?"

"He kept asking me out. Showing me the wad of bills he kept hidden in his pants pocket. As if he could buy me. But I showed him. You should have seen how his eyes lit up when I agreed to meet him down by Stony Pond." He rubbed the gun barrel against his cheek then leveled it at Sam again. "Hammand's eyes took on a different light when I tightened that cowberry wreath around his plump neck. And the old geezer had four hundred dollars on him. In twenties."

He laughed again.

Sam glanced at Agatha. She had become as still as her forebear's statue on the green. In the back of her mind, Sam wondered if the old woman had gone into shock.

Keep talking she told herself. "How did Doug get into McCutty's?"

"I dragged him in. I have a key, you see. Made a spare when I worked there. Old man McCutty fired me, so I left him a present. Besides, I love steaks, and he's kept me well supplied over the past few years. Two birds with one stone, as they say." His grin was more a mindless leer. "Stone. Stony Pond."

Sam tried to smile at the pun. "What happened to your wrist? The bandage."

He looked blank for a moment then lifted his arm slightly as his eyes shifted to the bandage. "The wounds of war. Some mutt must have smelled the steak I picked up in McCutty's after I dragged Hammand in there. I kicked his butt good. Would have shot him if I'd had my gun with me that night."

Sam had to know. "And Kent Butcher?"

Chris' lip curled into a snarl. "His brains were between his legs. All I had to do was crook my finger and he followed me home. A few knock-out drops in his wine and he was history. I left him in the cellar to think about his fate. I thought it was rather theatrical to leave him in his fancy car wearing the cowberry necklace. Almost matched the color of the Miata. Did you notice?"

So that's where Kent found the diary. In Chris Byrnes' basement. She wanted to know why he sliced his victims, but was too terrified to ask.

"Now, my heart," Chris leered at her, "we have to attend to Miss High and Mighty here." He waved the gun at Agatha then circled behind the chair in which Sam had been sitting, balanced the cowberry wreath on the top of the chair and leaned on the back. He shook the gun barrel at Agatha. "I'm going to put an end to her struttin' around town like she owns the place when other people don't have a pot to piss in. When other people have to work their fingers to the bone. I was meant for better things."

As he raised his gun arm level with Agatha's chest, he bumped the wreath and it toppled to the floor to his left, away from Sam.

In that one distracted moment, Sam reached for the cold metal handle of the fireplace stoker behind her. She swung it around, grabbed it with both hands, and lifted it high above her head. Every muscle in her body strained. Her fury took over.

This one's for my babies, you scum bag.

Her aim was off. The poker slammed down across Chris' gun fist, catching the tip of the barrel, and with a resounding crack, smashed into the wooden arms of the Morris chair. The arms of the chair collapsed and pulled the back of the chair forward, forming a V with the seat. The gun bounced up and out of Chris' hands and onto the floor in front of the chair.

"Call 911!" Sam shouted at Agatha.

Agatha, in one mighty leap, shot from her chair and ran toward the hallway.

Sam lunged for the gun, but the killer was on top of her.

He slammed her head against the floor with one strong arm.

"You bitch," he screamed. He grabbed the gun with his free hand.

An excruciating pain reverberated inside Sam's head. She fumbled for and found the chair rung that had clattered to the floor.

Chris was heavier than he looked. She could feel his legs squeezing her rib cage, choking off her breath. She groaned, then twisted her upper body enough so her right arm, the stronger arm, had swivel room.

"You don't know the half of it," she gasped, and with every ounce of strength left in her body, slammed the rung against the side of his face.

Crack!

Chris yowled in pain, a high-pitched little boy's howl, as both hands flew to his cheekbone.

Sam bucked the slack body off hers. The clown glasses flew off his face and seemed to hover in midair before they fell to the floor.

She somehow got her elbows on the wobbling seat of the Morris chair. Raw fear pulled her up. She grabbed for the poker again and wheeled, raising her arms above her head for a second time. She wasn't going to miss this time.

The end of a wavering gun barrel was pointed at her heart.

"Why?" he howled as his finger closed over the trigger.

Sam felt something whap into her as she brought the poker down on Christopher Byrnes' head with the might of a rampaging she-bear.

Then she slumped to the floor.

Chapter 31

Something went wrong. I finally come to blame myself. But I was young and scared when it started. That's no excuse for what I did as an adult, I know. But maybe it's a reason. I don't know why I'm writing this. Maybe it's therapy. Or some kind of redemption. Or maybe I'm afraid to leave this world without telling someone about the man my little boy has become.

Samantha Blackwell pressed the page gently against her breast and stared at the ceiling in her bedroom. A few more pages lay on the bed to her left.

Charlie had dropped off a copy of Cora Coldbath's diary for her. Grant said she had earned the right to read it.

Christopher George Byrnes was dead. Sam had killed him two days ago in Agatha's living room. She felt no emotion about killing him except that she was glad he was dead. She felt empty, not hollow like she did when she heard about the girls in the hospital or when Chris was stalking her. This feeling was like a big silver bowl reflecting light around it, empty, not part of anything. Displaced stasis.

She winced as she shifted on the pillows. The bullet had grazed her left side, tearing off a bit of skin. A few inches to the right, the doctor had said, and vital organs could have been damaged. Sam lightly touched the area where her red plaid nightshirt covered the dressing. She'd have a scar. Like Caroline. And Charlie. Part of an elite club.

When Sam woke in the hospital Sunday night, Nick and her mother were standing by her bedside. Her two bandaged daughters were at the foot of the bed. Sam had laughed weakly. A scene from a M.A.S.H. episode.

Agatha and Charlie had tiptoed in. Sam thought she remembered Agatha patting her hand but it must have been an hallucination brought on by painkillers.

By Tuesday, Sam insisted on going home. Grant was coming to get her statement today, late afternoon. Charlie too. Sam wanted time to read the diary before talking with them. Things were so jumbled in her head. She needed time to order them.

Once again, she lifted the sheet of paper.

> I left home when I was fifteen and pregnant. I couldn't tell my father. I think he would have killed me for disgracing his name. Tony and I took off in his van and headed for California. He told me wonderful things about the sun and warm beaches out there. He left me at a diner somewhere in Nebraska. Said he was going to the rest room. I never saw him again.

Sam lay the sheet of paper to her right and sighed. She wanted to breathe in deeply and exhale but her side hurt. She lay a hand there over the wound for a moment and thought about the young girl abandoned by the roadside. How frightened she must have been.

She picked up the next page.

> I was too proud to go home. I guess that's always been my downfall. My pride. Anyway, the woman who ran the diner was looking for help. I applied. Gert hired me on the spot. I told her I needed a place to stay. She didn't ask and I didn't tell. Gert was a hard woman but good. I had sixty-seven dollars in my wallet, enough for a room in a run-down boarding house. It was clean though, and nearby, so I could walk to work. Kept the baby in a playpen in the kitchen during my shifts. It worked out. I stayed there for about twenty years. Then Gert

died. I have to put the pen down now. I'm tired and my hand hurts.
I'm back now. Let's see. Gert died. That's when I decided to come back home. Not only because she died, that was part of it, I know. Also I suspected my son was in trouble. An old couple in town was murdered in their beds, their house robbed.

Victims one and two? Sam wondered. She picked up the next page.

The old man kept money in the house, and Chris was suddenly throwing money at the waitresses in a local bar. I shouldn't have suspected my own son but I think inside I knew he did it. You must understand that I had to protect him. I'm his mother. When we got back here...

She must mean Georgetown, Sam thought. She also thought the handwriting seemed more strained.

...I used the money I had saved, plus Gert had left me twenty-five thousand dollars. That was a surprise. The first nice thing anyone ever did for me these past thirty years. I'm rambling on, but who cares? This isn't English 101. And I'm not feeling good, so I'm going to take a nap.
I'm back again. I still feel bad but I have to finish this. I had enough money to buy this little house with no mortgage. It isn't much, but we own it. Chris handled the transaction. I'm too weak to leave the house. And we're way out in the woods. I never see anyone. I get so lonely.
Anyway, right after we moved here, Chris started acting funny, dressing up in women's clothes. It's my fault. I wanted a girl so bad. When he was little I bought frilly dresses for him. His hair

fell in beautiful dark ringlets. He would have been a beautiful girl.

"Jesus!" Sam rubbed her forehead.

I used to rock him and read nursery rhymes from a book I got at the dime store. He loved nursery rhymes. Especially 'One a Penny.' That was his favorite. I read that one over and over, and he would hum and his little toes would wiggle. So maybe it was my fault that he started dressing like a woman.
But what can I say now? He's a grown man. He's stronger than I am. I found that out. I don't need any more bruises.

Anger and disgust and disbelief roiled in Sam's stomach. The little boy inside was beating the mother who denied his masculinity.

Chris got a job at McCutty's Market first. McCutty thought Chris was a woman. He seemed to like Chris, that's what Chris said. And he was surprised when Chris offered to fillet the fresh fish for him. Chris liked that job, but then, like most little boys, he always liked knives.

A deep shudder ran through Sam as she thought about the single incisions down the chests of his victims. He liked knives all right.

McCutty even gave Chris a key to the store. He trusted Chris. I thought that would help him change. But that only lasted a few months. I think they had some kind of fight. Chris doesn't have much patience.
Anyway, he ended up at the Bog Café. He made enough money to bring us home steaks a lot and buy what we needed. I love steak. But then he started getting strange.

> He's locking his room now. I don't dare try to get in. I don't know what he keeps in there except that ugly black spider he calls Gracie. He thinks it's funny because his middle name is George. He says 'George and Gracie' like George Burns and Gracie Allen.

Oh, my God! George Allensby, the man who Caroline ran into at the supermarket parking lot. It was a deliberate meeting. Sam swallowed hard, then continued reading.

> I've been thinking about getting in touch with Agatha. My sister. I haven't seen her for so many years. I haven't seen anyone since we moved here. I can't go out. I'm too sick most of the time, and Chris keeps the car keys. He won't have a phone in the house. Says it disturbs his thinking. I wouldn't know what to say to Agatha anyway. She is proud, too. But responsible and strong. And she has a good business head. Everyone respects her.
> Chris went on a rampage today, throwing things, yelling. He smashed the Cinderella figurine I bought for him when he was five. That's when I really got scared and decided to write all this stuff down. Just in case. I don't want him to hurt anyone else. I'm going to hide this book in the basement and hope that someone will find it, but not Chris.

That's where Kent found the diary, in the basement, Sam thought. *Chris lured the reporter to his house and imprisoned him in the root cellar.*

Sam could visualize Kent trapped in a musty cubicle, scratching to find a way out then giving up, and to pass the time, going through boxes. Then he found the diary. He had the story of his life.

Butcher must have slipped the diary inside his safari jacket. Chris killed him, but never noticed the diary when he stuffed Kent into the red Miata. Chris then drove Kent to the Loop. Along comes old Chills who takes the diary from Butcher's dead body.

Without thinking, Sam let out a big sigh. She winced and reached for her side, breathing softly until the pain subsided.

This is unbelievable, she thought. *Like a soap opera. If I saw a movie like this, I wouldn't believe it. A combination* of Hush…Hush, Sweet Charlotte *and* Psycho.

She read on.

> I pray to God Chris doesn't find my diary. He has these blackouts and doesn't remember what he's doing. But I have to take a chance. He never goes into the root cellar. I've been thinking. Yes. I will to try and get a message to my sister. I don't know how. No one comes here to visit. I have no friends. And I can barely walk. My legs. I think it's arthritis. Probably all those years on my feet at the diner. So, this is the end. If you find this, please try to help my son. And if I don't get to my sister, tell her I thought of her every day since I left home so many years ago. Tell her that I love her.

When Sam looked at the tiny, shakily written signature—Cora Coldbath—she wept.

Minutes later, she wiped her face with Kleenex from the nightstand. She could imagine a bent woman, old before her time, creeping painfully down dark cellar stairs to hide her diary in the basement, then struggling to get back upstairs before her son came home so she wouldn't get a beating.

Samantha lay the last page on top of the other sheets to her right, then folded her hands over her stomach.

Sensory deprivation. That's what she needed right now. To be in one of those cylindrical chambers, floating in a saline solution, cut off from all outside stimuli. Just floating, no thoughts, no pain.

But the thought slammed hard against her.

I killed Agatha's nephew. Her last remaining heir. I robbed her of her family.

The tears started again, running from the corners of her eyes, down the side of her face, into her hair and on to the pillowcase.

Sam wanted to turn, sob into the pillows, but her side hurt too much. So she lay there and let the tears flow.

Chapter 32

Some time later, Sam slowly opened her eyes and stared at the ceiling, frightened, grasping for a solid edge. Clutching at the coverlet, she struggled up from an unremembered nightmare and realized she was in her own bed, safe, at home. She lifted her head slightly. The digital clock on the bureau showed 1:15 in big red numbers. Grant and Charlie would be coming at 3:00, and the rumble in her stomach told her she was hungry.

At the sound of the little brass bell left on her night stand, Nick poked his head around the corner. "You okay, Sam? You want something?"

"I'm hungry, honey."

Beaming, he kissed her on the forehead. "That's a good sign. How about some vegetable soup and toast?"

"Sounds great."

"And a Ring Ding for dessert?" His smile would have done a jack-o-lantern proud.

"Two."

After lunch, Sam carefully slipped into her fleecy plaid bathrobe, and holding her side, found her way to the sun porch couch. She could hear the television in the living room.

Nick appeared, wiping his hands on a dishtowel. He wore a yellow daisy apron around his waist.

"Sam!" he scolded. "You should have called me. I would have helped you out here."

"I'm fine. I have to get up and walk a little. Where are the girls?"

"They're watching *In and Out* with Kevin Kline."

Sam could hear them laughing. "How appropriate." She thought of Chris' confusion about his sexuality. "How are they?"

"Good as new, I'm happy to say. They're going back to their apartment soon. Your mom went out to do a few errands. For a while there, I felt like Florence Nightingale, ministering to war casualties."

"And a mighty pretty nurse at that," Sam said.

"Thank you, my lady. Oh, by the way, you've got some messages. Pat Hammand and Emmaline Loveless called. Emmaline said 'Remember our exchange.' What did she mean by that?"

"I haven't the foggiest," Sam said. Of course, she did.

"Hmm." He took a breath. "Charlie's called. About every hour, I think. And Agatha called for the second time today. If this keeps up, we're getting an answering service."

Sam was afraid to ask but she did. "What did Agatha want?"

"She wanted to know how you were doing?"

Sam's face went slack. "Nick. I killed her nephew."

Nick tossed the dishtowel on the trestle table and knelt before his wife. He took her hands and looked into her face. "Sam. You killed a psychopathic killer. He would have gone on to kill again. He had ceased belonging to anybody. He was as mad as old King George."

"But I killed him." She didn't want to start crying again.

"If you hadn't killed him, Sam, he would have killed Agatha. And probably you too. Agatha knows that."

"She knows Chris was her nephew?"

Nick nodded. "The police gave her a copy of the diary and will return the original to her when this business is done with."

"What must she think of me?"

"If I know Agatha, she thinks she's lucky that you were there to save her life, that's what she thinks. Now," he stood and grabbed the dish towel, "I don't want to hear any more guilt coming out of that pretty mouth. You hear me?"

Sam nodded without speaking.

"I've got a kitchen to clean up before the troops arrive, so you stay right there and relax."

"A man's place…"

"Don't start," Nick said. He kissed her again and disappeared into the back hall.

Charlie came early.

Nick had packed the girls into his car and left to take them back to their apartment in Portsmouth, but not before Caroline reminded her mother about the shopping trip promise. "And I expect you to be dressed to the nines," Caroline had said with a big wide smile, repeating one of Charlie's colloquialisms.

Sam had not been surprised that, even in a coma, Caroline had heard her promise at the hospital bedside. She had read about patients under anesthesia who could recall every word uttered in an operating room.

Bright sun poured in through the sun porch windows, covering half the room in a buttery glow. Charlie sat with his back to the windows. Light softened the edges of his balding head and broad shoulders.

"Is that a halo 'round your head, Charlie?"

"Whatta you talking about, Sam?"

"The way the sun bounces off your head, you look like an angel."

Charlie tried to make his face into a scowl. "Yeah. Well, you almost *were* an angel, Sam. What the hell were you doing out that night in the dark with that damned cracker running around?"

"I know, I know." She closed her eyes, pulled the green fleece blanket up to her neck and leaned into the pillows on the couch. "I didn't expect it. I was supposed to meet him at 10:00 that night at McCutty's, per our plan."

"Bad things happen when you don't expect them, Sam. Especially when you're dealing with a killer. You should at least have taken your gun. You could have been killed."

Sam tensed, looked straight at him. "Okay, *dad*. I'm sorry. I promise I won't do it again." Suddenly, her muscles felt like wet noodles. "I'm too tired to argue about it."

Charlie folded his hands. He rubbed a thumb back and forth over his top finger. "See that you don't," he said softly.

He didn't speak for a minute.

Then he said, "No sense in telling Grant about our plan to meet Byrnes at McCutty's. Could stir up a hornet's nest of trouble."

"I won't say anything. It's not relevant to the investigation."

Charlie was breathing heavily. He looked at the ceiling, looked out the window, then looked at his Timex with the black cloth band. "Grant will be here in a few minutes."

"I should sit up a little." Sam eased herself into a sitting position.

"Does it hurt much?"

"Not bad."

"You took an awful chance going after him with that poker."

"What were my options?"

Charlie's thumb now made little circles on his top finger. He looked at his shiny boots, nodding.

They watched the dust motes drift through the sunbeams.

When the doorbell rang, Charlie pushed himself out of the rocker. "I'll get it."

It was Grant Webber and it was precisely 3:00 P.M.

Charlie stepped toward the door, hesitated, then turned and said, "You sure you'll be all right alone? I can call your mother or get Lenny to come over."

Grant had come, got 'just the facts,' and gone with Jack Webb precision. To Sam's great disappointment, not one of the brass buttons popped off his suit jacket.

"I'm fine, Charlie, really. I have the portable, and Nick will be back any minute."

"Yeah." He stuffed his big hands into his chino pockets, as he shifted his weight.

Sam waited.

Charlie waited.

Then Charlie said, "You're quite a woman, Sam." He hurried out of the room.

Chapter 33

"Fate is strange," Sam said the next day as she spooned at the miniature marshmallows clinging to each other in her hot chocolate. They were out of whipped cream. "Chris would have inherited everything."

"I still have a hard time thinking of her, or him, as a man," Nick said. "He made a good-looking woman."

Nick was standing in the sun porch. He had made cranberry orange muffins and was holding a tray with plates, napkins, silver, his moose mug, the steaming muffins, butter, and a square jar of Coldbath Cowberry Chutney. "Your Monday brunch, madam," he announced, butler-like.

Sam pointed at the trestle table. "Put it here, Jeeves." She set her mug beside the yellow-lined legal pad on which she had been making notes for her next column.

Nick set the tray down and spread the red checkered napkin over Sam's lap. "Anything else, madam?"

She smiled up at him. "Yes. But we'll discuss that later."

"I'll hold that thought," he said. "Remember, Agatha is dropping by in about an hour."

Sam's stomach flopped. "Umm. I wonder what she wants."

"Probably wants to give you a case of cowberry chutney as a reward."

"I'm requesting Cran-Raspberry," Sam said, hoping Nick was right.

Nick slit the top of a muffin and put a hunk of butter inside, picked up his moose mug, and sat in the rocker opposite Sam.

Sam handed him a plate. "Crumbs."

He took the plate.

Nick reached for a napkin. "It certainly feels good to get back to my exercise routine. I can't believe the tension I stored in my shoulders and neck."

"Our bodies store memories," Sam said. "Remember Rolfing, in the seventies?"

"You mean that massage technique?" He eyed his muffin.

"It was more than that. We store memories, even from childhood, in different parts of our body. And when that part is deeply massaged, those long-forgotten memories are released. I remember stories about patients who sobbed uncontrollably, releasing experiences they had forgotten or hadn't consciously remembered. It was healing for many people."

"Maybe we both need a good massage." He licked his lips.

"I'm up for that."

Nick studied his muffin. "The forsythia is starting to bud."

They thought about that.

"You know they caught the kids who were breaking into homes," Nick said. "That's probably who Caroline saw outside our window."

"Thank the Lady," Sam said.

"Sam. I've been in the dark here for the last couple of days." He leaned back in the rocker and looked at her. "I didn't want to tax you with a lot of questions but now that you look bright-eyed and bushy-tailed, I want some answers, woman."

"Planning your strategy?"

"What?"

"Are you planning on how you're going to attack that muffin."

"Never mind that. Talk." He took a bite.

"Didn't Charlie tell you anything?"

Sam made a split in the top of her muffin, dropped a dollop of butter inside and held it closed to melt. She licked her right forefinger.

"No," Nick answered. "He said he couldn't talk about it until the investigation was closed."

Sam couldn't help but smile. "Can you imagine the embarrassed faces at the Bog when the news breaks that Chris was Christopher?"

Nick whistled through his teeth.

Sam ate half the muffin in one bite, then mumbled, "The birds are building a nest." She motioned with the muffined hand toward the shaded roof arrangement that Nick had built on one side of the pool in the back yard. She liked the outdoors, but not too much sun. "Aren't they cute? What's the temp?" She popped the second half of the muffin in her mouth.

Nick glanced at the outside thermometer. "Thirty-eight."

"Umm." Sam chewed.

Nick whistled Red River Valley.

"I can hardly wait for spring to really get here," Sam said, reaching for her thick, cream-cheese patterned mug. She picked up a spoon and poked at a marshmallow. It stuck and she spooned it into her mouth.

Nick scratched under his left eye, then put on a when-are-you-going-to-tell-me look.

"You ready?" she asked.

"You're really enjoying this."

Sam got sober. "Not really. There's nothing to enjoy about murder. There's just this side of me that enjoys the mystery, the intrigue. I like to figure things out, solve puzzles."

"I'm sorry, honey. I didn't mean it that way."

"I know you didn't."

She placed a hand on her side and slowly took in a big breath through her nose and exhaled through pursed lips.

"It started when I saw Madsen Chills at the gas station. My subconscious saw that diary with the initials C.C. in the back of his station wagon, but it didn't register at the time.

"Then Thursday, Sadie mentioned she was going to record this soap opera affair we've been through in her diary. The word "diary" brought me closer to remembering that book in the back of Madsen's car because it looked like a diary.

"Then that vision of the Cosmo sign. Remember I told you how the "C" doubled and bounced on top of Madsen's car. And then that night we were drinking wine and you said C.C.?"

"You've got me confused," Nick said.

"Yes. Well, so was I for a while. When I spoke with Emmaline Loveless at the supermarket, she said something about looking beneath the surface when judging others. So I began looking past the obvious.

"What tipped me off and started the assembling process was something so simple it's laughable. Even then I still wasn't sure."

"What?"

"It was the way Chris carried the plates at the Bog last Sunday." Sam watched the cute little furrow between Nick's eyes deepen.

"You never waited tables, Nick, so you wouldn't know. If you're right-handed, you would pour coffee with your right hand and carry plates in your left. You'd want control over the hot coffee."

"Yeah. I've seen Chris and Julie do that."

"Last Sunday, Chris didn't do that. She put the plates on her right arm and carried the coffee pot in her left hand."

"Maybe she always did it that way."

"No, she didn't. And it was obvious because it was awkward for her. Jesus. We're still calling her, her. Or rather, him, her."

"So why did that make him a murderer?"

Sam rubbed a finger over the swirl pattern on the outside of her mug. "It didn't. But then I saw that guy, who turned out to be Chris, who looked so familiar at the Cosmo. Remember, I told you?"

"Right."

"He acted so strange, he wouldn't look at me in the mirror. And he had a bandage on his left arm. I kept saying to myself that I knew him from somewhere. Remember, Emmaline had said 'look beneath the surface.'"

Nick was still puzzled. "I've got that connection, but how does that tie in with the two murders?"

"It didn't at the time, but pieces began to fall into place. Especially when I remembered what mom told me about Florence's dog."

"Sergeant?"

"Yes." Sam sighed again and set the mug down on the table. She straightened the blanket, then the napkin on her lap. "You see, when I took your shirt to the cleaners, Clarence told me about a dog barking all night. Well, Sergeant was out all that night. Florence didn't find him until the morning after Doug was killed. So I thought that the killer might have tried to stop Sergeant from barking, afraid the dog would alert the neighbors, and the dog could have bitten him. And Chris more or less confirmed that in Agatha's living room the other night."

"Thus," Nick added, "the man with the golden arm."

"Exactly, Watson. That arm was sore enough that Chris didn't trust carrying the plates there."

Sam decided not to tell Nick about her thwarted meeting with a demented killer in McCutty's market.

"And then there was his shirt."

"Whose shirt?"

"Chris's. He buttons his shirts left over right like a man's shirt instead of right over left. Of course, that wouldn't have made me suspicious by itself. Some women wear men's shirts. But all his shirts were like that. It was just another clue."

"And can you tell me what war he had returned from, the diseases he had contracted while there, and what he had eaten for breakfast?"

Sam grabbed a second muffin. "Give me time."

As if on cue, the doorbell rang and Nick let Agatha in. She came bearing gifts. Her man deposited a large crate on the hallway floor and left to wait in the car. Stamped on the natural wood slats was "Apple Cranberry."

"This is for Samantha," she announced to Nick.

"Why, thank you, Agatha. Sam's on the sun porch. She'll be pleased." He pointed and Agatha marched on ahead and settled into Nick's rocker. Nick sat in the second rocker to her left.

"Sam. Agatha brought a case of apple-cranberry chutney for you."

Sam didn't look at Nick. Memories of the southwest-facing crane lingered at the edge of her funny bone.

"How nice. Thank you, Agatha."

"May I take your coat?" Nick started to stand.

"No, thank you. This will be short visit." Her Chesterfield was buttoned to the neck. She wore hose and low black shoes. The ubiquitous black leather bag was compressed between her fingers.

One large heartbeat thumped against Sam's rib cage. She swallowed. "Agatha. I can't tell you how sorry I am about…"

"It is not about that, Samantha. I have done a bit of thinking since last Saturday night. Some events have a way of putting things in perspective."

Events? Sam thought. *The big mama of understatements.*

"As you know, I have no heirs." Agatha's lips tightened even more, if that were possible, then she said, "You and Nicholas, and your daughters, of course, are the closest to family I have. It was time to make a decision. Someone must carry on the proud tradition of the Coldbath recipe."

Nick's eyeballs rolled toward Sam then back to Agatha. His body was so still he didn't seem to be breathing. Sam thought he was afraid to move.

She was afraid to move.

Agatha sat straighter, an act that stretched one's imagination toward the impossible. "I would like to pass the recipe on to you with certain reservations."

Sam mouthed the word "me." Then it squeaked out. "Me? Why?"

Tiny brackets formed at the corner of Agatha's hairy lip. "Why not?"

Why not? Was that grammatically correct in Agatha's vernacular? Sam had never heard the woman speak a sentence with less than a dozen syllables. Saturday night *was* an 'event.'

"I am having papers drawn up. There is a code of secrecy that must be religiously observed. There are rules that must be followed. You will be Vice-President of the Keep Our Berry Bogs Clean Committee. I have confidence that you can do the job."

She stood. Nick stood. But for her side, Samantha would have stood.

Agatha was out the door before Sam or Nick could say another word.

Chapter 34

A week later, with all her sweats in the laundry, Sam reluctantly and carefully slipped on a loose, muted blue Eddie Bauer dress. She took the green foam roller out of her bangs and tossed it in the top bureau drawer, then ran a pick through her hair. In ragg socks, she padded through the sun porch toward the back hall and the washing machine.

Nick looked up from his morning coffee. "Where are you going?"

"Nowhere," she tossed over her shoulder.

"Why are you dressed up? Oh, I know," he chuckled, laying the paper in his lap. "Your five sweat pants and seven torn tee shirts are in the laundry."

"Funny boy," she called from the hall. She reappeared in the doorway and rested against the frame, her arms folded across her chest. "Just think. If I had the addiction you do, I too would own one of everything L.L. Bean has ever produced. And where would our budget be then?"

"You do pretty well at the mystery sections in the bookstores. Come to think of it, you *are* a mystery, one that I hope I never solve."

"No, I'm not. I'm an open book." She grinned and waited for him to laugh.

"Speaking of books," Nick said, "the chutney catalogs were distributed today. Agatha didn't find one mistake."

Sam didn't want to prick his bubble. Agatha probably wouldn't have told him if she had found a page inserted upside down. Not this year. Next year was another story.

Nick said, "We got an invitation to Pat Hammand and Jimi Duncan's wedding. We going?"

"We sure are," Sam said. "I wouldn't miss that for the world."

"Another surprise for our quiet little hamlet."

"We live in the twentieth century." Sam laughed. "Ooops. Change that to the twenty-first."

Her eyes drifted out the window. White patches of clouds spotted the bright blue sky. The sun's rays spilled over the treetops and along the top rim of the pool.

"We'll be opening the pool soon."

"What do you mean 'we,' Lone Ranger?" Nick chided.

One cheek rippled. "I'll help."

"I guess you won't do much until your side heals."

Sam wasn't about to argue with that directive. She squinted toward the back edge of the property where the tree line met the lawn.

"Nick. Look." She pointed. "It looks like the lawn's been dug up. Have we got moles?"

Nick swiveled in the rocker, glanced out the window, then turned back to Sam and grinned. "If we do, they're six foot moles."

"What's that supposed to mean?"

"It means, my darling, that you now have an asparagus bed."

"What? How? Who?"

"Which shall I answer first?"

"Nick!"

"A few days after you got home from the hospital, Henry Lincoln called, asking what he could do for you. He and his wife were so grateful that you saved his life he was ready to offer you his business. I told him how you always wanted an asparagus bed, had tried and failed. Next thing I knew, they were both here. He suggested that spot, I agreed. And you now have a professionally planted asparagus bed."

Her mouth watered. "Oh, Nick. That was so nice of them. I'll send them a note."

"How does it feel to be Vice-President of the KOBBC?"

Sam let out a little sniff through her nose. "I didn't have the heart to say no to her. God knows, I don't want the job."

"She must think a lot of you, Sam. And she can't say it to your face. This is her way of telling you."

"I know."

"When is your meeting with the committee?"

"Tomorrow afternoon."

"I'd like to be a fly on the wall."

"Not in Agatha's chutney plant, you wouldn't."

Sam got up, went to the couch and flopped down. "Ooh. I keep forgetting," she said, as a pain pulled at her side.

Nick winced. "Be careful, babe. You don't want that opening up."

Sam arranged the folds of her dress. She looked up to see Nick rubbing his knuckles into his eyes.

"Don't do that so hard, Nick," Sam snapped. "You'll hurt your eyes."

Nick eyed her. "Short fuse and long umbilical cord."

"What's that supposed to mean?" Sam said.

Nick changed the subject. "Just what will your duties be?"

"I don't want to think about it. I'm not getting any more involved than I have to. I have a life here with you, the girls and mom, my writing. Everything else is secondary."

Sam fanned her face with the small clipboard from the trestle table. "Is it hot in here?"

"Sam, honey. When are you going to accept that you're having hot flashes?"

Sam's eyes flashed sparks at him. "What do you mean?"

"Hot flashes, like in menopause."

"I am not!"

"Are too."

"Nick. I'm only forty-eight."

"Yup. And you got a letter from AARP the other day."

"That was a mistake. They probably meant to address it to you."

He laughed. "You're on their list, my darling."

Sam went to her desk.

She had gone to sleep the night before pondering the solution to the second note, the one pinned to Kent Butcher's dead body. The answer had been on her lips when she woke this morning. After Nick had left for work, she'd rummaged through her code books until she found what she was looking for.

The name of the code had been right in front of her all along when she drew those triangles: the Triangle Code.

She pulled a piece of scrap paper from the blue box on her desk and picked up her Saga pen. Sketching nine downward pointing triangles, she numbered them in the center, one through nine. On each point, the letters of the alphabet were drawn in ascending order. The ninth triangle had two letters, Y and Z.

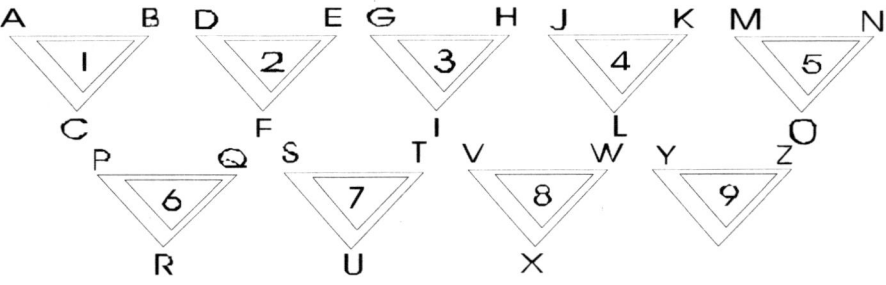

A copy of the killer's second riddle was tucked in her Thesaurus. She pulled it out, folded the creases the opposite way so it would lie flat, and lined it beside the scrap paper with the nine triangles.

3 by 9

FATHER SONHOLY GHOST

BUT WHERES MOTHER?

$$\overset{\text{\tiny/}\,\text{\tiny I}}{9}\;\underset{\text{\tiny I}}{5}\;\underset{\text{\tiny I}}{7}\;\overset{\text{\tiny \textbackslash\,I}}{8}\;\underset{\text{\tiny I}}{\underline{3}}\;\underset{\text{\tiny I}}{\underline{4}}\;\underset{\text{\tiny I}}{\underline{4}}\;\overset{\text{\tiny \textbackslash\,I}}{1}\;\overset{\text{\tiny \textbackslash\,I}}{2}\;\overset{\text{\tiny \textbackslash\,I}}{5}\;\underset{\text{\tiny I}}{\underline{3}}\;\overset{\text{\tiny \textbackslash}}{5}\;\overset{\text{\tiny \textbackslash}}{2}\;\overset{\text{\tiny /}}{7}\;\overset{\text{\tiny I}}{1}\;\overset{\text{\tiny /}}{5}$$

SAVE VICTIMS 5 AND 6
POST ANSWER MCCUTTYS BY APRIL 15

The first number on the note was 9, for the ninth triangle. The hash mark and dot at the top left indicated that the letter to use in the ninth triangle was a "Y."

The second number, a 5, represented the fifth triangle, and the bottom hash mark and dot was the letter "O."

The last number in this first word was a 7, the seventh triangle, with a hash mark and dot beneath, the letter 'U."

The first word was "you."

Minutes later, when Sam had finished deciphering the sentence, her lips curled back in a sneer.

"Only in your dreams, cracker."

She tore the sheets into postage-sized pieces, brushed them off the desk into her hand and looked at them for a long moment.

What a waste of a life.

She wiggled her fingers and watched the ragged white scraps flutter into the wastebasket.

Sam stood, slowly arched her back, let out a sigh, and then went to the kitchen to root for Ring Dings.

Addendum

YOUR PERSONAL READING

PERSONAL YEAR CYCLES

Your personal year begins on your birthday each year and continues until your next birthday. Every time you blow out the candles on your birthday cake, you are, in a sense, born anew. You are starting a new cycle complete with different learning experiences.

To find any personal year cycle, add your month and day of birth to the year in question.

For example: A birthday of May 20th.

If the personal year is 1999, add May 20th to 1999.

$5 + 20 + 1999 = 2024$.

Add again: $2024 = 2 + 0 + 2 + 4 = 8$.

8 is the Personal Year Cycle from May of 1999 to May of 2000. Find the Personal Year Eight reading below.

Same birthdate: May 20th, in the year 2004.

Add: $5 + 20 + 2004 = 2029$.

Add again: $2029 = 2 + 0 + 2 + 9 = 13$.

Add again: $13 = 1 + 3 = 4$.

4 is the Personal Year Cycle from May of 2004 to May of 2005.

Find your Personal Year Cycle and read the delineations below.

Remember, you can determine the cycle of anyone or any thing that has a birthday. Also, just like the seasons of the year that repeat in four predictable patterns—spring, summer, fall and winter—, your cycles repeat in predictable *nine*-year patterns. What you are doing now, you were doing nine years ago, eighteen years ago, and twenty-seven years ago. Similarly, you will repeat this pattern in nine-year increments into the future.

Of course, your repeating cycles won't encompass exactly the same events you are experiencing now, but the pattern will be similar. If home issues are the assignment for your current cycle, then that was the focus in your life nine, eighteen and twenty-seven years ago, and will be the focus nine, eighteen, and twenty-seven years into the future.

When you are aware of these repeating patterns, you can choose to improve, to elevate your consciousness with each recurring cycle. Instead of circling round and round, like oxen yoked to an endlessly turning water wheel, you can spiral upwards, learning from your past and growing into a bright new future.

PERSONAL YEAR CYCLE ONE

You feel like you've been dropped in the middle of a strange city, stark naked, with no cash or credit cards—now we're talking serious deprivation—and no idea where to go. Don't worry. You're exactly where you're supposed to be.

You have just finished your Nine Cycle of change where you had to let go of certain conditions in your life. You're beginning a brand new cycle, the first of this nine-year series. Family, friends and business associates surround you, but you still feel alone. Even your cat shuns your lap. But feeling alone doesn't mean lonely. It means you need to be separated from others so that you can make independent decisions about the next nine years in your life. Too much involvement with others can influence your decisions. You need to experience this personal year on your own.

Center on yourself. That's right—on yourself. You get to do this once every nine years, so enjoy it. You come first this year. You're Number

One. You begin to recognize that you too are an individual deserving of attention. Put all that nurturing on the little girl inside you, your inner child. She needs a lot of attention this year. Find out what she wants; buy her a new outfit, take her on a mystery ride, tell her how great she is. Remember, she is looking for adventure right now.

Please don't get involved. He may be a dream and he has the most gorgeous big brown eyes but, come on, you know you're not ready yet. Wait till your next birthday. If he wants to tag along and follow your lead, fine. Just keep him in his place. One important person can come into your life now but only if you maintain your individuality within that relationship.

More than equal rights now, you need to be the center of his life because the attention is on you. Write that in capital letters across your forehead: I AM IMPORTANT. I COME FIRST THIS YEAR.

This doesn't mean you should leave a trail of crumpled bodies in your wake, but it does mean your needs come first. As long as what you want doesn't put the kids out on the street or sell the business down the river, do it.

You're willing to try things that you wouldn't have before. Reach out, take a chance, and exercise your pioneering instincts. Try on that big A word: Aggressive. Set a goal and aim high.

Two final suggestions: no leaning—stand on your own two feet and don't let anyone tread on them; and secondly, speak up—it's time everyone knew how you felt anyway.

This is an exciting new start. You're brimming over with newfound energy so use it to create a bright and beautiful new future for yourself!

COLOR: Red. GEM: Ruby

PERSONAL YEAR CYCLE TWO

Get out the blindfold, the scales and the toga; it's time to weigh and balance and set things straight. You probably upset a few people last year, including yourself, so you need to pull back and take a look at what you started then. You become aware of the other point of view and want to work in harmony to bring about more peaceful conditions.

You have the ability to see both sides more clearly, so making a decision can be hard. You'd rather hang out in the background, be the silent shadow, and let others take the lead. However, because you *can* see what's happening, you are the peacemaker, the mediator who settles disputes.

Partnerships and marriage are possible now because you are as concerned about the other person's needs as you are about your own. Remember that special person you met before your last birthday—is he still around? Give him a jingle.

Expect the unexpected. Things will flow along quietly and then, like a bolt out of the blue, a situation will pop up which demands an immediate answer or someone from your past lands on your doorstep with roses in hand. This is a test. Eliminate negative attitudes and create harmonious circumstances so that your next cycle will blossom fully. If differences can't be settled now, separations can occur.

Develop your psychic abilities. There are forces working beneath the surface in your life that you may not see quite yet. Your subconscious is talking to you. Listen to your dreams. Meditate. The ancient teaching that mind controls reality is especially true this year. Your life is under construction, so get past those roadblocks.

Since the purpose of the justice system is to bring balance, legal situations can arise. Settlements, legacies, wills, insurance, and accident claims that occur now are bringing an end to disruption in your life. Contracts are highlighted. Large purchases may require the signing of documents. Read the fine print.

If you're flashing, chances are it's not menopausal but flashes of insight and intuition and understanding. Listen, because these revelations bring solutions to difficult problems. The flashes may also stimulate the artist in you. Exquisite works of art can result. So get out the paints, the pen, the wood and clay, the needle and thread, or whatever medium moves you.

You could be recognized suddenly for something you've been doing for a long time or something that you had long forgotten that has suddenly reappeared. Or you may perform a deed that puts you in the limelight unexpectedly.

This is a year of cooperation. Nurture the seed that was planted last year. Be prepared for sudden events and insights that inspire. You are highly electrified.

COLOR: Orange. GEM: Moonstone.

PERSONAL YEAR CYCLE THREE

Paint the word BIG in large letters on your bathroom mirror so it's the first thing you see every morning when you get up. This is your year to do things in a BIG way.

Take a trip, one that expands your consciousness—overseas or, if you've never left town, to the next county. It isn't the location but the newness of the experience that counts. The idea is to encounter events and people that will help you grow and see the BIGGER picture in life.

You will meet people who will open new vistas for you. They will show you how to use your potential. You'll hear nice things about yourself that you haven't heard in the last nine years. This is the time to get positive feedback. Because you're feeling pretty good about yourself, you send out confident vibrations. Others pick them up and return them to you—a positive Catch 22.

And, for heaven's sake, get yourself some new clothes. You can't go out looking like that. People are noticing you, remember? You'll be the center of attention—BIG time! They'll be asking for your autograph.

Pay attention to hair, makeup, clothes, and posture, anything that improves your appearance, because you are center stage and loving it! You might take elocution or acting lessons to enhance your social skills.

Remember last year's lesson that your mind controls your reality? Well, watch the results when you fling that dazzling smile.

You feel lucky. And you could be. Buy that one ticket and enter that contest. The person who wins will probably be in a cycle like, this so go for it. It's the law of cause and effect; you feel lucky so you draw luck to you. One note of caution: Don't get carried away with confidence. Too much of anything is not good. Too much food and drink harms the body; watch that your body doesn't expand along with your bank account. Too much spending brings on bankruptcy; save a little for a rainy day.

There is growth, fertility, expansion, and activity this year. The birth of a child is possible. Or that baby could be a creation of your mind that bursts forth into the sunlight. Pamper yourself. Relax and enjoy the flow of creative energy that is surging through you.

You need space, lots of it. Don't let anyone cramp your style or fence you in. Limiting factors in your life fall away so you are free to roam the universe on your own terms.

Your enthusiasm and optimism may draw business contacts in a social setting. Cultivate these contacts for they may prove most helpful in the future.

This year is full of fun, excitement, and freedom. You are in your best form so use the cycle wisely and have a BIG time!

COLOR: Yellow. GEM: Topaz.

PERSONAL YEAR CYCLE FOUR

Get serious. After last year, you need to. It's time to organize. Start by cleaning the attic, the closets and bureaus, the cellar, the garage, and the office. You have such an urge to organize your life that no corner is safe from your scrutiny. This compulsion stems from a need to build strong foundations in your life.

Material possessions become important. Yes, even more than they have been. Before now, you dreamt of having; now you go out and get. Your need for material comfort prompts you to buy little things like a car and a house and land. Where does that leave you? With a checkbook that needs attention, so now you have to work to pay off all those bills.

Work is a big theme this year. You work to pay off that big consolidation loan you took out to pay off those bills, some of which you probably incurred last year when you were feeling flush and living it up.

The money that comes now is earned money. How about starting your own business with these funds? Be practical. Use your money wisely. Start a savings account. Just think how much you would have in an account now if you had put $5 a week away since the day you started handling a weekly paycheck. You take care of your money and it will take care of you.

One of your most important material possessions is your body, and you find it needs attention. Out come the jogging shoes and the weights, the diet book and the bathroom scales you threw down the cellar stairs last year. This is a good time to heal your body, so have a checkup, eat right and get your sleep. Your last year of expansion, Personal Cycle Three, probably included the expansion of your body, so take care of it now.

And boy, do you need cuddling! Physical contact is especially important this year. You need to touch, smell, and taste life's sensual delights. Get out into nature, close to the land. Hug a tree. Nature is a healing force. Green, like nature, is the color of healing.

This can be a big money cycle, but it is money that comes in direct proportion to the effort you put out. If it seems lucky, you'll know that somewhere in the past you have earned it. The key is to work well. In return, you will be paid well.

Please, obey the traffic signs. This is a law and order cycle, so rules and regulations must be honored. You find yourself paying more attention anyway because this adds to the secure foundations that you are building this year. It is the laws that make society safe for all of us. You may even have to participate by serving on a jury.

Avoid using those credit cards to buy all the things you desperately want. Notice the word "want." You *need* air and water and shelter; you *want* these other material things. Don't let your possessions own you. Instead, enjoy what you own and have a wonderfully rewarding, physically stimulating year. Build that savings account. You'll need it next year.

COLOR: Green. GEM: Emerald

PERSONAL YEAR CYCLE FIVE

Feeling restless? Ready for change? Want some excitement in your life? Well, you're going to get all these things in the next twelve months. And, boy, do you need it!

Because you put everything in order last year, you have a firm springboard from which to launch big changes in your life. Think back four to five years ago. You made new starts then. Examine where you've been heading since. If you don't like your present course, change it. This year is a turning point in your nine-year cycle so be flexible, open yourself to new experiences and people, and for heaven's sake, make a decision about where you're heading.

SEX.

Did that get your attention? Yes, your five senses are vibrating. Even if you find yourself in a dark closet with a bag over your head, your sexual magnetism will draw relationships from at least five states away. So, if you're interested, get out your date book. If you have an existing relationship, you become closer. Intimacy can bring about changes in your home next year and you know what that means.

You are so busy with meetings and errands and phone calls and mail and arranging parties and getting involved in public functions that you should install a revolving door at home and in your workplace. All of a sudden everyone needs you.

You need experience during this cycle because the more information you gather and the more contacts you make, the easier it will be to make decisions about your future. A trip to the post office could change your life. Keep yourself open to going places; circulate and talk with people, because some of these experiences will help you make those important decisions.

Your mind is another erotic zone this year. Your curiosity prompts you to think about taking courses and enhancing your education in some way. New interests continue to entice you. Curiosity may have killed the cat, but you haven't even begun to meow.

Keep the gas tank full and the oil changed because your wheels will be spinning with the endless stream of places to go and people to see and things to do. Plus, keep a tank on reserve.

Your nervous system is highly charged so be careful driving and moving in general. You are in such a hurry that you don't see that last step or the door that inexplicably moves in front of you. Do avoid alcohol and drugs. You don't want to dissipate these wonderful opportunities.

Resist temptation unless, of course, you happen to find the dream mate you've been waiting for. Even then, the blood runs mighty hot, so enjoy life's experiences but keep moderation in mind.

This is your year for fun, excitement, change, learning, and sex. You're probably out of breath just thinking about it. Have a ball!

COLOR: Blue. GEM: Turquoise

PERSONAL YEAR CYCLE SIX

So, you had a wild time last year and now you've come home to nest. You're in the right place. For the next twelve months you need to pay attention to home and family, because there are changes on the domestic front.

Last year's cycle of sexual magnetism gave you the opportunity to try on different relationships, and one of them fit like a rubber dress—smooth and clingy. Now you want to establish your own home. This is a cycle of love and harmony, so settle in. Your attention may be drawn here anyway because that rubber dress may be expanding. A new addition to your family?

If you don't produce, you find that some family members may. Some of them could move in with you temporarily as they need your emotional or financial support. Or some of them may move out. That's just fine too. The point is—you are seeking balance at the roots of your being—your home.

You live in your body and your body lives in your house, so whatever is happening inside you psychologically will manifest outwardly in your home. If you renovate your kitchen, the changes within you may relate to your eating habits; if you attack the bathroom, you could be cleansing your body or mind; if the front yard occupies your attention, you are concerned about how others see you.

Think about redecorating. Do over a room or add an addition to your home. Out comes the paint and wallpaper and fabric and in comes new furniture. A new set of fine china and goblets grace your dinner table because food is a communion and you want to touch people with your sense of inner beauty this year. Don't forget yourself—clothes, a new hairstyle. All these things indicate the changing you.

Express your sensitivities in the community. A neighborhood clean-up campaign or charitable work can be most satisfying.

Any artistic talents you have should be nurtured this year. The depth of your feelings can produce beautiful works of art.

While you're at it, drape a thick thirsty towel over your shoulder. Your fine sense of balance and justice plays out through the Mother/Father Confessor syndrome. Everyone is crying on your shoulder, telling you their problems because, of course, you can solve them.

But take on only those things you can finish this personal year. Loose ends should be tied up before your next birthday.

This is the cycle of peace and war that means if you can't join them, you will lick them. If peace is not possible, separations occur. This is called "irreconcilable differences." Wars have been fought during these kinds of influences. The courts are a place where balance can be restored, so they may be part of this cycle as well.

Think positive thoughts. Get out your snugglies and nestle down for a long winter's communion. This is nesting time, a love cycle, when you are so tuned in to the needs of others that, hey, solving their problems is a breeze. Your personal life can be warm and fuzzy as well, so enjoy the best that this loving cycle can offer you.

COLOR: Indigo. GEM: Sapphire, white pearls.

PERSONAL YEAR CYCLE SEVEN

Take a break! You've had it up to here with responsibility and people and work and everything else. You just want to be left alone. And besides, you're tired. You haven't got the energy to flick a fly, so lock yourself in the bedroom and have your meals slid under the door for the next twelve months. Well, maybe that's an exaggeration, but you get the idea.

This is retreat time. Take a vacation or at least weekends away from everything. You need to think about your life—where have you been, where are you now, and where are you going. They don't call this the seven-year itch for nothing. Take the advice of the Creator who rested on the seventh day.

Besides, you know all those things you have been worrying about? They will magically take care of themselves. Your higher self is saying stop, look, and listen, and you can't do that if you're out there running around. If you persist in your mad frenetic pace, you may end up on your back, in bed, nursing a tired body.

What kinds of things should you be doing? How about pulling out those things you set aside for a rainy day or those projects you said you would get to someday. This is someday.

While the physical body rests, the mental body kicks in. Exercise those little gray cells. The mind is thirsty and sucking at the epidermis, waiting to talk with you. Take courses in philosophy, yoga, religion, astrology, or numerology. Listen to your dreams, experience visions and telepathic communication. This is the other side of life.

Polish your skills. Don't start new things but do train yourself in those areas that you already know or have had to put on hold for some time. This is a cycle of preparation for a big year coming up. You're in a planning stage so listen to your Mother and plan!

This does not mean that you have permission from the universe to stay home from work for the year or ignore your friends, but it does mean you should take time away from the craziness of the outside world and allow quiet time for your inner world to awaken.

Your mind is your strength now. You may begin to understand that mind does indeed create reality, and that you are what you think. If that's a horrifying thought, then change the program. Get out your tape recorder, make yourself a tape using present tense: "I *am* wonderful, I *have* a great relationship, I *make* lots of money for my valuable contributions, I *am* happy." Program whatever you want. And make sure you use the present tense—I *AM*—not I will be. "Will be" never comes. Then play the tape every night when you go to bed or while riding in the car or doing mindless chores. You will become what you program yourself to be.

If you must sign any legal documents, check the fine print. Thoroughness is important now.

Rest, think, and discover your beautiful inner self that's itching to get out.

COLOR: Violet. GEM: Amethyst.

PERSONAL YEAR CYCLE EIGHT

You're going to get exactly what you deserve. Sorry, but that's the way it is. Or maybe you think you deserve something really great. Well then, good for you, because it's coming.

This can be an important year out there in the material world of power, sex, and money. What else is there? Lots more, of course, but for now let's concentrate on your tangible rewards. You've worked for them and you deserve them. So if you're up for a raise or a promotion, you should get it, providing, of course, you put in the time. This cycle shows in no uncertain terms the law of cause and effect; what you sow, you shall reap. Public recognition and honors are possible.

If there is material loss, it does not mean you are a bad person, but it does indicate that you have not handled your past cycles with awareness, because this year is the culmination of the past seven years of effort. Don't worry. You'll get another chance. Now that you know your life works in cycles, you can prepare properly.

The pressure is on. You must take responsibility for the circumstances around you. Usually this starts at work where pressure mounts. Remember, working in the home is a job also—an important one. Others may heap more work on you because they finally recognize that you can do the job. As Byron said, "Ah, the weight of these splendid chains."

The intensity of this cycle works out through sexual relationships as well. This is the physical world, after all, and you should enjoy intimate contacts. But this kind of sex is more than fun and games. You need a partner who can fulfill you on all levels—physically, emotionally, mentally, and spiritually. The relationship must be an equal and respectful union. You must be responsible to and for each other. If you are going to get what you deserve this year, make it the very best.

Legacies and lotteries do come under this cycle because it is karmic—you get back what you put out. Even if you don't see the connection, you have earned it somewhere in the past.

If greed takes over and your drive to the top crushes those in your path, then loss of material possessions and resources is possible.

The big question is: do you want freedom or limitation? Limitation comes from fear of not having, a thirst that can never be quenched. Limitation comes from the need to control and have power over others, a power that is fragile and false. Freedom, on the other hand, is striking the balance between the material and the spiritual; understanding that your power in the material world can benefit you as well as others. You are the steward of material resources this year. Use them with respect and your rewards will be great.

Don't forget to enjoy the other part we talked about—the big "S" word.

COLOR: All colors, the rainbow. GEM: Diamond.

PERSONAL YEAR CYCLE NINE

It's time for housecleaning, serious housecleaning—physically, mentally, emotionally, and spiritually. You need to let go of those things in your life that just aren't working anymore. And if you can't let go, they probably will leave of their own accord anyway, so be flexible, flow with events. You have finished the cycle that began eight years ago, and in this ninth cycle, you shed the past.

We don't always know what we need—that's *need* not want—so the Higher Self steps in and says, "Okay, you don't need that job. You'll be better off in a new location." Or, "That person in your life is moving on to other places. Let him go." Whatever the message, you do need room in which to examine the past and prepare for the future.

You learn that "the only constant is change." And if you have roots growing out of your feet, you may find this emotionally trying because you don't want to uproot. Don't get stuck in a past that should become a memory.

Make time to sort out all the changes that are occurring in your life. Take a trip, go on a sabbatical or a retreat, and get in touch with the real meaning of life. Endings that occur here are a promise that a new beginning is imminent. When one door closes, another opens.

Let your light shine. Do charitable work. Tithe. Give back to the universe some of what you have gained. This is a demonstration of your faith in life. You can give much, and the universe will still provide for you. Work with others for the common good.

Give freely of your compassion, love, and understanding. You may find that old friendships become especially meaningful and that new friendships open your eyes to beautiful possibilities in the future. Any gifts or favors you receive now are rewards for the good that you have put out in the past.

Last personal year, you reached the mountaintop and experienced your fifteen minutes of fame. Hopefully you had your time in the sun, and if not, think about what you need to do next time around to get it. In the meantime, let your light shine for others. You might be surprised at the response.

Find out who you really are by examining this past nine-year cycle. Really think hard about what you started eight years ago and how each birthday brought you closer to where you are now. It's really important to understand this process because next year, Personal Year Cycle One, you are starting over with a similar nine year cycle, and if you know what you want and proceed with a clear objective, this next spin can bring you all the things of which you dream.

COLOR: Gold. GEMS: Gold, precious metals

Now that you know your nine cycles, go back and examine past patterns. Knowledge of your cycles brings you the "luck" and the success you desire.

MORE ABOUT PERSONAL YEAR CYCLES

Your personal year begins on your birthday each year and continues until your next birthday. Every time you blow out the candles on your birthday cake, you are, in a sense, born anew. You are starting a new cycle complete with different learning experiences.

Let's use the cycles of the moon as an analogy for your personal year cycle. Your birthday is a new moon. As the moon waxes or grows, the seed ideas of your new personal cycle begin to grow. During these first six months of your personal year cycle you should work with and learn about the qualities of your year's number and incorporate those lessons into your life.

You may find that three months after your birthday, like the first quarter moon, you need to examine the seeds you are sowing and make adjustments. Six months after your birthday, or halfway through your personal year, is the full moon point when the results of your year's efforts become more obvious. Your life is more visible just as the landscape is more visible under the full moon.

The remaining six months of your personal year cycle are the harvest or the waning moon. Time to reflect, to examine cause and effect, to recognize how your actions have produced a reaction. Three months into this final period, the final quarter moon, can also bring tangible results. If you were not pleased with the results during the halfway point or full moon in your personal year, you can make adjustments here as well.

You may notice that important events cluster around quarterly points in your personal year starting with your birthday, then three months, six months, and nine months later. Look back over your life to see if this is true.

Use our example above of May 20. Our woman's personal year cycle runs from May 20th of one year to May 20th of the next year. The first six months of her personal year, May 20th to November 20th, is the waxing, growing cycle when she should actively work towards achieving the goals of that cycle. August 20th—three months into her personal year—is the first quarter point when those issues may need attention. The events of her Personal Year Cycle peak on November 20th, the halfway point of her personal year.

The remaining six months, from November 20th to the following May 20th, are the harvesting cycle. It's time to think about and understand the effects of her earlier efforts. February 20th, nine months after her birthday, the final quarterly point, can bring rewarding events also. She might discover ways to prepare for the upcoming cycle that occurs on her next birthday.

Just think how fortunate you are to know this. Most people go through life with no awareness of their part in the cycles of life. Now you know. The rest is up to you.

Over the centuries, this information has helped countless thousands of people plan their lives more effectively. It can do the same for you. It's as easy as One, Two, Three!

Blessings, and go for the whole Nine yards!

In Love and Light,
dusty bunker

About the Author

dusty bunker is the author of many books on the metaphysical and symbolic nature of numbers and dreams. She brings her knowledge of the arcane into The Number Mystery Series.

Her many credits include a segment in the Time-Life books Series: Mysteries of the Unknown, columns for Mademoiselle Magazine, a dream column which ran for five years in the Manchester Union Leader, a humorous shopping column, as well as Tree Line, a cartoon strip for a New Hampshire publication.

dusty grew up in a Navy family, and has lived in the four corners of the United States—Maine, Florida, California and Washington State, and some of the states in between. She graduated from Saugus High School in Massachusetts and attended the University of New Hampshire. She now resides in a small New Hampshire town with her husband. Her grown family lives nearby.

0-595-10063-5